PLAY IT HARD

PLAYERS OF HANNAFORD U
BOOK 2

MICHELLE HERCULES

INFINITE SKY PUBLISHING

Paperback ISBN: 978-1-959167-41-9

PLAYLIST

Style - TAYLOR SWIFT

Lighthouse - LOVELESS

Baby Don't Hurt Me - DAVID GUETTA, ANNE-MARIE, COI LERAY

Stay - TRUE NORTH, LOVELESS

Radio - LANA DEL REY

Dance The Night - DUA LIPA

Bad Blood - TAYLOR SWIFT

Levitating - DUA LIPA, DABABY

Save Your Tears - THE WEEKND, ARIANA GRANDE

Anti-Hero - TAYLOR SWIFT

Love It When You Hate Me - AVRIL LAVIGNE, BLACKBEAR

Chandelier - SIA

PROLOGUE

ALEX

TWO YEARS AGO

I look at the time on my phone and curse under my breath. If Logan doesn't hurry up, I'll be late for my first class of the spring semester. Professor Weiland has a reputation for being a hard-ass, and he doesn't tolerate tardiness.

After our parents' divorce, Logan and I decided to sell our newer cars—gifts from our grandparents—and give the money to Mom so she could pay the first and last month's rent deposit on her apartment in Michigan. Not that Grandpa didn't offer to pay, but she didn't want to accept money from her folks anymore. Logan and I figured we didn't need two cars for our freshman year at Hannaford U, so we bought a piece of junk to get us by. It's clear this arrangement isn't working out.

I bang on the bathroom door. "Logan! What are you doing in there?"

"I'll be right out."

"I swear to God. If you make me late because you had to jerk off, I'm gonna kill you."

"I'm not jerking off, asshole." I hear the toilet flush, and a moment later, he opens the door. "The bathroom is all yours."

I twist my nose when the stench hits me. "Jesus Christ. What the hell did you eat last night?"

"Chili con carne."

I step away from the bathroom, fanning my hand in front of my face. "Thank fuck I don't need to use the bathroom. The air inside is lethal."

He laughs. "Then why were you yelling at me?"

"I have fifteen minutes to get to my first class."

He looks at me as if I'm crazy. "I didn't know you had class at nine today."

I walk to the open kitchen, which takes two steps to reach in our minuscule apartment, and I point at the schedule I taped to the fridge door. "Hello. Did you even look at it? It says right there, Purchasing and Procurement 101."

He rolls his eyes. "Fine. I didn't memorize the schedule yet. It'll only take me a second to put on clothes."

"I'll wait in the car. If you don't come out in five minutes, I'm leaving without you."

He flips me off before he disappears inside his room. I grab the car keys from the counter and head out. I'm not joking. I'll leave his sorry ass behind, and he knows it. I'd prefer if it doesn't come to that because his retaliation will be a bitch, even though I'm in the right.

Perks of having a twin brother who's a pest. But again, I'm no different.

I end up waiting more than five minutes, and when Logan finally gets in the car, I'm fuming from my ears. "You said it'd take you a second to change!"

"I couldn't find any clean clothes. I had to borrow yours."

I put the car in drive and peel out of the parking spot. I have six minutes to get to class. Unfortunately, speeding on campus is a serious offense, thanks to the countless bikes sharing the road, so I have to maintain the speed limit.

I don't bother finding a parking spot since Logan will keep

the car. But I have one minute to get from the front of the building to the lecture hall.

I fly out of the vehicle and run as fast as I can into the building. It's my luck that the room is on the third floor. Man, I'm getting my cardio in for the day.

I'm sweating when I finally find the lecture hall. Most seats are taken, and Professor Weiland is about to start.

He glances at me and narrows his eyes. "Cutting it close there, young man. One second later, and you wouldn't be allowed in."

"I'm sorry, sir. It won't happen again." I find a seat and drop there like a sack of potatoes as I try to catch my breath.

Man, that was close. Logan is lucky. I won't have to commit fratricide later.

BLAIR

It's the first day of the spring semester, so naturally, I've been up since dawn. My first class starts at nine, so I'm ready to walk out the door by eight. I want to get the lay of the land.

My plans are derailed when my mother walks into my apartment unannounced. She has a key, but I didn't expect her to come barging in without letting me know first.

"Mom. What are you doing here?"

"I have an early doctor's appointment nearby. I came to check on you."

"I'm about to leave for class."

"Nonsense. Your class doesn't start until nine."

"You've memorized my schedule?" My voice rises.

She gives me a droll look. "Of course not, dear. It's on my calendar."

"I was planning to arrive early."

She ignores me, setting her Birkin bag on the counter. "When did you buy those pillows?"

"I don't know."

"I hate them."

"I like them."

They have cute puppies on them, but that's probably why she's glaring at them as if they were an eyesore. She makes a disapproving sound in the back of her throat, but at least she doesn't order me to get rid of them. However, her inspection continues. Suddenly, her spine goes rigid, and I follow her gaze to a picture I have framed on the side table next to the couch.

"What's this?" she shrieks, making me wince. She snatches up the picture frame with fury and then turns around. "Care to explain why you have this picture on display for everyone to see?"

"It's my apartment, and I wanted a picture of Cory and me."

"This isn't *your* apartment. I pay the rent and let you live here." She takes the picture out of the frame and tears it into small pieces.

"You didn't need to destroy it!"

"Don't make me regret letting you live alone, Blair."

My eyes fill with tears. I wouldn't have displayed that picture if I'd known Mom would pay me surprise visits. I'm so stupid. She's never tolerated any reminder of Cory. Why would she change now?

"Do you have any more pictures of him here?"

"No. That was the only one."

She shoves the torn pieces into her bag and strides toward my room. I should have known she wouldn't take my word for it. I stay in the living room, afraid that my presence will set her off. There are other damning things in my bedroom, and if she really wants to look, she'll find them. I'd better stay away so I don't raise her suspicions.

Ten minutes later, she returns with several outfits draped over her arm. "Give me a trash bag."

"Why?" It's all the stuff I bought at the secondhand shop I went to with Gia.

"To put these trashy clothes in. What were you thinking buying them?"

"They're for a sorority event," I lie.

She huffs and dumps the clothes on the floor. Fucking hell.

"Mom, I have to go."

She looks me up and down and shakes her head. "You're not leaving the house wearing that."

I look at my slacks and cream-colored merino wool sweater, wondering what she could find offensive about them. "What's wrong with my clothes?"

"You look like your aunt Martha. Wear the light-blue Chanel suit."

I have two options. Stand here and argue with her, or do what she says. In the end, getting into a fight with Mom isn't worth it. I change, but the ordeal makes me late as hell for class.

When I finally arrive at the lecture hall, the door is closed. I'm five minutes late. Professor Weiland is one of the strictest professors on campus, but his department just received a big donation from my father's company. I hate using my family's name to get away with stuff, but after what my mother put me through this morning, I go for it.

When I enter the room, all heads turn toward me. Students are sitting in clusters, and my guess is Professor Weiland already gave them a group project to work on. Fantastic.

The first person I notice is one of the Kaminski twins. I'm not sure if it's Alex or Logan—they're identical, and I can't tell them apart. All I know is that they're my brother Ryder's hockey teammates and seem nice. I could use a friendly face today.

"Can I help you?" Professor Weiland asks.

I approach his desk, hoping he won't send me away. That would be humiliating.

"Yes. I'm in this class. My name is Blair Westwood."

"You're late. I don't allow students in my classroom if they can't arrive on time."

"I'm aware, and I completely agree with your policy. But I was hoping you would make an exception this time. I had a family emergency involving my mother."

His thick eyebrows arch. "I hope nothing serious."

"Everything is okay now."

He keeps staring at me with his beady eyes, probably debating the pros and cons of bending his rules for a Westwood.

"I'll make an exception this time, Miss Westwood."

I beam from ear to ear. "Thank you, sir."

"We're working in groups. Please join group *A*."

I turn, still sporting a smile, but it wilts when I catch the glower on Kaminski's face aimed at me. Shit. What did I do to him? I look at the groups, trying to find mine.

"You're in our group," he grumbles.

Fucking fantastic. I pull up the only chair available, which is directly across from him. "What are we doing?"

The girl to my right gives me a piece of paper with the instructions. I scan the document fast, trying to ignore the pair of blue eyes burning a hole through my face.

"Are you done?" Alex asks impatiently.

I look up, not caring one bit about his rude behavior. "Yep. It's pretty straightforward."

"I've already come up with a list of arguments why our company should have the oranges," the girl who gave me the handout says.

"We don't need a list of arguments," I say, baffled that she couldn't see the solution right in front of her eyes.

"Why is that? Should we just use your last name to get the other groups to do whatever we want?" Alex retorts.

"No. Do you have a problem with me, Kaminski?"

"I have a problem with people who believe the rules don't apply to them."

Who the fuck does this guy think he is? "That's rich, coming from a hockey player."

He narrows his eyes. "All the perks I get, I earn."

"Guys, can we focus for a moment?" another member of the group butts in. "Blair, why don't you think we need a list of arguments?"

"It's simple. Both companies in this scenario need the oranges, but not the whole orange. The other company only needs the pulp, whereas our company only needs the skin. We can both get the parts of the orange we need."

My team members turn their attention to their handouts, reading the document again, but I keep my gaze on Alex, who's glaring openly at me. And to think I believed he'd be someone I could befriend. He's an asshole, and he's dead wrong if he thinks I'll let him bully me. If he throws a stone at me, I'll toss back ten in return.

CHAPTER 1
ALEX

PRESENT DAY

I push my way through the crowd, not knowing exactly where I'm going. I'm hoping back to the dance floor, but this damn club is huge, and I may have had one too many tequila shots already. The tight corridor finally opens up to a large room, and ahead, I see the pulsating lights above the dance floor and the DJ booth high up, where a guy wearing a silver fedora is lording over the throng of people who dance and sing without a care in the world.

With my destination in sight, I walk faster, carving a path with my elbows… that is until I spot a petite brunette going in the opposite direction. It's dark, but what I see piques my interest. That girl is just my type. I change course, reaching her as she's about to turn into the corridor leading to the restrooms.

I touch her arm. "Slow down, pretty girl. Where are you going in such a hurry?"

She stops and looks at me, her defiant eyebrows pinched together. "What's your problem, Kaminski?"

Someone, shoot me now.

I yank my hand back as if I were electrocuted. I can't believe I came after Blair Westwood thinking she was a hot chick and a possible hookup. In my defense, she doesn't look like her usual self tonight. Her clothes aren't prissy, her hair is wavy and a little wild, and she's wearing red lipstick that makes her plump lips very kissable. As a matter of fact, I'm staring at them right now and wondering what they taste like.

"What are you looking at, perv?" she asks.

I snap my gaze back to her eyes, twisting my lips into a sardonic grin to hide the fact that she caught me staring.

"I was looking at your clown makeup. You shouldn't wear red lipstick if you don't know how to handle it."

Her blue eyes bug out. "What?"

"You have lipstick all over your chin."

I rub my thumb over the nonexistent smear. I don't know where I got the impulse to touch her face. I'm blaming alcohol for this stupid move.

She bats my hand away. "Don't touch me, jackass."

"Sorry... I was just trying to help." I attempt to keep a straight face.

She narrows her eyes. "Sure you were."

"Where are you going?"

She crosses her arms. "Why do you care?"

"It's not safe for a tiny little thing like you to wander this club alone."

She snorts. "Are you for real? Where's the danger?"

Fuck. I could say, look around at all these drunk assholes. But if I do that, I'll be damning myself as well. After all, I did come after her hoping to score.

"You're right. There's no danger. Looking the way you do right now, the only people you'll be attracting are the circus crowd."

She pinches her lips into a flat line. "Did you follow me just to insult me?"

I feel a twinge of remorse for putting her down, but I choose to ignore it. "Nah. I wouldn't waste my time chasing you. But now that I'm here, I can't pass up the opportunity to mess with you."

She scowls. "You're pathetic, Alex. Stay away from me."

My guts seem to curdle. Why do I care if she wants distance from me?

"With pleasure, darling."

She turns on her heels too fast and almost loses her balance. At any other time, that would make me laugh, but I don't. Blair is drunk, which supports my opinion that she shouldn't be wandering alone in the club. She regains her balance, then fixes her microskirt and lifts her chin before striding away toward the ladies' room. Immediately, my gaze drops to her ass. I wouldn't normally check her out, but in that tight skirt, it's easy to forget she's the bane of my existence.

I should turn around and head to the dance floor, but I don't move. Instead, I watch her walk away. She turns male heads as she goes, and that doesn't sit well with me. Those baboons have no right to ogle her.

Only you should have that privilege, right, Alex?

I ignore the annoying thought and walk in the opposite direction. I don't go far. Before I reach the end of the corridor, I stop and turn toward the restrooms again. Like a creep, I flatten my back against the wall, keeping my gaze on the women's restroom entrance. I'm not sure what I'm doing, and I know Blair can take care of herself, but... I feel like I need to protect her. If any asshole tries anything, I'll be there to make them sorry.

BLAIR

I don't know if Alex was putting the moves on me just now or if he was just being his obnoxious self. But he touched my face, and I didn't like it. Not because he shouldn't be touching me… I didn't like that his touch sent a thrill of excitement down my spine. What's up with that?

I have to pee, but thanks to his comment about my makeup, I veer for the mirror first. "That fucking asshole!"

There isn't a single hint of a lipstick smear on my chin. He lied. Why am I even surprised?

I don't look like a clown, but I don't look like myself either. I let Ashley do my makeup this evening, and she went heavy with the eyeliner. You'd think the red lipstick would be overkill, but I actually look hot, and not in a cheap hooker way. This makeup isn't something I'd ever attempt but for one night away with my girlfriends... it's perfect. Maybe I'll keep wearing red lipstick. I like it.

Now that I know I don't look like a clown, I do what I came here for, and a few minutes later, I walk out of the restroom feeling better than ever.

I haven't taken two steps before some random guy steps in front of me, blocking my path. "How are you, gorgeous?"

I wince, stepping away from his rancid breath. "I'd be better with you out of my way."

I walk around him, but he grabs my arm. "Where are you going so fast? I'm not done talking to you."

My gaze drops to his beefy hand on my arm, and then I look into his glassy eyes. "You have one second to remove your hand before you regret ever touching me." I stick my hand in my purse and curl my fingers around the pepper spray I always carry.

He smiles. "Oh yeah? What's a pretty little thing like you going to do to me?"

Before I can show him, someone yanks him back and shoves him to the side. He hits the wall, and that's the only thing that prevents him from falling on his ass.

"What the fuck, man!" He glowers at my savior, who's none other than Alex. "I was just talking to her."

"It didn't look like that to me. Now get lost before I rearrange your face."

I've seen Alex go into savage mode on the ice, but witnessing it up close is something else. Adrenaline shoots up my veins, making my entire body tingle. I get hot... maybe even turned on. This is hell.

The drunk idiot who grabbed me asks, "Is that your boyfriend?"

I open my mouth to say *hell no*, but Alex beats me to the punch. "I'm her *friend*," he grits out. "Now fuck off."

The guy walks away fast. Smart move. Alex is not one to issue empty threats. I bet he'd beat the shit out of that moron.

He gives me an assessing glance. "Are you okay?"

"I'm fine. You didn't need to intervene."

"I know."

I'm not sure what to say, so the silence stretches. But I don't break eye contact.

"Thanks," I finally reply.

"No problem. Should we go find the others?"

"Yeah."

He offers me his hand, and I freeze, staring at it like an idiot.

"It'd be easier if I don't lose you in the crowd," he explains.

I let him take my hand and try to ignore the strange sensation that shoots up my arm and the goose bumps that form on my skin. Why am I reacting like this to his touch? I don't like him... he's insufferable.

But I have to admit that letting him lead the way and carve a path for us through the crowd is much easier than finding my own way through. We reach the dance floor in no time, but before we join our friends, I pull my hand free. I don't want anyone to see me holding hands with Alex. The girls would tease me to no end.

It's providential that our friends are already drunk, and nobody realizes that Alex and I rejoined them together. I move close to the girls and dance with them for a few more songs, trying to ignore that Alex is there. Gia and Noah are lost in their own world, and only a blind person wouldn't be able to see they're in love. I smile, truly happy for her. My gaze moves to the right, and I catch Alex staring at me. My face warms, and once again, I break the connection first. What's with him tonight?

The DJ announces last call, and there's a collective sigh of disappointment from the crowd.

"I'm not ready to sleep yet!" Gia whines. "This was such fun."

"Who said the night needs to be over?" I ask, but I sound funny to my ears. Why isn't my tongue working right?

"Did you really just say that?" Alex asks. "Isn't it past your bedtime already?"

I look at him, but the room begins to spin. I focus on his stupid, gorgeous face. "I'd tell you to bite me, but I don't wanna ruin Gia's birthday party and bicker with you."

He laughs. "Aren't you sweet? But I like when we bicker."

His eyes narrow, and the emotion in them seems to change. I don't know why, but I get flustered under his gaze. Fuck. How much did I drink?

"Dude, you like it so much, you'll end up marrying her," Darren pipes up.

I whip my face toward him so fast I get a kink in my neck. He must be drunk out of his mind too.

"Nah... It'd be more fun if I married her, and then Alex realizes that he's been in love with her all this time, but he has no choice but to pine for her from afar." Logan laughs.

I press a hand to my forehead. Why is everyone saying stupid shit right now?

CJ furrows his brows. "Okay... that's not just alcohol talking. What did you take?"

Logan lifts his hands. "I didn't take anything. I swear. Don't judge me for having a vivid imagination."

"Your imagination is seriously disturbing," Ashley chimes in.

"Guys, we should start making our way out of the club," Sean butts in.

"I need to get my coat," I say.

"Ugh. It's going to take forever," CJ complains. "Why did you bring a coat?"

"Because I didn't want to freeze my ass off on the way here."

"Maybe you should have worn more clothes," Alex retorts.

"Don't stand there and pretend you weren't checking me out earlier."

"Say whaaat?" Logan laughs. "I knew you weren't blind, bro."

He glares at his brother. "Shut up."

I look around and notice that the birthday girl and her beau are gone. "Where did Gia and Noah go?"

"I'm pretty sure they went back to the hotel already. You know... to carry on the birthday celebrations." Ashley wiggles her brows up and down.

"Where's Jaime?" Darren asks, looking around for Gia's brother.

"Last time I saw him, he was hanging out with Gordon Montana and Gretchen McCoy. I'm pretty sure he went to the VIP room with them," Sean replies.

"Are you shitting me?" Logan chimes in. "When did that happen?"

Sean shrugs. "I don't know, man. A while ago."

Sensing someone is burning a hole through my face, I turn and see it's Alex who's staring.

Logan elbows his arm. "Can you believe we missed Gretchen?"

Still looking at me, he replies, "Yeah, bummer."

His attention is unnerving me, so I look away first. He's never stared at me as if he wants to invade my space and, I don't know... kiss me. I must be imagining things. There's no way Alex Kaminski sees me that way.

CHAPTER 2
BLAIR

SIX WEEKS LATER

I promised myself I wouldn't come to another Warriors away game, but after what happened to Gia and with the horrible way I handled everything after her breakup with Ryder, I need to prove I'm her friend. I'm still in shock and want to spend quality time with her. I knew her friend Martin was a weirdo, but never in a million years did I think he was a total psycho who'd try to kidnap her at gunpoint after she turned him down. He'll never see the light of day as a free man again if my brother and I have anything to say about it. He can rot in prison.

The Warriors are playing Clayton U tonight, and the arena is packed, but I'm alone in enemy territory. Zoey has started her intense figure skating training again and couldn't be here, and Ashley hates hockey with a passion. She came to Boston last month only because it was Gia's birthday.

Gia got me a media pass, but I thought it best if I waited for her in my seat instead of joining her in the locker room. I don't even know if I'd be allowed inside. I'm also trying to avoid seeing Alex outside of the classes I share with him. I still think constantly about our interaction back at the club in Boston. My memories of our tequila-shot contest that happened after the club are hazy at best. I don't even remember how that came about. Regardless, I don't like that the pest is living rent-free in my mind.

My phone rings in my purse. It's Ryder's ringtone. I don't want to talk to him, but I'm one of those people who can't ignore a call, ever. I answer them all, even the ones from numbers I don't recognize. If I don't, it feels like an itch I can't scratch.

"Hello?"

"Why didn't you tell me Gia was *pregnant*?" he shouts in my ear, making me wince.

"Hello to you too, brother," I scowl even though he can't see my face.

"Don't start with me, Blair," he snaps.

"I'm not starting anything. I'm just not rude like you."

"So, is it true?" I notice a slight trepidation in his voice and remember that Ryder isn't over Gia yet, so I give him a break.

I sigh. "Yes, it's true. Are you upset?"

He doesn't reply for a couple beats. He doesn't need to. I know he is.

"No," he grumbles.

Oh, Ryder, you sound so stupid when you lie.

"Then why were you yelling at me?"

"Because you didn't tell me. I had to find out from Preston, of all people."

I wrinkle my nose. CJ's brother is such a jerk. I think the only reason Ryder tolerates him is that our parents are friends.

"I'm sorry. She just told me last week."

"Is she… *happy* about it?"

"I think so. I mean... it's not ideal. No one plans to get knocked up while still in college. But Gia and Noah are so in love. If any couple can make it work, it's them."

"I hope you're right."

"Ryder… you were the one who ended things, remember? Why are you still hung up on her?"

A loud horn blasts in the arena, making me jump in my seat. I press my hand against my chest as if that will help my heart slow down.

"Where are you?" he asks.

"I'm at the Warriors game. They're playing at Clayton U."

"And you *went*?" His voice rises in pitch.

"Yeah. Why is that so hard to believe?"

"Because you never stepped foot in the arena when I was on the team." Oh, gee, he sounds butt hurt now. I didn't even know he cared whether I went to his games or not.

"Well, a lot of things have changed since then."

"Clearly." His voice drips with annoyance.

From the corner of my eye, I see Gia approaching. "I have to go."

"Fine. Have fun."

The call goes silent before I can press the end button. I hope his bad mood improves in the next few days. I can't handle the holiday season if Ryder isn't on my side. The entire month of December is filled with social events that are mandatory for the Westwood children.

"Hey, what's with the face?" Gia asks.

"Nothing."

"Come on. I know you. Who were you talking to on the phone?"

I sigh, not meeting her stare. "Ryder. He called to yell at me for not telling him that you're pregnant."

"Oh."

I look at her. "Does it bother you that my brother seems to still have feelings for you?"

She shakes her head. "It doesn't bother me. It makes me sad. I'm in love with Noah, and I've never been happier. I want the same for your brother."

"I know you do. He'll find someone…or my parents will find her for him."

Gia grimaces. "That's not the type of future I want for him or *you*."

I shrug. "I don't want that fate either, but sometimes there isn't a choice."

"There's always a choice, Blair."

I face the ice. "Not in my world."

The music changes, and the crowd gets rowdier. The Clayton U theme song is playing.

"Oh, the game is about to start. Great," I say, glad for the interruption. "How are the guys?"

"Excited. Games against Clayton U are rougher than usual, but they're all craving the opportunity to unleash the beast, especially Alex and Noah."

"He hasn't forgiven Atlas for talking shit about you at their last game, has he?"

"Nope. I told him to focus on hockey. Atlas always talks shit, hoping to get them riled up. That's how he rolls."

"I hope Alex puts him in his place."

Gia furrows her brows. "That's the first time you've mentioned Alex's name without attaching a negative comment to it."

Shit. I can't believe she caught that. "He's a menace. Might as well put his savagery to good use."

"Sure, sure." She faces the ice for a second before continuing. "I don't buy it, Blair. You've been acting strange about him since Boston. Did something happen between Alex and you at the club... or after? Wasn't there a certain tequila contest in the mix?"

My blood seems to freeze in my veins. I never told anyone that Alex flirted with me before he realized who I was. And never mind the charged stares we exchanged after that. It was alcohol. Just alcohol.

"Nothing happened. Please don't tell me you're buying into the bullshit that Alex and I will become a thing."

"I'm not buying into anything. If you say there's nothing

going on, then I believe you. Besides, I don't recommend Alex or Logan as potential boyfriends for anyone I care about."

Curious, I ask, "Why is that?"

"They don't want to settle down. They're more than happy to play the field for now. I'm not saying they'll never be good boyfriends. As a matter of fact, when they're ready to be monogamous, I'm sure they'll be the best boyfriends in the world. Both have amazing hearts, and they'll do anything for the people they love."

My heart skips a beat, and I don't know why it's reacting this way. I have nothing to say to that, so I bite my tongue and pretend to be very interested in whatever is happening on the ice. I've always known the twins were players, so why the hell am I fixating on the part of Gia's statement about Alex being a great boyfriend one day? I don't want to date Alex. I don't even want to hook up with him. Besides, it doesn't matter. Sooner or later, my mother is going to trap me into an arranged marriage, and there's nothing I can do about it. She holds all the cards, and what I stand to lose is not worth an act of rebellion.

"Oh, there are our boys." Gia touches my arm.

The Warriors enter the ice for warm-up, and my traitorous eyes immediately search for Alex's jersey. Most guys on the team are huge, but even so, he, Logan, and Sean stand out as giants. He's a foot taller than me, and if—and that's hypothetical—I decided to kiss him, I'd have to climb him like a monkey to reach his lips. I snort in my head at the visual.

"Who do you think is going to win?" I ask.

"It's hard to say. Both teams are good, and Clayton U is sore about their loss at the last game. They're hungry for retaliation."

The teams are supposed to stay on their side for the warm-ups, but when Alex skates near Kodiak in the neutral zone, they exchange words, and whatever Kodiak says doesn't sit well with Alex.

"Oh boy. It's starting already," Gia mumbles.

"What happens if someone starts a fight before the game?"

"They'll probably be ejected."

"Ejected? As in, kicked out of the game?"

"Yeah."

Sean drags Alex away from Kodiak, and he doesn't seem happy. I can't see the faces of their coaches since we're sitting in the section behind the Warriors' bench, but I bet they aren't amused that Alex is creating trouble before the game even begins.

"How much longer until the puck drops?" I ask Gia.

"I'd say half an hour."

"Should we grab something to eat?"

"Hmm... I'll pass on the food. Everything is making me nauseous lately. But I'll come with you."

I'm not really hungry; I just need an excuse to get out of my seat. I didn't expect to be so drawn to Alex on the ice like that, and I need a minute to get my mind in order.

CHAPTER 3
ALEX

"What the fuck do you think you're doing?" Sean yells as he steers me away from Kodiak.

"He needs to be taught a lesson," I retort.

"Not before the game starts, idiot." Our captain skates away before I can reply.

Logan and Noah approach, neither looking happy.

"What did that asshole say?" Noah asks. "He'd better not have mentioned Gia again."

I clench my jaw and avoid his gaze. That's exactly what that motherfucker did. Everyone knows that Gia is preggers thanks to CJ blabbering about it at The Heritage a couple days ago. That nimrod sure has a loose tongue when he's drunk.

My silence says it all, and within seconds, Noah is in my personal space. "What did that jackass say?"

"It's not worth repeating, man."

Noah looks toward the Clayton U zone, and I know exactly where he's aiming his death glare.

"That asshole has a death wish," Logan pipes up. "Don't worry. Before the night is over, he'll never open his big mouth again to talk shit about anyone."

"Hey!" Sean yells. "Why aren't you guys warming up?"

We break away and resume our exercises. I lift my gaze to the stands just in time to see Gia and Blair exit their row. I didn't know Blair was coming. A surge of excitement spreads through my veins. I like the idea that Blair is in the crowd tonight, and I can't fathom why. I won't lie and say I haven't thought about her since Gia's birthday party. I'm a guy, and now that I know Blair is fucking hot under those preppy clothes, I'm having a hard time remembering I don't like her.

She's a stuck-up bitch, that's why, moron. Even during that stupid tequila shots contest, she acted like she was better than everyone else.

Someone collides with me, jostling me sideways. "Wake up, bro."

Normally, I'd retaliate, but Logan's body check was exactly what I needed to snap me out of my trance. I shake my head and push thoughts of Blair into a dark corner of my mind. I've never allowed a hot piece of ass to distract me from the game. I won't let that witch do it now.

BLAIR

I did the best I could to stall. I picked the food stand with the longest line, then I got in line for the restroom even though I didn't need to pee. By the time we return to our seats, the puck is about to drop. The players are on the ice, and mercifully, Alex isn't in the starting lineup. It's a small reprieve—he will eventually have his turn.

"Coach is switching things around," Gia says.

"How so?"

"Alex always starts against Clayton U. I wonder if the change has something to do with his earlier altercation."

"If that's the case, he's probably not happy."

Gia shakes her head. "Probably not."

We don't speak for a while, mainly because Gia's focus is solely on the game. Noah is playing, and he has her undivided attention. The action is intense, and the body checks against the wall seem harder than needed. When a player from Clayton U shoves Noah against the glass, Gia winces.

"Oh, that's gotta hurt," I say.

"Yeah."

There's a line change, and Alex steps onto the ice. I straighten. Now I only have eyes for him. He might be hateful, but I can't deny that he flies over the ice with extreme grace for someone his size. Deadly grace. Within seconds, he slams into a Clayton U forward and enters the Warriors' defensive zone. The guy falls in a heap and doesn't get up right away. The crowd boos Alex, but he just smiles like a fiend.

"Will he be penalized for that?" I ask.

"I don't think so. It was a clean hit."

"Brutal."

"That's hockey for you."

It's clear that the Clayton U players aren't happy Alex wasn't sent to the sin bin. Alex stays focused on the puck as he skates faster than a bullet train. He doesn't seem to notice when a player from Clayton bears toward him just as fast. Their collision sends Alex flying backward. He crashes onto the ice and the momentum makes him slide until he hits the wall, out of my sight.

"Oh my God." I gasp, jumping from my seat to try to see him.

Gia does the same; meanwhile, players from both teams get into a scrum. There's a lot of roughhousing going around. The Warriors' trainer steps onto the ice and kneels out of my sight to check on Alex, I assume. Worry squeezes my heart like a boa constrictor.

"He's not hurt that badly, right?" I ask.

"I don't know," Gia replies, sounding choked up.

A moment later, the trainer and Alex get up and leave the ice.

It's hard to concentrate on what's happening on the ice now when I'm worried sick about the bane of my existence.

Mercifully, the first period ends, and Gia announces, "I'm going to the locker room to check on Alex."

"Can I come?"

Gia' brows shoot up. I probably shocked the hell out of her.

"Sure. I don't know if we'll be able to see him though. These passes don't grant us that kind of access, but I can't sit here without knowing if he's all right."

I don't say it out loud, but I feel the same way. Alex is a pest, a thorn in my side, but I don't *hate* him. I hope he's okay.

CHAPTER 4
ALEX

Son of a bitch. I pulled a back muscle, and I'm out of commission for at least two weeks. Last night, after my collision with number thirty-nine, the team's physician didn't let me return to the ice, and we lost to those Clayton U fuckers. Today, after my examination, he dropped the injury bomb. Needless to say, I'm beyond pissed.

Logan is waiting for me in the Warriors' common area with my puppy, aptly named Blair, when I get out of my meeting with Coach Bedford and Assistant Coach LaRue.

Blair barks, jumping up and wagging her tail. I smile despite my dark mood. When I'm closer, she rises on her hind legs and presses her tiny front paws on my jeans.

Smiling, I scratch her head. "Hey, girl. I'm happy to see you too."

"How was the meeting?" Logan asks.

I lift my eyes to him. "I'm benched for at least two weeks."

He runs a hand through his hair. "Fuck."

"I know. I'm not happy either. Dr. Martin said I could recover in a few days, but to be safe, Coach Bedford won't let me play until the two weeks are up."

Logan clenches his jaw and stares at me. "Silver lining. Now you can go on that trip to DC for your economics class."

I frown. "How is that a silver lining? I'd rather play hockey."

He gives me a droll stare. "Bro, seriously? You were moping around because you couldn't go."

"I wasn't *moping*. I just said it'd be nice to present my paper at the forum."

He taps my shoulder. "Now you can."

I didn't think I'd revealed to Logan that I was upset about missing the opportunity to go to DC, but I guess I'm not that great at hiding my emotions from my twin. I feel guilty for even wanting to go. I love hockey, and that's where my career is headed. Both Logan and I were drafted by the Miami Lions two years ago. We haven't been offered a contract yet, but Assistant Coach LaRue and our agent, Joanne Hughes, believe it'll happen at the end of the season.

"I have to speak with Professor McNelis. The forum starts in two days."

"Can't you send him an email?"

"I'd rather speak to him in person. I have his class later today. I'll just get there early."

Logan's lips twitch upward. "Are you capable of getting anywhere ahead of time?"

I clap his back. "Yes, when I don't have to wait for your sorry ass."

BLAIR

Today is not going my way. I didn't sleep well last night, thanks to one, staying up too late worrying about Alex and two, listening to Cookie cry all night long. Gia and I weren't able to see Alex before we left the arena, but later Gia texted me with an update. He pulled a muscle in his back. Not a terrible outcome, but it still prevented me from relaxing completely.

Pippa, my big sister at the sorority, woke me up at an ungodly hour to remind me that I was supposed to bring five hundred cupcakes to our charity event this afternoon. It totally slipped my mind.

I spent an hour this morning calling every bakery in the city, hoping for a miracle. In the end, I had to call in a favor with one of my mother's friends. I got the baked goods, but it cost me. She made me promise I'd go on a date with her horrid son. That's a deal I'll break for sure, and I'm not even sorry about it. Though if it had been a date set up by my mother, that'd be a different story.

Now I'm running late for my economics class. Punctuality is one of my strengths, and the idea that I might not be on time gives me hives. I can't find a parking spot, and when I do, it's far from the building. It's raining cats and dogs, and of course, I forgot to replace the umbrella I lost last week. I run through the parking lot, using my bag to protect my head from the rain, but I get drenched nonetheless.

People stare at me as I burst through the heavy double doors. I must look like a drowned, harassed rat. There's no time to check myself on my phone though. I have only a couple minutes before the lecture begins. Professor McNelis always starts on time. I sprint down the hallway, hoping I don't slip and fall on my ass. The biggest danger is losing one shoe—or both. They're wet, and thanks to my tights, my feet are slipping inside them.

I round a corner and skid to a halt when I catch Professor McNelis coming in my direction with none other than Alex next to him. They appear to be having a pleasant conversation. Alex is actually grinning. I guess his injury wasn't as serious as Gia led me to believe.

Then they spot me. Professor McNelis's eyes widen a fraction while Alex gives me an elevator glance and then smirks when our eyes meet.

My hair is dripping down my back, and I'm sure my makeup is ruined, but I keep my spine straight and my chin raised. I might look like shit, but I won't lose my dignity.

"Blair, I'm glad I caught you before class," Professor McNelis says. "I have great news."

I turn to him. "I like great news."

"Alex will be able to join you in DC after all."

My stomach bottoms out. That's the furthest thing from great news. I knew he was eligible to go, but I was glad he couldn't because of hockey. "What?"

"You two have the highest grades in my class. You're tied for number one. I usually like to send two students to represent Hannaford U."

Our grades have been a sore spot for me, and I don't like to be reminded of that fun fact.

"Why was I the only one going before then?"

He pushes his wire-rimmed glasses up his nose. "You two are performing far above your peers. I couldn't send anyone with you besides Alex."

I curl my hands into fists, trying my best to not show how unhappy I am. "That's… great."

"You're going to have a wonderful time," he says before he veers into the lecture hall.

Neither Alex nor I follow him. We're locked in a staring contest.

"I thought you got hurt. Are you sure going on a trip won't mess up your recovery?"

He tilts his head. "Aw, are you concerned about me?"

"No. Just making an observation."

"Right. I heard you came by to check on me last night." He smiles broadly, showing off his perfect white teeth.

Hell. I can't believe Gia told him that. *Traitor.* "Gia was worried about you. I was there to support her."

"Whatever you say." He follows Professor McNelis into the

lecture hall. "By the way, you might want to head to the restroom before class."

"Why?"

He laughs. "Just a suggestion."

I pull my phone from my purse and open the camera app. Crap on toast. No wonder that jackass was amused. My mascara is running down my cheeks. I look ridiculous. But the worst person to see me like this already did—Alex. So I follow him into the lecture hall and sit in the last row. I can fix my makeup while listening to the class.

This isn't my usual spot. I prefer to sit in the first row. Alex always sits in the back, and I never see him during class, but now I have a bird's-eye view of him sitting next to Carola Mitchell, president of the Zetas. She's blonde with big boobs and the personality of a door. I'm not surprised Alex is talking to her. From what I've observed, she's exactly his type.

I shouldn't be paying attention to them, but I'm unable to look away. When he leans closer to whisper in her ear, she laughs softly. It annoys me to no end. To add insult to injury, the jerkface looks up and catches me staring. My face catches fire. Quickly, I look at my purse and do what I was supposed to—grab my makeup bag.

Fuck. Can this day be over already?

CHAPTER 5
BLAIR

No one will ever know how hard it was for me to not ask about Alex's travel arrangements. The economics department bought my plane ticket to DC, so I'm assuming they did the same for Alex, but whether we're on the same flight is a mystery. Since I upgraded my ticket to business class, I head to the gate only when it's time to board.

As I stand in the priority line, I spot Alex sitting with his head down as far away as possible from the gate. Now I have my answer. He *is* on this flight.

I glance at the monitor when it changes to the waiting list. His last name catches my attention. He's fourth on the list. Judging by the number of people crowding the gate, it's a full flight. He's probably not getting a seat. Waiting at the airport for hours without knowing if you'll be able to take off is one of the worst things that can happen. This is a late afternoon flight—if he doesn't get on this one, when will the next be?

No. He needs to be on this flight. I'm not sure why I care, but I'm determined to make it happen. I approach the desk and force a smile. "Hi, do you still have seats available in business class?"

The attendant furrows her brows. "I believe it's a full flight."

"Can you check for me?"

The woman pinches her lips, then turns her frown to the monitor. "We do have one seat left."

"I'll take it." I slide my credit card across the counter.

"I also need your boarding pass."

"It's not for me. I'm already in business class. It's for a passenger on your waiting list. Alex Kaminski."

She types away on her keyboard, then says, "Yes, I see him. He doesn't have a boarding pass yet. He's on the waiting list."

No shit, Sherlock. I just said that.

"I know. Would you mind charging my card and not telling him I paid for his upgrade?"

She meets my gaze, and I can tell she has an objection on the tip of her tongue, so I add, in a sweet tone and a smile, "He's a friend of mine and I want to surprise him. He doesn't know I'm on this flight."

The tension around her mouth lessens. "Sure."

It takes another five minutes for her to complete the transaction, and I hope Alex is still distracted by whatever he's watching on his phone and doesn't glance in my direction. I truly don't want him to know I'm paying for his upgrade.

I return to the priority line, happy to now find myself at the end behind a couple of tall businessmen who'll hide my presence. I should blend in with the background. Normally I love to wear pastel colors, but not when I travel. My coat is black, and my tights are deep maroon. The only pops of color in my outfit are my red purse, hairband, and lipstick. Yes, after Boston, I decided to make red lipstick my trademark look.

The attendant at the desk calls Alex's name. I should stay put, but I can't help leaning to the side to spy on him.

"I'm Alex Kaminski," he tells the attendant.

"Here's your boarding pass."

He pinches his brows. "Wait. I'm getting a seat? I'm fourth on the list."

"You've been upgraded to business class."

"Why?"

Boy, would it kill him to just accept his good fortune and not ask too many questions?

One of the men in front of me looks over his shoulder and gives me a leering glance. I step back. "What are you looking at?"

"Are you sure you're in the right line, sugar?"

I scowl. "Why else would I voluntarily stand near a couple of old pricks?"

"What did you say?" he asks louder, likely hoping to intimidate me.

Bitch, please. I lift my chin higher. "You heard me. Now step back before I report you for harassment. I bet the last thing you need is to be put on the no-fly list."

The old creep's face gets red, and I'm sure the next thing out of his mouth will force me to make good on my threat, but suddenly Alex is striding up behind him.

"Excuse me," he tells the guy.

He whips around to face Alex, looking even more aggravated, but whatever he has to say dies in his throat. Maybe it's Alex's six-foot-four frame or his bulging biceps, which are obvious even under his jacket.

"Are you together?" the guy asks.

"Yes," Alex replies before I can. "Is there a problem here?"

"No, not at all." The man looks away and shifts forward in line without a fight.

I'm annoyed. All Alex had to do was show up for the asshole to put his tail between his legs and leave me alone.

"Did you pay for my upgrade?" he asks me.

I study my fingernails. "I don't know what you're talking about."

"Don't play dumb with me, Blair. It doesn't suit you."

He's too close to me, and I have to crane my neck to meet his stare. "What if I did? You weren't getting on this flight otherwise, and the forum starts tomorrow."

"I could have taken the flight I was booked on. It leaves in a couple of hours."

I raise an eyebrow. "Then why were you on the waiting list for this one?"

"Because I wouldn't mind getting to DC earlier. I can use the rest."

"There you go. I made your wishes come true. The correct reaction would be a 'thank you,' but I guess that's expecting too much from you."

"I don't like owing you favors. I'll pay you back."

"I don't want your money. I was trying to be nice."

He narrows his eyes. "You? Being nice? There must be a catch. What seat are you?"

"Why do you care?"

"Fine. Don't tell me. I'll find out soon enough."

The attendant announces boarding is open for our group. I let Alex go ahead of me because I don't want to follow the old perv in front of us. I hope I'm seated far away from the leering jackass.

I let out a sigh of relief when the two men keep going and take the last row in business class. Alex stops and then shoves his carry-on in the overhead bin above the first row—my row. He makes a motion to sit down, but I stop him.

"Wait. Let me get to my seat first."

He arches his brows. "We're sitting next to each other? What a coincidence."

"I didn't ask to be seated next to you if that's what you're implying."

"If you say so." He reaches for my carry-on and, before I can say anything, places it next to his in the overhead bin.

"I could have done that," I complain. "Aren't you injured?"

"I can handle your tiny bag. And I was trying to be nice. The correct response is 'thank you.'" He smirks.

Nicely played, Alex.

"Thank you."

I slide into my window seat and make a point of not looking in his direction. But he's sitting right next to me, and when his leg touches mine, a jolt of electricity goes through me. I could scooch closer to the window, but I don't want to give him the satisfaction of knowing his nearness affects me.

"I've never flown business class before," he says. "I appreciate the extra legroom. Thank you."

I wasn't expecting that, and I turn to see his face. Our eyes meet, and it's like someone lit a fuse inside of me. "You're welcome. How's your back?"

"Not as bad as it was after the collision."

"I don't know how anyone could enjoy getting pounded like that."

The corners of his lips twitch upward. "Oh, I can think of several scenarios besides hockey where getting pounded is quite enjoyable. Even *you* might like it."

My face bursts into flames, and I can't even blame Alex for going there. I totally teed that up for him.

I scowl. "Must you always turn every conversation dirty?"

His blue eyes widen innocently. "Dirty? I don't know whatchu talking about, Westwood."

I glare at him. "It's best if we don't talk at all."

"Fine by me."

CHAPTER 6
ALEX

I'm not one-hundred-percent convinced that Blair doesn't have ulterior motives for paying for my upgrade, but I have fun getting her flustered nonetheless. I already knew she was uptight, but I didn't realize how much pleasure I'd get from making her perfect porcelain skin turn pink. I'm beginning to see what my brother already did—that Blair is a stunning woman, and the temptation to push her buttons until she cracks is immense.

I leave her alone for most of the flight and focus on tweaking my speech for DC. From the corner of my eye, I see Blair typing away on her laptop. Her delicate brows are furrowed in concentration, and her full red lips poutier than ever. I don't think she's working on academic stuff, and I'm too curious for my own good.

"Who are you trying to stab through the laptop?"

She whips her face toward me. "What?"

"You're angry at someone."

"I'm not."

"As a person constantly on the receiving end of your glare, I can tell you're pissed. Don't try to deny it."

"What if I am? And why are you snoo—"

The plane shakes suddenly, making my stomach dip. I grab my armrests in a vicious hold while my entire body turns to stone.

"Whoa, that was a big one," she says.

The plane shakes again, and then the "fasten seat belt" lights turn on. My heart has taken off at breakneck speed, and my mind is already spiraling, picturing the plane nose-diving, our deaths imminent. No sooner does the thought enter my head than the plane drops, taking my insides with it.

"Fuck!" I blurt out.

Blair touches my arm. "It's going to be okay. It's just turbulence."

I look at her, unable to tell if she's being sarcastic or if she's actually being nice. My pulse is pounding in my ears, and panic is spreading through my veins at the speed of light. My airways are constricting already, making it hard to breathe.

"I hate flying," I grit out.

The plane shudders as if it's dying, and I hear a few frightened screams in the cabin.

The pilot announces we've encountered a patch of bad weather and it's going to be bumpy for a while. *Bumpy... this ain't just bumpy, motherfucker.*

"Shit," I mumble, shutting my eyes.

"Alex! Look at me."

I don't want to, but something in her voice compels me. I open my eyes and turn to her.

"It's just air. We'll be fine," she tells me.

Her voice has never sounded more soothing and sweet, and her eyes are gentle, caring even. This isn't the Blair I know. Me losing my shit must have triggered a side of her that isn't a hateful shrew.

"You don't know that."

"I *do* know that. Pretend this is a roller-coaster ride."

"I can't."

"Yes, you can."

I shake my head. "You don't understand. The fear... I can't control it."

And apparently, I can't control my tongue either. Why am I telling her this?

"You need a distraction. Why don't you tell me why you don't like me?"

"What?"

"Just list all the reasons you hate me."

I open and shut my mouth, hesitating. "I... I don't want to do that."

"Why? Because you're afraid to hurt my feelings?" She arches her eyebrows. "That never stopped you before."

"It's different. I'm not in the mood to spar with you right this second."

"Too bad, because we're going to. You're rude and cocky. You think everyone should hand things over to you because you play hockey."

I jerk back. I'm surprised that's how she sees me. That couldn't be further from the truth.

I snort. "Funny. I feel the same way about you. The moment I first met you, I saw an entitled, spoiled brat who was probably in need of a good fuck."

She widens her eyes. "You think I'm a frigid bitch?"

"Honestly... yes."

The plane rattles again and then drops sharply. More terrified shouts rise from the passengers. In economy class, a baby starts to cry.

"This is not good," I whisper.

Blair moves her hand to my thigh and squeezes it. I wasn't expecting the contact, and my dick wasn't either. It stirs in my pants, despite my brain telling me we're going to die.

"Breathe," she says. "We'll be fine, and when we get out of this, I'll prove to you I'm not a frigid bitch."

"How are you going to do that?"

She slides her hand up my thigh until her fingers brush my balls. "Use your imagination."

Damn it. If I wasn't so wrapped up in irrational panic, I'd move her hand to my cock. I can't even do that now. I can, however, imagine Blair in alluring situations. I don't know what I'd like to do to her first. In the back of my head, I know she's only saying those things to help me get through this. She'll never let me do all the filthy things I want to do to her. Pity. We could have fun. Hate and lust are a powerful combo. I bet hate fucking her would be out of this world.

"You're playing with fire, Westwood," I grit out while desire and fear wrestle one another for control.

"Am I?"

The plane keeps shaking, making me sick. One of the overhead bins opens, and a duffel bag falls from it. My heart is pounding so fast I fear it'll burst out of my chest. Shutting my eyes, I grab Blair's hand and lace our fingers together.

I'm not sure how long the turbulence lasts, but when it's over, the pilot announces we're landing in a few minutes. I keep my eyes closed, focusing on breathing in and out slowly and trying my hardest to make my body relax. That happens only after the plane touches the ground.

"Thank fuck," I say.

"Can I have my hand back now?" Blair asks.

Shit. I didn't realize I was still holding on to her. I let go, and she immediately massages her hand.

"Did I squeeze too tight?" I ask.

"A little."

She won't meet my stare, and I'm thankful for that. Now that the panic is receding, shame takes its place. I freaked out in front of Blair, and I'm mortified.

The moment the seat belt lights are off, I jump out of my seat. I can't wait to get off this fucking plane. I retrieve my carry-on and hers, and as soon as the door opens, I exit the plane without looking back. My stomach is still queasy, so I increase my pace, hoping to get to a restroom in time.

But hell. I won't. Out of the gate, I spot a trash can and make a beeline for it. This isn't my first time puking in public, but it's the first time I'm doing it sober, and there's a big difference. My face and ears are burning. Mercifully, I don't hack for too long. But when I straighten up, Blair is there, offering me a tissue.

I'm too shaken and embarrassed to refuse. I accept the offering, noticing it's one of those wet disposable towels they hand out when you board the flight. I wipe the corners of my mouth and then say in a gruff voice, "Thank you."

"Sure. Do you want a mint?" She extends an individually wrapped one.

"Yes, thanks." I take the offering, then add, "I'm going to rinse my mouth."

I turn around and stride toward the nearest restroom as fast as I can, wishing I had taken the later flight. I would have hopefully avoided that turbulence from hell and, most importantly, prevented Blair from seeing me at my worst.

CHAPTER 7
BLAIR

I don't wait for Alex to get out of the restroom. He probably hates that I witnessed him in a weak moment. If the situation were reserved, I'd be wishing for a hole to open in the floor and swallow me. But that's not the only reason I want to avoid him. I can't believe I came close to giving him a hand job on the plane, never mind what I insinuated. The next couple of days with him will be brutal.

I'm hoping that I don't see him again until tomorrow. I have to retrieve my checked luggage, and I'm sure he didn't check a bag. He'll be out of the airport before me. We're staying at the same hotel—the economics department arranged it—but it's big, and I bet I can avoid him.

The airport crew is awfully fast tonight, and because I want to stall, naturally, my suitcase is the first to emerge. I reach for the handle, but a muscular arm cuts in front of mine and lifts the suitcase off the belt. It's Alex. Damn it.

"I could have done that," I say.

"I know."

I'm pissed that instead of grabbing a taxi by himself, he came looking for me. "Did you check luggage too?"

He gives me a droll look. "What do you think?"

"Then why are you here?"

"I saw you waiting for your luggage. We *are* going to the same hotel. I don't see why we can't share a taxi."

I have a million reasons, but I don't voice a real one out loud. "It depends. Are you done puking?" It's a below-the-belt hit, but my self-defense mechanism has been activated.

He narrows his eyes, but then his lips curl into a smirk. "I'm not sure. We shall find out." He glances at my suitcase. "Is that it?"

"Yes. We're only staying for two days."

He laughs, then shakes his head. "Blair, you're definitely one of a kind."

His reaction pisses me off. "Of course I'm one of a kind. Most people are... not you though."

He arches his brows. "You don't think I'm unique?"

"Uh, no. You have a carbon copy named Logan."

He chuckles. "We look the same, but we're very different people. For starters, he likes you."

I snort. "No, he doesn't. He might want to rail me—that's not the same thing."

"Uh. I guess you're right. It's not the same thing."

He doesn't elaborate, and I'm not going to ask, even though I'm dying to know if there's a hidden meaning to his reply. Does Logan want to fuck me despite the fact that he hates me like Alex does? Or is that just how Alex feels, a.k.a. he wants to hate fuck me? I never interacted with Logan before I kissed him once at The Heritage, just to piss off Alex, but it's possible he shares his twin's animosity toward me. Sibling support and all. Shit. I shouldn't have implied I'd hook up with Alex only to prove I'm not uptight.

The line for the taxi isn't long. It takes us ten minutes to be on our way to the hotel. Alex and I don't talk during the ride, and the space between us feels like a chasm. I don't like this new dynamic because I don't know where I stand. I prefer when we're all about barbed words and open contempt.

When we arrive at the hotel, I try to pay the fare, but Alex shoves cash into the driver's hand before I can get my credit card out. It doesn't matter who pays—the school gave us a stipend—but he's sure going out of his way to assert his male dominance. We don't exchange words, but our eyes meet, and it's like he's daring me to open my mouth to complain. Maybe he hates the atmosphere as much as I do and wants to return to the status quo.

As soon as we're inside the lobby, he whistles in appreciation. The department booked us rooms in a Five Diamonds hotel, which is one of the best five-star hotel chains in the country.

"I can't believe we're staying here," he says, then turns to me. "Is this your doing too?"

"No. I had nothing to do with the planning for this trip. But I'm not surprised. The franchise is owned by the King family, and they're huge boosters to the school, especially the economics department."

Alex's eyes widen. "Wait, King, as in CJ's family?"

"Yes. Surely you know he comes from one of the wealthiest families in the country. Hannaford U even named the main library after his grandfather." Alex stares at me blankly. "Percival Wallace King?"

His neck and ears become red. "Hell, I never made the connection. Everyone I know calls it the Percy library."

"I'm surprised CJ never mentioned it."

"He can be a dick sometimes, but he rarely gloats about his family status."

"Did Ryder ever do that?" I blurt out before I can stop myself.

I'm not sure why I'm bringing up my brother. I'm certain he's still persona non grata with the hockey team, even after he helped catch Gia's stalker.

"I don't want to talk about your brother," he grits out and strides toward the front desk.

I follow him. There's only one person at the reception desk, and she's busy with a guest. I wait behind Alex, making sure I leave space between us and pull out my cell phone. I'm only mindlessly scrolling through Instagram to appear busy.

A minute later, Alex says in an annoyed tone, "There must be a mistake."

I look up and notice the front desk clerk furrowing her brows. "I'm afraid not. I have one reservation under that name, and it's for the presidential suite. There's another name under the reservation too.

"Let me guess, Blair Westwood?" His question drips with annoyance.

My spine goes rigid in an instant. *Hell to the fucking no.*

"Yes, that's the other guest."

Alex looks over his shoulder, fury sparkling in his eyes. Naturally, he'd assume I had something to do with that mix-up.

I walk over to the front desk. "My companion is correct. There must be a mistake. We can't possibly share a room."

"It's what I have in my system, and the hotel is fully booked. It seems a change was made to the original reservation a couple days ago, and you were upgraded to the presidential suite."

Shit. Maybe they had to upgrade so we could stay at the same hotel. But it's bullshit. There are plenty of other hotels in the area.

"Honestly, our presidential suites are huge, and you each have your own suites. It'll be like staying in your own hotel rooms, but you get a spacious common area and amazing views." The front desk clerk tries to massage our annoyance away.

"It won't be," I deadpan, then turn to Alex. "I'll try to find you another hotel."

He furrows his brows. "Why do *I* need to leave?"

"Because the reason we're in this situation, to begin with, is that you joined the trip at the last minute."

"Don't make it sound like I changed my mind on a whim."

"I'm not. I'm just pointing out the facts."

"Excuse me," the front desk clerk butts in. "There really aren't any hotels with availability in the area thanks to the Taylor Swift concert. And some of them are overbooked."

Alex turns to her. "I'll take the presidential suite."

The jackass! I'm sure I could find another room in a different hotel, but I want to stay at the Five Diamonds. If he's not willing to budge, then I'm not going anywhere either.

"I'll need a key too," I tell the woman.

Alex snorts, and it makes me madder. "What's your problem?"

"You." He takes his key and heads to the elevators, and all I can do is glare at his retreating back.

"May I have your ID, ma'am?"

I snap my attention back to her. "Of course."

By the time she finishes processing my check-in, Alex is gone. Good, the last thing I need is to be trapped with him in a metal box while I'm fuming. I need to control my emotions if I'm to survive two days of sharing space with him.

There's no sign of him when I enter the suite, but the double doors to the right of the living room are shut. I give the space a cursory glance. The front desk clerk wasn't lying when she said the suite was large. I didn't expect her to be exaggerating, though. Five Diamonds hotels are top-notch. The U-shaped white leather couch faces the wall with the large flat-screen TV, but it's the panoramic view from the windows that steal the show. I head into my room and close the doors. I'll enjoy the view of the city later when I'm certain Alex won't walk out of his room at any moment.

The king-size bed is beckoning me, but I feel gross after the plane, so a shower is the first order of business. Then it's room service and bed. If my travel companion was someone else, I'd suggest going out to dinner. There's no chance in hell I'll go anywhere with Alex voluntarily.

My phone rings in my purse, and the familiar ringtone puts me on edge. It's my mother. Most people would ignore calls from people they have no desire to speak to, but I'm not most people. The compulsion to answer is stronger than my aversion to a conversation with her.

"Hello?"

"Blair, where are you? I've been calling for the past hour and getting your voice mail."

"I'm in DC for the economics forum, and you got my voice mail because I was on a plane," I reply through clenched teeth.

"I didn't know you were going to DC. Why didn't you tell me?"

I pinch the bridge of my nose. "I did tell you."

"I have no recollection of that conversation. Would I have invited the Wilburgs to dinner if I had known you would be out of town? You know I detest them."

But you're more than okay with trying to marry me off to their son.

I keep the bitter thought to myself. It sounds like my mother is in a martini-fueled rage.

"I'm sorry. I must have forgotten."

I know I didn't, but it's better to just pretend that I'm wrong than to argue with her.

"Spare me your excuses. Since you're in DC, I want you to reach out to Mark Smith Junior. He works for a prestigious law firm in town, as you know."

Ugh, not that guy. I've met him once and he's a bore. "I don't have time to reach out to any of your friends' sons. This is not a leisure trip, Mom."

"Don't take that tone with me. You'll do as I say, or you can forget your next visit to Twin Falls."

My stomach twists so sharply that the pain robs me of air. "You can't do that."

"I can and I will. Don't sound so dejected. You know everything I do is for your own good. Call Mark."

She disconnects before I can reply.

I sit on the edge of the bed, dejected. Time is ticking by. The moment I graduate college then comes the arranged-marriage guillotine.

CHAPTER 8
ALEX

I can't help but think my current situation is a cosmic joke. When all I wanted was to stay as far away from Blair as possible, I'm now stuck sharing a presidential suite with her. Yes, the place is huge, but knowing she's just beyond the wall is doing unexpected things to me. I've always known where I stood in relation to her.

I hate her—or used to. She's an annoying, know-it-all brat who tries to best me in every single class we have together. Our majors are too similar. I'm studying economics and mathematics. She's a computer science and economics major, which means we cross paths too often. My family has a bad history with hers, so granted, I was biased against the Westwoods before we even met. But when I joined the Warriors and was forced to interact with Ryder, I worked hard against my prejudice. Eventually, he won me over, and we became close. Then he betrayed us all. With Blair, it was a different story—she's always been a Westwood, through and through. Stuck up, rude, and entitled.

The animosity is still there, but it's giving way to something besides lust. She not only didn't make fun of me for losing my shit on the plane, but she also helped me get through it. I'm secretly hoping she *will* use that against me soon. Then the world will make sense again.

I take a shower to get rid of the plane smell and have every intention of hitting the sack afterward. But it turns out the state-of-the-art, multijet installation in my bathroom does little to relax me. I'm wired. My back hurts from traveling—and from being tense for twenty minutes during that hellish flight. I brought the painkillers the team's physician prescribed, but I'll take them only as a last resort.

Ten minutes later, my ass is parked on a chair in the hotel bar, and I'm ordering a double whiskey. I'm not planning on getting hammered. I just need enough alcohol to remove the tension from my body. Besides, this drink is probably more expensive than getting a bottle at the liquor store. In hindsight, I probably should have checked the price. I need to pick up more tutoring gigs when I return; I'm getting low on funds. My scholarship doesn't cover all expenses.

I pretend to pay attention to whatever sport is playing on TV as I sip my drink, but my mind is elsewhere, more precisely on the fifteenth floor behind white double doors. A few minutes later, a flash of bright pink catches my attention. It's Blair, making a beeline for the other side of the bar. I don't know if she saw me and hence, decided to sit far from me or if she really didn't spot me.

I came here to forget about her—not that I was doing a good job—and she had to come down and make it that much harder. I don't have a visual of her now, but I can feel her presence nonetheless. And now that the whiskey has worked its way through my body, my mind is focusing on other things, such as the memory of her hand near my crotch. Shit. I'm already getting a hard-on just thinking about it.

Fuck this. I need to get out of here. I toss back the whiskey like a shot, then slam the thick glass back on the counter.

The bartender raises an eyebrow and asks, "Need another one?"

"No. I'm good."

He slides a black folder toward me, and I try to not wince when I see the damage. Then it occurs to me that I can simply charge the room. If the economics department can pay for a presidential suite, they won't bat an eyelash over this bill.

I'm determined to find a place to eat, but instead of leaving the hotel, I check on Blair. She's not sitting by the bar like I thought, but it's easy to find her when she's wearing such a bright color. I see her sleeve sticking out of a booth all the way at the end of the corridor. Maybe she came down to grab a bite to eat. I should go.

I don't.

In long strides, I reach her booth in seconds. Her hands are curled around a white mug, and judging by the little pieces of marshmallow I see floating in it, she's drinking hot chocolate.

"Only you would come to a bar and order hot cocoa."

She looks up, and then I see her red eyes and the slight smudge of makeup under them.

"What happened?" I sit across from her.

She pulls back, her spine going taut. "Nothing happened."

"Sure, you're crying over your hot cocoa for nothing."

"Just drop it." She pulls her hands from the cup too fast, tipping it over. "Shit."

Quickly, I reach for a napkin and toss it over the spill, stopping the liquid from spreading. "There, I saved your clothes, Barbie."

She glares at me for a couple beats, and if she were a cartoon, smoke would be coming out of her ears. Then she slides out of the booth. "You ruin everything, Kaminski."

She turns on her heels and storms off.

Oh no. She won't have the last word, not when I did nothing but show concern. I follow her, reaching her as she walks into the hotel lobby. I refrain from grabbing her arm, lest people think I'm harassing her. Instead, I get in front of her, forcing her to stop.

"What crawled up your ass? I was conc—" White-hot pain shoots from my tailbone to my spine, making me see stars. "Fuck!"

I bend forward a little, closing my eyes for a second. I shouldn't have walked so fast, or maybe it was the sudden spin that did the trick. I forgot for a second that I'm not supposed to execute abrupt movements.

"Is it your back?" she asks.

I open my eyes to level her with a glare. "No. I enjoy letting out grunts of pain for fun."

"That's what you get for running like an idiot."

"I didn't run," I grit out.

"Can you walk?"

I try to stand straighter and take a step, but it's like an elephant is sitting on my lower back. "Eventually. I'm waiting for the pain to subside."

"What time did you take your painkillers?"

"I didn't take any."

Her brows shoot to the heavens. "Why not?"

"I'd rather not resort to them."

"So you prefer to feel excruciating pain?"

Despite the discomfort, I smirk. "Obviously. I came after you, didn't I?"

"For an intelligent man, you can be such a dumbass."

My grin broadens. "Oh, you *do* think I'm smart then."

She narrows her eyes. "I think you're full of shit and not in any pain at all." She turns to leave, but I cave and touch her arm.

"Wait. I'm not kidding. I might pass out from the pain if I don't lie down soon."

"What do you want me to do about it?"

Shit. She's going to make me say it.

"Would you please help me get back to our room?"

Her eyes widen. "Wow. You're asking for my help? You must be dying for real."

Fuck this. I'm not begging. Gritting my teeth, I take one step, then another one, hoping I can make it to the elevators without collapsing.

Blair steps next to me, lacing her arm with mine. "Come on, Grandpa. Lean on me."

I'd offer a retort, but all my focus is on getting through this without more humiliation. Twice now, in a span of hours, Blair has witnessed me at my lowest, and it's going to eat me alive for months.

She's tiny, and for that reason, I try my best not to lean on her too much. The short distance feels like a mile, but eventually, we make it to the elevator just as a couple walks out. Blair keeps her arm laced with mine even when I lean against the wall and close my eyes.

"Are you going to pass out?" she asks.

"No."

"Throw up?"

To be a pest, I lie. "Yes."

"For real?"

I turn my face toward her. "Nah, I'm just yanking your chain."

She looks away first. "I don't know why you love to mess with me."

"Really? You don't know?"

The elevator dings a second before the door slides open. Thankfully, it's a short distance from our suite. Blair fishes the key card out of her purse and opens the door for me. As soon as I cross the threshold, I step away from her and veer for the couch, where I collapse on my belly. It's not complete relief, but this position is definitely better than standing up.

"Where are your painkillers?"

My face is pressed against the couch when I reply, "I'm not taking them."

"Alex, come on. Why are you being stubborn about this?"

I turn my head and find her standing next to the couch with her hands on her hips. Her pink coat is unbuttoned now, revealing a super short black-and-white-plaid dress with big white buttons on the front. She's wearing black tights, yet they don't hide the lovely shape of her legs. My thoughts become dangerous. I want to slide my fingers up her thigh and find out if she's truly not the ice princess I've always pegged her to be.

I look up before she notices I'm ogling her like a creep. "Because my father got addicted to them after an accident a few years back."

The confession surprises not only her but me as well. Maybe it's the pain that made me blurt out such a personal fact about my family, or I simply wanted her to stop pestering me about the painkillers.

"Oh, I see." She turns around and disappears into her room without another word.

Okay, not exactly the reaction I expected, but at least she did leave me alone. I close my eyes, hoping tiredness from the trip and the whiskey will put me to sleep.

A couple minutes later, Blair returns to the living room. "Can you strip from the waist up?"

I open my eyes. "It didn't take long for you to try to get me naked."

She squints. "Get your mind out of the gutter. I need your shirt off so I can apply a hot compress to your back."

I then see the blue pouch in her hand. "I can't believe you had that in your suitcase."

She shrugs. "It pays to be prepared. Now, can you take off your sweater on your own, or do you need help?"

I'm tempted to say I require her assistance just to watch her reaction, but I've already relied on her too many times today.

"I think I can manage." I sit up, and immediately pain flares toward my hips.

I grab the edges of my sweater and T-shirt to remove them at the same time, but halfway, I stop to take a deep breath. Damn, it hurts.

"Jeez, let me help you." Blair sets the compress on the coffee table and then leans down, bringing her face inches from mine.

Our gazes meet, and I feel the change in the air. She isn't looking at me with hate like the many previous times we engaged in a staring contest. It's desire that I see shining in her beautiful blue eyes. She lowers her gaze to my lips and lingers there for a couple beats. I'm a second away from twisting my hand around a lock of her hair and bringing her lips to mine when she yanks my sweater/shirt combo off and steps back. She doesn't say a word as her attention drops to my chest.

I'm used to women checking me out, but I take extra satisfaction that Blair is the one doing it now. "See something you like?"

"I didn't realize how awfully pale you are."

Her insult brings a grin to my lips. "I'm a winter boy."

"Okay, now lie on your stomach so I can put the hot compress on your back," she tells me.

Blair's assertive ways always annoy me, but tonight I do as she says without a retort because games aside, my back *is* killing me.

"Where does it hurt the most?" she asks.

"My lower back."

The moment she puts the hot compress over my aching muscle, relief follows. The pain is far from gone though. I moan out loud.

"What's wrong? Is it too hot?"

"No. It's perfect."

"I read that you need to alternate between hot and cold. I'll grab ice in a while."

"A massage might be more helpful," I say without thinking. Or maybe I am thinking but with my cock.

"Normally, I wouldn't consider touching you with a ten-foot pole, but I can see you're in a lot of pain. If you think it would help."

Not believing my ears, I look at her. She seems sincere, and fuck if my heart doesn't go from zero to a hundred miles per hour in two seconds. "It would."

"Okay."

I watch her take off her high-heel shoes and approach me with less confidence than I'm used to from her. "I've never given anyone a massage before. What should I do?"

Blair confessing she doesn't know how to do something and asking *me* for help makes all my previous weak moments worthwhile.

"Sit astride the back of my legs."

"What?" she squeaks.

"It'll be easier for you. Otherwise, you might end up with back pain yourself. The couch is too low. You don't want to hunch over me."

I can hardly believe when she follows through, and damn if her sitting on top of me doesn't make me horny in an instant. My hard-on presses against my jeans, and I have to fight the impulse to grind my hips against the couch.

She removes the hot compress and touches the area with the tips of her fingers. Goose bumps form as desire curls at the base of my spine. Why is her touch affecting me so damn much? She applies pressure with her thumbs and makes circular motions. It hurts, but it also feels so damn good, and not because the massage is working.

"Is this okay?"

"Yes," I hiss.

"I should have used lotion to avoid too much friction. I can grab it." She begins to lift her sweet ass off me.

I reach for her leg. "No. It's fine."

She relaxes again, and that's my cue to stop touching her, but my hand remains on her leg, and she doesn't bat it away. She continues massaging me, working the tension out of my lower back with her deft fingers like a pro. It turns out I like her hands on me, and I begin to imagine them exploring other parts of my body.

Without conscious thought, I caress her leg, making lazy circles with my fingers. The angle is awkward, and I can't explore farther up and under her skirt. I'd stop if she asked me to, but she continues working on my back without acknowledging what I'm doing.

The massage is definitely helping, and the pain is lessening, but another ache has taken a front-row seat. My cock is as hard as a rock and my balls are tight, ready to explode. I need relief, although I doubt Blair will help me in that department.

"Is it better now?" she asks.

"Yes... and no."

She goes still, then slides off me. I turn on my side, not bothering to hide the bulge in my pants.

"I did the best I could."

I sit up and reach for her hand.

"What are you doing, Alex?"

"I don't know."

She steps back, pulling her hand free. "We'd better go to sleep. We have a long day tomorrow."

Her reply works as a cold dose of reality. I'm attracted to her, and I'd fuck her right now if she'd let me, but I have to remember I don't like her at all, and tomorrow we'll be nothing but rivals.

"Right. Thanks for the massage, Westwood."

I don't move as I watch her hurry to her bedroom and close the door. My back isn't killing me anymore, but my crotch tells a different story.

CHAPTER 9
BLAIR

I can't believe I gave Alex Kaminski, my archnemesis, a massage last night. I also didn't stop him from touching me. His caress on my leg was far from scandalous, but sometimes, the simplest gestures are the most damning. I enjoyed having his hand on me, and I wished he had done more. Thank God I wised up at the last second and didn't fall for the lust fog that wrapped around my brain.

This morning I'm determined to forget that charged moment between us ever happened. I put on my best business suit—a navy-pin-striped tailored jacket and a pencil skirt combo—and pair it with a white button-down shirt. I've been up since five to make sure I had enough time to shower, do my hair, and tweak a few things in my presentation.

I couldn't be more ready, but I'm feeling unsteady when I eventually walk out of my room. I refuse to consider Alex might be the reason. That notion becomes impossible to ignore when he walks out of his room wearing a suit that fits him like a glove. It's also navy and his shirt is white, so we match. My heart lurches forward and beats faster.

"Good morning," I croak.

"Good morning." His gaze drops to my shoes and slowly

travels up the length of my body until our eyes meet again. "Looking sharp, Westwood."

I run my hands over my skirt, smoothing invisible lines. "Thanks, you too. How's your back?"

"Much better."

His blue eyes seem to burn into mine, and I feel a blush creep up my cheeks. "Good."

"Listen, about last night—"

I lift my hand. "Let's not bring up what happened last night, okay? Or our conversation during the flight."

He narrows his eyes, clenching his jaw for a second. "Sounds good to me."

Wait. Is he angry that I want to forget we shared a moment? "I ordered an Uber already. You're welcome to ride with me."

"Pass. I'm going down for breakfast. I heard the buffet is out of this world."

Disappointment floods me, which is stupid. "I'm not a breakfast person."

"That doesn't surprise me."

"Why?"

He shakes his head. "Never mind."

I hate when people don't say exactly what they mean, but I'm not going to press Alex to elaborate. I'm sure his reply won't be something I'll enjoy hearing anyway.

"I'm not waiting for you." I veer toward my room because I definitely don't want to ride the elevator with him.

"Wrong door, Westwood."

My spine stiffens. "I forgot something. I'll see you at the forum."

I'm one of the first participants to arrive, and for that reason, there's no line to check in. I collect my badge and welcome bag and go in search of a place to sit down and go over my presentation. I'm confident it's perfect as is, but I need a distraction, or I'll be obsessing about Alex the entire time. I need my head in the game, not miles away with him.

The forum is being hosted by Fairbrook University, and the presentations are split into two different buildings on campus. They aren't far from each other, and the organization gave ample time for people to get to their sessions. Alex and I are presenting in the same building, but his presentation is in the morning and mine in the afternoon.

Before I find a quiet area where I can work, I spot people carrying coffee cups, which reminds me I didn't have any caffeine yet. I ask them where they got theirs, and they point at the coffee cart outside that I totally missed when I walked into the building.

I get in the already long line and check my phone for messages. I set my phone to silent mode earlier. I must be a glutton for punishment because the first message that I see is from my mother asking if I called Mark yet. She sent it ten minutes ago.

I have no intention of calling Mark. It's a risk antagonizing her, but I'm hoping that if I ignore her and then later say I was busy and didn't have time, she won't follow through with her threat.

There's also a message from Gia, and that one brings a smile to my lips.

Have you killed each other yet?

Not yet. I'm giving him a break since he's wounded.

Is his back bothering him?

Obviously, I don't want to tell Gia that I gave Alex a massage. That secret I plan to take to the grave.

I don't know. He won't tell me if it is.

God, I feel awful about that lie. What if Alex doesn't have any issue with opening his big mouth? I just won back Gia's trust.

Yeah, I doubt he'd want to show you any weakness.

She's not wrong about that. I know he wasn't happy that I was there to see him lose his shit over a little turbulence.

It's my turn, so I put the phone away and order a large caffe latte and then hurry back into the building. I don't want it to get cold. There's a line for registration now, and I see Alex at the end of it, chatting with a tall redhead whose legs go on for miles. He says something, and she laughs while playing with a lock of her hair.

My chest suddenly feels tight, and I wonder once again why seeing Alex flirting with other women bothers me so much. Fuck. If this is jealousy, then I need therapy. I can't possibly be jealous of that baboon. Disgusted with myself, I stride away from the registration area and look for a place to sit. I finally locate a long counter-like table with a free chair facing the tall windows.

I have neighbors on both sides, but they're busy with their own laptops and ignore me when I set down my cup. The issue with these tall chairs is that they don't get along with tight skirts and heels.

I manage to sit down after an awkward maneuver and elbowing the guy to my left. "Sorry."

He turns, already sporting a glower, but his facial expression switches in an instant to a bright smile. "Don't worry." His gaze drops to my badge. "Oh, you're here for the forum?"

"Yep."

"Me too." He extends his hand. "I'm Daniel Lawrence. Harvard Law."

"Blair Westwood." I don't follow my name with my school and major because that was snobbish as fuck on his part, and I'd like to believe I'm not like him.

"What school do you go to?"

"Hannaford U."

His eyes widen. "Oh, you're Ryder's sister."

I furrow my brows. "You know my brother?"

His head bobs up and down. "I used to play hockey. I played against your brother in my last year as an undergrad. He was so good."

"Yeah, he was."

I pray he doesn't follow his comment with the dreaded question—why did Ryder quit?

"What brings you to the forum?" he asks.

"I'm presenting a paper."

His eyes bug out. "You are? I thought you were younger than Ryder."

"I am."

"Eh... so are you a senior?"

"Nope. Junior."

"Really? Wow. You must be supersmart then."

"You sound surprised."

Man, this dude is irritating me. I should have known he was a douche by the way he introduced himself.

"I am. Usually, übersmart girls aren't as pretty as you."

And he keeps digging his grave. "Right. If you don't mind, I'd like to get some work done before my friend's presentation."

"Sure, sure. Who's your friend?"

"Me," Alex replies, appearing out of nowhere.

Daniel Lawrence Harvard Law turns on his chair and faces Alex. "You're joking."

"Why would I joke?" Alex glowers.

"You're Alex Kaminski, defenseman for the Warriors, and you were also given a presentation spot?"

"That's right."

"Wow. What are they feeding students in Fairbanks? Maybe I should have gone there instead of Harvard."

"I guarantee our accomplishments have nothing to do with what we eat," Alex retorts, clearly not amused with Daniel's half-baked attempt at saving face.

"Well, I should go. I'm looking forward to both of your presentations." He scrambles out of his seat so fast he almost falls off his chair.

"Nice friend," Alex mumbles.

"He isn't my friend. I sat next to him, and he started a conversation."

"Hmm." He stares at me for far too long, unnerving me.

"What?"

"So I'm your friend now?"

I roll my eyes. "I couldn't tell the guy I was looking forward to seeing my *enemy's* presentation."

Alex arches one eyebrow. "But you *are* looking forward to seeing it."

"Only so I can watch you crash and burn."

He chuckles. "Blair, you're cute when you're funny."

My face turns into lava. I was not expecting that comeback from him. "I'm not cute!"

I was supposed to say I'm not funny, but he completely disarmed me.

My outburst makes him laugh. "The correct response was, 'So you think I'm cute?' Come on, I totally teed that up for you."

I get out of my chair and pack my things. "Well, I don't care if you think I'm cute or not."

"Okay, fine. You're not cute, just funny." He shrugs and walks away.

Damn it! I was going to storm off, and he took that from me too. Jerkface.

CHAPTER 10
BLAIR

Alex doesn't crash and burn. I never expected him to. He is many things, but dumb is not one of them. Just like when he plays hockey, he's imposing and confident. But one thing we can't see when he's fighting for control of the puck, or checking players against the wall, is how charismatic he is. As I watch him present his paper, I'm captivated by him, which annoys me. He's far too intelligent for my peace of mind and constantly competing with me for the number-one spot in academics. He also has other advantages. He has a penis, which will always give him an edge. But the most aggravating advantage he has over me is his personality. He's likable.

Throughout the day, professors and students go out of their way to speak to him. I can't say I experience the same. I shouldn't be jealous that he can charm a room. I could go that route as well, but I'm not a people person and I can't fake otherwise.

At least I don't suck at my presentation. I didn't expect to. I'm comfortable speaking to a crowd, especially if it's about a topic I'm passionate about. This is a great opportunity to shine in front of my peers and possible future employers. The networking opportunity was the main reason I was so keen to come here, and possibly being offered an internship that doesn't come with strings attached to my family. Once my presentation is over, I can't wait to return to the hotel and not leave my room for the rest of the evening.

I kept my phone on silent during the day. But as I make my way out of the auditorium, I crack and check my messages. Mother Dearest left me several texts. But the one message that catches my attention is from Mark Smith Junior. I open that immediately and have to read it a couple times before it sinks in.

Mom took matters into her own hands and arranged everything. He's meeting me here.

"Blair?" a male voice asks.

I look up and find Mark standing at the end of the aisle in the auditorium. Shit. I wish now I had checked my messages sooner. I'd have tried to prevent this from happening. He's tall and dark, and some might say he's even handsome, but his beady eyes give me the creeps.

"Uh, Mark?"

"Yeah, hello." He invades my space and gives me a hug that turns me into stone. "Long time no see."

"Right. I can't even remember how long."

He takes a step back and I glance around, searching for Alex. I didn't seek him out in the audience during my presentation because I didn't want him to distract me, but I know he was there. He wouldn't have missed it.

"Are you ready to go?" Mark asks.

"Go where?"

"Dinner. Didn't you get my message? Your mother said you didn't have any plans."

Damn everything to hell. That woman is a conniving snake. I should have known she'd pull something like this. Ignoring her has never worked in the past.

"Oh no. I'm here with a classmate, and we did make plans to have dinner together."

Mark smiles tightly, but it doesn't reach his eyes. "She's more than welcome to join us."

I don't correct Mark. Let him think Alex has a vagina for a little longer. I pull my phone out and call the blond pest, praying he answers.

He does on the third ring. "Hello?"

"Hey, where are you?"

"Uh, I'm outside the auditorium. Why do you want to know?"

"Wait for me there. I'll be right out."

"Blair, I'm not goi—"

I end the call before he can finish his sentence. I can't beg him to save me over the phone. I need him to see my desperation. I absolutely can't go out to dinner with Mark alone. Every cell in my body is rebelling against the idea.

My squeezed-tight heart shrinks even more when I see Alex with the redhead from earlier. He was about to say he wasn't going back to the hotel, and now I know why. I'm upset and angry at myself for being upset. Shit. Now I don't know if I'll be able to convince him to ditch his date to save me from a creep. Plan *B*, there will be no asking for help. I'll keep the charade going and hope he won't call me a liar in front of Mark.

He turns as I approach and immediately focuses on Mark. It seems his eyes darken, and his jaw tenses. I don't know if he's bothered that I'm interrupting his conversation with the redhead or if he's annoyed that I'm with someone as well.

"Hey, Alex. There's been a change of plans," I say. "An old friend of my parents wants to take us all out to dinner, and I can't say no."

Alex's eyes widen a fraction, but he hides his surprise fast. Now he's staring at me as if he's trying to read my mind.

"Oh, I thought dinner was only the two of us," the redhead pipes up.

Shit. Shit. I can't have him bail on me.

"It doesn't surprise me. Alex is notorious for forgetting

things. Has he told you yet about our flight here?" I ask her, then look at Alex again.

He narrows his eyes. He didn't miss the veiled blackmail.

"No. What happened?" the girl asks.

"It's not important. Are you going to introduce your friend to us?" He looks pointedly at Mark.

I open my mouth to make the introductions, but Mark beats me to it, extending his hand.

"I'm Mark Smith Junior. Nice to meet you."

"Alex Kaminski. Nice to meet you too." He turns to the redhead. "And this is Sheila."

"Sheila Fontaine," she adds as she shakes Mark's hand. "Are you the Smith of the Bingley and Smith law firm?"

"Yes—well, the Smith of the firm is my father, but he's getting ready to retire. How did you know?"

"I'm prelaw."

"That's fantastic."

While Mark and Sheila engage in pleasant conversation, Alex keeps glaring at me. He looks furious, and I can already tell he's going to make me pay for ruining his hot date sooner rather than later. I'm not afraid. On the contrary, his promise of retaliation sends a thrill of excitement down my back.

"I have a car waiting," Mark tells us. "How does everybody feel about Italian food?"

"Can't go wrong with that," Alex replies.

Mark and Sheila walk ahead of us and continue their conversation about law. I'm fucking glad that he seems more interested in flirting with Alex's date than paying attention to me.

Alex steps next to me and leans closer to whisper in my ear. "What the actual fuck is going on here, Blair?"

"I'm collecting a favor. You owe me."

"Yeah, I figured as much. Were you jealous that I had a date?"

I snort. "Not even close."

"I'll play along with your charade, but you *will* tell me why you're cockblocking me."

A sharp pain pierces my chest. I knew Alex was planning on screwing Jessica Rabbit there, but when he says it out loud, it hurts. I don't understand what's going on with me.

"That's not what I'm doing. Please don't tell me you were planning to bring Sheila back to our hotel room."

"No, sugar. Unless you were planning to join us."

"In your dreams."

"Yeah, probably." He laughs. "This restaurant better be good. It seems my date is far more interested in sucking up to your lawyer friend than sucking my c—"

"Don't you *dare* finish that sentence." I look at him so he can see my glower.

He smirks. "Not uptight, my ass."

"You know nothing about me, Kaminski. And you never will."

He snakes an arm around my waist, bringing me flush against his body. "There's where you're wrong, Westwood."

I shove him away, annoyed that the proximity sets my body ablaze.

CHAPTER 11
ALEX

At first, I was pissed that Blair had ruined my evening plans. I didn't have any intention of hooking up with anyone during this trip, but I didn't foresee wanting to fuck Blair to the point she started consuming my thoughts. I had to stop obsessing about her, so when I met Sheila during check-in, I figured she'd be the perfect distraction.

But it's clear now she's more interested in networking with the hotshot lawyer. We're almost done with the main course, and I haven't exchanged more than a few words with her. At least the evening isn't a complete bust. The food is phenomenal, and I'm stuffing my face. I'm fine not having to engage in small talk.

Blair is sitting opposite me, but she's been pretty quiet. Her phone is on the table, so when it vibrates, I notice. She glances at the text, and whatever she reads has an immediate effect on her. Her grimace is obvious.

"If you'll excuse me, I have to use the restroom." She sets down her napkin and almost jumps from her chair.

Mark barely spares her a glance before he resumes his convo with Sheila. I should leave Blair alone, but I stay in my chair for only a few seconds before I go after her. I don't bother telling them where I'm going.

I wait outside the women's restroom for a few minutes. When she doesn't walk out, I decide to go in and check on her. She's standing in front of the mirror, pressing a tissue under her eyes.

"Blair? Are you okay?"

She whips her head toward me. "What the hell are you doing in here?"

"You looked upset. I came to check on you. What happened?"

She lets out a sigh. "It's nothing, Alex."

I see that all the bathroom stalls are empty, so I walk over. "Don't bullshit me. Why are you crying in the bathroom? Does it have anything to do with why we're having dinner with that shmuck?"

"Am I that transparent?"

"When you aren't trying to hide it. You were pretty desperate to have me crash your dinner date. Is your mother trying to set you up with that idiot Mark?"

Her eyes turn rounder. "How did you guess?"

"Did you forget I played with your brother for two years? He might have mentioned something about how controlling your mother is about your dating life."

"Ryder has a big mouth when it's not about him." She rests her palms on the dark stone counter and leans forward, staring at her reflection in the mirror.

I tilt my head. "Did I guess it right?"

"Yes, Mark is a contender. My mother arranged our meet-up tonight, and I didn't want to be alone with him."

"Can't you just tell her to stop messing with your love life?"

She laughs without humor. "If it were only that simple."

"I think it's pretty fucking simple."

She turns, and our gazes connect. "Maybe for you, but in my world, we're not free to choose who we marry. It's a business transaction. Not even Ryder is free to make a choice, although he can date whoever he wants until he needs to fulfill his duty to the family."

"That's bullshit. You *do* have a choice—you're simply choosing money over happiness."

Blair's eyes turn brighter as tears well up in them. Fuck. Never in my life have I said or done something that made her cry. If she's breaking down in front of me, I've found her weak spot, and that makes me feel guilty as hell.

"Like I said before, you know nothing about me, Kaminski," she grits out.

"I know one thing. You don't want to go back to our table and pretend everything is fine. Let's get out of here."

"What about Sheila?"

"I'm pretty sure I'll be doing her a favor by leaving."

She holds my stare.

I wish I could read her mind.

"Okay. Let's go."

Was it a dick move to leave the restaurant without saying goodbye? Probably. But it wasn't like Sheila and Mark were acting like saints either. The moment we sat down, they were in flirtation mode and ignoring Blair and me.

Blair doesn't say much on the ride back to the hotel, but as soon as she walks into our suite, she says, "I'm ordering room service."

"We just ate."

"Not food. Booze. Lots of it."

I'm not one to discourage alcohol, and we should be celebrating the end of a successful forum. Both our presentations kicked ass. Blair was a rock star on that stage, and not in the way she presents herself at school. She wasn't snobbish, only perhaps a bit too serious, but I enjoyed watching her nonetheless, and not because she looked hot as fuck. She surprised me. I've been so wrapped up in my animosity toward her that I forgot how brilliant she is.

I was approached by several companies wanting to offer me internships if pro hockey doesn't work out. I bet Blair had the same experience. Although I know that's not why she wants to get drunk tonight.

"I'm getting out of this suit." I begin to peel off my jacket as I make my way to my room.

Blair isn't paying attention to me. She's on the phone placing an order.

When I return to the living room wearing comfy gray sweatpants and a T-shirt, she's kicked off her high heels and gotten rid of her jacket, but she's still wearing the skintight skirt and white button-down. Now I can tell that it's a little see-through. She looks like a sexy businesswoman, and I'm imagining all sorts of filthy scenarios.

Kneeling in front of the coffee table, she's lining up several miniature bottles.

"Did you empty the minibar?"

She glances at me. "Yes. I didn't want to wait to start the party."

"I doubt the school will pay for that."

"I don't expect them to. Don't worry, pal. You're a guest at my party—you don't have to worry about a thing besides keeping up with me."

"Oh, I can keep up. As I recall, you were the one who passed out first the last time we did this."

She gives me a dirty look. "I'm smaller than you. Naturally, you can handle more alcohol than me."

"It didn't stop you from betting you could outdrink me though." I sit on the couch and rest my elbows on my knees. "What do you have there?"

"Whiskey, cognac, tequila, vodka… oh, and Bailey's."

"What are you having?"

"Tequila. Let's keep our tradition alive." She smiles brightly, and fuck if that doesn't feel like she reached for my cock and wrapped her fingers around it.

There's a knock on the door. Perfect timing. I need the interruption. "That must be room service." I get up to open the door.

"Wow, they were fast."

My jaw drops when I see the number of bottles Blair ordered. I don't comment in the presence of the hotel employee, but when he leaves, I turn to her. "Did you invite more people to the party and forget to tell me?"

She jumps to her feet and inspects the goods. "No. I wasn't sure what I was in the mood for, so I got everything they had."

"It's a waste."

"No, it's not. Whatever we don't drink, the room service guy can have. I'm sure he'll appreciate it very much."

And there it is, the main reason I never got along with Blair. She represents everything I don't like about her kind. They don't value anything because they never have to work for stuff.

"What do you say... are you game for another tequila contest?" She looks at me expectantly.

Instead of antagonizing her about the careless way she spends money that isn't hers, I find myself agreeing to a tequila shot contest.

"Sure. Hit me."

It doesn't take long for my body to feel the effects of the tequila. I'm relaxed and can't think of a reason now why Blair and I should be enemies. She's drunker than I am and dancing on top of the coffee table to a Taylor Swift song.

"I didn't know you were a Swiftie, Blair." I take another shot of tequila.

We ran out of lime a few shots ago, and I keep forgetting to use the salt. At this point, it doesn't matter anymore.

"Who isn't?" The current song ends, and another starts that

has Blair shrieking in delight. "Oh my God. It's our song. Come dance with me." She reaches for my arm.

"We have a song?" I laugh.

"Yes. Listen to the lyrics."

"Bad blood?"

"Yes. Come on!" She tugs my arm.

I get up. "Blair, I can't get on top of that coffee table. It'll break."

"Fine. I'll get down."

She jumps into my arms, and we both fall back on the couch. She giggles, pressing her face into the crook of my neck. "Shit. I didn't mean to do that."

She ends up sitting astride my lap, and her skirt hikes up to her hips. My cock is one-hundred-percent awake now, and thanks to alcohol fucking with my better judgment, I grab her thighs, sinking my fingers in them so she won't slide off me. The desire to fuck Blair returns with a vengeance. I should have known getting drunk with her would be a bad idea.

She leans back and stares into my eyes. There isn't a shred of amusement left in them.

"Blair…"

"I can feel you pressing against my pussy."

Damn. I wasn't prepared for her to be so straightforward about it. It's hot as hell. "Do you want me to apologize?"

She shakes her head. "No. I want to make out with you."

I cup her face, then slide my hand to the back of her head and twist a lock of her hair around my fingers. "That can be arranged."

I crash my mouth to hers, hungry beyond reason for a taste. Her lips part, and the moment our tongues touch, an inferno ignites in the pit of my stomach, spreading through my body faster than a burst of light. I taste the tequila on her tongue, but beyond that, there's a natural sweetness as well that I didn't expect. All I know is that it's damn addictive. The only reason I don't have her flat on her back is because she never said she wanted to fuck me. But hell if I don't spiral out of control fast when she begins to grind her hips against mine.

"Blair, what are you doing?" I groan against her mouth.

"This feels good, doesn't it?" She kisses my neck, and it makes me delirious.

"Fuck, you know it does."

She leans back and traps my face between her hands. "I don't want to cross that line with you yet. Can we just do this instead?"

"What? Make out like teenagers?"

"Yes."

I move my hands to her hips and help her gyrate against my throbbing erection. "We can, but on the condition that you'll let me make you come."

She lets out a moan. "Only if you come too."

"You have no idea how close I am already."

I kiss her again, hard this time. I haven't climaxed from grinding like this since I was a teen, and I forgot how fucking sexy it is.

I move her hips faster when her moans turn louder. But I need more of her, of her taste, so I leave her lips to trail open kisses down her neck and her collarbone until I reach the swell of her breasts.

"Damn it, Alex. I want your mouth on me." She unbuttons her shirt, revealing the white lacy bra underneath.

Oh the damage I would have done to that piece of lingerie if Blair didn't release the front clasp. My mouth finds one of her nipples in the next second, and she arches her back, yanking my hair at the roots.

She's moving her hips much faster now, and I'm seconds away from exploding in my pants.

"Oh my God. Yes, yes, yes!" she shouts.

I let go of her nipple and kiss her again while jizz spills all over the inside of my sweats. Jesus fucking Christ. I haven't come this fast since I was a horny teen.

Blair sags against my body, keeping the side of her face pressed against my shoulder. "Thank you, Alex."

I chuckle. "You're welcome, baby girl."

She pulls back. "Baby girl? Is that what you call all the girls you hook up with?"

"No."

"Okay then." She slides off my lap and pulls her skirt down. "I'm going to sleep now."

As she staggers to her room, I don't move. I should head to mine, but I need a moment to recover from what just happened. I dry-humped Blair Westwood, my rival, my enemy… and I want more.

CHAPTER 12
BLAIR

Like a coward, I can't face Alex the next day. So I slip out of the hotel room at the break of dawn and catch an earlier flight. My head is splitting in two, so I keep my sunglasses on, removing them only to go through airport security.

I can't believe I got Alex drunk and then made out with him. If that's not an act of desperation, I don't know what is. That was the craziest shit I've ever done. I won't be able to avoid him forever—we have class next week—but I'm hoping by then, I'll have a game plan on how to deal with him.

As soon as I land in Fairbanks, I text Gia. She and Noah babysat Cookie for me. He's so young, and I didn't want to leave him at a dog hotel. She replies that she can drop him off, and I let out a yelp when I open the door to my apartment and Cookie comes running.

"Hey, sweetie pie. Did you miss Mommy?" I pick him up and let him lick my face.

Another puppy jumps on my legs—Marshall.

Gia walks into the living room and laughs. "I think Marshall is jealous of Cookie. Come here, boy. Leave Auntie Blair alone."

"It's fine. I don't mind."

"I'm sorry. I had to use your key and let myself in. I had to pee so badly."

"Is it because of the pregnancy already? I thought that happened when you were further along."

"No, I think it was the huge smoothie I drank on the way here."

I park my carry-on and suitcase next to the kitchen counter, then make a beeline for the couch. I love my apartment, and the couch is the best piece of furniture I own. It's Easter-egg blue, plush, and comfortable, and many times, I've slept on it instead of in my own bed. I set Cookie down and collapse on the sofa, face down on the pillows my mother hates so much.

When I enrolled at Hannaford U, I wanted to have the whole dorm experience, but my mother put the kibosh on that idea and leased this spacious two-bedroom apartment instead. At least she let me decorate it according to my taste. It's not exactly on campus, but it's close enough. The majority of the residents go to Hannaford U as well.

"How was the trip? Did you and Alex behave?"

"I don't wanna talk about it. I have a major hangover."

"Oh no. Was it tequila again?"

I roll on my side to face her. "Yes. Apparently, I have a steep learning curve."

"You never used to get hammered. Is something going on?" She sits on the chair opposite the couch, folding her legs under her.

"Yes. My mother is trying to matchmake even from a distance. She arranged a blind date for me while I was in DC."

"No shit. How did that go?"

"Not terribly. My date was more interested in sleeping with Alex's date than me. I escaped having to deal with that, but not my mother's wrath."

Gia lifts her hand. "Stop and rewind. You went on a double date with Alex Kaminski, your archnemesis?"

"Desperate times, desperate measures. He was the lesser of two evils."

"What happened?"

"Mark—the guy my mother set me up with—texted her to complain I had no idea he was coming. So naturally, she's furious with me."

"She's always angry with you. What's she going to do now? Take away your credit cards?"

I close my eyes. If only we were talking about being cut off financially. I let Gia believe that's the reason I allow my mother to bully me, just like I let Alex think I value money more than my own happiness. They'll never know why I put up with my mother's bullshit.

What my mother can take away from me, money can't buy.

"Probably," I lie.

"You can always get a job."

"I know. Maybe I'll start tutoring."

"You know that Alex does that, right?"

I snap my eyes open again. "No, I had no idea. How does he have the time?"

Gia shrugs. "When you need money, you find a way."

"Ouch. I felt that one."

"It wasn't a dig at your lifestyle. You know I never cared that your family has grotesque money."

I sit up, pinching the bridge of my nose. "I know. I guess I'm extra sensitive about the topic. I had to tell Alex why I was dragging him to dinner with me and my date, and I'm pretty sure he thinks I'm shallow."

Gia arches an eyebrow. "Since when do you care what Alex thinks?"

"I don't."

She tilts her head, narrowing her eyes. "Blair, did something happen between you and Alex during this trip? Both of you have been acting differently toward one another since my birthday party."

I'm glad I'm still wearing sunglasses and she can't see the truth in my eyes. "Did he say anything to you or Noah?"

"No. But... I don't know. Logan made a comment about Alex losing his mojo because he hasn't hooked up with anyone since Boston."

My spine becomes taut in an instant. "He *hasn't*?"

I sound too eager to my own ears, and Gia's expression tells me she noticed. "Okay, spill. I wasn't born yesterday, and I know you and Alex too well."

I grab a pillow and use it as a shield. "Fine. Maybe you can help me make sense of my situation." I pause, licking my dry lips. "At the club in Boston, Alex came on to me without realizing who I was. He quickly figured out it was me he was hitting on, but things have been different since then."

"I knew it! What happened during this trip?"

"Alex's back was bothering him, and he refused to take painkillers, so I gave him a massage."

"Blair! Oh my God. That's huge."

I wince. "Inside voice, please. I have a headache."

"Sorry."

"Nothing happened after the massage, but it was... intimate. Anyway, last night, after the dinner fiasco, I wanted to forget about my mother and her schemes, so Alex and I got drunk on tequila again, and then we..." I look away. "Shit. I asked to make out with him."

"No way!"

"Way, and now I want to die. How am I supposed to act around him next week?"

"You didn't see him this morning?"

"I snuck out of the hotel before he woke up and got an earlier flight. That's how mortified I am."

"Oh Blair... I'm sure it'll be fine. You were drunk and fooled around. Big deal."

I cross my arms and pout. "It *is* a big deal. I hate him."

Gia laughs. "Come on. Be serious. You don't hate him, and he doesn't hate you. You've been crushing on each other for a while now and everyone can see it."

My eyes turn rounder. "We have not! Besides, even if that were true, that shouldn't make you happy."

"Why not? I'd love it if two of my best friends got together."

"Excuse me? You've always said Alex wasn't boyfriend material."

"No, I said he'd be a great boyfriend when he got all the whoring out of his system."

"Who said he has? He had a hookup lined up in DC! I'm the one who ruined his plans."

Gia gives me a meaningful stare. "Blair, Alex would never, ever do something he didn't want to. If he wanted to hook up with that girl, he would have."

I can see why she'd believe that, but she doesn't know I blackmailed him, and I don't plan to confess. Alex would never forgive me if I told anyone about his phobia, and as much as I keep telling myself I don't care about him, it's a lie. After this weekend, I don't want him to hate me anymore.

ALEX

It wasn't the pounding in my head or the fact that I almost missed my flight that put me in a foul mood this morning. It was waking up and finding my roommate gone without leaving a damn note. I've never had a girl disappear on me like that after a hookup. *I'm* the one who sneaks out if I'm not in the mood for a morning round. The worst of it all is that I didn't even fuck Blair. Did she think I'd try to get in her pants today?

Logan picks me up at the airport, and he has puppy Blair with him. I pull her onto my lap, and she's as happy as can be, wiggling her tail and trying to lick my face. At least one Blair is happy to see me. The other ran away to avoid my presence.

"Man, you look like hell. Did you go out on a binge or something?"

"Too many fucking tequila shots." I massage my temple.

"Really? I thought there would be only nerds at the convention."

"I didn't go out."

"You got drunk by yourself? That's just sad, bro."

I should keep my mouth shut about Blair, but Logan has made no secret of the fact that he'd hook up with her if given the chance. We've always had a rule—we'll never go after a girl the other is interested in. I'm not sure yet how I feel about Blair, but I know I don't want Logan near her.

"I wasn't alone."

He looks at me, then reaches for my jacket and pulls the lapel away from my neck. "You hooked up! And she gave you a hickey." He laughs.

I bat his hand away. "Stop laughing."

"I'm not laughing at you. I'm happy you got your mojo back. I was beginning to worry something was wrong with you. You've been weird since Gia's birthday party."

"There's nothing wrong with me."

"So, who was she?"

"Blair."

"Blair what?"

"It was Blair. I hooked up with Blair."

"What the fuck!" He looks at me and the car swerves to the right.

"Watch the road, you idiot!"

He brings the car back into its lane, and my heartbeat returns to normal.

"I fucking *knew* you had a thing for her. How was she in bed?"

I pat puppy Blair's head. "I didn't fuck her, all right? We just fooled around."

"Oh shit."

"What?"

"Bro, you're screwed."

"Why am I screwed?"

"You guys have been hating on each other since you first met. If it was only physical attraction, you would have fucked each other's brains out last night. But you made out with her instead, and that tells me it's more than simply lust."

"You're wrong. We didn't fuck because Blair is an ice princess like I suspected all along."

The lie brings bile to my mouth. Blair is the opposite of that. I'm just angry she thought I was only good for scratching an itch. I feel used, and the irony isn't lost on me.

"Sure she is. That's why she gave you a hickey."

I rub my face, annoyed that I opened my big mouth. "I shouldn't have told you jack."

He laughs. "Another clue that you like her, as I've always suspected. You wanna make sure I don't go after her."

"This stays between us."

"I figured as much." He shrugs. "I have no intention of blabbering unless you piss me off."

"Ha ha. Very funny. I don't want to talk about Blair anymore. What are you doing today?"

"I have to finish a project, then I'll hit the gym. How's your back?"

"It was bothering me on Friday, but I'm better today."

"Did you take the painkillers?"

I give him a droll look that he misses because he's paying attention to the road. "You know the answer to that."

He glances at me. "You're not Dad."

"Addiction has been linked to genetics, Logan. I can't risk it."

The familiar and constant worry for Dad's well-being flares up in my chest. I haven't talked to him in a couple days. I'll call him when I get home.

"Whatever. I'm glad you aren't in pain anymore."

I cover my mouth with a fist and look out the window. "I need to do something today."

"Or you'll cave and call Blair?"

I glower at him. "Do you want me to punch you in the face?"

"You're hilarious. Besides, you should rest. We tied the game on Friday. We need you on *D*."

"Fuck, I'd do anything for some ice time right now."

"I hear ya, but you're no good to us if you return too soon and get more fucked up."

"I know." I sigh.

"Let's grab a pizza after my workout. I bet the guys will be game."

"Sure."

Hanging out with the team might be the distraction I need—that is if Logan keeps his mouth shut about Blair. He's usually pretty good at keeping secrets unless he's wasted… then all bets are off.

CHAPTER 13
BLAIR

After Gia left yesterday, I took a Valium and crashed. I don't usually resort to prescribed drugs, but yesterday, I needed it. This morning, I'm groggy and hate my weakness. I take Cookie out for his morning walk, feeling guilty as hell that I didn't give him much attention yesterday. The cold morning air does little to dispel the fog in my brain—my last hope is caffeine.

Cookie is fast doing his business, so before I develop a horrible headache, I return to the apartment. "Sorry, buddy. I'll take you for a longer walk later."

While I wait for my double espresso to brew, I park my butt on the chair by the kitchen island with my laptop in front of me. Last night I passed out without checking my messages and emails. Today I start with the emails, knowing the likelihood that my mother will appear in my inbox is slim. She prefers text messages and voice mails.

There's an email from Melody, my sorority's president, pertaining to the charity gala we're helping organize with the student organization. I click on it first since I'm on the committee and want to make sure I'm on top of things. My stomach drops to the earth when I see my name attached to not one but two tasks I'd rather not have anything to do with. The dance performance and the jock auction.

Fuck my life.

I reply to Melody, begging her to assign me to something else. Two minutes later, she calls me.

"Hey," I say.

"What's this nonsense of you wanting to change assignments?"

"I... I'd rather do something else."

"Well, tough shit. You're one of our best dancers. Let's put all those years of classical ballet to good use."

Ugh. I was afraid she'd use that argument. I should never have submitted my ballet recital video when I rushed the Deltas. Since then, everything that involves dance they stick my name on it.

"Fine. Can I get off the auction then?"

"I'm afraid you can't. After the fiasco with the challenge to find Kingsley's dream girl, Gia doesn't want anything to do with any of us. We need you."

"Why do we need to auction off the guys from the hockey team? What about the football or the swim teams?"

"We need volunteers from those sports as well, but you know the stars of Hannaford U are the hockey players. Without them, the auction won't be as successful. Remember, Blair, this is for charity."

"Ugh. Okay, fine. I'll stay on those tasks. At least we have a month."

"Uh, no. Didn't you read my entire email? We had to bring the date forward because the renovations at the Botanical Gardens are starting sooner. The gala is happening in two weeks."

"Two *weeks*? Fuck. That's not enough time."

"It's plenty of time, especially for a Westwood."

I don't like her implication. The last time I had to use my connections, I was roped into going on a date with another loser.

My espresso finishes brewing, but I'm afraid it's too late to avoid a headache. This conversation with Melody did the trick.

"I have to go, Melody. I'll see you at the meeting."

I end the call before she can utter a reply. I'm pissed that she didn't let me off those tasks. The only reason she needs my help convincing Gia to let the players participate in the auction is because she didn't listen to me in the first place. If she had stopped the challenge to date Noah when I said it was a bad idea, she wouldn't be on Gia's shit list.

I drink my espresso in one shot, burning my tongue in the process. Hell. Then I set the cup back and press the button to brew another one. I'll be mainlining caffeine today.

While I wait for the second cup, I return my attention to my inbox. There's an email from Professor McNelis from last night. I notice that Alex is on the same email, and as I read the message, I know why. McNelis wants to meet us for lunch today, but true to form, he didn't specify the reason. He's a man of few words. My guess is that he wants to discuss the forum.

Seeing Alex after I bailed on him yesterday was already going to be hard, but add Professor McNelis to the mix, and it's a veritable disaster. I haven't had a chance to process what happened and dissect all these new feelings that have woken inside of me. But I can't say no when I don't have a valid excuse not to go. So I confirm I'll be there and hope I'm feeling like myself in a few hours.

A text message pops up on my phone. Melody created a new group chat for the dance performance, and now we're trying to figure out a meeting time that works for everyone. I glance at the texts but hardly pay attention to them. I hate group chats with a passion because they're a constant distraction to me. Once they narrow down a date and time, I'll jump in with my two cents. I just can't be bothered with the back-and-forth nonsense.

But then Melody tags me, asking if I'm good with meeting in —gasp—an hour at the Delta house. Double hell. I don't have any classes that clash with that time, and Melody knows it. If I say I can't go, she'll be pissed. It looks like today will be hellish anyway, might as well suck it up and deal with it.

I reply that the time works fine and then dig out my leotard and tights from the back of my closet. If I'm going to dance practice, I'm going to dress the part. And if they think I'll let them pick the song this time, they're sorely mistaken. They want Blair Westwood, then they'll get *Blair Westwood*. In the wise words of Elton John, the bitch is back.

ALEX

When I first read Professor McNelis's email asking to meet Blair and me for lunch, my reaction was a grimace. But then I realized it'd be the perfect opportunity to antagonize her. She probably wants to forget last Saturday ever happened, and I intend to remind her every chance I get.

For the first time in my life, I arrive to an appointment with ten minutes to spare. I wanted to make sure I arrived at Professor McNelis's office first. We're meeting there and then heading out to lunch. My plan works, and by the time Blair knocks on his door, I've already established an easygoing rapport with the man.

I lose the upper hand when she comes in and I take stock of what she's wearing—yoga pants, Ugg boots, and a light-pink sweater that barely covers her ass. Her hair is pulled back in a ponytail, and she has a pink headband keeping the loose wisps of hair secure. But what strikes me the most is her flushed cheeks and lack of makeup. Damn it. She has to be *that* perfect au naturel.

"I'm sorry. Am I late?" she asks.

"No, not at all. Alex arrived a bit early and we had a nice chat. Come in, take a seat."

She glances at me, and it's like she knows exactly what I am up to. "Alex arrived early to an appointment? That's a first."

"Yes, it seems this past week has been all about firsts," I reply, getting back on top of the game when her face turns redder.

She ignores my comment and takes the chair next to mine. "What have you been talking about?"

"Hockey and other stuff that would probably bore you to death," Professor McNellis replies.

Blair's nostrils flare. Oh shit. I think she'll blow on her own, and I won't need to do a thing.

"Hockey isn't boring," she grits out.

"Oh? I thought you hated hockey," I chime in.

"I don't hate the game—I hate certain players." She gives me a meaningful look.

"Yes, some guys can be excessively aggressive," Professor McNelis pipes up, completely oblivious to the animosity between his guests. He looks at his watch. "To save time, I thought we could eat at the restaurant by the library. We can walk there. It's a lovely day."

"Sounds good," I reply.

"Shall we? You must be hungry." He glances at Blair.

She stands before replying, "I'm starving."

I'm surprised by her answer, but then she looks at me, and… hell. Was that answer meant for me?

CHAPTER 14
BLAIR

I grab the napkin on my lap and twist it around my fingers. My mind is spiraling, trying to come up with an excuse to say no to Professor McNelis. I thought the reason for this impromptu lunch was to talk about the forum. That's how the conversation started, and then it went downhill.

"You want us to collaborate on a paper?" Alex asks when I can't find my voice.

Professor McNelis nods enthusiastically. "Not just a paper. A proposal for the UN! I've received so many emails and phone calls singing both of your praises at the forum." He leans forward. "Not that it surprises me. I truly believe you two would be perfect for this project."

It's an amazing opportunity, but working with Alex would be disastrous. I don't think we'd be able to collaborate for ten minutes without arguing.

"I can't speak for Blair, but I'm honored to have the opportunity. I'm in."

Great. Now I can't say I'm not interested without ruining my rapport with Professor McNelis, and possibly sabotaging my academic track at Hannaford U. Mother Dearest wants me to marry someone of her choosing, but that doesn't mean I need to depend on my future husband—or my family—financially. I'll marry to get her off my back, then file for divorce a year later. For my plan to work, I need a career, and the opportunity Professor McNelis is presenting on a silver platter will help me with that.

"I'm in as well, sir. Thank you for the chance."

He claps his hands together. "Excellent! You should start working on it right away, and of course, I expect you to come to me if you need any assistance."

"When is the proposal due?" I ask, already dreading adding another thing to my plate.

"In two months."

Two months... I can work with that.

"I'm benched for another week, so I have extra free time in my schedule. We should get a head start while I'm more available."

Because all that matters is your *schedule, jerkface.*

I can't say that out loud without coming across as bitchy, so I say instead, "Unfortunately, I'm not as available as you are for the next couple of weeks. But we'll work something out."

The waiter comes to retrieve our empty plates, and then Professor McNelis asks if we want dessert or coffee. I'd die for more caffeine, but I don't want to spend another minute playing nice with Alex.

"I'm good. I actually need to go home and change before my next class. I came straight from dance practice."

"Oh, that's why you're dressed like the rest of us," Alex points out.

I have to bite my tongue to not retort. I focus on Professor McNelis instead. "Thank you so much for lunch. I'm afraid I have to run."

I push my chair back and stand up. Alex—who's sitting next to Professor McNelis—doesn't move. If he wants to dick around with the professor some more, be my guest.

"Of course. I'll email you and Alex the project details, and I'd like to schedule a meeting next week to go over your outline."

Hell. That means I *do* need to meet with Alex this week. "I'm looking forward to it."

I head for the exit calmly, but all I want to do is run away. I relax only once I'm in my car. I never knew it'd take that much effort to be in the same room with Alex and not bite his head off. He was doing everything he could to get on my nerves.

Before I put the car in drive, I check my messages. I texted Gia earlier, asking to meet with her. I don't want to ask about recruiting the guys for the auction via phone. It'd be easier for her to say no. I have to plead my case in person.

She says she's at the arena right now and I'm welcome to come by, but she's busy later. Crap. I could go straight there, but I won't have time to change. Practice with the girls took longer than I anticipated, and the only thing we accomplished was choosing the song and coming up with the first steps of the choreography.

I let out a sigh. So far, the day has been hellish anyway; I might as well stay in my comfy clothes. I'll swing by the apartment first to grab Cookie because he shouldn't be left alone for too long and my dog walker is off today.

I turn on the car, but a red light on my dashboard catches my attention. It says one of my tires has low pressure, which is super strange. I just had the car serviced. Most people would ignore that and drive off, but I'm not most people. I get out to check the tire, and I'm glad I did because it's flat. Son of a bitch. The first week I decide not to use a car service, and this happens.

"Car trouble?" Alex asks from the front of my car.

Jesus fucking Christ. Can I catch a break?

"Why are you everywhere I go?" I snap.

His eyes widen. "We just got out of a meeting that we attended *together*, in case you forgot already."

"I wish I could forget." I open the door and lean forward to grab my phone.

"Man, I knew you were about to blow back there. Come on. Let me have the full Blair witch blast. I'm ready."

"I don't have time to waste with you. I have to call road service assistance. I hope they can come change my flat tire fast. I need to get home."

"You can't change a tire?" He raises an eyebrow.

I give him my most deadly glare. "If you're just here to annoy me, run along."

"If you can get them here in half an hour, you're lucky."

"Half an hour? I don't believe you."

"Wanna bet?"

I should ignore him, but my mouth has a will of its own. "One hundred dollars they'll be here in ten."

He crosses his arms and laughs. "You're on."

Five minutes later, four that I spend on hold, I'm forking over a one-hundred-dollar bill to Alex.

His shit-eating grin is as infuriating as it is sexy. "Thank you. Easier than stealing candy from children."

"I'm glad my ill fortune amuses you. I have to get home."

"Come on, you can head to your next class wearing what you have on."

"I'm not going home to change," I grit out. "I need to get Cookie."

His amusement vanishes. "Oh. Why didn't you say so? I'll drive you."

"You could change my tire instead." I cross my arms.

"I'd have offered, but I can't. Bad back, remember?"

Ah shit. I totally forgot.

"Right." I glance at my phone and pull up the Uber app to check if I can get a ride, but it says the wait time is ten to fifteen minutes. "Okay. Can you drive me to my place and then back to the arena? I'm meeting Gia there."

He doesn't answer for a couple beats, but his gaze remains steady, locked with mine. "I'm not your chauffeur, but since I'm going to the arena myself, I'll allow you to tag along."

I press my palm against my chest and say in the fakest voice possible, "Oh my gosh. Thank you so much. Aren't I lucky today?"

"You *are* lucky. Let's go. I don't have all day."

ALEX

Am I surprised that Blair carries hundred-dollar bills in her wallet? No. I'm also not in the least shocked she carelessly threw away that much money on a silly bet. These reminders that she is a spoiled brat are now at war with other feelings that I have no business developing.

She lives in a luxurious apartment complex just off campus. The red-brick building has a modern design with tall, gunmetal-framed windows on the front that make me think I'm entering a mall, not a residential complex. Or maybe the metal canopy jutting from the entrance is what gives me that impression.

"You can drop me off here. It'll only take me a minute to get Cookie."

I ignore her and find a parking spot. "I need to come up and use the bathroom."

"You can't wait?"

"No. What's the matter, Westwood? Are you trying to hide something?"

"No," she grumbles.

She gets out of the car before I do and powerwalks to the building. I don't try to catch up with her, busy as I am checking out her sweet ass and long legs. I shouldn't be looking, not when she made it clear that what happened last weekend was a one-time deal.

The elevator ride is silent and awkward. I want to say something, but I'm most comfortable when I'm antagonizing her, and for some bizarre reason, I don't want to do that now.

I expect her puppy to come running to the front door when she opens it, but all I hear is a bark coming from somewhere in her apartment.

Without looking at me, she says, "The bathroom is down the hallway, first door to your right."

"Okay."

I didn't really need to pee that badly. I said that as an excuse to come up to her apartment. I've never been here, and I'm damn curious. The bathroom is as neat as if it's never been used before. If this is the guest bathroom, maybe it doesn't get a lot of traffic.

I hear sounds of Blair in the living room being distracted by her pup, so I use the opportunity to look at the rest of her place. The second door to the right is open and has a queen-size bed, a chest of drawers, and art hanging on the walls that looks pretty but is super neutral. This must be a guest bedroom. Jesus, she's a junior in college with a guest bedroom. I don't think I could get used to this lifestyle. I wasn't born poor; my family was middle class, and we lived comfortably. That is until my father lost his job, his pride, and his will to live. He's not dead, but he might as well be.

I should head back before Blair catches me snooping, but I've come this far—might as well look at everything. The door at the end of the hallway is closed but not locked. I push it open, and I'm certain that I'm in her room. The walls are pink, save for the one facing me where the king-size bed is. It's covered with floral wallpaper. The flowers are huge and in bold colors, and oddly, I like the effect a lot.

I look over my shoulder to make sure I'm not about to be found out, and knowing I'm in the clear, I walk in, closing the door behind me. This is a major invasion of privacy, but I can't stop. I tell myself it's wise to go behind enemy lines, especially now that we'll be working together. She has too much power over me already, and she's not opposed to using her knowledge to get her way.

Opposite her bed, there's a custom-built shelf and storage

unit but no TV. I walk over to inspect what kind of books she has there, and my eyes zero in on a spine that says *BDSM for Beginners*.

Hello, Blair. What do we have here?

I pull the book off the shelf and open it to a random page. In this scenario, the woman is the sub. She's on her knees, wearing nothing but a harness and a collar. The dom is holding the chain attached to her collar and she's giving him a blow job. My heart is running at an increased pace. I imagine it's Blair and me in that scenario and my head spins. I haven't attempted anything similar, but if she's interested, I'd love to explore it with her.

A dark thought penetrates my brain. What if she's already doing that with someone else? I hate that idea with a passion, and the violence of that feeling makes me fucking confused.

"What the hell are you doing in my room?" Blair shrieks, catching me red-handed.

I snap the book closed. "Nothing. Your apartment is so big, I got lost."

She notices what I have in my hands, and her eyes bug out. "Got lost, my ass." She walks over and snatches the book from me. "Did you find what you were looking for?"

"I found *something*..."

Blush spreads through her cheeks, and without makeup, her embarrassment is obvious. I love to see her flustered like this. It reminds me of the evening she came all over my sweatpants. Shit. I'm getting aroused and without hope of release anytime soon.

Blair shoves the book back in its place. "I don't have time for your games, Alex. *I* have a busy agenda."

"I'm not playing games. Are you?"

Her brows shoot to the heavens. "Why would you think that?"

I shouldn't answer, but I'm fucking pissed, and I don't know about what exactly.

"Hmm, let's see. You got me drunk, then asked to make out,

gave me a hickey..." I pull my turtleneck sweater to show the fading bruise, making her wince. "Then you bailed like a thief in the night. Did I forget anything?"

"No, and I don't recall forcing the tequila down your throat, nor do I remember you complaining when I gave you that hickey. But none of those things mean I'm playing games. I just want to forget that that night ever happened."

I step closer, invading her space and forcing her to crane her neck to keep looking into my eyes. "Good luck with that."

Before she can react, I step back and walk out of her room.

CHAPTER 15
BLAIR

"Did I just see you come in with *Alex*?" Gia asks from her desk.

I wheel the empty chair closer to hers and take a seat. "Yes. We had a meeting with our economics professor, and I got a flat tire. He gave me a lift."

Gia bends down to pet my pup. "You brought Cookie to your meeting?"

"No. We stopped by my apartment first."

Her eyes widen. "Alex went to your place? Did you guys talk about DC?"

"I was planning on never mentioning what happened, but he brought it up after I caught him snooping in my room."

Instead of getting an outraged reaction from her, she smiles. "Holy crap. That's big."

"Why are you happy? Didn't you hear what I said? He went into my bedroom and was looking through my things!"

"What things?"

"My books."

"See? He was looking because he's curious about you, and if he's curious, he's interested."

I give her a droll look. "I think the pregnancy is already

affecting your brain. You sound like Zoey. He's not interested. He was looking for something he could use against me because I know..."

"You know what?"

I can't tell her, especially now that Alex found my book.

"Never mind. I didn't come here to talk about Alex. I came to ask you for a favor."

She furrows her brows. "If you had to ask me in person, it must be big."

I pick up Cookie and hold him on my lap. My puppy shield. "It is, sort of. I mean, six months ago, you wouldn't hesitate, but now you might."

"Are you going to spill on your own, or do I need to knock you over?"

"It's about the Starlight Charity Gala."

Gia's spine becomes taut. "Fuck. I completely forgot it was coming up. You need the guys to participate in the Date with a Warrior auction, right?"

"Yes, and considering what happened with the challenge to find Noah's dream girl, I totally understand your reluctance to sign them up for it."

"It's not my place to decide. I'm only the social media coordinator. It's Coach Bedford you need to convince."

"Really? Shit. Then I'm fucked. Didn't he threaten to fire you over the whole panties fiasco?"

Gia nods. "He did. He was pissed about that challenge. Listen, I don't have a problem with the guys participating. It's for a good cause, and they all love the attention, but..."

"But if everyone on the team is taking part, then Noah will too, and you'd hate that."

"I'd hate that so much. I still get mad when I think about all the crazy stuff those girls did to get his attention."

"I know. They were off the rails. To be fair, most players wind up getting bid on by boosters. It's innocent, and the *date* is during the gala. But what if I can guarantee no one will outbid you for a date with Noah? Would you help me convince Coach Bedford to let the guys join the auction?"

"How could you guarantee that?"

"I can forbid anyone in my sorority to bid for him."

"It's not only sorority girls who come to the gala. And you only have power within your sorority, not the others."

"I can win him for you."

"Blair... you know how high some of the bids go. Besides, wouldn't you rather spend your money on someone else... Alex maybe?"

My heart lurches, and I tell it to simmer down. "Hell to the fucking no. All I want from him is distance, which is unlikely to happen anytime soon."

She tilts her head. "Why is that?"

"I'm working on an economics proposal for the UN with him. Professor McNelis's idea. It's a great opportunity I couldn't pass up."

"Hmm, I think I'll start calling him Professor McCupid."

"Gia, you're the worst, but I'll let you pester me about Alex if you convince Coach Bedford to let the guys participate in the auction."

"Okay, I'll ask him." She looks at my clothes. "What's going on here? I've never seen you dress so cazh to school."

"I had dance practice for the gala, and it ran late. I didn't have time to change before my lunch with Alex and McNelis."

"Oh, you're dancing this year? What song did you pick?"

"God, it was a battle. There were three rounds of voting, which took forever, but ultimately 'Dance the Night' by Dua Lipa won."

"It's a good song to open the event."

"I think so too. Melody put me in charge of choreography. I might pick your brain for ideas. My style is so classical."

"I'm glad to help on a one-on-one basis, but I won't set foot in the studio with your sorority sisters."

"I wouldn't ask you to do that."

Gia turns to her computer and logs off. "I'm done with my work here. If you don't have to hurry to a class, I can help you now."

I check the time. "I have forty minutes. But where can we practice?"

Gia stands. "There's a training room we can use. No one will be there right now."

I smile. "Okay, let's do it."

ALEX

The physio sesh lasts only half an hour, but I feel much better. It was basically a massage. Not as enticing as the last one I received though.

Damn. I'm already thinking about that witch again. She definitely put a spell on me, and I can't get her out of my mind.

She hurried to Gia's office before I could ask if she needed a ride home or back to her car, so I'm assuming my services are no longer required. Like an idiot, I go to check on her anyway and find Gia's office empty. Blair must have left already.

It's better this way.

I veer for the exit, but then I hear barking coming from the end of the corridor. Is that her dog? It could be Marshall. Sometimes Gia brings her pup to the arena. I change course and follow the sound of a puppy yapping, and then music pours out of one of the training rooms.

I see them before they see me, thanks to the windows facing the corridor.

Blair is dancing… and I'm transfixed. She's light as a feather on her feet, and her moves are unrestricted. It's like I'm seeing a different person—unbound, free. I didn't know she could dance like this. It's crazy that Gia never mentioned it.

Or maybe she didn't mention it to you because of your feud with Blair, dumbass.

I should leave, but I can't… and that's why I need to go. Gia glances in my direction and waves. *Fuck.* Too late. Blair stops dancing and looks over her shoulder, then gasps. Damn. I love that sound coming from her, especially when I cause it.

She walks over and opens the door. "You don't need to wait for me. I'm good."

"Okay. Just checking. It's rude to leave without saying goodbye."

The frown is immediate. "Oh, get over it, Alex. I'm sure you've done that plenty of times with all your hookups."

"I sure have, but you see, they all know I'm there for one night. Our case was different. You were never a hookup. You were my roommate."

"God, you're not going to let that go, are you? What do you want, an apology?"

Is that what I want from her? Fuck. Why am I still annoyed? I really do need to get past it.

"Don't lose sleep over it, Westwood. I'm just keeping the status quo. I don't want what happened in DC to change things between us. I still don't like you."

She winces, and hell, I feel horrible for saying it.

"Ditto." She shuts the door in my face and strides back to the middle of the room.

Gia glances at me and then at Blair. I wonder if she knows I fooled around with her friend. If she does, I bet I'll be hearing from her soon.

CHAPTER 16
BLAIR

By the time I get home, I'm exhausted. Today was the longest day ever. My car had to be towed since I couldn't wait for road service to show up and change my tire.

Thank God Gia offered to drop off Cookie at the apartment for me. The guys on the team can get away with bringing their dogs to class, but that wouldn't fly with my professors.

I'm determined not to use my family's driver anymore because I suspect he reports everything I do to my mother. Otherwise, she wouldn't know the places I've been, and she let it slip that The Heritage is not an establishment I should frequent. So, to get to my classes, I rent a campus bicycle. It's been ages since I rode one, and, oddly, that's the highlight of my day. Maybe I should do it more often.

I'm sweaty and tired when I walk into my apartment. The last thing I expect is to find my brother sprawled on my couch.

I gape at him. "What are you doing here?"

"What? Can't a big brother come check on his baby sister?"

"Not unannounced. Did you just decide to barge in and make yourself comfortable when you learned I wasn't home?"

Ryder shrugs. "That's what the spare key is for. You look winded. What did you do? Run a marathon?"

"No, asshole. I rode a bike."

His brows shoot up. "What's wrong with your car?"

"I got a flat tire."

"Why didn't you call roadside assistance?"

I dump my duffel bag on the floor by the kitchen island. "Who said I didn't? They had to tow my car to the dealership because I wasn't around when they came to change the tire."

"Gotcha. And those clothes?"

I huff. "What's with the interrogation?"

"You can't blame me. Comfy and practical isn't really your style, is it?"

"If you must know, I had dance practice."

"You're dancing again? I thought you hated that."

"I never hated ballet. I hated the pressure Mom put on me to be the best. I might return to it, actually."

He stares at me with his trademark intense look that used to make me squirm when I was younger. Now it just irritates me.

"Why are you really here, Ryder?"

He rests his elbows on his legs, leaning forward. "How bad is Mom trying to play matchmaker with you?"

The topic of conversation makes my chest tight. "Why do you ask?"

"Because whatever you did in DC sent her on a rampage. She blew up my phone last Saturday."

"I did nothing but have dinner with a date *she* set up, and the guy was more interested in another girl."

He seems surprised. "Really?"

"Yeah, really, but if you must know, she's been horrible lately."

He nods. "I'm not surprised. You're turning twenty-one soon. Are you still going to let her pick your future husband?"

"What choice do I have? You know what she'll do if I don't follow along with her plans for me."

"Blair, you shouldn't have to marry a stranger to satisfy the whims of a sociopath. We'll find a way."

I cross my arms and narrow my eyes. "You never cared about my deal with Mom. Why now?"

"Maybe I'm trying to atone for my sins. I know I wasn't the best brother to you growing up, but that doesn't mean I don't care about you. If you want out of your deal with Mom, just say the word, and I'll make it happen."

I laugh in derision. "You're as powerless as I am when it comes to our parents. Don't try to pretend otherwise."

He stands up. "My fate has been sealed, but you still have a chance to control yours."

Ryder has many flaws, but quitting was never one of them… until he quit the hockey team without any explanation.

"Fine. I'll let you help me with Mom if you tell me why you gave up hockey."

He groans. "Not this again."

I put my hands on my hips, widening my stance. "Yes, this again. You hinted to Gia you didn't want to quit but didn't have a choice. Why didn't you have a choice? I know it wasn't Dad pressuring you. He was pissed that you were no longer a Warrior."

Ryder twists his face into a scowl. "He was, but not for the reasons you think."

"Then enlighten me."

He shakes his head. "Nope."

I throw my hands in the air. "You're infuriating."

His lips twist into a crooked grin. "I know. By the way, are you on the Starlight Charity Gala committee again this year?"

Of course he'd change the subject. It's pointless to try to get anything out of him when he doesn't want to talk.

"Yes, why?"

"Then you know that the swim and football teams are participating in the auction this year."

"So?"

"That means Preston and Josh will be there."

Ugh. How could I forget Ryder's douchey friends are jocks too? "That's just great. I bet CJ is thrilled his big brother will be in the auction too."

"That's what you're worried about? Have you forgotten about the ongoing feud between the football and hockey teams?"

"Do you think I pay attention to pathetic rivalries among jocks?"

"If you want the auction to go smoothly, you should pay attention. I won't be there to keep the boys in check, and by boys, I mean Logan and Alex."

Damn it. Ryder had to go and remind me of that pest.

"I can handle the twins as long as Josh keeps his teammates on a leash."

Ryder tilts his head. "Since when do you have any influence over them? Don't you and Alex hate each other?"

"I never said I hated him. It's an intense dislike, but I have to learn to ignore that now. We're working on a project together."

His eyes bug out. "You and Alex? Working together?"

I nod. "Yep."

"Without killing each other?"

"We can be civilized when needed. We survived our trip to DC together."

"Oh, Alex was there, huh? How did that go?"

Ryder has no reason to suspect I made out with his former teammate, but my face bursts into flames just the same. "Fine."

He squints, scrutinizing me. "Hmm...."

"Stop looking at me like that."

"Like what?"

"Like you want to read my mind."

"Well, your face went all shades of red just now. Excuse me for finding that odd. I'm all for sticking it to Mom, but you can do better than Alex Kaminski. He's a notorious manwhore."

I cross my arms. "If you're insinuating that I'd sleep with Alex to piss off Mom, you're dead wrong."

No, *she* never crossed my mind when I asked to make out with him. I wanted to kiss him because... hell because he makes me horny.

"Okay, if you say so. I guess I'd better go. I'll see you Saturday."

"Saturday? What's happening Saturday?"

Ryder's brows furrow. "Are you okay? Did you hit your head or something?

"Wait. What date is next Saturday?"

"December 2nd."

Fuck my life. "Shit!"

Ryder shakes his head. "I can't believe you forgot. Does that mean you didn't invite any of your friends?"

"No. I also doubt they'd wanna come this year."

A shadow of sadness dulls Ryder's blue eyes. Last year, Ryder brought Gia to my parents' kickoff holiday party alongside Jesse, Sean, CJ, and Darren. The twins didn't come, even though I'm sure they were also invited. I brought Zoey, Ashley, and some of my sorority sisters.

"Really? Not even Melody or... hell, I don't know the names of the rest."

"I'm definitely not bringing them," I grit out.

He lifts his hands, palms facing me. "Okay, okay. But you really should bring some friends, Blair. You'll need the buffer."

My stomach coils tightly. I hear what he's saying. Mom will use the party to pimp me out. It's going to be hell.

"I'll think about it."

CHAPTER 17
ALEX

Even without being able to play hockey, my schedule is insane. I can't get on the ice, but I still attend every practice. It's fucking hard being benched, but I have only one more week to go.

Professor McNelis sent the instructions for the UN project the day we had lunch together, but I haven't heard from Blair since. We're competing with other proposals, so winning it would be a big deal. It's already Thursday. As much as I didn't want to be the first to reach out, I can't wait any longer. We need to start working on that ASAP. She might not need this opportunity, but I do. I've been drafted to play in the NHL, but I want this project on my résumé in case things don't work out in professional hockey. Being drafted doesn't mean I'll get a contract, even though Joanne is furiously trying to get the ball rolling.

I'm tutoring a new student—a freshman from California—who hasn't quite adapted to the fast-paced environment of an Ivy League school. He'll get there though. I've never failed any student of mine before. I've just finished our tutoring session in the library, might as well text the witch and figure out a time to meet.

We need to start on our project.

Immediately, she sends a reply.

I know. Sorry, I've been busy as hell.

She's apologizing to me? Something is wrong.

I'm free now.

I'm on my way to grab something to eat at La Taqueria. Meet me there?

Sure.

It doesn't hit me until I'm in my car that I'm about to have dinner with Blair again. Back in DC, we had her asshole date and Sheila tagging along. This time, we'll be alone. Hell. I have no idea what to expect. A few weeks ago, I wouldn't get near her voluntarily, and if I did, I'd break out in hives.

I'm not upset about meeting her tonight.

I park next to her white SUV and head into the busy restaurant. The hostess perks up as I approach her podium, smiling from ear to ear.

"Welcome to La Taqueria. Table for one?"

"No, I'm meeting someone. She's already here."

The woman's smile wilts. "Oh, sure."

The restaurant is big, and most of the tables are occupied. I scan the room, looking for Blair, but I don't see her anywhere. I pull my cell phone out to text her just as it starts to ring, *Blair Witch* showing on the screen.

"Where are you?" I ask.

"I'm in the booth all the way in the back. I'm waving at you."

I see her then, wearing her usual preppy, pastel-colored clothes. I begin to smile but catch myself in time. "Found you."

She's back in her seat when I reach the booth. I slide in

across from her, and as much as I don't want to be affected by her, I can't ignore how my pulse accelerates. I reach for the menu, hoping for a distraction. "Did you order already?"

"No. I was waiting for you."

My heart leaps. *Jesus, calm down, traitorous muscle.* "How considerate."

She sighs. "Really? You're starting already?"

Furrowing my brows, I look up. "Sorry. Old habits."

The waitress interrupts us before Blair can reply. "Welcome to La Taqueria. Can I get you something to drink?"

"Just water for me," Blair replies.

"What? No tequila tonight?" I arch an eyebrow.

A blush spreads through her cheeks, and she averts her gaze. "No."

"I'll have water too. Thanks," I tell the waitress.

Blair's gaze is glued to the menu, but I wonder if she's actually reading the options. She seems frozen. Is she thinking about our evening in DC? Now I am. Damn it.

A few minutes later, the waitress returns with our water. Blair orders fajitas, and I end up doing the same.

I lean back, relaxing against the seat. "So, how shall we do this?"

She sits straighter in her chair. "Do what?"

"Relax. I meant the project. How are we going to split the tasks?"

"Oh." Her face is still super red, and I'm almost certain she was thinking about us. "We need to do a lot of research. I think we should do it together so we're not both looking into the same things."

"I don't hate the idea. Let's do it."

Her brows arch. "What? Were you planning to object to anything I suggested?"

"Yes."

She pinches her lips. "At least you're honest."

"I'm always honest, Westwood. You should follow my example."

"Are you saying I'm not?"

I shrug. "The jury is still out."

"You're an ass."

A broad smile splits my face. "There's the Blair I love."

Her eyes bug out. *Fuck. Fuck. Fuck.* I didn't mean to say that. I meant to say *there's the hate I love,* not Blair. Jesus. I'm losing my mind. Can't backtrack now.

"All right. We're together. Let's dig into research while we wait for our food," I say.

I pull my laptop from my backpack and set it in front of me. Blair does the same, and for the next ten minutes, we discuss only work. Our food comes, and we eat in silence until it's broken by Blair's phone ringing. She looks at the screen and grimaces but doesn't answer.

It rings and rings until it finally stops, but immediately, she receives several text messages in a row.

"Someone is really trying to get a hold of you."

She reaches for her water, and her hand is shaking. "That's how my mother operates."

"Ah. Has she found another candidate for your hand in marriage?"

It's meant to be a joke to light up the mood, but I'm not amused by it.

I sit stock-still. Why do I care if Blair gets married?

She doesn't answer me, too busy reading her mother's texts, and whatever the woman said has an effect on her. The crease between her brows becomes progressively deeper, and the tension around her mouth more pronounced. Shit. I hate seeing what that woman does to Blair. Emotional bullying is sometimes worse than physical blows.

"What's wrong?" I ask.

"Who said there's anything wrong?" She tries to school her expression into neutral, but I see it past her mask.

"Your face."

She scowls. "Why are you paying attention to my face?"

"You're sitting across from me. Your sour puss is pretty hard to miss."

Her eyes narrow, and I wait for the retort, but instead, the most unexpected thing comes out of her mouth. "What are you doing Saturday night?"

"Uh, I don't know. Why?"

"Do you feel like pissing off a god-awful woman?"

"Not particularly. I have my hands full with you."

She smirks, and her eyes—her fucking gorgeous eyes—shine with mischief. In this moment, I'd do anything she asked of me.

"I want you to be my date at my parents' holiday kickoff party."

Ah hell. "I didn't go last year when I didn't want to punch your brother's face. What makes you think I'd go now that I do?"

"One, you'll get the chance to punch Ryder's face. And two, maybe I'll let you fuck me in my parents' house."

Jesus fucking Christ. Never have I gotten a hard-on so fast in my life. "Aren't you conceited? Who says I want to fuck you?"

She tilts her head. "Are you saying you don't?"

Fuck. I've never wanted anything more. "Remove the 'maybe' from your offer, and I'll consider it."

"Deal."

CHAPTER 18
BLAIR

For two days, I refuse to think about my impulsive decision. But as I'm getting ready to attend my parents' odious party, butterflies wreak havoc with my stomach. Alex confirmed he'd be my date only an hour ago. I should have known he'd wait until the last minute. He must have read the desperation in my eyes when I asked him.

I'm not sure what I'm most nervous about. Parading him in front of my mother or fulfilling my end of the bargain. I could tell him he took too long and I found a replacement, but the lie would hurt me more than him.

Mother sent me several dress choices, but she made it clear she wanted me to wear the white dress. Very bridal. Hard pass. In an act of rebellion, I ignore all the gowns, which are still inside their garment bags, and wear a black baby doll lacy dress with long see-through sleeves. It has an empire waist, and it's not snug like all the other dresses my mother sent, but it's sexy in a different way. At least I think so. And it's super short. If I bend over, you can see my underwear—and the garter belt. If I'm going to be fucking Alex later, I want to do it right.

I keep my makeup simple, save for the bold red lips—my trademark now. My hair is styled perfectly in soft curls and secured by a black headband with a big butterfly detail on the right side. The only jewelry I'm wearing tonight is the diamond stud earrings I got from Ryder for my eighteenth birthday and the pendant necklace with my initials.

Cookie is in the corner, playing with one of his chew toys. I turn to him and ask, "What do you think?"

He lifts his head, tilting it sideways. I wish I had my phone handy. That pose is adorable. He barks once and then returns to his toy. I take it that he approves.

The intercom buzzes, making my heart lurch in my chest. My hands are clammy and shaky. *Damn it, Blair. It's just Alex, your enemy.* There's no need to be nervous. This isn't a date. It's a trade of favors.

I pull up the app on my phone to make sure it's him in front of my building, then I buzz him in. I'm too nervous to face him, so I head to the kitchen and pour myself a shot of tequila. Cookie follows me and gets comfy in his bed by the couch. A minute later comes the knock on the door. I take a deep breath, then shake my head and arms as I exhale.

"Okay, I can do this."

I'm glad I drank the tequila shot because Alex in a suit is better than freshly baked chocolate chip cookies. I keep my eyes glued to his face, but his gaze wanders to my shoes then travels slowly up my body. He's done that before, and I'm just as affected as I was the first time. My pulse quickens, and my throat becomes dry.

I should say something, but I can't find my voice, so I just open the door wider and let him in.

"What time are we supposed to be at the party?" he asks, giving my living room a cursory glance as if he hasn't been here before.

"We have time," I say.

He turns around. "That doesn't answer my question."

"Fine. The car will be here in ten minutes."

"Car?" He arches his brows.

"Yes, I ordered a car to take us."

He shakes his head. "Cancel it. I'm driving."

"Why? Wouldn't you prefer to not worry about drinking and driving?"

"I'll still have to worry about driving under the influence unless you're assuming I'll be spending the night with you."

My face heats up. "I'm not."

"Either way, I'm still driving. I'm not going to a party with sharks and not having the means to make a quick exit."

"Fair. Then drive my car."

He scoffs. "What's wrong with mine?"

"It probably stinks of sweaty hockey gear and junk food."

"You're assuming a lot, Westwood."

"Fine." I grab my phone from the kitchen counter and send a text to the car company canceling our ride. "There. It's done. Are you happy now?"

"Hmm, let's see. I'm going to a stuffy party with you. No, I'm not happy."

I put my hands on my hips. "I don't remember forcing you to come. Are you that desperate to get laid?"

He walks over, invading my space. My back presses against the counter. I have nowhere to go.

"I'm not desperate. In fact, in the last half hour, I received several texts from girls wanting to hook up."

"You're disgusting," I grit out, trying to mask how much I'm enjoying his proximity. And why does he have to smell so good?

"It's not my fault I'm in demand."

"So why did you agree to be my date tonight?"

He places his hands on the counter, caging me in, and leans forward. "Because I've never fucked anyone I hated before, and I'm curious."

His words feel like a punch to my chest. *Hate*. He hates me. I suddenly can't breathe because it hurts too much. Not so long ago, the feeling was mutual. Now....

"I promise it'll be an experience you won't forget."

He brings his nose to my neck, sending goose bumps everywhere. "I'm counting on it, Westwood."

My breathing is shallow, and maybe it's the tequila already playing keep-away with my intelligence, but I'm seconds from pulling Alex's lips to mine.

Before I can attack his mouth, he steps back and fixes his jacket. "Why do you have a giant bug on your head?"

"What?" My ears are still buzzing, thanks to Alex's touch.

He points at my headband.

"It's a butterfly," I say like an idiot.

"Like I said, a bug."

"I'm not drunk enough to endure this." I turn to the bottle of tequila, but Alex grabs my wrist before I can pour another shot.

"No. I don't want you wasted tonight."

I yank my hand free. "You aren't the boss of me."

"I'm not going to fuck you if you're drunk. I want your head clear."

"Why? What difference does it make?"

"All the difference in the world. I want to know you're one hundred percent on board, and that your decisions aren't clouded by booze."

My heart is thumping inside my chest so fast and loud, I'm sure he can hear it. As crazy as it is, I want to get railed by Alex, but I'm afraid I won't be any good if I'm sober. I'll never tell him that though.

"What if I can't do it otherwise?"

"Then the deal is off."

I glance at the bottle of tequila, seriously considering going to the party alone. But then I picture my mother's face and her disapproving glare. No. I don't want to go alone.

I turn to Alex. "I can't promise I won't drink at the party. So let's do it now."

His eyes widen. "You want me to fuck you now?"

"Yeah, right here on this counter." I tap the marble surface.

He moves closer, and I lose my bravado a little. I swallow the lump in my throat, maintaining eye contact.

"I thought you wanted to get railed in your parents' house."

"That was the plan, but if you're insisting on having me sober..."

Roughly, he grabs my chin with his big, calloused hand and crushes his lips to mine. I wasn't expecting to be kissed like this, and hell... it's the best fucking kiss in the world. He takes possession of my mouth, my tongue, kissing me hungrily and hard. This is how hate tastes, and I want it all. I grab his biceps, digging my long nails into his muscles.

He pulls back, ending the kiss too soon. "I get to decide when and where I fuck you."

I'm still reeling from the kiss, but Alex is already by the front door, looking as stiff as a rock.

I sway a little. Was I the only one affected by what just happened? I drop my eyes to his crotch and see the bulge there. No, he's not immune either, but I recognize his move for what it is—a power play.

"You have lipstick smeared all over your face," I tell him.

He shoves his hand in his jacket pocket and pulls out a square white packet. "I came prepared."

He rips it open and takes out the wet napkin from the package, then wipes his face. "You'd better fix your makeup, Westwood. You're looking a little... *disheveled*."

I march to my bedroom but maintain my glower. He might have scored the first point tonight, but the match has just started.

CHAPTER 19
ALEX

I shouldn't have kissed Blair. It took every ounce of self-restraint to walk away instead of fucking her on the counter like she asked me to. When it happens, it will be on my terms, not hers. She thinks it'll happen tonight at her parents'. I'm not planning on that. If I'm going to cross that line with her, I want to have all the time in the world to do it right.

Her parents live in Evergreene, a small town thirty minutes from Fairbanks. The closer we get to our destination, the tenser Blair becomes. She's clutching the purse on her lap for dear life, and that delicious mouth of hers is locked tight in a harsh line.

Her phone rings, and I'd bet a limb it's her mother calling to ask why she's not at the party yet. Blair answers the call, and I'm proven right.

"I'm ten minutes away," she grits out.

I can't hear what the woman is saying; I see only how the conversation affects Blair.

"It's a party, Mother. I'll be there soon. Bye." She ends the call and holds the phone against her chest.

"Does she know I'm coming with you?"

"No. I figured I'd surprise her."

"Don't let her get to you."

"Trust me, I'm trying."

On impulse, I reach for her thigh and slide my hand under her dress.

"What are you doing?" she asks.

"I didn't let you drink the tequila. This is my alternate way of calming you down."

I don't move my hand for a couple beats, waiting for her to push it away. She doesn't, so I sneak a peek at her face. Her breathing is shallow, and her mouth isn't set in a thin line anymore. Her lips are partially open, and it's a shame I can't kiss her while driving. But I don't need both hands to steer the car. I slide my hand up her leg and discover she's wearing a garter belt. Shit.

"Is this for me, Westwood?"

"No," she whispers.

"I'll benefit from it anyway."

I keep moving my hand upward until I find the edge of her underwear. I toy with the seam for a bit while nudging her legs apart. She inhales sharply when I push the flimsy fabric aside and swipe my finger over her clit.

"Relax, baby girl. I'll make you feel good."

She's slick with desire, making my job so much easier. I play with her clit, alternating swiping my finger over it and pressing down on it. Her small gasps are little doses of libido going straight to my cock. My erection is pressing against my pants painfully, so when I slide my fingers down to her entrance, I imagine the tip of my cock pressing there.

Blair doesn't say a word, but her labored breathing and whimpers are enough motivation to keep me going. I insert one finger at first, testing her out. Gingerly, she begins to rotate her hips.

"Are you trying to fuck my finger, baby girl?"

"Yes," she pants. "I need more."

I chuckle. "As you wish."

I jump straight to three fingers, going in and out of her hot pussy as if it was my cock pounding into her. Her moans become louder, and her chest rises and falls faster. When her internal walls start to milk my fingers, I know she's close. I alternate fucking her pussy and giving her clit attention.

The GPS warns we're five minutes from her parents' house, so I need to finish this fast. They live in a gated community, and I don't want to pause my work to deal with a security guard.

"Faster, Alex," she cries out.

I piston my fingers in and out of her, loving how her juices are already all over my hand. I see our exit and slow down. As focused as I am on the task, I almost miss it. There's a red light ahead, and as the car stops, my ministrations accelerate.

She tosses her head back and yells, "Fuck!"

Her body shakes, and her clit pulses against my fingers. Then she closes her legs, making it harder for me to keep moving my hand, but I don't need to. She's coming all over it, and it's a beautiful thing to witness. Her eyes are closed, and her cheeks are flushed.

A honk behind me wakes me from my daze. The light turned green. I resume driving but keep my hand between her legs until her body relaxes against the seat. We pass the sign to her parents' gated community, then the gatehouse looms ahead. There's a car in front of us when I stop, and that's when I pull my hand free.

I look at Blair. "Wasn't this better than tequila?"

She meets my stare, face still red. "You're so cocky."

"I know." I bring my hand to my mouth and lick each finger slowly. "Hmm... what I didn't know is how sweet you taste, Westwood."

Her face becomes even redder before she breaks eye contact first.

BLAIR

I can't believe I let Alex finger fuck me in the car minutes before I have to see my parents. My panties are soaked through, and I'm pretty sure I smell like sex.

"How should I do this?" he asks right before we walk through the front door. "Do you want to hold hands, link arms, or—"

"I'm not holding your hand or linking my arm with yours," I grit out.

The snap wasn't necessary, but that's what I do when I'm spiraling. Things are getting more and more complicated with Alex and I'm losing control of the situation. I don't know where we stand or how I feel about him and add in the factor that I'm about to see my mother, and my nerves are fried.

"Okay. I'll just stand next to you like a Ken doll, then."

"You do that," I reply, sounding absentminded because I've already spotted my mother having words with one of the waiters.

My heart is hammering against my rib cage. Hell, she looks pissed. I don't want to talk to her right this second. I'm about to steer Alex away from my mother's line of sight, but Ryder appears out of nowhere and blocks our path.

"Jesus, Blair. When I said bring someone, I didn't mean *him*."

Alex turns to me. "Can I punch his face now? You promised."

Ryder steps back, blinking fast. "Come again?"

"I told Alex he could punch you if he agreed to be my date tonight."

Ryder stares at me as if I've lost my mind. Then he looks at Alex. "I suppose I deserve to get decked by you. But let me get a few of these in me first." He raises his glass of whiskey and takes a sip.

"Blair, is that you?" my mother asks.

Ryder moves out of the way, and now I can't hide. She's striding toward us with purpose. Her bleached-blonde hair is pulled back in a severe bun, making her dangling diamond earrings the center focus of her look. Her long emerald-green chiffon gown has a corset underneath that's cinched so tight I'm not sure how she's breathing.

"Hello, Mother."

She stops in front of me and looks me up and down as if she's appraising a horse. "What are you wearing? I specifically told you to wear the white dress."

"There was a stain."

She narrows her ice-cold blue eyes. "I seriously doubt that. What about the other options I sent?"

"None fit."

She pinches my cheek. "You did put on a few pounds. You need to go on a diet immediately. You know designers don't make clothes for fat people."

"For fuck's sake, Mom. If Blair were any skinnier, she'd disappear."

Mom glares at Ryder, but she doesn't reprimand him for cussing in front of her. If it were me... that'd be a different story. My face is in flames, and I'm sure it's showing. I knew she'd be awful to me in front of Alex—whom she hasn't acknowledged yet—but I was hoping I'd be drunk when it happened.

Alex clears his throat, drawing her attention to him.

"And you are?" she asks him, not warm, but not rude either. She doesn't know he isn't from a wealthy family.

"Alex Kaminski." He offers her his hand—the same hand that was inside of me a few minutes ago and that he hasn't washed yet.

Knowing him, he did it on purpose. Mom is oblivious, but why would she suspect anything?

"I don't think I know your parents."

"You probably don't. But I'm sure your husband knows my father."

I turn to him, unable to guess where he's going with that.

"Is that so?" Mom arches an eyebrow. "In that case, I'm sure Ray would love to speak to you."

"I'm looking forward to it." Alex's tone tells me differently. He isn't looking forward to it at all. What's the story here?

Mom gives me a scathing glance. "I'll speak to you later. Now go make your rounds."

As soon as my mother is out of earshot, I turn to Alex. "You never said your dad knew my father."

"Oh, they go way back." His eyes are cold and filled with rancor. I'm not sure if his anger is aimed at me or my parents.

Ryder scoffs. "Don't leave her in the dark."

"What's going on? Is there something I should know?" I cross my arms.

Alex clenches his jaw so tight his cheeks hollow.

It's Ryder who ends up answering me. "Alex's father used to work for a small manufacturing facility that Dad's company acquired and ultimately shut down. He lost his job, along with hundreds of other people, and they tried to sue Dad's company."

Shit. Everything is beginning to make sense. I didn't start the feud with Alex. He was the one who had it in for me the first time we met. I simply retaliated. Now I know why.

"Were you planning on telling me that, ever?" I ask Alex.

"What's the point? It happened a long time ago."

"Before you start arguing, I want to know what the fuck this is." Ryder points at the two of us. "You've always hated each other."

Still looking at Alex, I say, "Yes, that hasn't changed."

He doesn't contradict me, and once again, I get clobbered. It seems I don't have my shield in place anymore. I need to rebuild it fast if I'm to survive working with him.

I make a motion to walk away, but Alex asks, "Where are you going?"

My steps falter, but I don't stop. "To do what I came here for—find myself a husband."

CHAPTER 20
ALEX

I watch Blair walk away, trying to figure out why I feel slightly nauseated.

"You're not going after my sister?" Ryder asks.

"No." It comes out choked.

"Why are you here then? I thought you were her date."

I look him in the eye. "Didn't you hear her earlier? She promised me the chance to punch you."

He rolls his eyes, then finishes his drink. "Like I said, I need more booze to allow that to happen. And you only get one shot."

"Bullshit. You deserve an ass whooping after what you did to us last season."

"You lost the Cup, big fucking deal. You'll get another chance this year. I hear *Noah* is terrific."

I hear the sarcasm in his tone, loud and clear. "Do you try to be an asshole on purpose, or does it come naturally to you?"

He smirks. "It's a gift. One that you possess as well."

"I'm not an asshole."

His brows shoot up. "Are you saying you're not one to Blair?"

"She isn't a saint."

"No, but can you blame her?" He brings his glass to his lips, forgetting it's empty already, and grimaces. "Listen, I don't know why Blair brought you to this party when I told her she should bring a friend. I can't keep an eye on her the entire time, nor would she want that. But for some reason, she wanted you here. You ain't getting a shot at my face if you don't fulfill your end of this twisted bargain with her."

If he only knew—punching his face is not the main reason I'm here. That knowledge is the only thing saving him from being decked right now.

I crack my knuckles. "I'll find you later."

"Can't wait."

We go in opposite directions, but I'm sure this isn't the last I'll see of him tonight. I head in the direction Blair went and arrive in a grand room where guests dressed in their finest are standing in small clusters, sipping their fancy drinks. Being taller than most, I don't need to crane my neck to search the room. A quick sweep tells me she's not here.

I turn around and almost collide with a guest. "I'm sorry."

The redhead, wearing too much makeup and perfume, smiles at me. Jesus, not a single muscle on her face moves.

"It's all right. My champagne is still mostly in the glass, not on my dress."

"What a relief."

She tilts her head and scrutinizes me. "I'm not sure I've seen you at the Westwoods' soirees before."

"It's my first time."

A twinkle of mischief shines in her green eyes. Fuck. I know that look. Cougar on the prowl alert.

"Oh, I love first-timers. I can show you the lay of the land if you like." She touches my arm.

I step back, needing the distance. "I'm actually looking for my date."

Her smile wilts. "Oh, and who's your date?"

"Blair Westwood."

Another sparkle shines in her eyes, but this time, it's malicious, matching the upcurl of her lips. "You'd better enjoy the little time you have left. That girl won't be single for much longer. Her mother is intent on marrying her off by next year."

I knew that already, so hearing it shouldn't affect me. But the sudden pain in my stomach says otherwise.

"Thanks for the tip." I walk around her, trying my best to control my emotions.

Fuck. I have no reason to care about Blair's future. If she wants to marry a stranger to appease her parents, that's her choice.

I wander aimlessly. This house is huge, like a palace, and I'm beginning to suspect finding Blair won't be as easy as I thought. I finally make it to an outside area where white-cloth-covered high tables are sprinkled in strategic spots around the pool.

Toward the edge, I spot familiar faces. Adrian Steele, Josh Fitzpatrick Jr., Hunter Matthews, and Preston King—Ryder's friends. I can't stop a scowl from twisting my face. I never liked those preppy assholes when Ryder was on the team, and now I like them even less. I decide to avoid them until I see Blair burst out of a side door and head straight for their table. Her expression is mercurial, which I'm familiar with. Something's set her off.

She's on the other side of the pool and will reach the four assholes of the apocalypse before I can intercept her. Hell and damnation. I start toward their table, walking as fast as I can without shoving people out of my way.

I lose sight of them when an elderly guest trips and collapses against me. "Are you okay, ma'am?"

"Yes, yes. Thank you, young man." She pats my arm and then walks around me.

When I finally reach their table, Blair has an empty shot glass in her hand, and she's grimacing while Ryder's friends watch her with what I can describe only as matching horrified expressions.

"What was in this?" Blair asks.

"Hell, why did you shoot that?" Adrian asks.

"What's going on?" I butt in, and they finally notice me standing there.

Preston turns to me. "My, my, you *are* here. I couldn't believe it when Ryder told us."

I'd answer him, but Blair is massaging her chest and frowning.

"What did you give her?"

Hunter's eyebrows shoot to the heavens. "We didn't give her anything. She stole one of our special shots."

Fuck. That's code for drugs.

"What was in the shot?" I ask through clenched teeth, barely containing my anger.

"Xanax and tequila." Adrian rubs his face. "Ryder's going to kill us."

Fuck.

"You mixed *Xanax* with tequila? Are you out of your goddamned minds?"

"Shh, lower your voice," Josh retorts.

"Don't get started with me, asshole."

Josh makes a motion to come at me, but Hunter holds him back. "Don't."

"Am I supposed to be feeling this light-headed?" Blair sways.

I reach for her, steadying her against me with my arm. "It's okay. I got you."

Preston laughs. "Oh, this will be so fun."

"What will be so fun?" Ryder approaches the table, erasing the amusement from Preston's face.

"Blair drank one of your buddies' 'special' drinks," I tell him.

"What the fuck!" Ryder blurts out. "Who gave her that?"

"Don't blame us!" Preston retorts. "We didn't offer her anything. She stole a shot and drank it before we could stop her."

"Jesus fucking Christ." Ryder pulls his hair back, then turns to me. "You need to get her out of here before the drug takes effect."

"I'm not leaving! I feel like dancing." Blair tries to step away from me, but I hold her tighter.

"Shit. I think it's too late for that," Adrian chimes in.

"Fuck, your father is coming, bro," Josh points out.

I look over my shoulder and see the man my father hates the most in this world approach. He knows who I am—how could he not? I play for the Warriors, and the man was not only a fan but also a booster. He was always at the games and even visited the locker room a few times. Thanks to my father punching his face at a protest in front of the Westwoods' headquarters, he's not a faceless, disgruntled former employee. But Raymond Westwood never acknowledged my connection to my father or treated Logan and me differently because of it.

I doubt he'll maintain his neutral position toward me if he sees me holding his daughter in this state. No doubt he'll blame me.

"Come on, Blair. I'll dance with you." I steer her away from the table, and mercifully, she doesn't resist.

I have no intention of dancing with her, but she's already as high as a kite and doesn't notice we're leaving the party until we're outside the mansion.

"Hey! You tricked me." She tries to pull free of my grasp, but I hold her tight.

"No, I didn't. I'm taking you somewhere else to dance."

Her eyes turn rounder. "Are we going back to the club in Boston?"

"Sure."

"Yippee!" She twirls with extreme grace for someone high on Xanax.

"Get in the car, Westwood." I open the door for her.

"Why do you keep calling me Westwood? I prefer when you call me baby girl."

"Is that so?" I step into her space and lean down to whisper in her ear. "I'll call you baby girl when I make you come again. Now get in the car."

It's an effort to step away because I very much want to kiss her again. I won't though. I'm not touching her tonight. I wasn't kidding when I said I wanted her to know what she was doing.

She pouts. "You're so bossy. Maybe you can be my dom."

Whoa. I wasn't expecting that. Sure, she has a book about BDSM in her room, but I didn't know she actually wanted to experiment with that. I'll gladly go down the rabbit hole with her if she's serious about it, but right now, I'm not going to entertain the idea. I can't take anything she says under the influence seriously.

"We'll see." I nudge her into the car and thank fuck, she doesn't resist.

I run to my side before she decides to escape, and once I'm behind the steering wheel, I lock the doors for good measure.

But Blair doesn't seem intent on running away. She reaches for the radio and changes stations until she finds a song that pleases her. "Oh, I love this song."

I look at my dashboard and read "Anti-Hero" by Taylor Swift. "You love a lot of her songs. Are you a Swiftie, Blair?"

She turns to me and smiles from ear to ear. Man, that's something. If we weren't enemies and she smiled at me like that when she was sober, I'd be at serious risk of falling for her. Instead of answering, she sings the song at the top of her lungs.

She continues during the entire ride, and even though she doesn't sing as well as she dances, I'm glad that's all she does. I've heard some crazy stories about people high on that shit. I still can't believe those fuckers would touch it. Aside from Adrian, they're all athletes. I guess sports for them is just a pastime. When you don't need to work for a living and everything is handed to you on a silver platter, you don't have to take anything seriously. Half the football team operates like that. Hence the animosity between hockey and football players is rampant. They also lose more games than they win.

Blair doesn't notice when I park the car in front of her building. She's singing with her eyes closed.

"We're home," I say, then turn off the engine.

She looks out the window. "Wow. That was fast."

"I guess time flies when you're having fun."

With her hand on the door handle, she turns and gives me a come-hither glance. "It's about to become even better."

Yeah, it's not gonna happen tonight, baby girl.

She gets out of the car and takes off her shoes before sprinting across the street without looking for traffic. I hurry after her, catching up before she has the chance to gain access to the building and leave me behind.

She giggles and twirls on the tips of her toes all the way to the elevators. My crazy ballerina.

"I forgot how much I enjoy dancing."

"You're amazing," I tell her, only because I know she won't remember it tomorrow. Then I press the button to call the elevator, which she seems to forget to do.

She closes one eye and wrinkles her nose. "Do you really think so?"

"Yeah."

The elevator arrives, and now I have to come up with a plan. I can't leave her alone in this condition. Maybe I can call Gia.

I'm thinking through my options when Blair pushes me against the wall and flattens her tiny body to mine. "I'm horny."

"I bet you are." My voice comes out like a growl.

"I want to cross that line with you tonight."

So do I, baby girl, but there's no chance in hell that will happen.

We arrive at her floor, and I don't have to push her away. She steps back on her own and takes off down the corridor, yelling, "I'm getting railed by Alex Kaminski tonight!"

"Shit!"

I run after her and take the key from her hand since she's having trouble finding the keyhole. I need to get her inside ASAP.

"Oh my God. I don't know why I was dreading going to the party tonight. Even overhearing my mother talk about me like I was some prize horse to a potential suitor didn't ruin my evening. I had such a blast."

That was what set her off? God, her mother is vile, and now I know what true hate feels like. It wasn't what I harbored toward Blair at all.

She lobs her shoes to the side and then bends over her puppy's crate. "Do you need to go for a walk, buddy?"

Hell. I can't let her out of this apartment, but I also can't walk her dog and leave her alone.

"Maybe we can do that later. He's probably hungry."

She takes the puppy out of his crate and cradles him against her chest. He starts to lick her face, making her laugh.

"That tickles." She puts the dog on the floor, and he comes running in my direction.

I get into a crouch to play with him. "Hello, little guy." I'm about to ask what she named him, but then I see his collar. "You named him Cookie?"

"Yes, chocolate and cream cookies are my favorite, and that's what he reminds me of."

I unfurl from my lower position and ask, "Where do you keep his food?"

"The lower cabinet next to the sink."

I turn my back to get the food, and when I look up, Blair is gone. I whip my face toward the door. It's closed, so she didn't leave the apartment.

"Blair?"

"I'll be there in a second," she replies from her bedroom.

Relieved that I haven't lost her, I find a couple of bowls to put the food in and also fresh water.

Cookie attacks the food and cleans his bowl in seconds. "You were hungry."

Movement in my periphery catches my attention. It's Blair

leaning against the wall where the corridor gives way to the open living space. Her dress is gone, and she's standing there in black lingerie that makes my knees go weak and my cock spring to life.

"How about you, Alex? Are you hungry too?"

"Blair, I..."

The words die in my throat. She sashays in my direction, and I can't do anything but drink her in. She's more breathtaking than in my dreams. I've dreamed about her plenty, on her back, screaming my name as I fuck her into oblivion. I want to do all the things I've imagined, but not tonight.

"It's okay. I'm starving too." She invades my space, pressing her palms flat against my chest. "Your heart is beating so fast. Are you nervous, Alex?"

"No," I growl. "We can't do this."

She rubs her other hand against my erection, which is throbbing against my pants. "I think we can."

I grab her wrist, making her stop. "I told you I wouldn't fuck you if you're drunk."

"It was only one shot of tequila. I'm not drunk."

No, you're high out of your mind. "I'm sorry, baby girl. Not tonight."

She steps back, revealing not a mask of seduction but an expression of deep hurt. "You don't think I'm attractive, do you? Or you don't want to fuck an uptight bitch."

"What? No! That's not what I think at all. You have no idea how hard it is to say no to you tonight."

"Prove it."

"Prove what?"

"Prove that you want me. Kiss me."

Shit. Kissing her could snap my control, but if I refuse that as well, she won't believe I'm dying to be with her. She's high, but if she remembers anything about this tomorrow, this moment will be the detail she'll hang on to.

You can do this, Alex. You can kiss her and not lose control.

I pull her to me and cradle her face with one hand. "You're so damn beautiful, Blair. I can't stand it."

I know she has a rebuff on the tip of her tongue, but I don't allow her to voice it. I claim her lips, teasing them open with my tongue. One swipe, one taste, that's all it takes to set me on fire. I never knew how desperately I wanted her until I couldn't have her.

CHAPTER 21
BLAIR

I open my eyes, and my first thought is, what died in my mouth? Because it tastes foul. My second thought is, why does my head hurt so much? I don't remember drinking anything at the party. One shot of tequila wouldn't give me a hangover.

My skin is clammy, and the sheets feel rough against my skin. I'm almost completely naked, save for my panties. My body freezes, turning me into stone. *Alex*. Hell. Did I sleep with him? I look over my shoulder and find the other side of my bed empty. But that means nothing.

If I fucked him and don't remember, I'm going to scream. The whole point of sleeping with him was so I could stop thinking about it. Get over him by getting under him sort of thing. I toss the sheets to the side and sit up.

Ouch. Too fast. It just made my head hurt more.

There's a glass of water and painkillers on my nightstand. I know I didn't put them there. I take the pills and drink the full glass because I'm parched. Water on an empty stomach makes me a little sick though. I cover my mouth and wait to see if I need to throw up. There's nothing I hate more than that. The nausea passes, so I deem it safe to stand up.

I put on my robe, and on my tiptoes, I walk out of my bedroom. My first concern is Cookie. I don't remember getting home, much less feeding him or taking him for a walk.

He's out of his crate and sleeping soundly on Alex's chest.

Sweet baby llamas.

My heart takes off, running at breakneck speed. That's the cutest and sexiest pose I've ever seen. Hot guys and puppies seem to be my weakness. Alex spent the night and, obviously, took care of Cookie for me. He's still wearing his clothes, so it's possible we didn't do anything last night. I hope that's true. His jacket is draped carefully over a chair, and his hair isn't tousled as if he had a night of wild sex.

I return to my bedroom feeling a little better, but not much. I don't remember last night, so God knows what I've done. I pray I didn't embarrass myself in front of Alex. I take a quick shower and then brush the hell out of my teeth until I taste only mint toothpaste.

I look like crap, with dark circles under my eyes and a paler than usual complexion. I debate putting makeup on, but it might seem like I'm trying too hard. Forget it. I just put on leggings and an oversize sweater and return to the living room.

I catch Alex midyawn. He's sitting now, and Cookie is playing with a chew toy nearby. Alex slept on the couch, wearing last night's clothes, and he still looks like a Norse god. Life isn't fair.

"Good morning," I croak.

Shit. What's wrong with my voice?

"Good morning." He pierces me with his intense blue eyes as if he's searching for something. "How are you feeling?"

"Like hell. What happened last night?"

"What do you remember?"

I try to piece the bits of memory back together. "I remember the drive there and then..." Ah damn. His hand on my pussy, his fingers making me feel alive and delirious. "...your attempt to calm me down."

He doesn't interrupt me with a sexual comment or a quip. In fact, his facial expression doesn't change at all. That can't be good.

"And that's it. I don't remember anything about the party."

"Really? Nothing? Not even the conversation with your mother when we arrived?"

I shake my head. "No. Was it awful?"

"It wasn't pleasant."

Feeling vulnerable and exposed, I cross my arms. "Why don't you fill in the blanks for me?"

"After the convo with your mother, you went off to socialize on your own. I had a chat with Ryder."

My eyes widen. "You didn't punch him, did you?"

"No."

I release a shaky breath. "Oh, thank God."

"After that, I went looking for you. It took me a while. You found Ryder's friends first, and that's where everything went downhill."

"What do you mean?"

"You overheard your mother talking to someone about you and that made you upset. You stole one of their special shots."

"What do you mean? What special shot?"

"They were drinking shots of tequila mixed with Xanax. You drank one, and well... you get the picture."

"I got high on Xanax?" I shriek, making Cookie whimper.

I feel faint and weak, so I stagger to the closest chair and collapse. Cookie comes running and jumps on my legs, but I'm not in the mood to play.

"I got you out of there as quickly as possible. No one saw a thing."

If my mother had seen me high, she would have already blown up my phone.

"Thank you for that." I drop my gaze to my lap, unable to maintain eye contact with him.

"You're welcome."

"But what happened between us? Did we..."

"We didn't hook up."

I lift my face. "But something happened."

He runs his fingers through his hair and looks away. "We don't need to talk about that."

"I want to talk about it. Don't leave me in the dark. What did I do? Spare no details."

Our gazes lock once more, and I feel like I can't breathe. Those eyes and that mouth... they're making me hot and bothered, and I don't know why. It's like a memory that's trying to resurface.

With a heavy sigh, he says, "If you insist. To start, when we got off the elevator, you ran down the hallway and yelled you were going to get railed by me."

I wince. *Shit. That's bad. How am I going to face my neighbors?*

"Once here, you took your clothes off and tried to get your wish fulfilled."

I curl my fingers around the fabric of my sweatshirt. It keeps getting worse.

"But you didn't succumb to my charms."

The corners of his lips twitch upward. "Trust me, it was hard to resist. You were very persistent. Case in point." He tugs the collar of his shirt and reveals another hickey. "I'm beginning to think you aren't a witch but a vampire. What's with you chomping on my neck?"

"Ugh!" I cover my face with my hands. "This is so humiliating."

"It's all right, Westwood. I won't tell anyone."

I look up. "You think I'm worried about you blabbering?"

"You aren't?"

"No. You have many flaws, but bragging about details of your sex life isn't one of them."

He quirks an eyebrow. "How do you know that?"

"Gia told me a long time ago."

I can tell he's amused by that detail. He's smiling now, his eyes twinkling with mirth. "So you've been asking about me."

"Of course not. Why would I ask about you?"

He gives me a boyish shrug. "Because you're secretly in love with me?"

I snort. "You're delusional. I think it's time for you to go home."

"Fine." He stands and stretches his arms. His shirt rises up, showing a hint of his washboard abs. I spend a few seconds too long staring at that patch of taut muscles.

"Don't worry, Westwood. I'll let you lick my stomach next time."

I whip my face to his. "What?"

Smiling, he says, "You begged to lick my abs last night." He snaps his fingers. "Oh shoot, you don't remember."

"I didn't. You're lying!" I stand too fast, and the dizzy spell hits me out of nowhere.

I flap my arms, trying to regain my balance, but there's nothing to hold but air. Suddenly, Alex is there, catching me before I fall on my face.

"Are you okay? Maybe I should get you something before I go."

Heat spreads through my body like wildfire. Damn it. I like being pressed against his body too much. Now I totally believe I begged to lick him. With effort, I step back, keeping my eyes glued to his chest. "I'm fine. I'll walk Cookie and then go back to bed."

"How about I walk him, and you eat something?"

Unable to resist, I look up. "Don't you have to be somewhere?"

"Not until later." His voice drops to a husky tone as his eyes fixate on my mouth.

"Okay."

He steps back but keeps his hands on my arms. "Can you stand on your own?"

"I'm fine. I won't fall."

"Well, if you do, try to aim for the rug, not the corner of the coffee table."

"Got it."

He chuckles. "I have to use the restroom first."

"Sure."

I don't move or blink as I watch him walk down the hall. It's not until he disappears inside the bathroom and shuts the door that I snap out of my daze.

Oh my fucking God. What's happening to me? Why am I yearning for Alex like this? It's like a wire in my brain short-circuited and I can't think straight anymore. Nothing makes sense.

I hear the toilet flush, and that's my cue to move so he doesn't see that I stood still like a damn statue this whole time.

"Hey, Blair? Do you have a toothbrush I can use?" he asks from the open bathroom door.

"There should be new toothbrushes and toothpaste in the drawer."

"Thanks."

I try to not think that now Alex will have fresh minty breath, perfect for kissing, and focus on getting food in my body. I don't feel like cooking anything, so today, I'm having cereal with milk and orange juice. I don't want to assume he's going to stay and eat, but it's also rude not to offer, so I place a second bowl and glass on the counter.

A minute later, Alex walks out of the bathroom. His hair is wet and pushed back. He looks fresh, as if he just showered.

"I've got cereal and OJ if you're hungry," I say.

He glances at the food briefly and then at me. "Nah, it's okay. I'll just walk Cookie and then go home."

Disappointment rushes through me, and I hope it doesn't show on my face. I look away while Alex gets Cookie on his leash, but I'm aware of his every move in my periphery.

"Okay, see you in a few," he says.

"The access code to the building is two-two-nine-seven. The front door key is on the console."

"Thanks."

This is just surreal. Alex spending the night and now walking my dog. We're acting like we're dating sans the sex.

I wait to be disgusted by the idea of having Alex as my boyfriend, but what I get are butterflies in my stomach doing the cha-cha. No. I can't be pining for him.

My brain is still foggy, and my movements are sluggish. I'm bone tired. Maybe I woke up too soon. I can only stomach eating half of what I put in my bowl. I clean up the kitchen and then sit on the couch to wait for Alex. Gingerly, I pick up the pillow he used last night and bring it to my nose. Yes, it smells like him now. I lie down, clutching his pillow against my chest… and close my eyes.

ALEX

Cookie is fast about his morning business, but it's clear he's full of energy and wants to play. I'd feel bad about returning to Blair's apartment too soon. She doesn't seem like she can give her puppy a lot of attention today.

There's a small park across the street from her apartment, and I see that there are other dog owners with their pets. I grab a stick and play catch with Cookie for a little bit. I'm tired and deprived of caffeine, but the cold morning air is helping.

My mind is only partially in the present. I keep replaying what happened last night over and over again. I never had to fight so hard not to sleep with someone. Blair was relentless, a complete nympho. The lap dance and striptease were hot as fuck, and I wished so much that she wasn't toast and I could actually fuck her without remorse. Do I feel bad that she did all those things only because she was high? One hundred percent.

But save for keeping my eyes closed the entire time, there wasn't much I could do.

But I did kiss her a lot, and for that, I'm not sorry at all. Her kisses are fire, and I'm looking forward to tasting her lips again.

My phone rings in my pocket, and I wonder who's calling me this early. The moment I see Ryder's name on the screen, it makes sense. He knows I spent the night at her place, because he texted me last night to ask how she was.

"Hello?"

"How is Blair?"

"She's okay. Probably feels like shit though."

"Did she throw up last night?" His voice shows worry, and it surprises me. I never noticed he cared about his sister before. Maybe I wasn't paying attention.

"Nope."

"I called her just now and she didn't pick up. Did you leave already?"

"No. I'm at the park with her dog. I'm sure she went back to bed."

"Did she give you the key to her apartment?" He sounds agitated.

"Yes. Why do you sound concerned? I slept at her apartment last night. If you think I'm a danger to your sister, you should have babysat her yourself."

"I'm not concerned. I'm surprised, that's all. In case you've failed to notice, she's a control freak."

Last night she was the opposite of that. If he only knew. "I'm going to head back to the apartment now. A pleasure talking to you."

I end the call first and get Cookie back on his leash when he returns with his stick. "Sorry, buddy. We have to go."

I'm sure Blair just went back to sleep, but I'm a little worried. I don't know what kind of nasty, lingering effects Xanax mixed with alcohol has on the body. I hate drugs, but the prescribed kinds are the worst.

I find Blair sleeping all right, but not in her bed. She's curled up on the couch, holding the pillow I slept on last night against her chest. I close the door softly and then put Cookie in his crate. He whines, and I fear the noise will wake her, but nothing. She's out cold.

On impulse, I touch her forehead. I don't know why I'm checking to see if she has a fever. She isn't sick. Maybe I just want an excuse to touch her. I crouch next to the couch at eye level with her and stare unabashedly. I wasn't kidding when I told her she's damn beautiful. She is, and I can't believe I've never noticed it before. I'm glad she doesn't remember what I said though. I don't want her to know how much power she has over me.

CHAPTER 22
BLAIR

It's Monday morning and I still feel like roadkill. The next time I see any of Ryder's friends, that's what they'll become. I want to know who had the moronic idea of bringing Xanax to the party and consuming it out in the open. Did they think no one would notice they were high? Or maybe they don't give a fuck. In our circle, you can get away with everything if you have a penis.

The dog sitter was late, which means I'm late. I'm pissed, and she's toast. I didn't fire her yet, but I already put finding a replacement on my to-do list this week. I hate hurrying places and add in that I'm not feeling like myself, and I'm in the foulest mood possible. I must be giving off psycho-killer vibes, because no one dares to sit close to me in my first class.

While the professor goes on and on about something completely irrelevant to his class, I check my email. The top of the list is from Professor McNelis. He's sent a few articles he wants Alex and me to check out.

Then I read the email from Melody about today's dance practice. It's going to be a bitch to move while I'm still recovering. The email says we need to postpone today's practice by an hour thanks to some repairs that need to be done in the studio we rented. I open my calendar and curse. If we change the time, that means I have to meet Alex straight after practice, but I need to go home to let Cookie out. We were going to meet at the library, which would help keep our meeting strictly business.

I pull my phone from my purse and text him.

Hey. Can we meet tonight at my place?

Is this a booty call?

Ugh. I don't even blame him for that question after my appalling behavior last Saturday.

NO! My schedule changed. Can you meet there or not?

Sure.

I wait for him to add a teasing remark, but he doesn't text anything else. I guess it's better to keep things strictly professional.

I make an effort to pay attention to the lecture, but a new text from him catches my attention.

I have to bring your namesake.

Hell, I forgot that the dumbass named his puppy after me.

Perfect. I'm sure Cookie will love seeing his sister.

Alex replies with a puppy-in-love emoji and my heart does a backflip before accelerating to a hundred. Why is such a silly thing making me giddy? I cannot possibly be catching feelings for him. I have to remind myself of all the awful things he's said and done to me and hang on to those memories, not yearn for his touch and kisses. I've perfected the aloof mask over the years. I can do that with him.

When I finally park in front of my building, I'm a hot mess. Dance practice went longer than planned. I am already stressed when I remember that I have nothing in my fridge. I can't host a work session at my place and not offer any food. I've been conditioned by my mother to be the perfect hostess, and it's ingrained in me. So I stop at a convenience store on the way there and grab a few things.

It's raining a little, but I won't get drenched if I make it to my apartment in one trip. I make a mental note to buy a damn umbrella and leave it in the car. I get out quickly and run to the back of the car to get everything out of the trunk. I hoist my duffel bag strap over my shoulder first and then grab all the grocery bags.

The rain turns heavier—naturally—and while I wait for the street to clear of cars so I can cross, the cold droplets seep through my clothes. I'm shivering in no time. I have to run to avoid getting drenched completely. But once in front of my building, I don't have a free hand to punch in the code for the door.

Suddenly, someone reaches for the grocery bags in my left hand. On instinct, I pivot and hit him with the bags in my right.

"Ouch!" Alex steps back, curling his arm protectively around his puppy. "I was just trying to help."

"Goddamn it, Alex! You scared me to death. Say something next time. Don't sneak up on me."

"Sorry. I thought you saw me when you crossed the street."

"No, I didn't," I grit out, then look at the puppy and feel horrible. "Did I hit her?"

"No, she's fine."

In response, she barks. She's gotten so big already—bigger

than Cookie—and I don't know how he can hold her with one arm.

Blair, look at those biceps.

"Here, take them." I give him the bags and then quickly enter the door code.

Once inside the building, Alex sets his pup down and they both shake their heads in perfect sync. It's comical, and it makes me laugh.

"What?" he asks.

"Nothing." I head for the elevator.

"I see that you're once again dressed like a college student."

"I had dance practice."

"When is the performance?"

I glance at him. "The Starlight Charity Gala."

"Ah, that. Right. I'm looking forward to it."

I arch an eyebrow. "You're looking forward to the gala or just the auction part?"

He tilts his head. "I'm looking forward to seeing you dance."

"Oh." My cheeks heat up, and I don't know what to say.

Mercifully, the elevator arrives just in time.

"So, who are you bidding on?" he asks.

My heart wants to say *on you*, but my head wins. "Definitely not you."

He laughs. "Didn't expect you to."

We don't exchange another word until we're in my apartment and he asks for a towel to dry off his dog.

Cookie goes berserk in his crate when he sees his sister. I let him out, and they go nuts.

"I hope the rain stops soon. I need to take him for a walk," I say as I empty the grocery bags.

"If you have a couple of umbrellas, we can go now."

I flatten my lips, annoyed at myself. "I don't."

Alex looks at his phone. "According to the weather app, the rain should stop in half an hour."

"Let's eat first, then. I'm starving."

"I didn't expect to be served dinner."

More embarrassment comes my way. "Oh, did you already eat?"

He smiles. "No."

God, he has a nice smile. I don't realize I'm staring until he points at all the containers on my kitchen counter. "Do you need help with those?"

I blink fast and then glance at all the food I got. "Uh, no, it's okay. I didn't know what you like to eat, so I grabbed everything that looked good."

He walks over. "Once an overachiever, always an overachiever."

I open my mouth to protest, but he cuts me off. "But when it comes to food, more options are always the answer."

He sits on a chair and leans forward. "What d'you got there?"

"Buffalo wings, sliders, lasagna, mac n cheese, Greek salad..."

"So basically every comfort food known to man."

"Yes, so what do you want?"

Staring into my eyes, he says in a husky tone, "Everything."

The way my body reacts to his answer tells me he's including me as well. I was cold before, and now I'm burning up. How can one simple word carry so much meaning?

I break the connection first. "Right. We can sample everything tapas style."

"Sounds good, Westwood. I can't wait to dive in."

CHAPTER 23
ALEX

Blair bought way too much food, but I can't blame her for all of it disappearing. I didn't realize I was so hungry. Now I'm having a hard time concentrating on the words in front of me. After we ate, we took the puppies for a quick walk and returned to her apartment to work on our proposal. The fact that I'm sitting on her comfy couch isn't helping my situation either.

A yawn sneaks up on me, and she catches it. "Do you need coffee?"

"Hell no. If I drink caffeine now, I'll never fall asleep later."

"Well, you need to do something to wake up because you haven't typed anything in the last ten minutes."

"I'll catch up. Don't worry."

"I want to finish this proposal as soon as possible."

"Why? Tired of seeing my face already?"

She gives me a droll look from her corner of the couch. "As a matter of fact, yes."

Ah, Westwood. I know you're full of shit. But I won't call you on it now. "Let's Pomodoro it. I bet I can write more words in a twenty-five-minute sprint than you can."

She arches an eyebrow. "Is that so? I seriously doubt it."

"Want to put a wager on it?"

Her eyes turn to slits. "What kind of wager?"

"If I win, you'll role-play with me."

She sucks in a breath. "Role-play what?"

"Something from that book I found in your bedroom. A dom/sub scenario. I'll be your dom, and you'll be my sub."

Her eyes turn as round as saucers, and she doesn't speak a word. Her cheeks are fiery red though.

I expect a solid refusal, but then she surprises me. "What makes you think I want to be the sub?"

"Fine. If you win, you'll be the dom."

She blinks fast and takes a few more seconds to reply. "You got yourself a bet."

I didn't think she'd go for it, and now I'm wide awake. Excitement in liquid form is coursing through my veins, making my heart pump faster.

"I'll set the timer on my phone."

Blair cracks her knuckles, keeping her eyes on me. "One detail though. Whatever we write needs to make sense. It can't be gibberish."

"Agreed." I smile. To me, any outcome is a win. Either way, I finally get to fuck her. "Whenever you're ready."

"I'm ready."

"All right. Ready. Get set. Write."

For twenty-five minutes, the only noise in the room is our fingers tapping away on our keyboards. Blair must think she has this bet in the bag, but she doesn't know I hold the record in my old high school for words per minute. I already have the chapter outlined, so I just need to write without stopping.

Time flies so fast I barely notice it, and when the timer goes off, I can't believe it's up.

"Fingers off the keyboard," she tells me.

I lift my hands. "Okay, let's hear the word count. You go first."

"One thousand and five."

"Impressive, Westwood." I smile from ear to ear. "Too bad it's not enough to beat my fourteen hundred."

"What?" She sits up. "There's no way. Let me see."

"Be my guest." I hand over my laptop and relax against the couch, linking my hands behind my head and grinning like the cat that ate the canary.

Blair speed-reads my chapter, keeping her glower in place. "Unreal. How did you write so fast?"

"Years of practice." I lift my hand. "Can I have that back now?"

She shuts the laptop with too much force and shoves it back to me. Then she pivots on her heels and strides to her bedroom.

"Okay..." I set my laptop on the coffee table and debate my next move.

"Are you coming or what?" she asks.

"We're doing this now?"

"Yes."

I jump to my feet and make a start toward her room but stop in my tracks and glance at the puppies. I can't leave them loose out here while I'm busy fucking Blair's brains out. I put both of them in Cookie's huge crate and then continue toward her bedroom.

Blair is still fully clothed, staring at some scraps of leather lying on her bed. Coming closer, I see what they are. A harness made for what we're about to do, and a collar and chain leash. No surprise, they're pink.

Without looking at me, she says, "I bought this ages ago, but I was too chicken to take it out of the package."

"Blair... we don't need to role-play or even hook up if you don't want to."

She whips her face to mine, her eyes so big that they make her look younger. "Don't go back on your word now, Kaminski. I want this."

"Okay. Before we start, we should pick a safe word."

"Pickles."

My eyes widen. "That's your safe word?"

"Yes. It's a funny word and not in the least sexy."

"All right then. I'll use yours too."

She swallows hard, and she's shaking a little. "Where are the pups?"

"I put them in the crate."

"Good."

I walk over, invading her space, then slide my palm over her cheek and into her hair. "There's no need to be nervous. You're safe with me."

"I know."

"You do?"

"You hate me, yet you took care of me when I couldn't think straight. As strange as it is, I trust you."

I wince because that's not true at all. Maybe I thought I hated her, but I know better now. "I don't hate you."

Her brows shoot to the heavens. "You don't?"

I cup her face. "No."

Her lips part, and I want to kiss her, but she asks, "Have you done this before?"

I hesitate. Speaking about my past sexual encounters isn't something I want to do with her, but for this to work, I have to be completely honest. "No, but like you, I've always been curious. I've read about it—not extensively though."

Her lips make a perfect *O*. "What should I do?"

I've never heard Blair sound so insecure. It does things to me. I want to protect her, hug her and press her face against my chest. I settle for kissing her instead. It's a slow, deliberate kiss, sweet even. I want to savor her before we start. Her tongue dances with mine in perfect harmony. It's funny. We never see eye to eye on anything, but when doing this, we're a perfect match.

Her body relaxes into mine, and I know she's ready. I step back and rub my thumb over her lower lip. "Take off your clothes."

She shuffles back, and I sit on the edge of her mattress. I'm hard already, and my cock is pressing against my jeans. I need release soon. I haven't hooked up with anyone since I started these games with Blair, and I've had a major case of blue balls since last Saturday.

She takes her sweater off first, revealing the leotard underneath. Then she peels off her leggings. I can't rush her, but hell if I don't want to yank off the rest of her clothes and plunge my dick deep into her pussy. But then I'll miss out on all the fun. I don't know if I'll get Blair to agree to do this again.

I unzip my jeans and pull out my cock.

Her eyes widen, and she stops undressing.

I smirk. "Who told you to stop? Take everything off."

She's once again wearing a bra with the clasp at the front. When her perky breasts come into view, I stroke myself, spreading precum over my shaft.

Her gaze drops to my crotch, and I smile. "Do you like to watch me playing with myself, baby girl?"

"Yes."

"Look how hard I am already for you. Do you want to taste it?"

Her gaze lifts, connecting with mine. "Yes."

I smile. "You need to earn it. If you're a good girl, I'll let you suck me with that gorgeous mouth of yours. Now take everything off. I won't ask again."

She rolls her panties down her legs next, and the sight of her bare pussy makes my balls tighten. I still my hand, lest I end up pleasuring myself beyond the point of no return. I want Blair to make me come.

"Good girl. Now put on the harness and your collar, then attach the chain."

She follows my orders and then turns to me for further instructions.

"On your knees. Crawl to me."

I see the fight in her eyes but also the desire burning in them.

There's a fifty percent chance she's going to call the whole thing off. I wait for her to utter the safe word, but when she drops to her knees, I grow more impatient for her. I need her on her back with me between her legs. I need to hear her scream my name at the top of her lungs.

When she's within reach, I grab the chain and pull gently, bringing her forward. "Suck me."

She keeps her defiant eyes locked with mine while wrapping her fingers around my dick. Jesus, I love her hand on me. I'm already burning up, and she didn't even do anything yet. I clench my jaw when she licks my length, but as good as her tongue feels, that isn't what I ordered. I reach for her hair, grabbing a fistful of it.

"I said, suck me. Open your mouth." I guide her head, forcing her to swallow me until I hit the back of her throat.

Her eyes water and her gag reflex kicks in, but I don't release her hair. "That's it, choke on my big cock." She can't breathe like this, yet I hold on just a bit longer before I allow her to withdraw. "Now suck me right, or I'll fuck your mouth hard."

I don't need to guide her this time; she sucks me into her hot mouth, and damn it, it feels amazing. If I closed my eyes, I'd believe I was fucking her pussy. The way she works my shaft with her tongue is making me delirious. I'm going to come if she keeps this up.

"You're taking me so well, baby girl."

I tighten my hold on her hair, having every intention of making her stop, but she's a little greedy monster attached to my dick. Instead of pushing her away, I help her, forcing her head up and down faster.

"Fuck!" I throw my head back as I climax, filling her mouth with my cum.

Blair takes it all, and when I relax my hold on her, there's not a single drop left. But there are tears in her eyes and down her cheeks. Shit. I was too rough, and with her mouth occupied, she couldn't ask me to stop.

"Did you want to use the safe word?" I rasp out.

"No," she croaks.

"Are you sure?"

"Yes."

I narrow my eyes. "You made me come in your mouth, and I'm not happy."

She blinks fast, confusion etched on her pretty face. "I can still taste your happiness on my tongue."

"Are you talking back to me?"

"That wasn't talking back. I was just pointing out a fact."

"You're misbehaving, baby girl, and now I have to punish you." I pick her up and lay her across my lap on her stomach.

"How?"

I flatten my palm against her butt cheek, making her tense. I will punish her, but first, I need to tease her. Instead of smacking her ass, I cup her pussy, finding it slick. She gasps when I insert three fingers inside of her.

"Do you like that, baby girl?"

"Yes," she whispers.

I pump my fingers in and out, making her even more drenched. "Do you want my cock inside of you?"

"You know I do."

"You're being sassy again." I pull my fingers out and slap her ass hard. She cries out, but not from the pain because she's rubbing her pussy against my leg. She's enjoying this. "Are you going to behave, or should I punish you more?"

"I'm going to behave."

"I don't believe you."

Using both hands, I fuck her with my fingers and spank her. Her moans keep getting louder, and my cock is awake again. I could flip her over and rail her like I want, but seeing her like this, at my mercy, is too hot. I can't stop.

I stop smacking her when her internal walls start to milk my fingers. Not much later, she yells my name and falls apart on my lap. Her body relaxes after a moment, and I pull my hand from between her legs to caress the red spot on her butt cheek.

"I think you've learned your lesson, baby girl."

Her spine goes taut. Then she jumps to her feet and runs into her bathroom, shutting the door hard.

Fuck. Maybe I went too far. This was her first time trying BDSM. I shouldn't have spanked her. I get up and knock on the bathroom door.

"Blair, are you okay?"

"Pickles."

"Okay."

"You need to go."

My stomach drops, and my chest now feels heavy as remorse the size of a boulder sits on it, caving it in. "Blair, let's talk about this."

"No. Please, Alex. Just leave."

The choked sound of her voice makes me too worried. In other circumstances, I would go, but I can't leave her like that. "I'm sorry, baby girl. I can't go until I know you're okay."

"I'm telling you I'm fine."

"Open the door then."

She yanks the door open and levels me with a glower. "I said I was fine. Don't worry about me, Kaminski. I'm tougher than I look." She shuts the door in my face again, and I feel it in my bones.

I won't force her to do anything else. I already fucked things up enough.

"All right. I'll go."

CHAPTER 24
BLAIR

I haven't talked to Alex in days. It's now Friday, and I'm glad my busy social life is keeping me occupied. He sent me several texts to check on me after he left my apartment on Monday, but I ignored them all. In class, I pretend he doesn't exist, even though I feel his stare. He must think I have buyer's remorse, but the truth is the opposite. I loved what we did so much that it terrified me. Not only because I want to continue doing naughty things with him but because there's also a growing feeling in my chest that's more than lust.

The Warriors are out of town for an away game, and Gia told me Coach Bedford will probably let Alex play. That means the chance I'll see him tonight at the open party the Deltas are cohosting with the Iotas fraternity is slim. I'm sure I'll see other jocks, like Josh and Preston, which means Ryder might come too. A few guys on the football and swim team are Iotas. Lucky me. When I asked Ryder if he was planning to stop by, he was evasive.

His friends had better stay the fuck away from me. I'm not in the mood to deal with their assholery.

The Deltas opened their house for the party because, apparently, they lost a bet. I didn't ask for the details. I don't have spoons left. It sucks though. The Iota house is already a dump—they wouldn't care if it got trashed. But I don't live in the Delta house, so it doesn't really affect me much. I still do my rounds to make sure everything is where it's supposed to be.

The stage for the band is set and ready for them. We hired a band called No Damsels Allowed that's gained a lot of popularity recently on social media, but I don't know who they are and haven't heard any of their songs. The place is already packed, so I hope they get here soon. Right now, one of the Iotas is DJing.

I'm surrounded by people, yet I've never felt lonelier. I'm *definitely* not missing a certain tall, blond hockey player.

When I spot Ashley in the crowd, I sigh in relief and make a beeline in her direction. "Hey, I'm so glad you're here. I haven't seen you in forever." I hug her.

"Uh, hi, Blair." She hugs me back, but when she eases off, she's smirking. "What's going on with you?"

"What do you mean?"

"You were never the affectionate kind."

"Maybe I'm drunk already."

She narrows her eyes. "You aren't because you're a mean drunk. You wouldn't be hugging me."

Alex would also say I'm a horny drunk. Ugh. Why the hell am I thinking about him?

"Ryder said I'm too much like my mother, so I'm trying not to be," I lie. Ryder never said that, but it would be something he'd say to piss me off.

A somber thought occurs to me. I *am* like my mother. *Oh God.*

"What's wrong?" Ashley asks.

I shake my head, trying to get rid of the dark cloud hanging over my head. "Nothing. Why do you ask?"

"You looked horrified for a second."

"I think I need a drink. Come on, let's get something."

She glances at the dance floor. "There will be live music?"

"Yes, Melody hired this new band that's taking the digital world over by storm. No Damsels Allowed."

She grabs my arm hard. "Shut the fuck up! You hired my sister's band?"

"What?"

"My stepsister Kenzie."

"Oh, Kenzie. I didn't know she was in a band."

Because Ashley rarely talks about her family.

"Yes, she's always been into music. When she said she wasn't going to college in order to pursue her music career, her dad almost had a heart attack. It was a thing. He blamed his ex-wife and her European lifestyle. It was drama central for months in our house."

"Is that why you and Sean don't talk much about her?"

Ashley grimaces. "Sean took his father's side, and Kenzie got angry that I didn't take hers. I was trying to remain neutral."

"Oh no. How long since you've spoken to her?"

"A few months. I thought we were okay." Her face falls. "I guess not, or she would have told me she was playing here tonight."

"Make sure you speak to her before the night is over. Maybe you can patch things up."

Ashley bites her lower lip and glances around, distracted. "Yeah, maybe."

I lace my arm with hers. "Let's find that drink."

ALEX

It's a party on the Warriors' bus. We have another win under our belt, and I'm fucking glad I was able to contribute, even though I played only in the second period. We've been singing stupid songs the entire ride back from the game, and I'm hoarse. Gia is recording everything. She travels with the team now because

Noah would lose his mind with worry if she were to drive alone at night. He's become überprotective of her since he found out she's pregnant, but to be fair, so has the entire team.

"So where are we going tonight, boys?" Logan asks. "We need to celebrate."

"The Heritage is always a good idea," Sean replies.

"I'm not going to The Heritage," Noah pipes up.

"Why? What do you have against that place?" I ask. "There's booze, pool tables, and if I remember correctly, wasn't that where you kissed Gia for the first time?" I smirk, knowing it's a sore subject for him. He doesn't remember kissing her because he was too drunk.

He scowls. "Bite me, Kaminski."

"The Deltas and the Iotas are cohosting a party," CJ chimes in. "We should check it out."

"I'm definitely not going to a sorority party," Noah retorts. "Those bitches are crazy."

"Not all of them. I wouldn't mind going to support Blair," Gia replies.

An electric current seems to go through my body just from hearing her name mentioned out loud. That party should be the last place I want to be, but it seems I'm a glutton for punishment because I'm going.

"I'm game," I say.

"For real? You want to spend more time with your archnemesis?" CJ, who's sitting next to me, raises an eyebrow.

"It's because she's my archnemesis that I want to go."

Logan laughs. "Yeah, right."

Damn, he had to open his big mouth. One of the drawbacks of living with my twin brother is that he knows me too well and misses nothing. He suspects something is up with Blair and me, even though I didn't say a word about what happened on Monday.

"Shut up, jerkface."

"Oh, I'm intrigued. We definitely should go," CJ replies.

"I think I'm gonna pass," Sean declares.

"Why?" Noah asks. "If I can suffer those lunatics, you can too. You're coming. I can't be the only responsible person on the team going to that party."

I glare at him from across the aisle. "*You* are the responsible one? The freshman who knocked up his girlfriend?"

"Damn!" CJ pipes up.

Noah's face falls, and regret fills me. Fuck. I took it too far.

"You can be a real jerk sometimes, Alex," Gia retorts.

"I'm sorry. I didn't mean it like that."

Gia turns her face toward the window. "Whatever."

"Look what you've done." Noah glowers then switches his attention to Gia.

"Man, you really fucked up this time. Not even I would have said that," CJ butts in again.

I don't reply because I know I fucked up. When Noah and Gia told us she was pregnant during our team Thanksgiving dinner, they seemed fine and excited about the news. But maybe that was a facade for us. I'd be losing my shit if I got a girl pregnant while my future is still so uncertain. I feel like a dick. Maybe I should stop obsessing about a certain witch and pay more attention to my friends.

I can go to the party and not make it about Blair. My guess is the place will be bursting at the seams. It shouldn't be hard to avoid her.

CHAPTER 25
BLAIR

I don't know if it's the two shots of the tequila I've drunk already that are making me enjoy this music so much, but I'm really digging the sound of No Damsels Allowed.

I had to drag Ashley to the front of the stage because the middle of the dance floor was too crowded, and I couldn't breathe. She and her stepsister talked briefly when the band arrived to set up. It was tense for sure, but funnily enough, it was Ashley who acted weird as fuck. Kenzie seemed chill.

"I can't believe you never told me how cool your sister is," I yell in Ashley's ear.

"Since when do you recognize what's cool and what's not?"

"Ouch. You're in a mood tonight, and Sean isn't even here."

"What does Sean have to do with it?"

I shrug. "You always get bitchy when he's around."

She clamps her jaw shut and stands still while everyone around us is dancing. After a moment, she says, "I'm thirsty. I need water." She walks away from the stage without waiting for me. *What the hell?*

"Wait! I'll come with you."

Either she doesn't hear me, or she's trying to run away from me. Is she mad at me for bringing up Sean? She carves a path through the crowd, but somebody grabs my arm, and I lose sight of her.

It's Faith Williams, a freshman and my little sister who stop me. "Oh my God, Blair. They're here!"

"Who's they?"

"The hockey team! I just saw them walk through the door."

Shit. I was counting on them not crashing the party, thanks to their away game. "Who did you see?"

"Sean, CJ, the cute rookie Noah—but he's with his girlfriend." She scrunches her nose, but then her face lights up. "And the twins!"

Fuck my life.

"They're so hot!" She squeezes my arm tighter.

"Their personality does not match their faces." I pull my arm free, annoyed that she's drooling over them, and try to go after Ashley.

I'm not jealous at all.

"Wait... where are you going? I need you to introduce me to them."

"No can do. As your big sister, I think that's a terrible idea."

"Fine. I'll introduce myself." She pouts.

The desire to bring her upstairs and lock her in a room is immense. But she's an adult, and if she wants to hook up with Alex, I can't stop her.

I sure as hell can be fucking pissed about it though.

"Knock yourself out. I need to find Ashley."

I head for the living room where we got our drinks before, hoping that's where she went. No sign of her, and all the bottles that were set on the table have disappeared. Great. I text her, but if she doesn't have her phone in her hand, she probably won't see the text.

A second later, a message from Gia pops up.

At your party. Where are you?

Living room.

I see you now.

I turn around and spot her at the entrance waving at me. Noah is glued to her side. No other hockey players are with them though. I head in her direction, hoping I won't see Alex tonight.

Gia smiles from ear to ear when I walk over, then she hugs me. "God, it feels like I haven't seen you in forever."

"It's only been a couple weeks. But I've been busy." I look at Noah. "How was the game?"

He grins proudly. "We won. Thank fuck Alex was able to play. He made a big difference."

My chest aches. I don't know why he had to bring up Alex. Noah is a sweetheart, and I know he didn't say that just to be annoying. He probably didn't even think about it.

"I bet he *loved* that," I reply.

"Yeah, he was pretty happy. Sang the whole way home," Gia pipes up.

"Yes, that was interesting. But then he had to open his big mouth and ruin everything." Noah scowls.

I shouldn't ask, but I can't help myself. "What did he do?"

"It's nothing," Gia waves her hand dismissively.

"It's not nothing. He made a stupid-ass comment about me being irresponsible because, you know..." He drops his gaze to Gia's stomach.

"Are you kidding me?" I put my hands on my hips. "Do you want me to yell at him?"

Blair, are you trying to find an excuse to go after him? Ugh. I'm an idiot. But I'm all fired up now.

Gia shakes her head. "Blair, do *not* talk to him about it, okay? I don't want you guys fighting tonight."

I cross my arms. "As long as he doesn't cross my path, there won't be a fight."

"I'm pretty sure he'll be busy before you get a chance to yell at him anyway." Noah looks over my head.

Curious, I turn around and see what has his attention. Alex is speaking with Faith, and she's all over him, pressing her hand against his chest. She's much shorter than him—who isn't, really—and his head is bent down and close to her face. He's smiling, and even from this distance, I can see he's laying on the charm thick.

Red-hot rage surges from the pit of my stomach and spreads through my body like wildfire.

"I need a drink," I say, but I don't wait for them to reply or follow me. To be honest, I want to be alone.

Unfortunately, Alex and Faith are standing in the hallway that leads to the kitchen. I have no choice but to walk past them. I'm praying he doesn't notice me. Of course, I should have known better. Somebody shoves me right into him.

He catches me, and when our gazes lock, I see my emotions mirrored in his blue eyes. He's not annoyed that I bumped into him. He's downright angry.

"Watch where you're going, Westwood," he says through clenched teeth.

"I barely touched you." I step back, hating how my body comes alive in proximity to him.

"You know that's a fucking lie."

I wince. Hell. He's not talking about me bumping into him. Is he really going to bring up the subject in front of Faith? My face is in flames when I turn to her, but she seems oblivious to the context of the conversation. She doesn't even notice that I'm staring at her. Her googly eyes are locked on Alex's face even though he's glaring at me. She's a goner.

For once in my life, I can't find a single word to say. I'm too fucking angry at myself for letting Alex get to me. I should never have allowed my hormones to do away with my intelligence. Alex and I will always be enemies.

I pivot and stride away, more determined than ever to dull

my conflicting emotions with tequila. The kitchen is chaos central. Everyone figured out that's where the booze is. Most of the good stuff is gone, and I don't trust the open bottles that are left. Getting roofied tonight is not in my plan. The incident with the Xanax was bad enough. I know Pippa, my big sister at the sorority, has a stash of booze in her room. She keeps her bedroom locked during parties for obvious reasons, but I have a master key.

I leave the kitchen before anyone notices my presence. I have no desire to entertain drunk frat boys. Back in the hallway, Alex and Faith are gone. I also don't see Noah and Gia. They probably went to the dance floor. I'm glad since I'm in no mood to socialize right now.

I get to the stairs and have to jump over couples making out on the steps to reach the second floor. Luckily, Pippa's bedroom is one of the last ones down the hallway, and there's no one lingering in front of her room. I let myself in and close the door behind me.

Her bedroom is immaculate, and because she's a senior and the vice president, she got one of the biggest suites in the house and has enough space for a king-size mattress. Fluffy pillows in rainbow colors cover her bed. And she has one of those wrought iron headboards that she decorated with twinkling lights. When she got her bed delivered, it was a source of much teasing. Melody gave her a pair of pink-fur-covered handcuffs as a joke.

Pippa keeps her booze in the cabinet next to her desk. I make a beeline for it, but when I open it, my heart sinks. It's fucking empty.

"That's just great."

A door shuts, making me jump on the spot. I turn around fast with my heart stuck in my throat and find Alex in the room, blocking the exit.

"What the fuck are you doing in here?" I ask.

"We need to talk."

Slowly, he walks over like a predator stalking prey.

"The hell we do. You need to leave."

"Not until you tell me why you're avoiding me. That's not your MO, Blair."

"I'm not avoiding you," I grit out.

"Bullshit. You've ignored all my texts and calls, and you won't even look me in the eye in class. I'm sorry if I took things too far last Monday. But that's what safe words are for. You should have used it."

My eyes widen. "That's what you think is going on? You think I'm traumatized?"

He runs his hand through his hair. "I don't know what to think. You hid in your bathroom for crying out loud."

"I'm not upset about what happened last Monday."

"Then what the hell is this? Is this a game to you? Are you fucking trying to make me go crazy? I've been worried sick, thinking that I hurt you." He steps into my space, crowding me. "I haven't been able to get you out of my head since the last time we were together."

Shit. It never occurred to me that he might be concerned. But my shields are up, and that means the bitch is out.

"Because we didn't fuck? Is that what this is? Do you want to collect?"

I watch his eyes and see several different emotions shine in them in the span of seconds. The crease between his brows becomes deeper. "This has nothing to do with our deal. I'd never force anyone to do anything they didn't want to. But I also can't lie to myself. I want your pretty cunt milking my cock."

Hell and damn. I want that too, so fucking much that my pussy is throbbing, and my panties are already soaked through.

"What about Faith?" I ask feebly.

He cups my face with his huge hand. "She isn't you."

I don't know who attacks whom first. We collide in the middle, a clash of lips, tongues, and teeth. I can't blame my actions on booze or drugs this time. The shots of tequila I drank earlier have left my system already. I'm sober but completely intoxicated by this infuriating man.

He lifts me onto the desk, nudging my legs open so he can press his rock-hard erection against my pussy. I run my fingers through his hair, messing up his perfectly styled hairdo, while I drown in the ferocity of his kisses.

"Fuck, Blair, I want you so bad," he whispers against my lips, then kisses my neck.

"Damn it. I want you too."

He pulls back and stares into my eyes. "Have you been drinking?"

"Not enough to impair my judgment." I capture his face between my hands. "Alex Kaminski, you're going to fuck me tonight. No excuses, no bets, no role-playing. I want your cock inside of me. I want you to shatter me into a million pieces and make me forget who I am."

He grabs a fistful of my hair, yanking it so hard that it hurts, but it's the good kind of pain. "Oh, baby girl, I'll make you forget your own name all right."

His lips claim mine again, hungry, bruising, and impatient. I'm done pretending I feel nothing for him. It's not only lust, and it's no longer hate. I don't know what it is. I just want to feel everything. I reach for his jeans, opening the fly to free his cock. He groans when my fingers curl around his girth.

"That's it, baby girl. Play with me."

"I don't want to play."

"What do you want?"

"You know what I want."

He reaches for his back pocket and pulls out a foil packet. "You do it."

I focus on the shiny square between his fingers for a couple seconds, and then at him. "I've never done it before."

His brows shoot up. "Are you a v—"

"No! I just never put a condom on anyone before."

He gives me a crooked grin. "I'll talk you through it."

"You enjoy giving me lectures, don't you?"

"In the bedroom? One hundred percent." He kisses my neck, just below my ear. "It turns me on like nothing else, baby girl."

A shiver runs down my spine. I close my eyes for a moment, then, yanking his hair, I bring his lips back to mine while I pump my hand up and down his shaft.

"I thought you didn't want to play," he murmurs against my mouth, then bites my lower lip softly.

"Right. I got distracted."

"Since your hand is busy, I'll open this for you." He rips the foil packet in two and gives me the condom. "Hold the tip and roll the condom down my length."

I don't tell him I already knew that. It turns out I do like it when he tells me what to do in the bedroom. It turns me on too.

"Done," I say.

He drops to his knees and nudges my legs apart farther.

"What are you doing?" I ask.

Holding my stare, he slides my panties to the side. "I want a quick taste first, baby girl."

I moan loudly when he licks my clit, toying with it and doing lazy circles over the sensitive spot. I wasn't ready for this kind of pleasure. I clutch the edges of the desk and throw my head back. "Oh my God."

"Has anyone ever eaten your pussy before, baby girl?"

"No."

"They've missed out."

I don't tell him I've been with only one guy before him.

He licks me again before sucking my clit into his mouth. A strangled cry rips from my throat. "I'm gonna come if you don't stop."

"That's totally fine. Come all over my tongue, baby girl."

I reach for his head, curling my fingers around his hair. "Jesus, fuck!"

The orgasm hits fast and hard. I've never climaxed so fast in my life, and it's different than all the times I came using sex toys.

It's ten times more intense and bone-shattering. Alex gets back on his feet and replaces his tongue with his cock, pressing the tip against my throbbing clit.

"This is it, baby girl. The final line to be crossed between us."

His face glistens with my juices and I want to taste myself on his lips. "I'm ready." I cross my legs behind his ass and pull him into me while kissing him hard.

He slides in with ease, stretching me to the max. Oh my God, this feels so good. He pulls back and slams back into me, moving faster and faster with each thrust. The desk bangs against the wall, and the penholder falls to the floor.

Alex moves from my lips to my neck, placing open-mouthed kisses that make my skin tingle. The noise from the desk hitting the wall becomes muffled as the loud drumming of my pulse in my ears drowns out the other sounds. But I hear Alex's grunts loud and clear, mixed with my moans. He digs his fingers into my hips, increasing the pace, fucking me harder.

"Fuck, I hate how good you are at this," I whisper.

He looks at me and grins. "Why is that, baby girl?"

"Because one time won't be enough."

"Who says it has to be one time only?"

I can't answer that question without ruining the moment, so I kiss him again, getting lost in him until he levels me to the ground with his passion. Who knew the man I hated for two years would be the one to make me feel alive for the first time? I whimper against his mouth while my body disintegrates into nothing.

"That's it, baby girl. You're doing so well."

I grab his face with my hands, feeling completely euphoric and unhinged. "Don't ever stop fucking me."

"I wouldn't if I could... fuck!" He groans, then kisses me as if he wants to punish me while destroying my pussy with his cock.

I grab his arms, holding on to him for dear life until he slows down and then stops moving altogether. My heart is pounding, making it hard to breathe. Hiding my face in the crook of his neck, I close my eyes and wait for the room to stop spinning.

"Are you okay there, Westwood?"

I tense. I'm only baby girl to him when we're in the moment. But if he's using my last name, it means he's returned to reality already.

I push him back and slide off the desk, fixing my underwear and skirt. I don't look at him. I'm too embarrassed to do so.

"Blair?"

"I'm fine, Alex. You don't need to worry about me."

"Okay, then. Is there a bathroom in this room?"

"Yes, it's through that door." I point ahead.

"I'm going to clean up. Are you sure you're all right?" He tilts his head, and I finally meet his stare.

"I'm okay, Kaminski. I'm not breakable."

He chuckles. "Good to know."

Heat spreads through my cheeks, and I'm craving his bone-melting touch again. But the way my heart is beating so fast terrifies me. It feels like I'm unraveling, and I can't allow that to happen.

While Alex is in the bathroom, I check my phone. Shit. There's a voice message from Ryder. I listen to it right away, and my heart shrivels to nothing with every word.

Blinded by tears, I run out of the room without a second thought. My only goal is to get to Twin Falls as fast as I can, and the only name on my mind now is Cory.

CHAPTER 26
ALEX

I take longer than needed in the bathroom because I need to get my thoughts straight. I didn't plan on fucking Blair tonight, but I don't regret it. I thought one hookup would be enough to satiate my curiosity, but all I can think about now is how to convince her to keep doing this for an undetermined length of time.

I'm an idiot for believing she'd be waiting for me when I walked out of the bathroom. The room is empty and the door ajar. I should have foreseen she'd run away. The last time we fooled around, she hid in the bathroom. Why did I think she'd have the courage to face me tonight?

As I leave the room, I pull my phone from my pocket and bring up her contact info. My thumb hovers over the text pad. I hesitate. There's nothing I can say that won't make me sound pathetic. I've never had to beg a girl to be with me before, and I'm not going to start with Blair.

Downstairs, I spot Sean and Ashley having an intense convo in a corner. Fuck. I don't need to get pulled into their family drama, so I veer in the opposite direction toward the back of the house. I need to find booze ASAP.

Jackpot. You can always count on kegs at a frat party. I join a circle where people are taking turns drinking from the keg upside down.

"Hey, one of the trouble twins is here!" a drunk guy I don't know from Adam yells.

The crowd cheers. They don't know which twin I am either. Only close friends can tell Logan and me apart.

"Hey, where's your cup?" someone else asks.

"Who needs a cup?" I walk to the keg and push the dude standing on it off the damn thing.

He staggers back, wiping his mouth on his forearm, but seems too drunk to be pissed at me.

I grab the handles and push myself into a handstand. As two guys support my legs to help me stay up, the guy who acknowledged my presence puts the beer tap into my mouth, and I drink, and drink... until I stop thinking about Blair and her fucking pussy.

CHAPTER 27
BLAIR

I get home around three in the morning, and I'm drained, not because of the late hour. My emotions are wrung out to the point that I can't pick them apart anymore. My heart feels heavy, even though the worst didn't come to pass.

Bone tired, I stagger to my couch and collapse on it face-first.

"Do you want me to stay?" Ryder asks.

We rode together to Twin Falls. When he got the call, he had just stepped into the party, which was providential. I wouldn't have been able to drive, and waiting for a car to pick me up and take me to Twin Falls would have driven me insane.

"No, I'm okay."

"You're not okay. You didn't say a word the entire ride back." He takes a seat on the other end of my L-shaped couch.

I look into his eyes. "Fine. But I don't see what your company will do to make me feel better. That was a close call."

He rests his forearms on his knees. "I know."

"It's all her fault. If she'd let us visit more often..."

"She won't." He cuts me off. "That's how she controls you."

"Not us?"

A shadow of sadness crosses his eyes. "I don't have the same connection to Cory as you do. I know it makes me sound like an asshole, but that's the truth."

My stomach clenches painfully. I've always known that to be true, but hearing Ryder's confession out loud hurts.

"Do you wish he'd die?" I force the words out.

He stares at me for a couple beats, his jaw locked tight. "Honestly, yes."

My eyes burn, not out of sadness, but out of fury. I sit up fast, ready for a fight. "How can you say that?"

"You'd be free of Mother if he did. She wouldn't have a hold on you anymore."

Tears roll down my cheeks, and I wipe them off fast. "I'm not surprised you feel that way. You never loved him."

He runs a shaky hand through his hair, pushing the long strands back. "That isn't true. But... I pick you."

"You should leave."

He stands, keeping his gaze on my face. His expression is cold, unyielding, but his eyes... there are a million emotions shining in them. "You should try to get some sleep."

I watch him walk to the door. He stops with his hand on the knob and says, "I love you, Blair. Remember that."

A fist the size of Texas seems to lodge in my throat. Ryder finally leaves, and I never say I love him back. I do, but I can't utter those words out loud when his confession is still ringing in my ears.

I grab my phone from my purse and click on Alex's name. I disappeared on him without a word—again—but this time, it wasn't due to cowardice or regret. I'm heartbroken, seeking comfort, and he's the first person that pops into my head.

I'm sorry. I didn't run away this time. I swear.
Can we talk?

I stare at my phone for several minutes, but he doesn't text back. *What do you expect, Blair? It's the middle of the night.*

I set my phone on the coffee table, then curl up on the couch… and cry myself to sleep.

CHAPTER 28
BLAIR

I'm still half-asleep when I walk into the studio for dance practice. Melody, in her infinite wisdom, booked our session at nine in the morning on the day after our party. I'm glad I'm not the only one with puffy eyes. My reasons aren't the same as anyone else's, but I don't have to explain why I look like hell.

At least I don't have a headache, which can't be said by the majority here. I stand next to Pippa, who's massaging her temple.

"Rough night?" I ask.

"Yes, the worst. Not only did I have way too much wine, some asshole broke into my room and had sex on my desk."

Shiiiit.

"How do you know?"

"My door was wide open, and I know I locked it. Plus, I saw the evidence." She twists her face into a grimace. "I found the condom in my trash can."

"Okay, but how do you know they did the deed on your desk?"

"It's the only area that was disturbed. They knocked down my penholder, and the desk wasn't in exactly the same spot."

I should have picked up the penholder, but I was not in the right frame of mind when I booked out of her room.

"At least they didn't use your bed."

"Thank fuck. If I find out who was in my room, they're dead meat."

Let's hope you never do. I don't remember if there were any witnesses in the hallway.

I set my duffel bag down and get out of my coat. "Let's focus on nailing this dance number before you go on a murder spree."

"Has anyone heard from Faith?" Melody asks from across the room.

No one says a word, so naturally, Melody pins me with her glare. "She's your little sister, Blair. Get her ass here ASAP."

"I'm not her keeper," I retort.

"I know why she's late," Torrance pipes up. "She hooked up with her crush last night."

My entire body freezes. "What?"

"Oh yeah," Pippa chimes in. "I saw her making out with one of the twins."

My stomach bottoms out. Alex wouldn't hook up with Faith right after screwing me, would he?

Faith walks into the studio, and all eyes turn to her.

"Hey, everyone, sorry I'm late." She has a sly smile on her face that says she isn't sorry at all.

Before I can stop myself, I blurt out, "Did you hook up with Alex?"

Her face turns beet red. "Yes. Please don't be mad at me."

I blink fast, my heart thundering in my chest. I should be devastated, and maybe that'll come, but right now, I'm numb, as if I'm having an out-of-body experience.

"Holy shit! You bagged one of the twins?" Torrance replies. "How was he?"

Faith opens her mouth to answer, but I cut her off. "We don't have time to gossip. Discuss Faith's sex life on your own time."

Torrance pouts. "You're no fun. Just because you hate Alex doesn't mean we all have to."

My entire body enters fight mode. "Say one more word about that walking billboard for venereal disease and you're banned from the gala."

Her eyes bug out. "You can't do that."

"Wanna bet?"

She looks at Melody with a plea for help, then at Pippa, but she won't find an ally in them. I'm Blair Westwood, and they know to not stand in my way when I'm pissed.

"Blair is right. Discussing anyone's sex life is in poor taste, and it doesn't align with Deltas' values," Melody pipes up. "If I hear anyone discussing hookups out in the open, they *will* be banned from the gala. Is that clear?"

Everyone nods. Torrance doesn't open her big mouth again, nor does Faith. It doesn't matter though. The anger coursing through my veins refuses to leave my body. By the end of practice, I've pulverized these girls to the point that they all hate me, including Melody and Pippa. My body is sore too, but I welcome that pain. It's the one in my chest I could do without.

CHAPTER 29
ALEX

I'm having a pleasant dream when a loud knock on my door wakes me. "Get up, dumbass, or you'll be late."

Groaning, I drag my head from under the pillow. I squint and look for my phone to find out the time. There's nothing on my nightstand. Shit. That's right. I lost my phone at the party on Saturday, and I was too hungover yesterday to look for it.

I kick my legs to untangle them from the sheets, then throw them over the side of the bed and sit up.

Logan opens the door. "Are you alive in there?"

"Barely," I croak.

Blair comes running between his legs and tries to jump on my lap. "Good morning, girlie." I pat her head.

"I already walked her, but you need to buy her food. We're out."

"I need to look for my damn phone."

"It's probably still at the Delta house. Why don't you call your buddy Blair and ask if they found it?" He smirks.

I try my best to level him with a glower. "She's not my buddy. And I won't call her."

"Jesus, it sounds like you're back to hating her. What happened?"

I stand up and look for a shirt. "Nothing happened. Stop asking about her."

"Fine. By the way, Joanne called. She wants to meet."

I'm alert in an instant. "Does she have news?"

"She wouldn't say over the phone, but she sounded excited, so fingers crossed."

"We should introduce Noah to her," I say out of the blue.

Logan's brows shoot up. "Shit. That's not a bad idea. I can't believe he hasn't signed with an agent yet, but hell, that kid should have been drafted already."

"No shit."

"Let's see what she wants first, then we mention Noah. Knowing her, he's probably already on her radar. Anyway, gotta run."

"See ya."

Thanks to me being a slowpoke this morning and having to buy dog food, I don't have time to stop by the Delta house before I have to head to class. I'm not one of those people who can't function without a phone, but I might be missing important texts or calls. I'll go after Professor McNelis's class, which I'm very much looking forward to. Blair said she wasn't playing games, but so far, that's exactly what she's been doing, and now she's got an adversary.

I don't bother arriving early, and as usual, Blair is already in her spot in the first row. I pick the row I prefer, farther back, but this time, I purposely pick a seat without a female neighbor. As much as I'd love to show Blair that I don't need to beg for a fuck, I'm not in the mood to talk to anyone. It seems the hangover hasn't left my body yet. I haven't drunk that much in years, so I'm not surprised I still feel like shit.

I try to follow the lecture, but I keep missing bits of information here and there. I'm tired and my brain keeps going on snooze. I should have had more coffee before coming here. Professor McNelis asks a question, and Blair immediately raises her hand to answer. That gets my undivided attention. Her answer is only partially correct, and that's my cue to bring some sense of normalcy into my life… because pining for her isn't normal.

I raise my hand, catching Professor McNelis's attention. "Yes, Alex?"

"I disagree with Blair."

She looks over her shoulder, and the death glare shooting from her eyes is almost palpable. I twist my lips into a grin, then explain why her answer is incomplete. The more I talk, the redder she becomes. Naturally, she argues, but Professor McNelis cuts the discussion off before it takes over the entire class.

I relax against my chair, feeling somewhat vindicated. Blair doesn't glance in my direction again for the rest of the class, but when it's over, I wait for her to come up the stairs so I can intercept her.

"You're in my way," she grits out.

"It'll be quick. I lost my phone at the party on Saturday. Did anyone find it?"

The hurt that sparks in her eyes takes me aback. "Why don't you ask *Faith*?"

"What?" I jerk back and raise a brow, waiting for an explanation.

She walks around me, shoving her huge bag against me on purpose. I'd follow, but Professor McNelis is coming up, and it seems he wants to talk to me.

"Is everything okay between you and Blair?"

I hesitate and glance back at where Blair is now stomping out of the room. "I'm actually not sure."

McNelis pushes his glasses up his nose. "I know you've had

your differences, but I hope you can manage to work through them. Do not disappoint me, Alex. My reputation is also on the line if you can't deliver."

"I won't, sir. Even if I have to work on the proposal on my own, it'll be up to par."

"I'd prefer you fix whatever issue you have with Blair."

Fucking great. Now I can't even ditch the witch and work on the proposal on my own, which had crossed my mind. Whatever crawled up her ass, she'd better get over it fast.

Outside of the lecture hall, I find Logan waiting for me, sporting a shit-eating grin. "Man, what happened in there? Blair looked like she was ready to kill someone."

"She gave an incomplete answer, and I pointed it out."

He shakes his head. "Ah... so the truce is over."

"Definitely. What are you doing here?"

He pulls my phone from his pocket. "Look what I found."

"Where did you find it?" I take the device from his hand and click it, but the battery is dead.

"I didn't."

I look up. "Who did then?"

He fixes his backpack strap with a shrug. "If you won't tell me what your deal is with Blair, then I won't reveal my source."

"Whatever. Did you just stop by to hand over my phone?"

"No. We're meeting Joanne now. Since you didn't have your phone, there was no way to tell you the time and place."

"Right. Where are we going?"

"I can text you the address."

I lift my phone and point at the black screen. "My phone is dead."

"Don't you have a phone charger in your car?"

"No."

He rolls his eyes. "You're hopeless. Fine. I'll drive."

CHAPTER 30
BLAIR

One of these days, I need to reevaluate my life choices and start to say no to shit. I'm speed walking toward the restaurant where I'm meeting the girls for an early dinner while trying to solve a crisis at the sorority. The costumes for our performance arrived, but they're two sizes too big. Apparently, a glitch in the system modified our original order. Now everyone is freaking out.

I trip over something right in front of a restaurant window and almost end up on my knees. My phone takes a nosedive and crashes against the ground. I curse under my breath and pick it up, hoping it isn't broken. I should have known better. The screen is cracked.

"Motherfucker!"

I sense I'm being observed, so I look into the restaurant. The couple sitting by the window is indeed staring at me, but they aren't the ones who catch my attention. Two tables deeper inside, I see Alex sitting with a woman. He says something that makes her laugh, and the sharp pain in my chest burns.

My stomach drops through the earth, and my heart seems to shatter into a million pieces. Tears sting my eyes, making me fucking mad. I walk away from the restaurant before he can see me.

Boy, he doesn't waste any time. But why would that surprise me? He fucked Faith the same evening he fucked me.

I'm angry and confused, not knowing when Alex became someone who could hurt me like this. The restaurant where I'm meeting the girls is a block away, and I need that time to control my emotions. Even so, I take deep breaths before I venture inside.

Gia, Ashley, and Zoey are already there. The fact that I'm the last to arrive isn't lost on them.

"Hey, look who's late for once." Ashley grins like a fiend.

I pull up a chair and drop like a sack of potatoes. "My life is chaos central."

"Is it the Starlight Gala prep that's keeping you busy?" Gia asks.

"That's one of the many balls I'm currently juggling. It'd be fine if the universe wasn't out to get me. It's been one problem after the next." I flag the waiter because I need a drink stat.

"I'm sorry it's been shitty, but at least the gala will be over by next week, and then it's wedding shenanigans, babe!" Zoey says enthusiastically.

"I love Riley, but hell, she and Jesse couldn't have picked a worse time for their wedding," I grumble.

"I think it's romantic to get married on New Year's Eve," Zoey rebuffs. "You said you didn't mind when Riley asked. In fact, I remember you thanked her."

I glower but don't say a thing. Last year, I didn't have an issue with Riley's wedding being the same day as my twenty-first birthday. It gave me the perfect excuse to avoid a lavish party thrown by my parents. I couldn't have foreseen that my life would be so complicated right now. Besides, Mom is still planning a bash for the week after, so Riley and Jesse's wedding didn't get me off the hook.

The waiter comes, and I order a margarita. It's only Monday, and I shouldn't drink, but after the day I've had, I need it.

"What's the plan?" Gia asks Zoey.

She pulls out a mini binder that's full and has several tabs sticking out.

"Hello. What the hell is that, Martha Stewart?" Ashley asks.

"What? This is my maid of honor binder." She flips the front toward us and shows off the golden lettering that says so. "See?"

"Did you buy that?" I ask.

"No. Riley gave it to me when she asked me to be her maid of honor. She knows I'm obsessed with stationary."

"Trust me, we *all* know." Ashley snickers.

Zoey blows her a raspberry, and I take a sip of the margarita the waiter just put in front of me.

"Are you ready to order?" he asks the table.

"I haven't looked at the menu yet," I say.

"I'll give you a few more minutes." He walks away, but I don't look at the menu. I'm focused on getting as much margarita as I can into my body before I get a brain freeze.

"Whoa, slow down, Blair." Gia chuckles.

"Don't be a hater because you can't drink for the next seven months," Ashley chimes in.

Gia's amusement vanishes. "Jeez, what's with you?"

Ashley turns her attention to the menu. "Nothing." She doesn't make eye contact.

"Anyway, Riley will be in town the week before Christmas, so that's when I'm having her bachelorette party. Jesse and Deacon will be here too, so the bachelor party will happen the same night," Zoey pipes up.

"What's your brother planning for the bachelor party?" Gia asks.

Zoey shrugs. "I don't know. But Deacon is the mastermind, so it'll be something over the top and stupid."

I tune Zoey out, glad that, for once, I'm not in charge of anything. Our bridesmaid dresses have been ordered, so that's not something we have to worry about. My phone's screen is cracked, but at least it's still working, and I can read my messages. It seems someone's cousin is a fashion design student, and she can alter our costumes in time for the gala. Disaster averted.

"By the way, Riley wants us to do a dance number at the wedding," Zoey says, getting my attention.

"Oh, how fun," Gia says. At the same time, Ashley replies, "Fuck me."

"Come on, did you think your only duty as a bridesmaid would be to wear a pastel-colored dress and get the bride drunk at her bachelorette party?" Zoey arches an eyebrow.

Still sporting a scowl, Ashley replies, "Pretty much."

"Please tell me either you or Gia will do the choreography," I chime in.

"Don't worry, Blair. You're off the hook on this one." Gia smirks. "How's the number for the Starlight Gala going?"

"We're almost there. We just had a costume emergency that was mercifully resolved without me needing to use my connections to fix the problem."

My phone vibrates, announcing another message. Thinking it's from one of my sorority sisters, I casually glance at the screen without bracing for it.

> I didn't see your text until now. Long story. Yes, we can talk. Tell me when.

My entire body freezes, save for my heart, which is now beating at breakneck speed. I was determined to forget about Alex and keep him in the enemy zone forever. But the way my body reacts to his damn message is messing with my ability to think straight. I want to see him so I can yell at him, but that would show my hand. He can't ever know how much of a hold he has on me.

"Blair, what's wrong?" Gia asks, her brows furrowed.

I shove my phone into my purse and say, "Nothing. Nothing at all."

For the first time in forever, having dinner with my girlfriends fails to improve my mood. Alex is the cause, and I don't know what to do about it. I've always known he was a player, but I thought he wouldn't sleep around while *we* were messing around. I'm so fucking stupid.

I didn't reply to his text. What would be the point? Why would I bother explaining to him I had an emergency? He was obviously glad to move on to the next warm body in line.

I'm glad this hellish day is finally over. I can't wait to get into my pj's and curl up with Cookie on the couch. But a tall blond hockey player is standing in front of my door.

"What the hell are you doing here?" I ask.

"You didn't answer my text," Alex replies. "So I decided to stop by."

The anger from seeing him having dinner with another woman comes back with a vengeance. I'm fuming as I stride down the hallway.

"If I wanted to talk to you, I'd have texted you back." I shove the key into the keyhole with so much force I'm surprised I don't break it. Wouldn't *that* be the cherry on top?

I walk in, and naturally, Alex follows me before I can shut the door in his face.

"Tough shit. We are talking whether you want to or not." He slams the door shut.

The noise sets me off. I whirl around and poke his chest. "Sure, let's talk about how much of a manwhore you are."

His brows shoot up. "What?"

"Don't *what* me. I know you hooked up with Faith after I left the party last Saturday."

"Where did you get that idea? I didn't hook up with anyone after you left!"

"She wouldn't lie about that."

He grabs my wrist and leans down, his nose almost touching mine, and grits out, "I didn't fuck anyone at that party but you."

His eyes are burning with anger and desire, and my body is reacting, melting on the spot.

"What about the woman you had dinner with tonight?" I ask feebly.

He pulls back, frowning. "You saw me with Joanne?"

I yank my arm free. "Yes. I was on my way to meet the girls and saw you."

"Joanne is my agent. Logan was there too. Didn't you see him?"

I'm beginning to feel more foolish by the second. "No."

"You must have seen us when he went to the restroom."

My heart is fluttering now, damn happy about that explanation. "Oh."

"What's going on here, Westwood? Are you jealous?"

Crossing my arms, I look away. "Don't flatter yourself."

He steps into my space and places his hands on my forearms. I look up… and maybe I shouldn't have. He has an infuriating smirk on his lips that makes him sexy as hell.

"Why did you bail on me last Saturday?"

I stare into his eyes, noticing there are silver flecks in them. "I... I had a family emergency."

"Is everything okay?" he asks in a soft tone.

"It is now." I step back, not wanting to get reeled in by him.

He runs his fingers through his hair, pushing the long strands back. "Look, I didn't sleep with your friend, all right? I may be a manwhore, but I'd never hook up with two girls on the same night unless it was a threesome."

"You're a pig."

"I'm just being honest. I haven't slept with anyone since we started whatever it is we're doing."

My heart does a little somersault, giddy as hell. "Why not?"

"Because I don't want to fuck anyone but you."

I open and shut my mouth, but I can't speak, and Alex keeps staring at me, waiting.

"I... what does that mean?" I finally ask.

He rubs his face, sighing heavily. "I don't know what it means."

"Maybe we shouldn't continue until we do."

I can't believe I'm saying that when every cell in my body wants to jump into his arms.

"You're right. Maybe we shouldn't." He turns to the door, but before walking out, he says, "Good night, baby girl."

CHAPTER 31
BLAIR

I can't believe I survived the week before the gala without another catastrophe striking. As for Alex, I put my feelings toward him in the icebox. I can't talk to him until I understand what I want from him. He's left me alone, for the most part, and our communications have been done solely via email, staying focused on our project.

Tonight, I'm a nervous wreck. I have to perform in front of him and then suffer through the auction. I'm not sure how I'm going to react when women start to bid on him. If I hadn't promised Gia I'd get Noah for her, I might be tempted to throw my money at Alex, even though I still don't know what to do about him.

"How's your costume? Do I need to fix anything?" Torrance's cousin, Sophia, asks, pulling me back to the here and now.

I run my hands over the front of the corset. "No, it's perfect. Thank you so much for helping out. I can't believe you were able to alter all the costumes so fast."

She smiles. "I've been practicing speed sewing. I want to compete on *Project Runway*."

"I love that show."

"Me too!" Her eyes sparkle with genuine intensity.

"We were lucky you came to the rescue."

"True. I can't believe the manufacturer screwed up your order like that."

"Me neither." Another thought crosses my mind. "I didn't know you lived in Fairbanks."

Her blue eyes turn rounder. "Actually, I live in New York City. I go to school there."

"Makes sense. Fairbanks isn't known for its fashion scene."

I want to ask what she's been doing all week here in Fairbanks and missing classes, but that would be prying. Torrance and Faith join us, and the subject changes.

"Are the guys here yet?" Faith asks.

"How am I supposed to know?" I retort, already annoyed.

Alex swore he didn't hook up with her on Saturday, but a shred of doubt lingers. We've been enemies for so long, it's hard for me to trust him now.

"I'm so planning on bidding on Alex tonight." She smiles slyly, turning toward the vanity mirror to check her makeup.

My stomach coils tightly, making me sick.

"I bet he looks even hotter wearing a tux," Torrance adds. "You're so lucky, Faith. I wish either twin would look my way."

"Who are you talking about?" Sophia asks.

"Oh, the Kaminski twins, hockey gods," Faith sighs.

"Ah, *them*." She nods as if she, too, knows them in an intimate way.

Damnit, the reach of their dicks must be far if they're screwing girls outside of Fairbanks.

"Do you know them?" I ask, unable to stop myself.

She shakes her head. "Never met them, but I know who they are—my brother's nightmare."

I pinch my eyebrows together. "I don't follow."

"My brother plays center for Clayton U," she clarifies.

"Oh *shit*. You're their rival's sister." Faith's eyes bug out, then she turns to Torrance. "How come you never mentioned Vince Daniels is your cousin?"

Torrance snorts. "Do you think I want people to know my cousin is a Jackal?"

"I suppose not. I don't really follow hockey. I only went to one game this year."

"I wouldn't mention that your brother plays for Clayton U if you're around any of the Warriors," I say to Sophia. "They're our biggest rivals."

"Don't worry. I'll keep my lips sealed about that."

"Are you planning on bidding on anyone?" Faith asks Sophia.

"Me? No way. I'm not staying for the auction. I have a date."

"Oh, with that hot doc?" Torrance smiles, making Sophia blush.

"Yes, but keep your mouth shut. I don't want your mother to know—she'll tell mine, and they'll start planning the wedding."

I can't help wincing at the word *wedding*. I haven't heard from my mother since the holiday kickoff party, which means she's plotting, and I should worry.

"How can you tell the twins apart when they're not wearing their jerseys?" Sophia asks.

"Alex has a scar on his chin," Faith replies.

"No, he doesn't," I blurt out.

She pinches her lips. "I'm certain he does. I licked it. Have you?"

I would have if he had one, you dumb fuck. I'm pissed about her jab. But then my heart starts beating faster when it dawns on me. She *didn't* hook up with Alex.

I laugh. "Oh my God. You take the prize of the most dimwitted person I've ever met. Logan is the one who has a scar."

"What?" Faith shrieks.

Torrance shakes her head. "Girl... how could you get them mixed up?"

"I don't know! It was dark, and when I called him Alex, he didn't correct me."

"Gee, that guy sounds like a prize," Sophia chimes in.

They carry on the conversation, but I'm no longer interested. Now that the seed of doubt has been removed, I can entertain the idea that maybe I want Alex back in my bed. I certainly have not had my fill of him yet. The question is, is he tired of me already?

ALEX

Logan and I met Sean, Darren, and CJ at The Heritage for preauction drinks. Unfortunately, Josh and his football buddies had the same idea, so we didn't stay. Now we're at the Botanical Gardens and one-hundred-percent sober.

"Is there any chance Noah can bring us booze?" CJ asks.

"You want the underage player to smuggle alcohol into the venue?" Darren raises an eyebrow.

"What? I'm not twenty-one, and I'd have done it."

"I just got a text from him," Sean says, looking at his phone. "He's got a cold and isn't coming."

I trade a glance with Logan, and I can tell he's thinking the same as me.

"Sick my ass." Logan laughs. "He didn't want to upset Gia."

"Yeah, that tracks." Sean nods.

"I told you we should have gone to a different bar," CJ complains, then glances around, no doubt searching for the open bar in the room.

"We were already running late," Sean retorts. "It's better this way. I don't want any of you embarrassing the team." He gives me a meaningful glance.

"Why are you looking at me like that? I can hold my liquor, unlike lightweight here." I toss my arm over CJ's shoulder.

He shoves me to the side. "I'm not a lightweight. And did

you already forget that Noah and I had to drag your drunk ass out of the Delta-Iota party?"

That comment pisses me off, but I control the annoyance. I won't let CJ know he got under my skin. "Nope, don't remember a thing."

"Come on. Let's find our table," Darren chimes in. "I think they're about to start."

I glance at the stage, and sure as shit, some stuffy lady from the school administration is walking toward the middle with a microphone in hand. We follow Darren toward a table close to the wall and the entrance to the backstage area. I spot Preston with his friends from the swim team, but Josh and his teammates aren't here yet.

Assistant Coach LaRue and Coach Bedford are already at our table, and both have a drink in front of them.

"You're late," Coach Bedford grumbles.

"Sorry, Coach." Sean pulls out the chair next to the man.

Thank fuck. I don't think anyone wants to sit next to Coach when he's in a bad mood. I sit next to LaRue and whisper. "Why is he mad now?"

"He had to socialize with boosters. You know he hates that kind of stuff."

Man, I'd hate that too. But it seems I'll have to do that once I'm playing for the NHL. Joanne told Logan and I that we can expect contracts any day now. If that happens, this will be our last season playing for the Warriors. The thought is exciting and also depressing. Man, I really need a drink.

Lost in my thoughts, I miss the entire intro speech. Now the presenter is announcing the Deltas, and my entire body turns to the stage. A disco song pours from the speakers, and the Deltas come out wearing colorful outfits that twinkle under the spotlight. I only have eyes for Blair though. She's in the middle of the front row, and it's clear she's the best dancer in the group. I wish we were sitting closer.

"Wow, I didn't know Blair could dance," Logan pipes up.

"Yeah, me neither," I reply, distracted.

I already knew that detail, but I'm not going to tell Logan that.

She's radiant on that stage, a completely different person than the uptight girl I used to know. And I want her so terribly that it's taking every ounce of self-control I have to remain seated and not move closer to the stage.

I know now why I don't want to sleep with anyone but her. The ache and yearning in my chest are impossible to ignore. I probably look like Noah when he stares at Gia. I never planned to fall for anyone, least of all my enemy. How the fuck did I let that happen?

CHAPTER 32
BLAIR

When I exit the stage, my heart is speeding like a bullet train. I forgot how exhilarating it is to perform in front of an audience. Bonus points that my mother wasn't in the crowd, judging my every move.

It's a little messy backstage. We need to change for the gala, and soon the jocks will come back here to wait for their names to be called for the auction. There's a changing area for privacy. But I don't head there right away because Gia is waiting for me.

She has a bouquet of flowers in her hand. "You did amazing, Blair."

"Is that for me?"

"Duh. Who else?"

Warmth spreads in my chest. I'm so touched. I accept the flowers from her and take a whiff of the white lilies, my favorite. "Thank you. They're lovely."

"So, about the auction... Noah is sick and can't be here. You're off the hook."

"Oh." I frown. "What's wrong with him?"

"Just a cold. He should be fine in a few days."

"Then what are you doing here? You should go home and be with him."

She waves dismissively. "He'll be fine on his own for a few hours. I don't want to miss the auction. They're always fun."

I smirk. "Fun because your guy isn't being auctioned off."

"Well..." She smiles back, her eyes twinkling with mirth. I'm beginning to suspect Noah isn't really sick.

"He doesn't have a cold, does he?"

Her eyes become round. "He does!"

"Okay, if you say so."

"Anyway, now you can bid on the person you really want to."

Schooling my face into the most innocent expression I can muster, I say, "I don't want to bid on anyone."

"Wait until you see Alex in a tux. You'll change your mind pretty fast."

I don't say anything for a couple beats, but then the man in question moves into my line of sight, and hell, my entire body is consumed by liquid fire. He searches the room until he finds me and then makes a beeline in my direction.

Gia turns. "Speak of the devil."

Alex's lips are curled into a sexy grin, and I'm glad Gia is here because that expression is doing crazy things to my mind and body. I want to climb him like a tree and do unspeakable deeds.

"Hi Alex. Looking good," Gia greets him.

"I *am* good." He keeps his gaze locked with mine. "You did well out there, Westwood."

Radioactive butterflies take over my stomach. I swallow hard, then croak, "Thanks."

He eyes the bouquet in my hands. "Who gave you those?"

"I did," Gia replies. "Are you ready for the auction? I hear you're up first."

His brows shoot up. "Really? Ah hell. I was hoping I wasn't."

"Why? Are you afraid no one is going to bid on you?" I ask.

"On the contrary. I think it's going to be a bloodbath."

I'm sure it will. "Aren't you cocky?" I raise an eyebrow.

"I just know my worth."

A panicked guy wearing a headset and holding a tablet approaches. "You're Alex Kaminski, right?"

"The one and only."

"You're up."

Alex turns to us. "All right, ladies. It's showtime. See you on the other side."

I watch him walk away, transfixed. Gia snaps her fingers in front of my face. "Blair, wake up."

"What?"

"If you want to bid on Alex, you'd better get your ass out there. He wasn't kidding. He'll get a lot of bids."

I hesitate, not wanting her to know how badly I want to win him. Ah, fuck it. Why am I bothering to hide the obvious? "I guess I'd better hurry, then."

There's no time to change into my gala dress, not that I really care. The Deltas have a few tables in the middle of the room, and all the dancers have already changed clothes.

Melody looks at my costume. "Why are you still wearing that?"

"I lost track of time." I take my seat.

The emcee cracks a few jokes as he describes Alex, but they barely register. I'm suddenly nervous, and my pulse is pounding in my ears. I wipe my clammy hands on my skirt, then grab my auction sign and use it as a fan.

"Are you okay, Blair?" Pippa asks.

"I'm just hot."

Alex enters the stage then, and the female crowd cheers and whistles. They're using some cheesy song in the background for his catwalk, and I'm a little mortified by it. But Alex oozes charisma, and he owns the stage. No surprise—he's a spotlight whore and is right at home.

The bid starts at fifty dollars, and Faith is the first to raise her hand.

"I thought you wanted to bid for Logan," Torrance chimes in.

"I've already had Logan. Now I want Alex."

"God, you're such a ho." Torrance snorts.

"A ho for the Kaminski twins."

"Faith, we've talked about this," Melody chides. "Being crass is not an image that aligns with the Deltas' values."

Faith's mouth turns down, creating deep creases. I never noticed that before. It's like now that she's competing for my guy, all I can see are her flaws. I should be better than this, but the jealousy is winning.

The bidding war continues, and I have yet to enter. It's now at three thousand dollars.

"Wow, it seems you really like the Warriors' D-man!" the emcee jokes to the crowd. "It's a good thing we have another one just like him, eh?"

Alex frowns at the guy, then shakes his head.

"Are you done bidding, Faith?" Torrance asks.

"Yeah. Three grand is way over my budget."

"We're at three thousand, ladies and gentlemen. Do I hear four thousand?" He looks at the crowd.

This is it. If I don't bid now, the bimbo sitting at the table next to us wins. My eyes lock with Alex's and the quirk of his brows feels like a challenge.

I raise my sign, and say, "Ten thousand dollars."

Faith gasps loudly. Even the emcee seems taken aback. He asks if anyone would like to offer more, but I know no one will.

"Congratulations to bidder number thirty-nine," the emcee announces.

My heart is thundering in my chest from the rush of victory. My sorority sisters are all staring at me, mouths agape, but I don't care.

"I can't believe you paid that much for a guy you hate," Torrance says.

I smirk. "Why not? It's for a good cause."

Alex returns backstage, and I get up to pay for my prize.

CHAPTER 33
BLAIR

Alex finds me just as I finish paying for my bid. His eyes zero in on the shiny black card in my hand and harden. Shit. I can imagine what he thinks of me now. He doesn't comment about it as his gaze meets mine.

"Before you say anything about money, let me remind you this is for charity and totally tax deductible."

"Hey, it's not my business what you do with your father's money. I'm just here reporting for duty."

"You're right. It's not your business, but I want you to know anyway. Ryder and I *must* spend a certain amount a year on charity donations. It's one of our obligations as Westwoods."

"Like I said, I don't care."

"Your tone says otherwise."

Putting his hands on his hips, he looks at the floor and sighs.

"We don't need to do anything if you don't want to," I add.

He whips his face up. "You paid for a date with a Warrior. You'll get your date. Just tell me what you want to do."

I glance around and notice people staring at us. We're already gossip fodder, but again, my bid for Alex will probably be the highest tonight. I turn my attention to him again. "I want to go back to that club in Boston."

"It's an hour away."

"I can get a car to drive us there."

"And then what? Are we spending the night in Boston?"

The thumping in my chest feels so loud I'm afraid he can hear it. "That'll depend on how the evening goes."

He swallows hard, and I notice a slight squinting of his eyes. Then he tilts his head. "Are we still playing games, Westwood?"

I gulp down the lump in my throat and shake my head. "No games, Alex. I swear."

ALEX

By the time Blair changes out of her costume and we leave the Botanical Gardens, our ride is waiting for us. Her royal-blue gala dress is strapless and snug, with a skirt that flares at the bottom. She looks like a siren who wants to seduce me to my death.

"This wasn't what I had in my mind when you said you'd get a car," I say, taking stock of the luxurious interior of the limo Blair rented.

"It was all they had available last minute."

"Does it have a fully stocked bar?"

"I don't know." She presses a button, and a compartment to my right juts out.

I open the door and find all the booze one might need to party in a limo, plus glasses. "Jackpot." I look over my shoulder and smirk. "There's tequila."

"Oh good. I need something to take the edge off."

I pause and take my time to look at her. There's a small clench in my chest, and I wonder if she's feeling something similar. "Are you nervous, Westwood?"

"Stop calling me that."

"What should I call you then?"

She flattens her lips but doesn't answer. I fill two shot glasses with tequila and hand one to her. She tosses her head back and drinks before I can lift my glass to my lips.

"Hit me again." She stretches out her arm.

"I didn't even drink mine." I toss the shot back and then take her empty glass and put it away.

"Hey, I want another shot."

I shake my head and scooch closer. "You can have another shot after you tell me what's going on. Why pay so much for me?"

"Because it was for charity."

"Wrong. Try again."

Her chest rises and falls faster, emphasizing the swell of her breasts. I make an effort to keep my eyes locked on her face though.

"I don't want to answer that."

I run my fingers up her legs, lamenting the snug fit of her gown. "Why? It's a simple question."

She trembles under my caress. "It's not a simple question. Not when it comes to you."

I flatten my palm over her stomach, leaning closer to kiss the corner of her mouth. She lets out a shaky breath. The need to suck her lower lip into my mouth is immense, but I do want answers.

"Were you jealous, Westwood?"

"I already asked you to stop calling me that."

I kiss her neck, just under her ear. "Fine. Were you jealous, baby girl?"

"Yes. Is that what you want to hear?" She pushes me back and scowls.

The fury sparking in her eyes adds fuel to the fire that's already burning in my veins. I glance fleetingly at the front of the limo, making sure the divider between us and the driver is still up. Then I look into her eyes and cup her cheek, rubbing my thumb over her lower lip.

"Yes. I like that you're jealous over me."

She bats my hand away. "I'm glad I can help inflate your ego even more."

"You can't blame me. My ego has taken quite a beating from you."

"What?" she squeaks, widening her eyes.

"Last Saturday, when I came out of the bathroom and you were gone, I got wasted to the point that I lost my phone and had to be taken home by CJ and Noah. I haven't done that since I was a stupid teen. What does that tell you?"

I'm confessing like an idiot and to Blair, of all people, a woman I can't decipher and who has the ability to hurt me like no one else.

"You're an emotional drinker like me."

I chuckle. "I guess I am."

She takes in a sharp breath. "I didn't win the auction only because of jealousy. I did it because I want you, and I don't care what that means."

Fuck. That's all I need to hear. I capture her face between my hands. "That's good enough for me."

I kiss her, savoring her luscious lips as if they're the nectar of the gods. She reaches for my arms and tugs at the sleeves. One kiss turns into several more, each hungrier than the next. I want her on my lap and her pussy grinding against my cock, but her dress is too constricting.

I pull back so she can help me out of my jacket, which comes off easily. Free from it, I try to shove her skirt up her legs, but it won't budge.

"Why are you wearing this damned tight thing?"

"Because it makes me feel sexy."

"You're always sexy, even wearing sweats. How am I going to get to your pussy?"

She slides away from me and leans back against her side of the limo while pulling her dress up her glorious legs. When that damn garter belt makes an appearance, I take over, grabbing her legs and placing them over my shoulders. She's flat on her back across the seat now, and my mouth is exactly where it needs to be.

"Have I told you I have a weakness for garter belts?"

"No."

"Well, now you know, baby girl." I lick her pussy over the flimsy fabric of her panties, loving the taste of her arousal.

"Alex," she moans, closing her eyes.

"Look at me, baby girl. Watch me as I eat you out."

Her eyes open but remain hooded and glazed with desire. I push her panties aside and lick her again, rimming her entrance with my tongue. The limo gains speed, which means we must be on the highway. But we have plenty of time before we arrive at our destination, and I plan to make every minute count.

For a moment, I get lost in her flavor, in her scent. I've never tasted anything sweeter or more addictive. With every swipe of my tongue over her clit, Blair's whimpering increases. I want to tease her, bring her to the edge, but prevent her from taking the leap for as long as I can. Whenever I sense she's getting close, I change my focus.

"What are you doing, Kaminski?"

"What does it feel like?" I kiss the inside of her thigh.

"Like you're hell-bent on torturing me. Make me come already."

I pinch her ass, making her yell. "There's only one boss in this limo, baby girl. Remember that."

Her eyes widen, and the flames in them burn brighter. "Please... I'm so close."

My lips curl into a grin. "That's better."

I fuck her with my tongue with intent now, not only because she begged me but because I want to plunge my cock into her pussy next. I already know what she likes, so it doesn't take long for her to shatter into pieces.

"Fuck! Alex," she cries out, tilting her chin back and closing her eyes.

I lick and suck until I've drunk all her juices and she stops shaking in my arms. This is the hottest thing I've ever done, and I want so much more. I set her legs down and then unzip my pants to take my dick out.

"Come here, baby girl." I take her hand, keeping my left curled around my erection.

She sits up, still looking a little dazed. I caress her flushed cheeks. "I love how you look right now."

"You dig the disheveled style?" She grins.

I chuckle. "You have no idea. Come sit on my lap, baby girl. Put me out of my misery."

"I don't have a condom in my purse."

I shove my hand in my pocket and fish out a foil packet. "You should know by now I'm always prepared."

Her brows furrow. "Were you planning on hooking up with whoever won the auction?"

I tap the tip of her nose with my index finger. "You're cute when you're jealous. The answer is obviously no. You own my cock now, baby girl, for as long as you want."

She blinks fast, and the way her mouth turns into a perfect *O* shape speaks louder than words. She wasn't expecting that.

"In that case..." She leans forward and kisses my neck.

Shivers run down my spine. I wrap my arm around her waist while goose bumps break out on my skin. I know she's giving me another hickey, and I'm more than okay with that. But her warm tongue on that sensitive spot is making me see fireworks already. I need to be inside her. I rip open the package and roll the condom down my shaft as fast as I can.

"Ride me, baby girl."

She eases off my neck and looks into my eyes. For a moment, neither of us speaks, but I can't ignore the crackle of electricity that sparks between us. This isn't just sex, at least not for me.

I grab her hips and lift her, positioning her where I want. She grabs my cock and guides it to her entrance, then lowers her hips slowly.

"Who's the torturer now?" I ask.

"I'm sensitive after you destroyed me with your tongue. You don't think going slow is torture for me too?"

I laugh. "I just gave you an earth-shattering orgasm, woman."

"Who says it was earth-shattering?"

I grab a fistful of her hair, enjoying the silkiness around my fingers. "I know it was." My mouth claims hers again and I'm finally sheathed in her completely.

She begins to move, but her pace is too gentle. I'm already on the verge. I need fast and hard. I release her hair so I can grab her hips with both hands and take charge. My fingers dig into her skin, the need to mark her just like she did me running deep. She rests her hands on my shoulders and uses them as leverage, trying to wrestle back control.

"Don't even think about it, baby girl."

She threads her fingers through my hair, messing it all up. "I need more, Alex, and faster."

"You're a hungry vixen, aren't you?"

"I can't help it. You make me feel so good." She throws her head back, pushing her chest out.

Her tits are close to my face, and it's a temptation I can't resist. I kiss the swell of one breast before biting the soft skin lightly.

Blair shouts my name then and climaxes so hard her shakes reverberate into me and all over my cock. I can't take it anymore. I explode, my body convulsing with the intensity of my orgasm. I force her face back to mine so I can possess her lips again. It's a battle of tongues and teeth, a compulsion to win at this too.

When my balls are empty and my breathing is ragged, I stop moving Blair's hips. She hides her face in the crook of my neck, and we go utterly still, save for our heavy inhales and exhales. The background music—which I didn't notice until now—and the outside highway noises become more obvious.

I caress her shoulder blades with the tips of my fingers and wait for my body to return to earth. I may be boneless, but my mind is sharp. I know *exactly* what I want from her, and it isn't just sex. Now I need a plan… because I'm not letting her go.

CHAPTER 34
BLAIR

When the limo drops us off, there's a line to get into the club. It was the same when we came here for Gia's birthday party, but that night, I called ahead and paid for the VIP treatment without anyone knowing. I've already flaunted my financial status too much in front of Alex, so I don't try to skip the line.

In our hurry to leave the gala, I forgot my coat at the Botanical Gardens. I'm shivering in no time, but Alex drapes his tux jacket over my shoulders.

"There," he says, his eyes twinkling with kindness that I'm not used to coming from him.

"Thanks."

He smiles, not taking his eyes off my face. "You're welcome."

I'm not sure how to act around him now. It's the first time we've hung out post sex. In all the previous instances, I bailed.

"Is this weird?" I ask.

"Your standing in line like a commoner? Yes, super weird." He smirks.

"No. Us, together. I mean, we aren't dating, and... I don't know how to behave around you, to be honest."

He tucks a strand of hair behind my ear. "Let's not overanalyze things tonight, Westwood. We're hanging out and enjoying each other's company. That's all."

I don't know why his answer disappoints me. He's not my boyfriend, and he can't be, yet I want more from him.

"I can do that," I reply.

He wraps his arms around my waist and pulls me closer. "Maybe we can find a dark corner in that club for round two."

I shake my head, laughing. "I can always count on you to have a one-track mind."

"When it comes to you, always." He kisses me on the lips, but it's tender, not the hot and heavy kisses from before.

This is sweet and unexpected, and it's doing crazy things to my body, especially the muscle in my chest that has no business beating faster for him. When he pulls back, I'm dizzy, and I even sway a little.

"Are you okay?" He chuckles.

"Yeah, of course."

"Blair?" someone calls from nearby.

Alex turns, and I see a man wearing a sharp, tailored coat approach. It's dark out here in the street, and I have no idea who he is.

"Blair Westwood?" he repeats my name when he's standing in front of us.

"Yes. Do I know you?"

"My apologies. We haven't officially met yet. My name is Ilya Bolkosky. I'm a friend of your father." He offers me his hand.

I shake it automatically, but my mind is racing. I've heard Ryder mention the Bolkosky name a few times, and each time, he sounded angry.

"Nice to meet you," I say.

"I'm Alex Kaminski." Alex extends his hand as well, and although his facial expression remains impartial, I sense tension coming from him.

"Nice to meet you, Alex," Ilya replies smoothly.

"Aren't you a bit young to be friends with Mr. Westbrook?" he asks.

Ilya chuckles. "My father has business dealings with Mr. Westbrook, and where I'm from, that automatically makes him a friend of the family."

Somehow, I don't think *friend* means the same to him as it does to us.

He turns to me. "That means you're my friend too, Blair. Come on, let's get you inside before you freeze to death."

Shit. I so don't want to go into the club in his company.

"You want us to cut the line?" I ask.

He chuckles. "It's not cutting the line if you come in with the owner."

"I don't want to impose," I retort, but it's weak. I'm hoping Alex will butt in and help me refuse his offer. He can't possibly be happy about it.

Of course, he has to go and surprise me again. "Come on, Blair. My jacket is doing nothing to keep you warm."

My jaw hangs open. He doesn't see my reaction though. He's staring at Ilya in a challenging way. Ugh. Now it's a testosterone contest.

"Great!" Ilya beams. "Follow me."

I walk slowly on purpose so we can hang back and I can talk to Alex. "What are you doing? Didn't you notice I was trying to say no to him?"

"I did. But, one, you're freezing, and two, I want to keep an eye on this dude. Something about him is off."

I have a reason to feel that way about Ilya. But Alex couldn't possibly know about Ryder's comments. "Why do you say that?"

"Just a feeling."

Ilya waits for us to catch up at the club's entrance. The bouncer doesn't spare us a glance. Why would he—we're with his employer.

The music in the club is different tonight. It's playing techno instead of '80s and '90s songs. That means there's a different crowd here too. I don't know what I was expecting when I suggested we come back. It isn't the same vibe.

Alex throws his arm over my shoulder and keeps my body flush against his in a protective way as we follow Ilya. I try to not bask in his possessiveness and fail. I'm melting against him.

We head toward a set of stairs that's corded off and manned by a bouncer. As soon as he spots Ilya's approach, he removes the cord.

"These are my VIP guests. They need wristbands," he tells the bouncer, then turns to us. "I want you to feel free to go anywhere in the club and be able to return to the VIP room without issues."

"Thanks, that's very thoughtful," I say.

We let the bouncer put the band around our wrists, but instead of following Ilya to the VIP room, I say, "If you don't mind, I'd like to hit the dance floor first. We'll see you in a bit."

He smiles, but even in the dark room, I can tell it's forced. "Of course. Have fun."

I turn around and, holding Alex's hand, stride toward the dance floor.

"Blair, wait."

"I want to dance."

"I get that, baby girl, but let me carve a path for us."

I was doing just fine taking the lead, but once Alex is in front of me, our progress is much faster. As soon as we step onto the packed dance floor, he spins me around in his arms and kisses me deeply. I'm taken by surprise. I didn't expect a public display of affection from him.

When he leans back, he's smiling smugly.

"What was that for?"

"I just wanted to kiss you, Westwood."

"It has nothing to do with the fact that the VIP room has a bird's-eye view of the dance floor, right?"

"What? Do you think I'm marking my territory?"

"You aren't?" I raise an eyebrow.

He rubs his thumb over my lips. "You got me there. I am. You're mine tonight."

My heart flutters in my chest like a trapped hummingbird. I'm shocked to learn I like being called *his* way too much. Possessive alpha guys were never my type… until Alex came along.

I throw my arms over his shoulders, linking my hands behind his neck. Even though I'm wearing heels, he's still so much taller than me that I need to get onto my tiptoes to kiss him.

Loud dance music is blasting around us, but we don't move. I'm too busy melding my body with his and drowning in his essence. I could have never foreseen how much I'd enjoy kissing Alex Kaminski. He's everything I never knew I wanted.

Blaring alarms sound in my head. I can't allow my thoughts to picture Alex as a golden knight in shining armor. Our thing has to be about sex only, nothing more.

I feel a tap on my shoulder, and the interruption brings me back to reality. Alex and I break apart, and lust is fogging my brain, but when I see Ryder standing there, staring daggers at us, it becomes sharp again.

"What are you doing here?" I yell.

He leans over to talk in my ear. "I could ask you the same question, but I won't. You need to leave. *Now.*"

"We just got here. We'll leave when we're good and ready," Alex retorts.

"You came in with Ilya Bolkosky."

"So?" I ask.

Ryder spares a few seconds, trying to intimidate me with his glare, but I don't change my stance. If he wants us to go, he needs to tell us why.

He switches his focus to Alex. "If you care about my sister, get her out of here, Alex."

Whoa. Ryder is appealing to Alex's feelings for me? Doesn't he know there aren't any, besides raw attraction?

Alex puts a hand on my lower back. "Come on, Blair. Let's go."

I'm too stunned to put up a fight. After what Ryder did to the team, I can't believe Alex is listening to my brother.

Outside the club, he asks, "Can you call the limo to pick us up?"

"Yeah, the driver is on standby." I take out my phone and send a text message while Alex hugs me from behind, keeping me warm.

"Why did you listen to Ryder?" I ask.

Alex stares at me intently. "Because he was acting like the old Ryder, and I used to trust that guy."

CHAPTER 35
ALEX

Damn it. I can't believe Ryder saw right through me. Then again, we used to be tight when he was on the team. The motherfucker knows me. Back then, he'd have kicked my ass for even getting near Blair. But I'm not the same guy I was, and she isn't a random hookup. It's like he knows how much she means to me now.

But if he knows me well, the same truth applies in reverse. He was agitated, worried even, and my gut told me to listen to him and get Blair the fuck out of that club. I'm not sure if Ilya was the danger or someone else.

Blair is quiet on the ride back to Fairbanks. Neither of us even suggested spending the night in Boston. But she's snuggled tightly against my chest, and my arm is over her shoulder, and that's all that matters to me.

I run lazy circles over her arm with my fingers, an innocent caress with no ulterior motives. I just like touching her, even if it isn't leading to sex.

"Thanks for tonight, Alex. I had fun."

"Even though we didn't stay long at the club?"

"The vibe wasn't the same as Gia's birthday party. I was happy to leave early."

"Really? I didn't get the impression you wanted to bail."

"If you had an older sister bossing you around, would you have left without putting up a fight?"

I chuckle. "That's an amusing scenario. And to answer your question, no. I'd do the opposite."

"So you get it." She leans back and looks at me. "I'm worried about Ryder though."

My brows furrow. "Do you think he's involved in something shady?"

She swallows hard and it's audible. "Yes. He's been acting strange for a while, but whatever it is, I don't think it's something he wants to be doing."

"Do you want me to talk to him?"

She blinks fast as if my offer surprises her. "Ryder won't open up to me. What makes you think he'll talk to you?"

"Did you forget we used to be friends?"

"Used to be, past tense."

"When he quit the team, I was so angry all I wanted to do was deck your brother. I never once reached out to him to find out the reason. I should have tried."

"If you talk to him, and he does fess up, will you tell me?"

I hesitate. "That depends."

Blair tenses, her spine becoming taut. "On what?"

"If the truth has the potential to hurt you, I won't tell you."

She crosses her arms and flattens her lips into a harsh line. "Why do you care if I get hurt or not?"

Shit. How can I answer that without putting myself in a vulnerable position?

"God, woman. I'm not a heartless monster. I've tasted you on my tongue. I've been inside you. Isn't that enough reason to not want to hurt you?"

I wish it wasn't dark in the car and I could see her expression better. She doesn't answer for a couple beats, and I wonder if I said the wrong thing.

"I guess, but I still want to know. I'm a tough girl. Whatever it is, I can handle it."

I pull her back to my chest. "I know you're tough, Westwood. I'm not sure if I'll get anything out of Ryder, so this argument is premature."

"True. I doubt he'll talk to you."

"Do you want to bet on it?"

"You and your bets." She kisses my chest, derailing my thoughts.

"When I get you, whether I win or lose, how could I not bet?"

She unbuttons my shirt and licks my abs. "I bet I can rock your world right now."

I thread my fingers through her hair, lust already pumping through my veins. "No need for that bet. You already are, baby girl."

She unzips my pants and pulls my cock free, curling her fingers around my length. "Let's see if I learned my previous lesson."

"Blair…" I twist a lock of her hair around my hand, but I don't yank. I just want to feel the silky strands between my fingers.

She peppers my abs with open kisses, traveling south while working my cock with her hand. I'm already burning for her, but I exercise patience. Sometimes, it pays off.

She stops when she reaches my navel and looks at me. "Any requests?"

"Just your pretty mouth on my cock, beautiful."

Her lips twist into a grin. "As you wish."

Holding my stare, she runs circles over the head with her tongue, licking the precum. I hiss, loving the way she teases me.

"Do you like that?" she asks.

"Fuck yeah."

Keeping one hand wrapped around the base and the other cupping my balls, she sucks me into her mouth until I hit the back of her throat.

"That's it, babe. You're such a good girl." I breathe out.

I can't take my eyes off Blair as she sucks my dick with gusto. The way she knows when to lick and suck to give me the most pleasure is a gift that I hope she bestows only upon me. No, I don't hope. I'll make it so. She's mine, and I don't give a fuck what her parents want for her future. I won't let her go.

My balls tense, and I can't help tightening my hold on her hair and urging her to go faster. She doesn't complain or try to fight me. Like a good girl, she sucks me harder, using her hand to jerk me off at the same time.

"Fuuuck." I explode in her mouth, my cum rushing out in an intense stream.

Blair's eyes find mine as she swallows everything I give her, sending another jolt of libido down my spine. My heart is beating at supersonic speed for more reasons than one.

I don't know what's going to happen from now on, but Blair Westwood owns me, and she doesn't even know it.

I'd eat Blair's pussy again if she'd let me, but after she obliterated me with her mouth, she wanted nothing more than to snuggle with me. Ten minutes later, she's sound asleep.

I have the rest of the ride to get lost in my thoughts, but a few minutes after Blair falls asleep, my phone vibrates in my pocket. It's a text from my brother.

Where did you go?

Now you ask? I left the gala hours ago.

I thought you were busy :D. I just got home.

I went to Boston. I'm on my way back to Fairbanks.

Why did you go to Boston?

Blair's idea. Who bid for you?

Some Delta chick. I already forgot her name.

I shake my head. Logan and his terrible memory for names is notorious.

She was boring AF. Got rid of her as soon as I could.

That's cold.

I didn't fuck her. She put my dick to sleep too.

I chuckle.

That's too bad.

How was your date with the enemy?

I don't reply right away, debating how honest I want to be with him. He won't give me peace if I confess I have feelings for Blair.

Endurable. We bumped into Ryder in Boston.

I hope you punched that asshole in the throat.

No fun when he already gave me permission to deck him.

Okay. I'll do it then.

Something isn't right. We should talk to him.

You're going soft, bro. Is it because you're in luv with his sister?

Shit. He can't possibly know that.

Fuck off. I'm not in love with Blair.

Then she's in love with you. Yours was the highest bid.

It's crazy how my heart reacts to Logan's message, beating faster. If Blair has feelings for me, she's doing a good job not showing her hand. Bidding at a charity auction is hardly proof of heartfelt emotion.

If she is, then too bad.

It feels wrong to send that reply to Logan, but I can't let him know the truth. He's a pest, and if the situation were reversed, I'd give him hell.

And I'm the cold one. Does that mean it's okay if I go after her?

FUCK NO.

Not in love my ass.

Damn it. That knee-jerk reply was a dead giveaway. I'm a fucking idiot.

[middle finger emoji]

Tired of the topic, I put my phone away and ignore his follow-up messages.

"Alex... don't go," Blair whispers.

At first, I think she's awake, but her eyes are shut. She's mumbling in her sleep. I run my fingers through her hair gently. "I'm not going anywhere, baby girl."

CHAPTER 36
BLAIR

I wake up in my bed alone. Rays of light breach the crack between the curtains, and judging by their intensity, it's already midmorning. I remember falling asleep on Alex's lap in the limo after blowing him, and I vaguely recall getting out of the limo and into my apartment. Alex was with me, but maybe he didn't spend the night. A pang of disappointment flares in my chest, but I stomp on it until it dies. I can't afford to have deeper feelings for Alex. I can only do sex—anything more will lead to heartache.

Rubbing my eyes, I sit up. I'm wearing only my panties, and my gown is draped carefully over my chair underneath Alex's white shirt. The butterflies in my stomach wake. He hasn't left.

I get up and, instead of finding my own clothes to wear, I grab Alex's shirt and put it on. It smells like him, and I don't know why, but being enveloped by his scent gives me a sense of peace.

Before I venture out of my room, I make a quick stop in the bathroom to brush my teeth and pee. I don't hear any noise from the living room, but maybe Alex fell asleep on the couch. I walk on soft feet, just in case, and find him sleeping like I suspected. I stop for a moment to admire him. He's so damn gorgeous it hurts. I can't believe I never saw him in this light before. Now it's impossible to ignore.

I move closer, noticing his damp hair. He smells like soap, so he must have taken a shower. I bring my face inches from his and blow a minty breath over his lips. He blinks his eyes open and, a second later, focuses on me. The radiant smile that splits his face makes my entire body quiver. I try to ease back, but he cups my cheek and slants his lips over mine.

I fold like a house of cards, collapsing on the couch next to him and surrendering to the feel of his tongue moving in perfect harmony with mine. My accelerated pulse is loud in my ears, and my nipples are already hard little pebbles. I'm turned on by just one kiss. God have mercy on me. How am I going to walk away from this when the time comes?

He runs his fingers over the front of my shirt—*his* shirt—and releases a few buttons. "Are you wearing my shirt, Westwood?"

"Yes." I turn my face so I can kiss his neck.

"It looks good on you."

He rests a hand on my hip and keeps it there for a while. I pull back to look at him. "Is something wrong?"

"Yes. I'm out of condoms."

"Oh."

"I'm hoping you have some."

My cheeks become hotter. I'm embarrassed, but not by this question. "No. I forgot to buy them."

He caresses my face with the back of his hand. "It's okay. We can do other stuff, although I'm clean. Just got tested a few weeks ago."

"I see. Do you want to do it without protection?"

His brows furrow. "It's not a want. I'm just letting you know because I have a reputation, and I think telling you is important, whether we're going to keep using condoms or not."

"Are you saying you don't plan to sleep with anyone else while we're fooling around?"

He tilts his head. "Is that what we're doing? Fooling around?"

I open and shut my mouth. This sounds like a trap. No matter how I answer the question, it'll blow up in my face. "Is there a better term to describe a sex-only relationship?"

He doesn't answer for a couple beats, making me nervous. Maybe he doesn't want to keep seeing me. I just assumed he did, which, thinking clearly now, was a damn stupid assumption.

"No, I guess there isn't. I like you, Westwood, and I'm not done savoring you yet—not by a long shot."

The vise-hold worry around my heart slackens, and I can breathe easier. "Are you okay with keeping things casual?"

"As long as I'm the only one in your bed, yes."

As if I want to sleep with anyone but you, dumbass. "The same rule applies to you."

The corners of his lips curl upward. "I know."

We don't speak. We just keep staring into each other's eyes. When I feel myself falling into his blue gaze, I look away and stand from the couch. "There was only one guy before you and—"

He grins. "Really?"

I roll my eyes. "Yes, really. Anyway... I'm healthy too, but I'm not sure I'm ready to have sex without a condom. I can't end up like Gia."

Alex shivers. "We definitely don't want that."

"How about breakfast then?"

Cookie makes a noise inside his crate, letting us know he needs attention. Alex and I turn to him.

"Let's walk him first. Isn't there a pharmacy nearby? We can stop there and restock condoms," he says.

Shit. Going out to buy condoms with Alex sounds like tempting fate. I don't want people to know I'm sleeping with him... although it's probably too late to stop rumors after I paid so much money for a date with him.

"Yeah, there's a pharmacy a block from here. Let me go

change." I turn to walk away, but Alex pulls me onto his lap. "What are you doing?"

"I didn't kiss you enough." He claims my mouth again, kissing me deep and making my toes curl.

I'm breathless when he pulls back. "You don't play fair. Now I need a cold shower." A ringtone interrupts our moment. It's Alex's phone, ringing and vibrating on the coffee table. I glance over and see the caller ID. "It's your brother."

"Huh. He never calls unless it's important."

I slide off his lap so he can reach his phone.

"Hey, what's up?" he answers, already sporting furrowed brows.

Wanting to give him privacy, I go to my room. I need to change anyway if we're going to take Cookie for a walk.

I just have time to take off Alex's shirt before he knocks on my open bedroom door. I turn, startled, and use his shirt as a shield. I'm not sure why I want to hide my body from him. He's seen me naked plenty already.

"Sorry, I didn't mean to spook you. I have to go," he says, regret shining in his eyes.

"Did something happen?"

He runs his fingers through his hair, pushing it back. "Nothing serious, but yeah, I need to leave right away."

"That's okay." Realizing I'm still holding his shirt, I shorten the distance between us. "Don't forget this."

"This T-shirt will do. You hold on to my tux shirt." He leans down and kisses me softly on the lips. "I'll text you."

"Okay."

I don't move from the spot, not even to walk him out. I don't know why that is until my front door shuts, and Alex is gone. I'm unbearably disappointed, and not because we didn't get to have sex. I'm sad because he left, and I miss him already.

I miss Alex Kaminski.

CHAPTER 37
ALEX

I meet Logan at our apartment so we can ride to Dad's place together. Logan called him several times this morning, and when Dad didn't pick up, he got concerned. I am too.

We both hate going to the trailer park. It's depressing and a reminder of how far our father has fallen. He lives in a hopeless pit, and no matter how hard we try to get him out of that hole of despair, he doesn't have the will to climb out. All we can do is check on him from time to time. Mom stayed with him for as long as she could. We don't blame her for asking for a divorce.

Old Mildred, Dad's neighbor, is sitting outside her trailer smoking a cigarette when we arrive. It's her usual spot. The eighty-year-old woman keeps tabs on Dad for us.

"Good morning, Mildred," Logan and I greet her in unison.

"Morning, lads," she replies in her fake British accent.

She's been talking like that since she started watching *The Crown*.

"How's it going?" I ask.

"I cannot complain. Poor Elizabeth, though." She shakes her head. "What Philip did wasn't right."

Oh God. She's talking about people on that show as if she were friends with them.

"Did Dad get into any trouble?" Logan gets to the point.

"No. He's been awfully quiet these days. I checked on him yesterday to make sure he was still alive."

My heart shrivels into a tight ball of guilt. Maybe Logan and I have been selfish for not coming here more often. I can't speak for my twin, but I'm constantly on edge, expecting the dreadful call from Old Mildred or the police saying our father is dead.

"Thanks, Mildred," I reply.

The trailer park itself isn't the worst I've seen. Some of the trailers are in good shape, and the folks who live here aren't shady individuals. But Dad's trailer is rusty in several spots, and the little garden at the front that was there when he leased the place has long turned into a barren patch of dirt and weeds.

The hinges creak when Logan opens the door, and the stench that follows forces me to cover my nose with my hand.

"Dad?" Logan calls.

A cough comes from the bedroom. We have to navigate through a path of trash that covers most of the dingy carpeted floor. We find Dad in bed, looking more pitiful than ever. His face is flushed and sweaty, and his silver hair is matted to his forehead. His usual five-o'clock shadow has turned into a fuzzy beard. I hardly recognize him.

Logan sits on the edge of the mattress and shakes him. "Dad, wake up."

He opens his eyes but seems to have a hard time focusing.

"Dad, can you hear us?" I ask through the lump in my throat.

"Logan?" he croaks, looking at me.

"No, I'm Logan," my brother replies. "What's wrong with you?"

"It's nothing. Just a cold."

Logan presses his palm to Dad's forehead. "You're hot. I think you have a fever."

He bats his hand away. "I don't. I told you I'm fine."

A coughing fit hits him, contradicting his answer.

"Shit. We need to take you to see a doctor."

"I'm not going anywhere."

Logan looks at me, and I know what's going through his mind. *What now?*

"You need to shower, at least. You reek," I say.

"I don't care."

"We do!" Logan replies, frustrated. "And we aren't asking. You're taking a shower, or we'll hose you down."

Dad glowers at him as if that's going to change anything.

"I'm getting the hose." I turn.

"Wait! Fine. I'll shower if it means you'll leave me alone."

Logan needs to help him get out of bed, and then I join them on Dad's other side. I have to breathe through my mouth because he does smell like he's rotting. The guilt in my chest expands, making my stomach clench in response. We should have come sooner.

If I had money, I'd pay to put Dad in an assisted living facility. We can't rely on neighbors to keep an eye on him, and he clearly can't take care of himself. He's been depressed for a while.

The bathroom is tiny, and Logan and I can barely fit in there.

"We can't both help Dad in the shower. I'll start cleaning the place," I tell Logan.

"Okay. I got him."

The entire place is a pigsty, and it's hard to pinpoint which room is the worst. I start on his bedroom, so he can rest in a clean bed when he gets out of the shower. I grab the biggest garbage bag I can find and toss in all the trash, filling it up pretty fast.

Fuck. His place wasn't this bad the last time we visited. Is he hopped up on painkillers again? He's been clean for over a year, but you never know. If he's taking drugs, I don't find any evidence in his room.

The bedsheets are in such terrible condition they're not even worth washing. I hope there's a clean set because this one should be set on fire.

I find a brand-new set in the hallway closet. It's still in the packaging from the store. We bought these two months ago—I can't believe he hasn't used them yet.

Damn it, Dad.

I rub my face, frustrated with myself for being so distracted lately. Blair and hockey have been occupying most of my thoughts, and it was much easier to focus on the positive aspects of my life than to think about Dad's situation.

One thing is clear. Things have to change.

Logan and I are quiet on the way home. Dad's fever broke after his cold shower, but neither of us was happy to leave him alone.

"We need to do something about him," I say.

"I know. I'll grab a change of clothes and my laptop and go back to spend the night."

"I can come too."

"Better not. What if he's sick for days? We should alternate. I can cover tonight."

I sigh, looking out the window. "Today it's a cold. What about tomorrow? He can't live by himself."

"What do you suggest? Bring him to live with us on campus?" Logan replies, sounding frustrated.

"He needs to move to an assisted living facility."

"And he will, as soon as we sign the contract with the Miami Lions."

"If they give us contracts, it won't happen until spring," I reply, defeated. "We can't wait until then."

"I know. We'll think of something."

Since we were drafted, I've been dreaming of playing for the NHL and making real money so I can help my parents. I still want that, but signing the contract means leaving Fairbanks. I'll miss my teammates and the friendships I've forged.

And now there's something else dampening my excitement. I

don't want to leave Blair—which is crazy. She comes from a world I hate, and for a long time, I couldn't separate the person from the background. Now all I see is her, and I want her in my future. Although I can't help but think that if she saw my dad's place, she'd run for the hills. If I were smarter, I'd cut ties and stop seeing her. Even if it is just sex. But when it comes to Blair, I'm the dumbest guy in the world.

CHAPTER 38
BLAIR

Knowing I can't afford to pine for a guy I have no future with, I keep myself busy. Shower, walk Cookie, buy groceries—and lots of condoms—stop by Gia's to pick up the duffel bag I left behind at the gala, and then home to do homework. Unfortunately, I'm very good at focusing when I commit to it, and I finish everything on my to-do list by midafternoon.

I'm back in my empty apartment, staring into space and thinking about Alex. *Daydreaming* about him. His hands on my body, his kisses, the way he can unravel me with a simple look. My heart is already beating much faster, and my panties are soaked. I might need another shower—an ice-cold one.

I know Gia has plans with Noah this afternoon, and I don't want to be the third wheel. I text Ashley and Zoey and ask if they want to do something. Ashley replies that she's busy, and I don't even get a response from Zoey. She must be training.

I could use my toys, but that won't do. I have to stop obsessing about Alex, not rub one off thinking about him.

I can't stay home. There's gotta be a movie worth seeing at the theater. I pull up the listings and find the perfect distraction. A French movie that critics are raving about. That will do.

I check on Cookie to make sure he has everything he needs and then head out. Once I'm in the elevator, I notice what I'm wearing—leggings, Uggs, and a sweater dress under my tailored coat. I've been walking around like this all day, and it dawns on me that I'm dressed like what Alex dubbed as "everyone else."

The makeup I applied this morning is probably gone, and I don't care. Well, besides the red lipstick that I carry in my purse now, I reapply it as soon as I get in my car.

The movie theater is only ten minutes from my apartment, and I'm not surprised to find the parking lot packed. It's Sunday, and there's a blockbuster showing. I manage to snag a spot near the front by sheer luck, and I take that as a good sign.

I already bought my ticket online, and I don't have any interest in popcorn or candy, so I just head to the theater. As I predicted, there are only a handful of people in the room. Foreign films aren't what attracts college students, even if Hannaford U is an Ivy League school.

I choose an isolated seat all the way in the back, and to kill time, I check my phone. There are some messages in the Deltas' group chat, but now that the gala is behind us, none of them require my input.

Melody and Pippa sent separate messages asking about my date with Alex. I don't reply. They can choke on their curiosity for a little longer. I'll be hounded anyway during our next meeting; they can wait until then to get my evasive answers. Funnily, Faith didn't text me. She must be angry that I got Alex. I smile. I'm not sorry at all.

I haven't heard from him all day, and I don't know if the pang in my chest is annoyance… or hurt. I click on his name and debate sending him a text. Then a new message from him pops up, and my heart soars.

What are you up to, Westwood?

Grinning like a fool, I reply.

I'm at the movies.

Alone?

Typical Alex to assume no one would want to come to the movies with me. To be fair, no one did.

Yep.

Oh yeah? What movie are you watching?

A French one.

I expect him to have something obnoxious to say. He surprises me.

Cool. Has it started yet?

No.

What theater are you at?

My pulse quickens.

Why?

I might join you if it's okay.

My hands are shaking now, and the butterflies in my stomach are awake and having a party.

Sure. It's the movie theater near my apartment.

I'll be right there.

You don't want to know the name of the movie?

Is there more than one French movie showing today?

I don't think so.

[smirk emoji] I'll see you soon, Westwood. I hope you're wearing a skirt.

Heat spreads through my cheeks. Of course Alex wouldn't be interested in watching a French movie with me. Do I care? Not in the least.

The only issue with knowing that Alex is coming is that my gaze stays glued to the steps leading to my seat, and I can't relax. The room goes pitch black as the trailers start. I should have told him where I'm sitting. But he didn't ask, and I wanted to see if he could find me in the dark.

The opening credits begin, and there's no sign of Alex. If he doesn't show up, there will be hell to pay. I was fine being at the theater alone. Now I'm on edge, worried that he's going to stand me up.

I cave and start to type a text when someone asks, "Is this seat taken?"

Alex is towering over me, and even though I can't see his face properly, I know he's smirking.

"No," I whisper.

He sprawls into his seat like he's at home on his couch, and his left leg touches mine, setting my entire body ablaze.

"What did I miss?" he whispers.

"It just started."

He tosses his arm over my shoulders and pulls me toward him. "Come here."

I turn to him, and he captures my lips with his, kissing me like he wants to consume me. We've devoured each other's mouths hungrily before, but this feels different. I touch his cheek, tilting my head so I can drown in him.

With his free hand, he caresses my leg, going up my thigh and under my dress until he's cupping my pussy.

"Alex…" I murmur against his lips.

"You aren't wearing a skirt, Westwood. Pity."

"It's a dress. Same difference."

"You've got leggings on."

"It's cold outside."

"It's okay. I can work with these."

He presses his thumb over my clit, then makes circular motions over the fabric. Even with the barriers, it feels amazing. We keep kissing while he plays with my bundle of nerves, and the movie is quickly forgotten.

He pulls back and whispers in my ear. "I want you to ride me."

"What?" I squeak. "You want me to dry hump you in public?"

He chuckles. "You're cute, Westwood. No, I want to fuck your hot pussy in public."

My heart is beating much faster now as adrenaline mixes with desire. I've never done anything remotely daring like this.

"People could see us."

"People? What people? There's barely anyone here."

I nibble on my lower lip as I look around. He's right. Only a few seats are occupied, and none of them near us.

I look at him. "I don't have a condom on me."

Thanks to the movie on the screen, I can see his cheeky smile. "I came prepared. You're running out of arguments, Westwood."

"They aren't arguments. They're valid concerns."

His hand is still between my legs, and to make his point, he swipes his thumb left and right, sending a jolt of desire through my veins.

"You're already soaking wet, baby girl. If you don't want to ride me, that's okay. I can keep using my fingers."

It won't take much effort from him to make me come like this. But I want to take him up on his challenge. I want to experience this with Alex because I know there won't be a repeat. I'll make as many memories as I can, hoping they'll be enough to help me through a life without him.

"I want you inside of me, Alex."

He runs his fingers through my hair. "That's my girl."

He unzips his jeans and frees his massive erection. Unable to resist, I get out of my seat and kneel in front of him. "Can I taste you first?"

"You never have to ask me that, beautiful. The answer is always yes."

I curl my hands around the base and bring his cock into my mouth, swallowing it until it almost makes me choke. I know he loves when I go deep, and it's no different now. He seems to grow larger inside my mouth, and his hand is already fisting a lock of my hair.

He grunts when I increase my pace, then says, "If you keep that up, I'm coming inside your mouth."

I pull back, releasing his dick. "That won't do."

"Then you'd better replace your mouth with your pussy hole, baby girl."

I unfurl from my kneeling position and get rid of my boots so I can peel off my leggings and panties. Meanwhile, Alex fishes the condom packet from his pocket and makes quick work of getting ready for me. My heart is thumping at breakneck speed. Sure, my dress is covering my nether regions, but it's impossible to ignore that my pussy is bare in a public place.

Pushing through the nerves that are wreaking havoc on my body, I move to sit astride Alex, but he places his hands on my hips and stops me.

"Turn around, baby girl. Face the screen."

"I'm not sure I can ride you properly like that."

"Trust me. You can." His voice is thick with need, and it sends my libido shooting across the sky.

I turn toward the screen, and Alex's big hands disappear under my dress. He digs his fingers into my skin and helps me sit on him. I find his cock in the darkness and guide it to my entrance. Coincidently, the movie shows a love scene, and it's more salacious than you'd get in any American film.

Alex lowers my hips slowly, and his cock stretches me to the max. I love this new angle and how the tip of his dick hits me in a spot that's already making me see stars. The scene on the screen disappears to me as I get lost in the sensation of getting fucked by Alex.

"How are you feeling, baby girl?" he whispers in my ear.

"So good. Can you move faster?"

"I was trying not to. Your pussy is so tight, baby. You're milking me good."

"I need more. Please." Arching my back, I reach for his head.

"Ah hell. I can't say no when you beg like that."

He moves me faster, bringing my hips up and down his length with hard and precise movements. I try to help, but he wrestles control from me. "No. Let me do it."

I could fight him, but he's doing fine on his own. I close my eyes, letting go of restraints and inhibitions. I forget that anyone could turn around and see us. The risk of discovery makes everything more exciting.

"Alex…" I whisper, but all I want to do is scream his name as the orgasm shatters me to bits.

My body is shaking from head to toe and Alex is moving me so fast now I can hear our lovemaking noises over the movie theater sounds. I hope it's only me that can hear them.

Alex grunts, then bites my shoulder. The surprise pain sends another spark of pleasure down my spine, and I climax again. I grab the armrest, clutching it hard until my knuckles hurt.

He stops moving, and my body goes lax against his. I remain still, trying to catch my breath and recover the sensation in my legs. Damn. That was a wild ride.

Alex kisses the spot where he bit me. "Did I hurt you?"

"No," I murmur, then stand on shaky legs to look for my panties and leggings in the dark.

"Don't put them on yet."

"Why not?"

"We still have another hour or so of the French movie."

"And?"

"And I need a distraction."

CHAPTER 39
BLAIR

The movie is over, and I couldn't have told anyone what it was about. I was Alex's distraction, and he proved that his fingers are pure magic. He has a gift for making me come multiple times. My clit is sensitive now after so much stimulation.

"Do you wanna come back to my place?" I ask as the movie credits roll on the screen.

"I wish I could. I have to take care of some stuff."

Disappointment rushes through me, but mercifully, it's still dim in the theater and I'm hoping he doesn't notice.

I smile, even though I'm not feeling it. "That's okay. We should probably make time this week to work on our proposal for the UN."

"Yeah. I'll text you." He stands up and adds. "I should probably head out first."

A sharp pain in my chest robs me of air. We're in agreement that this is only sex, but it hurts when he's the one taking measures to not be caught in my company. Maybe he doesn't want to be seen with me in case one of his puck bunnies is in the movie theater.

It's stupid thinking. He already said he has no interest in hooking up with anyone but me. Aagh. I'm overthinking.

"Blair?" he says, getting me out of my head.

"Sorry. I spaced out for a sec. That's probably a good idea. I'll wait a bit."

He glances at the now-empty theater and then leans down and kisses me on the cheek. "See you later, Westwood."

Like a schoolgirl, I melt as giddiness overtakes me. I watch him take the steps down, and before he disappears from view, he smiles and waves at me.

Shit. Shit. Shit.

I'm falling for Alex. Or maybe it's already a done deal. Regardless, I can't believe I was fucking stupid enough to let it happen. I should stop sleeping with him, but I know I won't be able to walk away now. I'm addicted to his brand of drug.

I wait five minutes before I walk out. The movie theater is busier than before, and I'm glad I'm on my way out, not in. The big blockbuster movie must have just ended because the flux of people veering for the exit is heavier than I expect. I plan to pay a visit to the restroom but decide it can wait until I get home.

It's a slow process to get out of the corridor and into the theater's main atrium. I'm not paying attention to the crowd—my gaze is locked on the exit. But someone calls my name, and I stop to look.

It's Ashley, standing next to a lanky guy with glasses I've never seen before in my life. She's waving, and since I'm curious about her companion, I change course and head in her direction. Also, she blew me off because she was busy. Is he the reason?

"Hey, Ash. I thought you couldn't come to the movies."

Her face goes beet red. "I couldn't go when you asked."

"No worries. I doubt you'd like the French movie I saw." I turn to the guy. "I'm sorry. Where are my manners? I'm Blair."

"Oh shit. Sorry. I totally spaced you haven't met Brian yet. Brian, this is Blair, one of my closest friends."

"Nice to meet you, Blair."

"Likewise." I give Ashley a questioning glance.

"We've been seeing each other for a while," she explains.

"And you never mentioned him before?" I ask and immediately realize it's a bitchy move. Best-case scenario, it sounds like I'm complaining. Worst-case scenario, it makes it seem as if Ashley doesn't care enough about Brian to mention him to her friends.

"I was protecting Brian from the inquisition." She smirks.

"So, where did you meet?"

"Mixed-media class," Brian replies, pushing his glasses up his nose. "We got paired on an assignment."

Just like Alex and me. "It seems professors at Hannaford U also moonlight as cupids," I say.

Ashley tilts her head and squints. "Who else has started dating a classmate thanks to an assignment?"

Hell. I said too much. "It happened to one of my sorority sisters."

"Hmm." Her focus changes to something behind me. "Hey, speaking of partners, isn't that Alex?"

I turn, even though I shouldn't look. Ashley misses nothing, and I'm not sure if I can hide how Alex affects me. But my concern is moot. Alex is chatting with a couple of puck bunnies I recognize from The Heritage, and he's eating up the attention. My throat tightens to the point that I can't breathe.

I twist my face in disgust. "As usual, surrounded by his adoring fans."

"That's why I'd never date a hockey guy. They just can't help themselves."

"Noah isn't like that." I feel the need to point that out since Gia isn't here to defend her beau.

Ashley rolls her eyes. "Noah is the exception. God broke the mold when he made him."

"I didn't know you were religious, Ash," Brian chimes in.

"Born and raised Catholic. I'm not saying I'm religious, but you'll hear me make a lot of remarks related to religion. I can't help it. I've been exposed to it for too long."

Brian laughs. "It's okay. I'm not passing judgment." He turns to me. "I'm an atheist."

I'm not sure what kind of response he's looking for, but I'm too upset to come up with one.

"I'd better go," I say.

"You're not going to say hello to your *friend*?" Ashley asks, smirking.

"Pass. Nice to meet you, Brian."

I begin to move toward the exit, but then Ashley calls out, loud as fuck, "I'll see you later, Blair!"

I swear she did it on purpose. Alex hears and looks in my direction. Our gazes lock, and I don't try to hide how angry and betrayed I feel. He frowns as if he's confused. When I feel the sting of tears, I look away and hastily make my way to the exit.

I cross the street without looking, but it isn't like any cars are speeding in the parking lot. I'm glad I parked near the front—not that I expected Alex to follow me, but I wish he did.

On my way home, he texts me—and then calls me. I ignore both, which is hard for me to do. My issues with not answering calls and texts are legendary.

At home, I take a quick shower to erase all traces of Alex from my skin. I don't need any reminders of our rendezvous. It's past six already, and I haven't eaten much all day. I'm not hungry, but I should eat. I do need to take Cookie out, so I might as well grab food while we walk.

It's already mighty cold, so I put on the thickest winter coat I own, a long white puffer jacket. Once I pair it with the bright-red scarf and ear mittens, I look like a snowman. I also dress Cookie in a fleece hoodie before heading out. The puppy is as happy as he can be, excited with the prospect of fun times outside, even if the temperature isn't pleasurable. His enthusiasm is contagious, and even though my heart took a hit today, being with him is helping.

Outside, I shiver. The forecast predicted snow tonight, and I can sense it in the air. It's about time. I don't care for the cold, but Christmas isn't the same if it isn't white.

"Come on, boy. Let's get going before we freeze our tushies." I tug on Cookie's leash, but instead of heading toward the park, where I usually take him, I veer toward the street of shops.

The shops are just a block away, but Cookie wants to stop and sniff every corner. When we finally get there, he's marked his territory several times. I'm freezing despite my warm coat, so I'm not fussy about dinner. I buy a small pizza from the little hole-in-the-wall pizza bar. It's a to-go-only place, not a sit-down, but the pizza is delicious. I'm lucky there isn't a line tonight. Maybe it's too cold for most people to venture out.

I'm on my way home five minutes later. I don't bother running since the pizza will be cold no matter how fast I go. But as I start to leave the shops behind, a dark figure steps in front of me, forcing me to a sudden stop. I gasp, then look around. There's no one in sight. Shit. Am I about to get mugged?

"Hello, Blair."

The man steps into the streetlight, allowing me to see his face. It's Ilya.

"You scared me."

"I'm sorry. I didn't mean to startle you. I saw you from across the street and rushed over to say hello."

Ryder's intent to get Alex and me to leave the club in Boston in a hurry comes to the forefront of my mind. My spooked heart was already beating at an accelerated pace; now it's running at breakneck speed. Ilya showing up in my neighborhood isn't a coincidence.

"What are you doing in Fairbanks?"

"I have a business meeting early tomorrow morning. I figured it'd be easier to come tonight."

"And you're staying somewhere close?"

He rubs the back of his neck, looking sheepish. But his personality is too cold and calculating, and I don't buy the act.

"Actually, I'm looking to invest in rental properties, and your mother mentioned there are some apartments for sale in your building. I came to check it out."

My blood runs cold. Of course my mother would have something to do with Ilya's presence here. The idea that he might own an apartment in the same building I live in sends chills of dread down my spine. My sixth sense is telling me this guy is bad news.

"Oh, well. I'd better get going."

"Can I walk you to your apartment?"

"There's no need. This is a safe neighborhood, and my place is just around the corner."

If he says he'll feel better if he tags along, there's really nothing I can do.

"If you're sure... have a good evening, Blair. I'll see you soon."

"See me soon?"

One corner of his mouth twitches upward in a sinister smirk. "Your parents' Christmas gathering? It's coming up, isn't it?"

A lump gets stuck in my throat, and my tongue feels thick in my mouth. "Yes, that's right," I croak.

"I can't wait." He turns around and walks away.

I can't move from my spot, caught in a mini panic attack. My mother has been awfully quiet lately. After I disappeared from her previous party, her MO should have been to hound me and tell me how disappointed she was in me. She hasn't done that, which means she's planning a nasty surprise for me, and my gut tells me Ilya is involved.

Oh my God. What if *that's* who my parents want me to marry? I feel sick just contemplating the idea. From a physical standpoint, I could do much worse, but his handsome face can't mask his black heart. I know deep in my bones that Ilya isn't to be trusted. Ryder seems to have the same aversion to the man, and he knows him better than I do.

Cookie tugs on his leash, tired of standing still. I force myself to move, and a couple steps in, I'm striding as fast as I can. By the time I get to my building, my heart is racing, only to find another tall figure waiting for me. Alex.

I forget that I'm supposed to be angry at him and run into his arms.

"Blair. What's wrong?" He holds me tight against his chest.

"Nothing."

"Bullshit. Something happened. You're shaking."

"I'm cold."

"Let's get inside then."

He punches in the code to open the door, and keeping me glued to his side, he steers me into the building. He doesn't ask again what happened, but he stares at me while we wait for the elevator. I pretend I don't notice and keep my gaze glued to the metal door.

Inside the elevator, he punches my floor number and turns to me. "Your lips are blue. How long were you outside?"

"Not that long. What are you doing here?"

He doesn't answer. The elevator dings, announcing we've arrived at my floor. We walk in silence down my hallway, and only after we're in my apartment does he reply. "I came because you weren't picking up your phone."

"You called once. That hardly warrants an in-person visit." I set the pizza box on the kitchen counter, avoiding eye contact.

"I called you several times."

"I didn't get any other calls." I touch my jacket pocket and find it empty. Then I spot my phone lying on the coffee table. "I guess I forgot to bring my phone with me."

"So you weren't avoiding my calls?" He sounds unsure, and it's a tone so unusual for him that I look at his face.

His expression of uncertainty and fear takes me by surprise. "Would you care if I was?"

He frowns. "Of course I would care. I got the impression you were angry with me when you left the theater."

I wasn't angry. I was hurt, but I'm not telling you that. "Nonsense. Why would I be angry?"

"Because I was talking to a couple of girls."

I take off my gloves, then my coat. "That'd be crazy, Alex. You aren't my boyfriend."

"I know, but I told you I'd be exclusive with you while we're fooling around, and I meant it, Blair. You don't need to worry about me going with other girls."

"I'm not worried." I open the lid of the pizza box, hiding from him that I *was* worried back in the theater.

"I saw Ashley and figured you didn't want her to know we were there together. So yes, I was flirting with those two girls because that's my MO... or it used to be."

"You don't need to explain yourself to me." But my heart is enjoying it very much. Stupid muscle.

"I know, but I want you to know just the same." He walks over and pinches my chin between his thumb and index finger, turning my face to his. "Are we good?"

I let him capture my gaze with his intense blue eyes, and I soon get lost in them. "Yes, we're good."

"All right. Now tell me what got you spooked."

I step back, turning my face away. "I already told you it was nothing. I heard a branch crack, and it startled me. I got pizza. It's small, so I'm hoping you're not too hungry."

I sense his scrutinizing stare burning a hole in my face, but I refuse to acknowledge it.

"I can't stay. I just came to check on you."

"Oh? Okay."

He pulls me into an embrace, circling his arms around my waist. "Don't look so disappointed, Westwood. I think I gave you enough orgasms to last you through the night." He leans down and kisses me softly, but it's too quick for my liking. "I'll see you tomorrow."

CHAPTER 40
ALEX

As soon as I step out of Blair's building, I call Logan for an update on Dad.

"Hey," he answers, sounding tired.

"How is it going?"

"Dad went to sleep after he ate the soup I made. He's fever-free, but I'm spending the night."

"I can come ov—"

"And sleep where? That old couch barely fits one person. It's fine, Alex. You can spend the night tomorrow if Dad isn't better by then."

"Okay. But call me if you need anything."

"You got it. Try to rest. You might need it tomorrow. Talk later."

"Bye." I end the call and look left and right before I cross the street.

There's a car approaching, so I put my beanie on as I wait. It's cold enough to freeze balls. The car slows down, and I can see it's a Ferrari. Damn. That's a sexy car. But I don't spend much time appreciating the Italian craftsmanship of the vehicle because the window is down… and the person behind the steering wheel is none other than Ilya Bolkosky.

Our gazes lock, but before I can say anything, he brings the window up and speeds down the street. What the fuck is he doing here? I glance at Blair's apartment building, and then it dawns on me why she was spooked earlier. She must have seen him or maybe even talked to him.

The snow that was forecast finally begins to fall in small flurries. That'd be a sight to bring a smile to my face, but I'm too worried about Blair to be amused by the weather. I rub my chin, debating going back to her apartment to ask about Ilya. But she didn't want to tell me—what makes me think she would now? She doesn't seem to know much about him either. But there's one person who does. Her brother.

It's a little after seven. If Ryder hasn't changed his habits, I know exactly where he'll be. I run to my car, hoping he's still as strict about his workout schedule as he used to be when he was on the team.

The ride to the gym complex just off campus takes five minutes from Blair's apartment. Hannaford U offers several gyms, but Ryder always preferred to work out in the luxurious facility that looks more like a spa than a mere gym.

The parking lot is half-empty, which makes it easy for me to spot his car parked near the entrance. A million years ago, he gave me a guest pass that had five visits included. I came only once and decided it wasn't my scene.

I scan the card to gain access, glad that it hasn't expired. I don't have a duffel bag with me, and I'm not wearing workout clothes, but the guy at the front barely glances in my direction.

There's a café to the right of the entrance, and I see a few people who came here to work on their laptops instead of working out. Rich people are fucking weird.

It's a four-story building with a heated swimming pool on the roof. The weight-lifting machines are on the second floor, so that's where I head. I just hope Ryder isn't done with his workout yet and isn't in the sauna. I'm not having this conversation with him naked, save for a towel wrapped around my waist.

The weight-lifting room takes up the entire second floor, and it's a fucking dream, with the best machines on the market. It doesn't take long to locate Ryder. He's doing bench presses, but like the cocky motherfucker that he is, he doesn't have anyone spotting him.

I position myself behind him and grab the bar, keeping it pressed against his chest.

"What the fuck are you doing?" he asks.

"I came for a little chat."

"This isn't funny, Alex." He tries to push the bar up, but he can't budge it while I'm holding it down.

"Do you see me laughing? I want to know why you begged me to take Blair away from the club in Boston."

"She had no business being there. That club isn't a place for her."

"Bullshit. We were there for Gia's birthday party, and everyone had a great time."

His eyes narrow when I mention Gia's name. "I'm sure you did."

"Did you ask us to leave because of your buddy Ilya?"

The change in his expression is like night and day. The aggravation gives way to concern. "Why are you asking about Ilya?"

"Because I caught him driving by Blair's apartment just now. What's his deal?"

Ryder's pupils dilate, and then his Adam's apple bobs up and down as he swallows hard. "Release me, and we'll talk."

"Are you going to tell me the truth?"

"Yeah."

I help him raise the bar onto its supports and step back. Ryder sits up, shoulders hunched, and dries his face off with a white towel. When he's done, he stares into space, saying nothing.

"I don't have all night," I grit out. "Is Blair in danger?"

He whips his face to mine. "Maybe. Has she told you about her deal with our mother?"

My stomach churns. "The one where she needs to throw away her life in an arranged marriage?"

"Yes. Ilya's family is powerful, and they want to strengthen their relationship with my father. Marrying into the family would give them the hold they've been after."

"Your mother wants Blair to *marry* that guy?" My voice rises.

"No. For all her flaws, the last thing my mother wants is to see Blair marry into the Bolkosky family. Hence why she's been shoving suitors down Blair's throat for the past couple of months. But now Ilya has taken an interest in Blair and…" He looks away, pushing his hair back with his hand. "It's all my fucking fault."

"Why is this your fault?"

"I fucked up. I tried to outsmart them, but all I did was allow them to sink their claws deeper into my family."

"You're not making any sense. Who are they?"

He meets my stare. "Dangerous people, Alex. We can't let Blair marry that son of a bitch."

My pulse quickens while jealousy and rage mix in my guts. "How can we stop it? Blair is dead set on fulfilling your mother's wishes. She's too afraid to give up the money."

Ryder's face contorts in anger. "Is *that* what you think? Blair doesn't care about money or status."

"Then why can't she tell your mother to take a hike?"

Turmoil and guilt shine in his eyes. What the fuck is he hiding? He turns away first. "Blair isn't who you think she is, Alex."

She definitely isn't who I thought she was. If it isn't about money, then... fuck. I can't believe the possibility didn't occur to me until now.

"Your mother has another hold on Blair, doesn't she?"

He doesn't answer, and I can almost see the gears working in his head. He's weighing the pros and cons of telling me the truth. Finally, the words whoosh out of him in a sigh of defeat. "Yes, but you have to ask Blair about it. I can't tell you."

"You can't or won't?"

He laughs without humor. "Is there a difference?"

"When it comes to you, I guess not. How do you propose we stop Blair from marrying Ilya or anyone else?"

Ryder arches one of his brows. "Anyone else? Why do you care, Alex? Are you in love with my sister?"

Fuck. How did Ryder jump to that conclusion so fast?

"You're out of your mind. Blair and I are just having fun."

"Blair doesn't have casual fun. If she let you into her bed, you mean something to her."

I don't dare to believe Blair might have feelings for me. Hell. I'm acting like a fucking simp. "You don't know your sister as well as you think."

His lips curl into a sardonic smirk. "And you do?"

"I probably know her better than you do."

"Maybe, but that doesn't change the fact you care about my sister. For the sake of the friendship we once had, I'm begging you to keep an eye on her, Kaminski."

"What? You want me to play her bodyguard?"

"Don't stand there and pretend it's going to be a chore for you."

I clench my jaw hard, buying time to think of a clever retort, but I don't come up with any. He figured me out already.

"And how do you plan to stop Blair from getting engaged to Ilya?"

"I'll think of something."

"You just said you already fucked up once. You're clearly in over your head. I need to know what we're dealing with. Who are the Bolkoskys?"

His gaze turns cold when it locks with mine. "The less you know, the better."

"Bullshit. I need to be prepared."

He stands up. "This conversation is over. Go home, Alex. You're about to get everything you ever wanted."

"You don't know what I want!"

"Really? Are you saying you don't want to play for the NHL? I hear the Miami Lions are going to offer you and Logan contracts at the end of the season."

"Hockey isn't everything."

"It used to be," he replies, solemn, and I don't know if we're still talking about me.

He walks away, and I let him. I got all the information I could from him. He won't say more.

He's wrong about one thing though. Playing in the NHL is no longer everything I've ever wanted. There's one more thing, and I'm about to lose her.

CHAPTER 41
BLAIR

I know something is wrong when I don't wake up before my alarm. I'm so used to being up before six on weekdays that I set my alarm only because I'm a freak. As I try to get out of bed, my entire body hurts and my throat is on fire. Hell. I cannot be sick.

When I trudge to the bathroom, I realize it might be too late. Lack of energy and sore muscles. I'm already sick, and looking at my reflection in the mirror, I confirm it. My skin is pasty and has a green hue. I touch my forehead. No fever yet.

Maybe I'll feel better after I take a hot shower and eat breakfast.

Wishful thinking. I feel worse, and I manage to eat only a couple of spoonfuls of cereal with milk. I fill my glass with OJ and walk to the window. The sky is gray, and down below, the street is covered by a thin layer of snow.

Cookie scratches the door of his crate, trying to get my attention. I need to walk him. I haven't hired a new dog walker yet. But the idea of putting on clothes and heading into the cold isn't appealing in the least.

"I wish you were a cat with a litter box."

He barks once as if he understands me.

I drink half the orange juice and then put on my Ugg boots, my puffy jacket, and a thick beanie. I can't be bothered with makeup. Never mind that I'm wearing fleece pj's underneath my coat. At this hour, who am I going to see?

I grab Cookie's leash first and then get him out of his crate. He jumps on my legs, all excited, and it's a pity I can't reciprocate. I just want to crawl back into bed and sleep.

"Come on, buddy. This will be a quick outing." I put on his tiny vest and head out.

ALEX

The first thing I do when I wake up is send Blair a text. It's a little past six, so I don't expect an immediate reply. Then I text Logan for a Dad update.

> He's doing much better. I think we caught the end of whatever he had.

> Good. Are you coming to practice?

> I'll meet you at the arena.

I go about my morning routine, which includes walking puppy Blair. Then I head to the arena for the early morning practice on the ice. I always feel better after a good hockey sesh, but today, my mind is miles away, and the heaviness in my chest doesn't relent. At least I don't have to worry about Dad being sick anymore.

"What's the matter with you, Alex?" Assistant Coach LaRue asks when I fail to block Logan in the offensive zone.

"It's nothing."

"Bullshit. You're distracted. Get your head in the game."

"Yes, sir."

Logan skates by me. "Are you okay, bro?"

"I'm fine," I grumble.

"I'll believe you when you join us on the ice."

I shove him away from me, but the idiot just laughs. I want to tell him about my conversation with Ryder, but we didn't have time to talk before practice. It's also not a topic I want to discuss in the locker room.

Half an hour later, we're walking out of the arena. CJ and Noah are bickering about something unimportant, and Sean is trying to play referee. I hold Logan back, letting the guys walk ahead.

"What's up, bro?" Logan asks.

"I went to see Ryder last night," I whisper, not wanting the guys to hear us.

His brows shoot up. "How did that conversation go?"

He's not asking if I punched Ryder in the face. That's a good sign.

"You know Ryder. When he wants to keep a secret, it's impossible to get anything out of him."

"Yeah, he's a fucking clam."

"But I got enough out of him to piece together a theory."

Logan raises an eyebrow. "I'm listening."

"I think his family is doing business with people they shouldn't, and he got caught in the middle. It might be why he quit the team."

"Does that surprise you? His father is a heartless prick."

"It doesn't surprise me. And I know Ryder can handle himself. The issue is, I'm afraid Blair will also be a victim of her father's sins."

Logan's eyes widen. "Ah, that's why you were distracted today. You're worried about her."

There's no point denying the obvious. "Yeah."

"Tell me, bro. When did you fall for her?"

I blink fast, stunned that Logan figured the truth out so

quickly, when I tried my best to hide it from him. "I don't know."

He whistles. "I can't believe my little bro fell in love."

"You're only two minutes older than me. Stop calling me little bro. You know I hate it."

He throws his arm around my shoulder. "And that's why I do it."

I elbow his side, stepping away from him. "You're an ass."

He laughs. "I guess I've lost my wingman."

"I'm not sure about that. Blair and I aren't on the same page."

He gives me a quizzical look. "Are you saying you haven't managed to woo her yet with your charms? I don't believe it."

"*Woo* her? Who talks like that?"

He shrugs, adjusting his duffel bag strap over his shoulder. "I do when I'm feeling inspired."

I shake my head. "You're ridiculous. Let's forget for a second that I've fallen for the only girl in this school who doesn't want a serious relationship with me."

"Aren't you a bit cocky?"

"Am I?"

"Nah. You're right. But they're all interested in the hockey player image, not the real person. Hence why I don't give them a second thought. I get my fill and move on."

I used to be like that, until Blair. Maybe because she's the only one who sees the man underneath the hockey uniform.

"I think she might be in danger," I say.

That wipes the amusement from his face. "How so? Because of her father's dealings with unsavory people?"

"Yes. Ryder is freaking out."

"Well then, we need to find a way to protect her."

"You're offering to help?"

He looks at me as if my question is insane. "You're my brother, and you care about her. Now tell me everything."

It was hard telling Logan that Blair agreed to an arranged marriage to appease her family and that Ilya Bolkosky might be the groom. I knew he was judging her, just like I had done. But he never said anything out loud. And he also didn't tease me about it. He would have if he didn't know how I felt about her.

I haven't heard from Blair since I sent her the message this morning. I called her too, but it went straight to voice mail. I try to convince myself she isn't in immediate danger. If her parents' plan is to marry her off to Ilya, then he won't harm her. But why the hell was he in her neighborhood last night?

It's almost time for McNelis's class, and I still haven't heard from her. The worry keeps growing with every minute that passes, and I'm quickly losing my mind.

When she doesn't show up, I know something is wrong. She never misses a lecture. I can't stay. I jump out of my seat, earning the professor's attention.

"Is there something wrong, Alex?"

"I'm sorry, sir. I have to leave."

I'm acting impulsively, blowing off class like a damn Romeo in distress. The conversation with Ryder set me on edge. And now Blair is a no-show. I don't want to think those events are related, but it's hard not to.

I get to her place in record time and don't bother to buzz her apartment. The code to her building is imprinted in my brain, and I'll keep using it until she asks me to stop.

But getting into her apartment is another matter since I don't have a key. I ring the doorbell, and when that doesn't work, I knock on the door hard. "Blair, are you there?"

I hear Cookie barking, but that doesn't mean she's inside. I should have looked for her car in the parking lot. The sound of a lock releasing makes me sigh in relief. But when Blair opens the door and I see the way she looks, I'm back to worrying.

"Alex? What are you doing here?" she croaks.

"You didn't answer my text and you didn't show up for class."

"I'm sick. You should leave." She tries to shut the door in my face, but I press a palm against it.

"I won't go. You look like hell."

"Gee, thanks."

"Come on, Blair. Let me in." *Let me take care of you.*

She opens the door wider. "Fine. If you get sick, don't blame me."

"What are your symptoms?" I take off my jacket and hang it on the coat rack by the door.

"Sore throat, headache, and my body aches as if I've been run over by a truck." She collapses on the couch and wraps a thick blanket around her body.

"What about fever?"

"I don't know. I can't find my thermometer."

I walk over and touch her forehead. "You're burning up. Where do you keep your medicine?"

"The cabinet in my bathroom."

I go retrieve a fever med, and I can't help but feel relieved that she wasn't at school because she caught a cold. It's better than the crazy scenarios I conjured up in my head.

It isn't my intention to snoop, but maybe she didn't find her thermometer because she was too sick to look. I search her drawer and the cabinet under the sink. I don't find it, but it's impossible to miss the big new box of condoms. A smile tugs the corners of my lips. When she gets better, I'll make sure we go through those quickly.

I return to the living room to give Blair the fever medicine. She looks absolutely pitiful with the blanket now over her head, reminding me of how my father looked yesterday. Shit. What if I gave her what he had? I didn't get sick, but it's possible I was carrying the virus.

"Here. Take these." I give her two pills and a glass of water.

She winces when she swallows. "I can't even take a sip. This is hell."

"Come on. It's just a cold. You're acting like a baby."

She glares at me, and with the blanket covering her head, she looks like a little demon from medieval times.

"I can't afford to get sick," she grits out.

"Are you worried about school?"

"Yes, plus all the nonsense family activities my mother expects me to participate in. I'm dreading the to-do list. And there's Riley and Jesse's wedding." Her eyes widen. "And our UN proposal," she shrieks.

I touch her arm. "Calm down. Getting worked up about all those things won't make you get better faster."

"It's easy for you to say. You aren't sick." She scooches away from me. "You really shouldn't touch me."

"Relax. If I was going to get sick, I would be already."

"You don't know that."

"I might have given it to you."

She furrows her brows. "How? Were you sick and didn't tell me?"

"No. I went to see my dad before I met you at the movies. He was sick, but he's better today."

"Oh. I didn't know he lived in Fairbanks."

My face warms, and I hope I'm not red. "Yeah."

"What's wrong?"

I shake my head. "It's nothing."

"What about your mother?"

"She lives in Midland, Michigan. It's where Logan and I were born. My grandparents still live there as well."

"How long have they been divorced?"

"A couple years, but God knows they should have separated way before that."

"I'm sorry. At least they did. My parents will never split, even though they don't love each other anymore. I'm not sure they ever did, to be honest."

"Was theirs an arranged marriage too?"

She looks away. "Yes."

"And are you sure that's the life you want for yourself?"

"I don't want that life, Alex. That's why I pour myself into being the best at school. I want a career, independence. I don't want to ever depend on anyone for anything."

"Then why are you going along with this charade?"

She closes her eyes and lies down. "I don't want to talk about this."

I watch her for a few beats, wrestling with the feelings in my chest. I wish she'd open up to me. What's so horrible that she can't say it?

"You can tell me anything, Blair. You can trust me."

"It's not a matter of trusting you. Just let it go, Alex."

I sigh. "Okay, baby girl. Rest then. I'll take Cookie out for a walk."

"Where's your puppy?" she asks with her eyes still closed. "You should have brought her."

"Logan has her. Maybe next time. Go to sleep."

"Okay."

I don't move from my spot for a while because I'm busy watching her. Blair is so out of it that she doesn't notice I'm still there. The ache in my chest flares up. Damn it. I do love her, and I'm terrified I'm going to lose her before I even have her.

CHAPTER 42
BLAIR

I don't know where I am at first. My brain is mush as if it's filled with cotton candy, and I'm hot and sweaty. I shove the blanket covering my body aside and try to focus. I'm in my living room. I must have fallen asleep on my couch. A clanking noise coming from the kitchen tells me I'm not alone. I sit up slowly because everything hurts, including my head. Alex is in my kitchen, cooking. That's a sight I'll never forget. Maybe I'm hallucinating.

"What are you doing?" I ask, but I sound like a frog.

"You're up."

"How long have I been sleeping?" I glance at the window. It's dark outside already.

"A few hours. I'm making chicken soup. I hope you can eat."

"You're cooking for me?"

He checks the contents of the pan, then walks over. "Yes, Westwood. I am."

"Why?"

"Because you're sick."

Warmth spreads through my chest, and it has nothing to do with the cold. A hummingbird seems to be trapped there, or it's my heart that's fluttering.

"You're taking care of me?"

"Yes." He flattens his palm against my forehead. "Your fever is gone."

Tears fill my eyes, but I don't want him to see them. "That's very... thoughtful."

He chuckles. "That's something you never thought I could be, huh?"

"It *is* a surprise. Thank you."

"Your clothes are drenched. You should probably take a shower before you eat."

I wrinkle my nose. Jesus. I must look like roadkill. I hate that Alex is here to witness it. "Yeah. I'll do that."

I get up, but the room begins to spin, forcing me to sit down again.

"Are you all right?"

"No. I'm woozy."

He reaches for my arm. "I'll help you. Lean on me."

"I don't want to lean on you. I'm disgusting."

He laughs. "Come on, Blair. Do you think I care you're a little sticky?"

"Well, I care."

"I've seen you dirtier than you are now."

Blush creeps up my cheeks. "That doesn't count. You were in the same state."

"Would it make you feel better if I broke a sweat? I can do some jumping jacks and push-ups."

"Ha ha. You're hilarious. Can you just hold my hand?"

"Sure."

He helps me off the couch and then walks me to my bathroom. "Are you going to be okay taking a shower on your own?"

"I should be able to manage."

"Okay. Holler if you need help, and please leave the door open."

"I will. Now go before you burn dinner." I shoo him away with my hand.

I'm touched by what Alex is doing for me. No one has ever taken care of me when I was sick without getting paid. As a child, I had a nanny who looked after me whenever I got a cold, and as a teen and an adult, I suffered through any illness alone.

This isn't something a mere hookup would do. I need to protect myself from Alex. If he wants more, I can't give it to him, even though I want to.

In the shower, I allow misery to take over and let the tears fall. I'm being weak, but… fuck it. I'm sick. I think I'm falling for Alex. What will I do if the same thing happens to him? I told him. He knows what's in my future. I have to put an end to this, especially now that Ilya is in the picture. He's the one my parents want me to marry, I'm certain of it, and he doesn't strike me as a guy who'll tolerate competition.

The shower does help clear the fog in my brain, but it doesn't ease the heaviness in my chest. I'll ask Alex to leave after dinner. The more time we spend together, the harder it will be to let him go. I steel myself, erect the barriers around my heart… but all the protection is for nothing. The moment he looks at me and smiles as if I'm the most precious thing in the world, I'm disarmed. I want him so much I can barely breathe.

"Dinner is ready," he says.

I go to him, wishing I could kiss him. I obviously don't want to give him my germs, so I settle for hugging him. "Thank you."

He hugs me back. I press my cheek against his chest and can hear his accelerated heartbeat. "You're welcome, Westwood."

"Don't call me that."

"All right. You're welcome, baby girl."

I ease back and glance up. "What are we doing, Alex?"

He takes a deep breath, and his gaze intensifies. It's like he's searching for something. "I want more, Blair."

My breath gets caught in my throat. "I want more too. But—"

He presses his index finger against my lips. "No buts. Not tonight. Let us have this moment."

"I'd fight you on this, but I'm sick," I quip.

He caresses my face, smiling softly. "I know. You need to eat because I want you feeling better as soon as possible."

"Okay, boss."

"Hmm, I like how agreeable you are." He boops my nose.

I step away from his embrace before I melt. "Don't get used to it."

He turns his attention to the pan on the stove. "This is a recipe from my mother. It'll cure you in no time."

I laugh. "I don't believe chicken soup truly has medicinal properties."

"This is a special one." He winks.

I tilt my head. "Why? Because it was made with love?"

My reply was meant as a joke, but when Alex turns all shades of red, I know that's what he is thinking.

"Yes," he croaks, then clears his throat. "That's the secret ingredient."

My heart is hammering against my chest, at war now with my head. I know I'll have to let common sense win, but tonight, I'm letting my emotions run the show. I sit on the counter and watch Alex fill a bowl with soup and slide it toward me.

"Do you want a piece of bread?" he asks.

"Sure."

He takes a baguette out of the package and cuts a couple slices. "I didn't have that at home," I say.

"I know. I stopped by the market when I took Cookie out for a walk."

"You really didn't need to go through all that trouble."

"It wasn't any trouble at all. Besides, I feel guilty that you're sick because of me."

"We can't know that for sure. There were a lot of people at the movie theater. I could have caught the cold from someone there."

"Maybe." He grabs a bowl of soup for himself and a lot of bread to go with it and sits next to me.

"I'm feeling somewhat better. We could maybe work on our UN project."

"Blair, you really need to learn to take it easy. You should rest."

I focus on my soup. "Right. And you probably need to get home."

"I don't."

I turn to him. "Do you want to spend the night?"

"I'd feel better if I did. But if you want me to go, I will."

Tell him to go home, you idiot.

"I want you to stay."

He smiles, and there I go again, melting at the sight.

Blair, you're a total goner.

CHAPTER 43
BLAIR

Alex did spend the night, but not in my bed. I didn't want him near me in case I started to hack with coughs or if I developed a fever in the middle of the night. I'm not ready for that type of intimacy. I am feeling much better this morning, and if I did have a fever last night, I didn't notice. Alex is sleeping on the couch, so before I jump in the shower, I check on him. He's still sound asleep, but it's only five in the morning.

I'm not one-hundred-percent recovered, but I'm well enough to attend classes today. I take my time in the shower now that I'm strong enough to stand for a prolonged period. Then I spend extra time preening in front of the mirror—blow-drying my hair and putting on makeup. I want to erase that disgusting, sick version of myself from Alex's memory. But when it comes to making clothing decisions, I'm stumped. He likes when I don't dress like a pampered princess, but dressing casually isn't really my style. I feel better when I'm wearing pretty dresses, colorful tights, and heels.

My gaze snags on the short plaid dress I wore in DC. It was the first time I realized Alex really had a thing for me. There was the incident in Boston, but up to that point, I had dismissed our moment as a drunken encounter without meaning.

I take the dress out, deciding this is what I'm going to wear. But I don't put on tights yet. Maybe I can convince Alex that I'm not sick anymore and bedroom activities can be resumed.

When I walk out of my room, the hallway bathroom door is closed, and I hear the sound of the shower. I smile. He also decided to freshen up before I saw him. I take more vitamin C with my OJ, then grab all the berries Alex bought yesterday. I usually drink coffee first thing in the morning, but since there might be kissing in the near future, I put a hold on the caffeine. No one likes coffee breath.

Five minutes later, I have a spread of healthy breakfast foods in front of me, and that's when Alex walks out of the bathroom. My heart skips a beat. I'll never get used to how sexy this man is and how blind I was to his looks until recently.

"Good morning." I greet him with a smile.

"Good morning, beautiful. How are you feeling?"

"Much better. You were right. Your mother's chicken soup recipe is miraculous."

"I told you so." He wraps his arms around my waist and leans down for a kiss.

I sigh against his mouth, melting into his body. His tongue tastes like minty toothpaste, and the scruff on his face tickles. I love it all. He pulls back too soon and studies me for a couple beats without saying anything. It makes me self-conscious. Maybe I didn't do a good job hiding my still-too-pale face.

I step back. "What?"

"Nothing. Just appreciating the view."

Cheeks warm? Check. Accelerated pulse? Check. Why am I getting flustered from receiving a compliment from him?

I look away first. "Anyway, I didn't know what you wanted for breakfast, so I have fruits and toast, but I can make scrambled eggs."

"You don't need to cook for me. Besides, I don't want you exerting yourself."

"I already told you I feel fine."

"Even so."

His phone rings on the coffee table. "It's Logan. Let me get that."

"It's cute that you have a specific ringtone for your brother."

"All my friends have different ringtones."

"Oh yeah? What's mine?" I tease, not expecting him to have actually assigned me a ringtone unless it's a doomsday-type sound, like the Darth Vader theme song.

"'Style' by Taylor Swift." He smirks.

Another lurch inside my chest. It's getting harder and harder to remember I made the decision yesterday to put a stop to our thing. In fact, I completely ignored that detail when I woke up this morning and buffed myself into prettiness just to impress him.

"Hey," he answers the phone. "No, I haven't checked my email yet."

A moment later, his eyes bug out. "No way! For real?"

He sounds super excited now. Then he punches the air. "Yes! It's finally our time, bro."

I pop a strawberry in my mouth and watch him. It's my turn to appreciate the view.

"I'm still at Blair's." His gaze meets mine, and he smiles. "Yeah, I'll see you soon."

Once he puts the phone away, I ask. "What was that all about?"

He walks around the kitchen island, takes me in his arms, and lifts me off the floor. "Come here." His mouth slants over mine possessively, setting fire to my veins. I let him take control, and it's the most exhilarating thing to be able to taste his happiness on my tongue.

But I need to know what happened, so I pull back. "Are you going to tell me what Logan wanted?"

"Our agent called last night. The Miami Lions have offered Logan and me entry-level contracts for three years."

"Oh my God. That's huge! Congratulations."

"Thank you." He sets me down. "When Logan and I entered the draft, we knew the chances we'd end up playing for the same team at the beginning of our careers were close to zero. I was picked thirty-four overall, and he was thirty-six."

"I don't understand how the NHL draft works."

"Teams get priority picking players based on how they performed in the previous season. Teams who did poorly get the first picks."

"Shouldn't it be the other way around?"

He shakes his head. "No. If that were the case, teams with the strongest players would always end up on top. The system makes sure teams can turn things around."

"Gotcha."

"Logan was first drafted by the Toronto Destroyers, but after the pick, they made an exchange with the Miami Lions. That's how we ended up on the same team."

"I bet the Lions' marketing department already has an entire campaign around the fact that you're identical twins."

"Yeah. And Joanne is lining up sponsorship deals for us. It's gonna be crazy."

"I'm really happy for you. But what about school and the Warriors?"

His smile wilts, making my stomach clench. "The moment we sign the contract, we aren't eligible to play for Hannaford U anymore."

"So you're going to leave midseason?"

He shakes his head. "No. We'll sign the contracts once this season is over. It's not set in stone until the ink is dry, but at least now we know there are contracts on the table."

A lump the size of Texas forms in my throat. I want to be one-hundred-percent happy that his dreams are coming true, but a small and selfish part of me wishes he wasn't leaving at the end of spring semester.

"You look sad," he says.

"What? That's crazy. I'm not sad." I look away. "Besides, with you gone, there's no competition for the number one spot on the Dean's list."

He touches my lower back, sending rivulets of desire down my spine. "Blair... I don't wanna waste the time I have left here at Hannaford U playing silly games and pretending I'm okay with our arrangement."

I close my eyes, wishing I was free to give my heart to him. "You know I can't offer you more."

"Yes, you can." He turns me around, and with his index finger, he tilts my chin up, forcing me to make eye contact with him. "Look into my eyes and tell me you don't feel the connection between us. I dare you."

I open my mouth to do just that, but the words get lodged in my throat. "It doesn't matter how I feel."

He releases my chin and captures my face with his hands. "It's the only thing that matters, baby girl."

He sweeps in for the kill, slanting his lips over mine. His kiss is savage and hungry, making my bones melt and my skin yearn for his touch. He lifts me off the floor, his big hands clutching my ass under my dress. I wrap my legs around his hips, pressing my pussy against the erection I can feel through our clothes.

"I need you, baby girl. Tell me you want me. Tell me I'm not alone in feeling this way," he begs between feverish kisses.

"I want you, Alex. So damn much, I can't think straight."

"Then don't think."

He strides to my bedroom, and together we fall onto my bed. My dress is already bunched up at my waist, and my panties are soaked through. Alex kneels between my legs and reaches for the back of his T-shirt, pulling it off in the next second. He messes up his damp hair in the process, making himself even sexier, if that's possible. I sit up, wanting to touch every inch of his exposed body. His skin is smooth, and I can't resist drawing my tongue across his chest and playing with his nipple.

He grabs a fistful of my hair, pulling my mouth away from him. "You drive me wild, baby girl. You're all I think about. I want to fuck you every moment I'm awake, and when I sleep, I'm deep inside your pussy in my dreams."

"Then shut up and do it already."

"I shouldn't... you're recovering." I grab his arms and dig my long nails into his biceps. "Ouch!"

"You're not going to get me all hot and bothered and then back down. It isn't fair. And I can take you, Alex. I already told you I feel fine."

He rubs his thumb over my lips. "Say you're mine first."

"What?" I squeak.

"Say it. I need to hear it."

My heart is thumping hard against my rib cage. I want to be his, and as insane as the idea is, I never thought I'd like to belong to any man until Alex came along.

"I'm yours, Alex."

Even when I can't be.

He seals his lips to mine while his hand searches my back for my dress's zipper. I have to guide him to the correct location. "It's on the side," I whisper against his mouth.

He lowers the zipper, but instead of helping me out of my clothes, he caresses my breasts through the thick fabric.

"Alex! Do you want to rail me or not?"

He takes one of my hands and places it over his dick. "What do you think, baby girl?"

"Get the condoms." I nudge him off the bed. "There's a box under the sink."

"Okay, okay."

He jumps out of bed and disappears into the bathroom. I get rid of all my clothes at the speed of light. When he returns to the room, Alex halts and gawks. I lean on my elbows and spread my legs wide. "Do you like what you see, big boy?"

His Adam's apple bobs up and down, and it's like he's rooted to the spot by sheer willpower. He tosses the box of condoms onto the bed. It bounces across the mattress until it almost ends up on the floor.

"I'm not going to dignify that question with an answer. I'll show you." He unzips his jeans and gets rid of them and his briefs in one fell swoop. His rock-hard cock springs free, hitting his washboard abs, and on cue, my clit throbs, and I get wetter. With eyes blazing, he fists his dick and plays with himself, running his hand up and down his length. Precum spills from the tip, making my insides quake.

"I want to taste you," I say.

"Only if I can taste you at the same time."

I swallow hard, feeling nervous suddenly. "I've never done that before."

He walks over, still working his dick, and stops by the edge of the bed in front of me. "I can show you how, baby girl."

"Okay."

Putting one knee on the mattress between my legs, he leans forward, bracing both hands on each side of my head. He brings his nose below my ear, then licks the column of my neck, drawing a needy moan from me. I arch my back as I reach for his cock.

Like a ninja, Alex lifts my body off the mattress as if I weigh nothing and flips me around, making me yelp. Now I'm on top of him. "Jesus, give me a warning next time."

"And what would the fun be in that?"

I open my legs, sit astride him, and gyrate my hips, rubbing my wet pussy against his shaft. He groans, narrowing his eyes. "Don't do that, baby girl, or I'll fuck you before I eat you out."

"I can't help it. It feels so good."

He digs his fingers into my hips, making me stop. "Turn around." I follow his command, and when I'm facing the other way, he pulls me back until my pussy is by his mouth. "Ah, that's what I call a view."

I take his cock, wrapping my fingers around the base and then licking the top. Alex digs his fingers harder into my hips and licks my pussy hole, rimming it with his tongue. I clench my legs, already delirious with desire. It's hard to concentrate on him when every cell in my body is melting. I won't fuck up this lesson though. I swallow his length, sucking so hard that my cheeks hollow. In response, he flicks his tongue over my clit, frying all my senses. My legs are quickly turning to jelly, and then I start to shake. I'm determined to give good head though. I won't fail this lesson.

Alex shifts my body, forcing me to stop my work. I look over my shoulder, afraid I've already messed up. "What did I do?"

"You're exerting yourself, baby girl. I'm sorry. I didn't think."

"I'm fine."

"No, you aren't."

I get off him, feeling deflated. Maybe he's just saying that because he doesn't want to hurt my feelings. But he sits up and pulls me into a hug. "Don't be sad, baby girl. I'm still going to fuck you into oblivion."

"I'm not sad," I reply through a pout. "Just don't lie to me. Tell me how bad it was."

His brows shoot up. "Bad? Are you crazy? You give the best blow jobs I've ever had."

A tiny smile blossoms on my face. "Really?"

"I wouldn't lie to you." He kisses me gently, and I taste myself on his tongue. It's strange but not bad.

I deepen the kiss, trying to sit on his lap. Without unlocking our fused lips, he pushes in the opposite direction until I'm lying flat on my back, and he's between my legs, pressing his cock against my slick folds. I bring my knees up, opening myself even more for him.

He leans back, resting his weight on his forearms. "Condom."

I close my eyes, and I swear he's gone for only a couple

seconds before he's pushing inside of me, driving me to the point of sweet insanity.

It's too late for me to say goodbye. I can't do it. But he's leaving anyway, so that gives me an out. I'll keep him until he goes.

CHAPTER 44
ALEX

"Who are you texting nonstop?" CJ leans closer, trying to see my screen.

I elbow the sucker. "None of your business."

Noah, who's also next to me at the high-top table, yawns and tries to hide it with a fist.

"What's the matter, rookie? Someone keeping you up at night?" I ask just to draw CJ's attention away from my phone and my messages to Blair.

"Yes, stupid finance class."

"You'd better get used to sleepless nights." CJ smirks.

"Taking care of my baby when the time comes is definitely worth a lack of sleep. Finance isn't." He tosses his head back and finishes his drink. "Where's Sean anyway?"

We all came to The Heritage after practice at the request of our captain. He was all mysterious about the reason for this meeting, and so far the theories have been completely ludicrous, mainly because CJ was the one coming up with them.

Noah's attention turns to the entrance of the bar, and he perks up. "There he is. Finally!"

I turn and spot Sean walking to our table. There are a couple guys behind him, but Sean is blocking my view of them. Then he steps aside, revealing his companions.

"Shut up. Jesse!" CJ is out of his chair so fast he almost tips it over.

"Hey, man. What's up?" He greets CJ the same way he used to when he was captain of the team, with a high five and then a fist bump.

"Not much. I didn't know you were in town."

When CJ started last year, Jesse took him under his wing and soon won him over. CJ never hid that he idolizes Jesse, and taking into account he's usually a grumpy asshole, it's entertaining to see him act like an excited puppy around our former captain, who now plays for the Vancouver Vikings.

"Just for a couple days." He turns and points at the man standing next to him. "You guys remember Deacon, right?" He smirks.

Like any of us need an introduction. Deacon Price, center for the Boston Zodiacs, was drafted first pick overall straight out of high school. Since he joined the team, the Zodiacs have risen from the ashes. Last year, they made the playoffs but lost the Cup to the Los Angeles Titans.

Noah jumps from his chair and walks over. "Hi, I'm Noah Kingsley. Nice to meet you."

"Oh, *you're* the infamous Noah." Deacon smirks while they shake hands.

Noah's forehead creases. "Why am I infamous?"

"Maybe because of all the drama involving you in the last few months," CJ deadpans.

"Noah Kingsley and CJ King." Deacon looks at the duo. "Any jokes about your last names?"

They glance at each other, but it's Noah who replies, "Not when we both rule the ice."

CJ draws his brows together as if surprised by Noah's compliment.

"I hope to see you two in the NHL draft next year," Deacon replies.

CJ makes a face. "We'll see."

"What's the matter? Are you afraid I'll get picked first?" Noah teases, smiling like a fiend.

Instead of coming back with an angry remark, CJ mumbles, "Sure, that's it."

"Let's get a few more chairs," I say, trying to lift the mood after CJ's strange reaction.

Tuesdays aren't busy at The Heritage, and we find some extra chairs easily. Fewer people also mean fewer puck bunnies trying to score. Once upon a time, that would have sucked, but now it's a fucking blessing. There's only one girl I want. And to think that not too long ago, I was teasing Noah about his over-the-top love for Gia. Look who's obsessed now.

Once everyone is sitting at the table with drinks in hand, Logan asks, "How's the wedding prep going, Jesse?"

"It's intense. I never knew how much work getting married involves. Thank God for Riley's aunt."

"You didn't just come to Fairbanks for a casual visit, did you?" Darren pipes up.

"No. I'm flying back to Vancouver tomorrow evening. Riley and Zoey had the brilliant idea to do a dance number involving the wedding party."

"What do you mean?" CJ asks.

"The bridesmaids and the groomsmen will do a dance before the newlywed couple is introduced," Deacon explains.

"Oh, thank heavens I'm not in the wedding party," Noah chimes in.

"Yeah, thank God. With your dance moves, you'd ruin the whole thing," CJ retorts.

"You're full of it, but I've seen you dance. You aren't that much better than me."

Noah's relieved, but I'm caught in a mix of excitement and apprehension. Blair and I are in the wedding party, but for obvious reasons, I'm not her escort. I'm walking with Gia. I think Logan is escorting a friend of Riley's we haven't met yet, and I don't know about the rest.

Either way, if we're part of a dance number, that means spending time together in front of our friends. Can I be in the same room as her without giving away that I'm head over heels in love with her? I got Blair to say she's mine, but that was in the heat of the moment. I'm taking her confession at face value. If word gets out that we're seeing each other, it might scare her away from me.

"Who's choreographing?" I ask.

"Gia offered," Jesse replies. "Anyway, the bad news is that thanks to Deacon's and my tight schedules, we only have tomorrow to learn it, and then we have to practice on our own time before the wedding."

"No offense, but who had the bright idea to get married in the middle of hockey season?" Noah asks.

"Dude! Rude much?" CJ barks.

"I said no offense. I'm just curious. Most hockey players get married in the summer."

Jesse nods. "True. But the place Riley and I want is only available on December thirty-first, and we don't want to wait another year and a half to get married."

Noah's face turns beet red. "Oh. Makes sense. I'm sorry if I came across like a King."

CJ's spine goes taut. "What's that supposed to mean?"

"King, asshole. Potato, potahto." Noah waves his hand dismissively.

Deacon and Jesse chuckle.

"As you can see, Jesse, I now have two brats to deal with instead of one." Sean takes a sip of his beer.

"I don't even know why Noah is here. He's not part of the wedding party," CJ spits back.

"But he's coming to the bachelor party, which is the next topic on the agenda," Deacon replies.

Noah sticks out his tongue at CJ, making me feel a little sorry for Gia. Pretty soon, she'll have two babies to take care of.

Logan rubs his hands together. "Oh yeah, now we're talking."

"When is it happening?"

"The twenty-sixth, in Boston. I'll email you the details because my man Jesse here can't know." He claps his friend on the shoulder.

"Nothing wild, please," Jesse begs.

"Trust me, bro. It's gonna be epic," Deacon smiles brightly.

"That's what I'm afraid of."

My phone vibrates in my pocket, and unable to resist taking a peek, I fish it out.

I guess we have dance practice tomorrow.

Yep. I just heard. Will that be a problem?

No. I can't wait to see you dance.

I'm not as good as you, but I can bust a move.

LMAO.

Too distracted by my convo with Blair, I don't notice Noah looking at my phone until I glance up and find him smiling knowingly. "What?"

He shakes his head. "Nothing. Welcome to the club."

CHAPTER 45
BLAIR

Gia got permission to use one of the gym rooms in the arena so we can practice the dance number for Jesse and Riley's wedding. I'm a little nervous about being around Alex in a closed environment and among our friends, so I asked if I could get a ride with Gia, intending to talk with her about him.

Unfortunately, I didn't foresee that Noah would be the one driving—he's not even in the wedding party—and one minute into the drive, he asks, "How did you manage to tame Alex, Blair?"

"What?" I squeak.

"You're together, right?" He peers at me through the rearview mirror.

I glance at Gia. "You told him?"

"I didn't say a word. I swear. Noah figured it out on his own."

"It's not my fault Alex is whipped and totally gave away that he's into you."

My brows arch. "He did? When?"

"Yesterday at The Heritage."

Shit. "Does everyone know?"

"No, relax. He was texting someone nonstop, so I glanced at his messages and guessed."

"Noah! I can't believe you did that," Gia chides him.

"What? He was sitting next to me. I couldn't resist."

"Please don't tell anyone," I say. "It's not serious. We're just having fun."

"Aww, for real? I was hoping we could double date." Noah sounds disappointed.

Dating Alex out in the open and being able to call him my boyfriend sounds like a dream, but I know it'll never happen.

"It's better if we don't," I reply.

Mercifully, Gia changes the subject and keeps the conversation going with Noah, whereas I slump into my seat and look out the window, worrying about the day when I have to say goodbye to Alex.

It seems as if my heart grows more in love with him every day, and I live with a constant ache in my chest. That's what I get for lowering my barriers. I thought I'd be safe with him. I didn't even like him to begin with. I couldn't have foreseen falling in love with the guy who made my life hell for two years straight.

We arrive at the arena. I didn't even notice the drive. I wince as I get out of the car. The weather definitely took a turn for the worse, and this early in the morning, it's colder than the North Pole. My boots crunch against the snow, and I cross my arms to protect myself from the chilly wind. It's a vain attempt.

Ahead of me, Noah throws his arm around Gia and brings her flush against his body. A pang of jealousy pierces my chest. I want what they have, and maybe I could have it… with Alex.

No. I won't entertain that idea. Happily ever afters don't exist in my family.

Once we're inside the Warriors' zone, I make a beeline for the coffee machine. I need to defrost my body. Since I won't be kissing Alex in front of everyone, I deem it safe to drink caffeine.

Someone stops next to me while I'm putting the lid on my

cup. I turn and find Alex there, smiling and looking like a god. I get distracted by his proximity and forget that we aren't alone.

"Hey," I say, leaning closer.

"Hi." His grin broadens.

"Blair, come here!" someone calls.

I snap out of my daze and step back. Riley is the one waving me over. She's standing next to Gia and Zoey while Jesse is talking to Deacon and Logan farther away. I approach the girls, hoping no one noticed me invading Alex's space and looking at him like a fool in love.

"Hey, Riley. I'm so happy to see you." I hug her, careful not to spill hot coffee on her.

"Me too! It's a pity our visit is so short and you couldn't come to dinner with us last night."

"I know. It's been too long, but I had to study for a test."

"You know Blair, she can't let that GPA drop," Ashley says, joining us.

"I really can't." *For more reasons than you know.* "How is life in Vancouver, Riley?" I ask, trying to move the spotlight away from me.

"I love Vancouver, but it's been an adjustment for sure, and the wedding stress isn't helping."

"I can't imagine the hassle of trying to pull it off in the middle of hockey season," Gia says.

"Yes, Jesse and I really weren't thinking when we picked our date. But oh well, it's almost over."

Gia looks around. "Is everyone here? We should start."

"I think so," I say as I spot Darren, CJ, and Sean. "But aren't we missing some of the bridesmaids?"

"Yes, they'll join us online. They're pretty good dancers, so it shouldn't be a problem," Riley replies.

"I can't wait to meet them in person," I say, distracted now that Alex has joined the guys and is in my line of sight.

He must sense me staring because he looks at me and winks.

Shit. Why is he doing that? My face is in flames as I hastily look away.

"I believe you've already met Sophia. Didn't she help the Deltas with a costume emergency?"

"Oh my God. I didn't know she was your friend. She just said her brother plays for Clayton U."

"Shhh," whispers Riley, looking over her shoulder to make sure the guys didn't hear me. "No one knows that small detail besides Jesse."

"Oh, right."

"How do you know Sophia?" Gia asks.

"She made me a custom outfit for a competition. We became close friends after that."

"She's the best. She's designed a few of my costumes too," Zoey pipes up.

"And who did you pair her with?" Ashley asks.

"Logan." Riley grimaces. "I know, I know. But Sophia is in a serious relationship with a hot doctor, and she's bringing him as her date. She's safe."

"Jesse better tell Logan to behave as well," Ashley chimes in.

"Enough talking about pairings. We need to start," Gia butts in and then turns to the guys. "Let's go, everyone."

She walks toward the gym, and we all follow her. Noah tags along, and I wonder if he's just here to have a laugh at the guys.

Riley instructs Jesse to bring the bench to the front of the mirror so she can set up her laptop there. While she logs on to the virtual meeting with the rest of the girls, Gia starts teaching the guys their part of the dance while Noah pulls his camera out and begins filming.

Ah, so that's why he's here. Gia probably asked him to record the lesson so she could post it later on the team's social media pages.

I take off my coat and sweater and set them on the empty part of the bench, then I exchange my boots for ballroom dance shoes. Today, I'm wearing light-gray leggings over a long-sleeve baby-blue leotard. This outfit hides nothing, and yes, I've selected it on purpose.

Alex's eyes bug out when he notices me standing there without my coat, and he stares unashamedly. To torture him more, I begin my stretching routine, which includes first holding my right heel and then bringing my leg up until it touches my ear.

"Alex, are you listening to me?" Gia snaps her fingers in front of his face.

He blinks fast and turns to her. "What?"

I can't help the smile that crosses my face. Ashley steps next to me and asks, "How was he in the sack?"

I whip my face to her. "What?"

"Come on, girlie. I'm not blind. You bought him at the auction, and now you're doing everything you can to get his attention."

"I don't kiss and tell," I grumble, annoyed that she noticed what I was doing.

"Who did you kiss and you're not telling?" Zoey comes over, looking all cute in her ballet skirt and emerald-green leotard that's similar to mine save for the high collar and the naked back. Maybe she wants to catch someone's attention too.

"No one," I say. At the same time, Ashley replies, "Alex."

"No way!" Zoey blurts out.

"Gia, could you please tell your friends to stop gossiping? It's distracting," CJ complains.

"It's only distracting if you're trying to eavesdrop," Zoey retorts.

"Zoey, come on." Deacon gives her a meaningful look that's not so different from the ones Ryder used to give me. Why must all older brothers act the same?

She rolls her eyes. "Fine. I'll shut up."

"What song are we dancing to anyway?" Logan asks.

"'Levitating' by Dua Lipa," Riley replies. "Emma, Sophia,

and Melanie are logged on to the video conference. Everyone say hello."

We all greet Riley's remote bridesmaids, and then Gia resumes showing the moves to the boys. Their part is fairly simple. Once they get the hang of it, she turns to us. Since we're all more experienced in dancing—including Ashley, who was a cheerleader in her previous life—our steps are more complex.

Jesse and Riley don't join our group until the very end since this is the intro to their first dance. We don't get to see it though. As soon as Gia is certain we've memorized the steps, she kicks us out of the room, including Noah.

"What are you going to do while Gia is busy with the love-birds?" I hear Alex ask Noah from behind me.

I purposely left the room first so I could walk ahead of him, putting more swing in my hips.

"I'm gonna hit the gym. Do you wanna join me?"

Shit. Noah was my ride.

"I can't."

"Ah crap. I totally forgot about you, Blair." Noah comes to the same realization I did.

I stop and look at him. "It's okay. Maybe one of the girls can drive me home."

"I can take you," Alex offers, making Noah's eyes shine with mirth.

"Yes, Alex can give you a lift home." He smiles broadly, earning a stink eye from me.

"What about Logan?" I ask.

"What about him?" Alex furrows his brows.

"Didn't you come together?"

Now it's Alex's turn to grin from ear to ear. "Nope."

This is bad. Now everyone will see me leaving with Alex. Pretty soon, the entire team will know we're hooking up.

I sigh. "Let's go then."

I turn around and walk ahead of him at a brisk pace. In the

common area, the girls are chatting near the coffee machine. They turn to look at us.

"Leaving already, Blair?" Riley asks.

I walk over to say a proper goodbye. "Yes. I have a million things on my to-do list today."

"Thanks for coming to this last-minute rehearsal. I appreciate it."

"You're welcome."

"And thanks again for letting me celebrate my special day on your big birthday."

"Don't mention it. Trust me. You're doing me a huge favor."

We hug goodbye, and at first, I believe no one will notice who I'm leaving with, but then Ashley opens her big mouth. "Are you waiting for Blair, Alex?"

"He's giving me a ride since I came with Gia and Noah and they aren't ready to leave yet."

"Sure, sure." She nods.

I grimace. "Anyway, talk later."

I hurry to leave the place before we bump into Alex's teammates, who, mercifully, have disappeared. Alex is quiet for the entire walk from the arena to his car. I don't know what to say either. But when we're in the car, he leans across the seats and reaches behind my head. "Come here."

He kisses me softly but no less passionately than usual. His lips taste of naughty promises. I pull back. "Someone might see us."

"Right. But I couldn't resist. You were driving me crazy in there, baby girl."

"Was I?"

He runs his fingers up my legs. "Yes. What were you thinking wearing something so revealing?"

"It's just leggings and a leotard." I smirk.

"I think you secretly do want people to know about us. It took an enormous amount of self-restraint to keep my hands off you."

"Maybe you're right," I admit. "And soon they'll know. All my girlfriends figured it out already, so it's only a matter of time before you give it away to the guys if you haven't already."

"Noah read my texts, that sneaky bastard."

"I know. He told me."

Alex caresses my cheek. "I didn't know your birthday was December thirty-first."

"Yeah. The big twenty-one."

"I can't promise to keep my hands to myself at Jesse and Riley's wedding."

"You have to. Please."

His forehead crinkles. "Why? What are you afraid of?"

I look away hastily. "I'm not *afraid* of anything."

"You're afraid your mother will find out. Is that it?"

I cross my arms. "No. Could you please drive already? I didn't lie to Riley. I *am* busy."

"Fine."

He turns on the car and pulls out of his parking spot almost too fast.

I reach for the door handle. "What are you doing?"

"Taking you home as fast as I can, Westwood." His reply is curt.

Great. I managed to turn a tender moment into our first argument as a quasi couple. It's my fault. I'm the one who knows I can't have him but am unable to let him go.

CHAPTER 46
ALEX

Damn it. I'm annoyed as hell. Now that I admitted to myself how I feel about Blair, I don't want to hide it. In fact, I want to tell the world, hoping her parents do find out about us and stop forcing her to marry someone she doesn't want. They're coercing her, and it drives me up the fucking wall that I don't know how to help her or stop it from happening.

I keep my mouth shut during the drive to her apartment, and when we get there, I don't park. I stop in front of her building by the curb.

"You're not coming up?" she asks, sounding hopeful.

"I thought you were busy."

"I am but… I don't want to leave while there's this tension between us."

"I can't help it, Blair. I'm angry."

"I've seen you angry before. This is different."

I look at her. "Yes. I'm angry at myself for agreeing to your terms."

Her brows furrow. "I thought we were on the same page. Why complicate things when you're leaving at the end of the school year?"

"That's four months away! A lot can happen between now and then."

"The only thing that's guaranteed to happen is a broken heart."

Yes. Mine.

I don't voice those words. I've already made myself too vulnerable. Glancing straight ahead, I say, "I think it's better if we keep our relationship strictly academic from now on."

She winces. "You don't mean that."

I hear the crack in her voice, and it kills me that I'm hurting her, but I have to get this off my chest.

"I want more, Blair. I won't be your dirty little secret."

A long stretch of silence follows. I don't move; I don't even dare to breathe, waiting for her reply. I keep my gaze glued to a point in the distance while clenching my jaw so hard it hurts.

"I can't give you more. I'm sorry." She opens the door and gets out of the car. "For the record, you were never a dirty secret," she says in a choked-up voice. "I just care too much about you to let you get caught in the cross fire."

She bangs the door shut, and the sound resonates in my ears. I don't move for a couple beats, wrestling with my emotions and trying to reconcile her parting words with everything that's happened between us.

I close my eyes, pinching my nose. I'm a fucking idiot. I know about her family and the pressure she's been under, and I managed to make it all about me.

I press the pedal to the metal and turn into the parking lot in front of her building. When I get out of the car, she's long gone. But her code is still the same, and even though she already took the elevator up, I'm hoping she'll let me come through the door of her apartment.

To my surprise, she's not inside. She's on the floor of her hallway with her back pressed against her door, hugging her knees.

She turns to me, and I see her red eyes and the tears rolling down her cheeks.

Fuck.

I run, reaching her in the blink of an eye. I drop into a crouch and ask, "Baby girl, what's wrong?"

"I fucked up. I know."

The agony in my chest at seeing her like this and knowing I'm to blame is almost crippling.

"You didn't fuck up. I did."

My reply makes her cry harder. She shakes her head. "I can't let you take the blame for this one."

"Too bad because it's mine."

"Are we going to fight over this too?"

"This isn't a fight. Come on. Let's go inside." I help her to her feet and then take the key from her hand.

As soon as we're in her apartment and the front door is closed, I pull her to me and kiss her in a way I've never done before. It's deep, raw, and desperate. I want her to feel my love, even if I don't dare say it out loud yet.

I cup her face with my hands, trapping her there so I can savor her mouth without interruptions. My heart is running faster than the speed of light, and the rush of excitement coursing through my veins is akin to when I step foot on the ice. Hockey was my only passion until now.

Needing to be inside of her, I pick her up in my arms and almost run to her bedroom. I don't fall onto her bed though. We're wearing far too many clothes. I set her down, and with our lips still fused together, I get her out of her coat. She does the same to me, and now we're competing for who can undress the other first.

I pull back, breaking the kiss for a second, to take off my sweater and shirt. Blair peels off her leggings and then gets rid of her leotard. She isn't wearing underwear. Okay, she wins this race, but just by a few seconds. My jeans and briefs have barely touched the floor, and I'm already nudging her backward while claiming her lips again.

Now we do fall together, and Blair immediately opens her legs so I can fit right between them. My cock is hard and pressing against her pelvis, and my balls are tight, ready to go. I need a condom.

I lean back to reach for the box of condoms that's now on her nightstand, but Blair touches my arm. "No. I want to feel you fully, no barriers."

I inhale, staring into her eyes. My pulse is thundering in my ears. "Are you sure?"

"Yes." She takes my cock and guides it to her entrance. "Don't hold back."

"I won't, baby girl." With a single thrust, I sheathe myself in her, but I pause a moment to make sure I'm not going to lose complete control. I'm wound tight, ready to explode. I gyrate my hips, stretching Blair's pussy without pulling back. She's so wet already.

"Oh, Alex…" She closes her eyes. "That feels good."

"I can make it feel better." I hook my arm under her right leg and put it over my shoulder. Then I fuck her in earnest.

"Yes!" she cries out.

"Damn. Your pussy is tight, baby girl. I love how well you take me."

"Fuck me harder, Alex. Please."

I piston in and out of her, moving my hips as fast as I can but mindful not to hurt her. I could do some serious damage to her small body if I'm not careful. The bed starts to move, the headboard banging against the wall hard. Her bedside lamp shakes as well, moving closer and closer to the edge of the nightstand.

A sheen of sweat covers my forehead, and our bodies are slick, rubbing against one another. My breathing soon becomes labored, and my grunts mix with her moans in a delicious symphony.

Her hooded eyes connect with mine, and my mind flashes

back to all the times we argued over stupid shit. I never once thought she would one day look at me like this. I love this girl so damn hard, more than I ever imagined. I thought this feeling of completeness would come later in my life after I'd experienced many things. I didn't expect it so soon. I didn't foresee falling for Blair Westwood.

The confession is on the tip of my tongue, but hell, a profession of love during sex is the worst move a guy can make. I kiss her instead, so I won't blurt out the truth. That forces me to slow my pace down, but I don't mind prolonging this moment for as long as I can.

Suddenly, Blair tenses under me, around me, and a second later, she's shaking and scratching my back with her long nails.

"That's it, baby girl, come for me. Scream my name," I murmur against her lips.

"Alex, God. You fuck me so good. Don't stop."

"I don't want to stop. I never want to stop fucking you."

Wishful thinking. Tremors of pleasure run down my spine, and I lose the little grasp of control I had. I come hard inside her pussy, and it's the best fucking thing I've done in years. I keep thrusting, milking the orgasm, and it does seem to last longer than normal. Maybe making love *is* better.

I stop moving only when I'm all empty. I roll off her, collapsing by her side but keeping my arms wrapped around her body. For a moment, the only noise in the room is our breathing.

"I think this was the best one yet," she says.

"Agree." I kiss her shoulder.

"We should argue more often." She chuckles.

"No. I don't ever want to see you crying because of me."

She turns her face toward me. "I don't want to hide our relationship from our friends."

"You don't?"

She shakes her head.

"Does that mean I can kiss you in front of everyone at Jesse and Riley's wedding?"

She smiles, making her eyes twinkle. "Yes."

I trace her hairline with the tips of my fingers. "Does that also mean you're coming to my game on Saturday wearing my jersey?"

"This Saturday?" Her voice carries a tinge of worry.

"Yes."

"I'm sorry. I can't make it to the game. It's my parents' Christmas party. My attendance is mandatory."

I try not to show disappointment in my expression. "That's okay. There will be other games. I wish you could come to the Warriors' Christmas bash afterward though. It's always fun."

I remember being extremely jealous that Ryder got to attend them. "Where is it being held?"

"The Heritage, like every year. We close the bar. It's open only to Warriors and their guests."

She cups my cheek. "I'll come."

"You just said you have your parents' party."

"I can't come to the game because the party starts early and I won't be able to leave the house too soon, but later, I can sneak out."

That's better than I hoped for. "I like your rebel side, Westwood. It suits you."

She tosses a leg over my body and rolls onto me. "Rebels without a cause are lame, but you make it worthwhile, Kaminski."

I grab her sweet ass and dig my fingers into her cheeks. "How much time do we have?"

"I don't know, but... I'm still feeling rebellious."

My lips curl into a grin. "That's my girl."

CHAPTER 47
BLAIR

Even though I told Alex I didn't want to hide our relationship from our friends, I asked him to wait until the Christmas party to confirm what they already knew. I won't go as far as calling us a couple because I'm still very much trapped in my agreement with my mother. My excuse for waiting? It'll be easier to tell everyone at once, but also, I have another motive—to avoid drama with my parents when I have to spend hours trapped with them at their party.

So far, the party has not been hell on earth. I've been able to stay clear of my mother and her attempts to shove me in front of a potential husband candidate. The fact that she's not parading me around like a prize horse is almost a confirmation that her search is over. The Bolkoskys haven't arrived yet, and I'm dreading seeing Ilya again.

When my parents are distracted, I sneak into my father's den and check my phone for the game score. Third period is almost over, and the Warriors are winning. Contradictory feelings mix in my chest. I'm happy they're leading the game but sad that I can't be there cheering them on. Who knew I'd become a hockey fan?

The door opens, and my mother appears in the frame. "There

you are, Blair. I've been looking all over for you. The Bolkoskys are here, and Ilya is eager to say hello to you."

Dread runs down my spine, giving me goose bumps. My stomach revolts, coiling tightly. I'm glad I didn't eat anything yet, or I might hurl.

"I'll be right out. I need to make a phone call."

"Who are you calling at this hour?"

"Melody. She's having a bit of a meltdown, and she needs me."

My mother flattens her lips. "Be quick about it."

She turns on her heels, leaving the door ajar. I wait a minute before I follow her out. The last thing I want is to socialize with the Bolkoskys, but I need to play nice so I can sneak out later. I'd better get this over with quickly.

Squaring my shoulders and taking a deep breath, I walk over to my parents and Ilya's family. He looks even more handsome wearing a tux, but even if he didn't give me a bad vibe, his good looks wouldn't work on me. There's only one person who gives me butterflies and makes my heart beat faster for the right reasons. As it is, my pulse is accelerating now, but it's from apprehension, not desire.

Ryder is nowhere in the vicinity, which sucks. I could use his help. I saw him only once tonight, talking to an old friend of my parents.

Ilya's soulless eyes spark when I come closer. "Blair. Aren't you a vision in red?"

I run my clammy hands over the chiffon dress that hugs me in all the right places. Mom's pick. I love the dress, but I know why she insisted that I wear it. I'm supposed to win Ilya over, convince him to marry me. I'm fairly certain I don't need to resort to games of seduction when it comes to him. He doesn't strike me as the type of person who can be manipulated like that.

"Hi, Ilya." I smile tightly, then turn to his parents. "Good evening, Mr. and Mrs. Bolkosky."

"Good evening, Blair. I hear you met my son at his nightclub in Boston a few weeks ago," his father says in a thick Russian accent.

"Yes, such a coincidence. I had no idea he owned the club."

"It's a new acquisition. We're expanding our businesses in the US with your father's help."

Dad nods once but doesn't reciprocate Mr. Bolkosky's smile. He hides his lack of enthusiasm behind his whiskey glass.

"Did you look into those listings in Blair's neighborhood, Ilya?" Mom asks.

"Yes, ma'am. I've made an offer on one."

I swallow hard. "You have?"

"Yes. It's a great investment. And I love the area. I'm waiting to hear back from my agent."

I should say something, but I'm busy freaking out. God, I wish I had grabbed a glass of champagne before I came over.

"How long until you graduate, Blair?" his mother asks in a tone that hinges on disapproval. Looking at her reinforces my suspicion.

"A year and a half to go."

"Hmm. In my time, women didn't need a degree. The husband provides."

"I'm glad I'm not from your time." I see a waiter walking by, and instead of waiting for him to come closer, I meet him halfway.

I debate using this as an excuse to escape, but Ilya follows me. "I'm sorry about my mother. She has extremely archaic views about women's roles in society."

"I got that."

"I don't share her views though. I think women should be empowered and encouraged to reach their potential."

I tilt my head. "As long as they know their place, right?"

He frowns. "You're concerned."

Alarm bells sound in my head. "Why should I be concerned?"

"Let's cut to the chase, shall we? We both know about our parents' plans for us. I feel very fortunate that my future wife is bright and determined. I won't undermine you. You have my word."

My stomach dips, and I feel sick. It's one thing to anticipate something, quite another when it's spoken out loud as if it's a done deal.

"Are you okay? You look pale." He touches my arm.

I step back. "I'm fine. I just need a bit of fresh air."

"It's the hockey player, isn't it? The one you were with at my nightclub."

"I don't know what you're talking about."

He narrows his eyes. "Don't play dumb with me, Blair. I don't appreciate these games. You ought to forget him. I'll protect you, cherish you, and allow you freedoms that none of the women who marry into my family possess. But I won't tolerate betrayal."

"You speak as if we're married already."

"It's a done deal. You need to accept it." He caresses my face, making my blood freeze and my skin crawl. "I can be good to you, darling."

"Like I said, I need fresh air." I turn around and walk away from him.

I want to cry, to scream. Marrying Ilya *can't* be my fate. The dress I'm wearing feels like a straitjacket or a prison uniform. I need to get out of it. I head back to my childhood room, and before the door is even closed, I unzip the back and breathe a little easier once the corset slackens.

I let the gown fall into a heap at my feet, then I kick my high-heeled shoes far away. Angry tears blur my vision, but when they fall, I hastily wipe them away. My makeup will be ruined, and I don't have time to fuss over it. I'm getting out of here.

I don't want to draw attention to myself, so I wear dark clothes under my black coat. I take the staff staircase down, but going out the back of the house won't do. I'll be spotted by the people working in the kitchen. I don't want them to tell my mother I left if she comes looking for me. The best option to sneak out of the house unseen is to take the side door that leads to the gardens.

I walk close to the walls, trying to blend in with the furniture. I'm acting like a spy; I hope I'm a good one.

I'm almost there when a voice stops me dead in my tracks.

"Where are you going, sis?" my brother asks.

"Shit, Ryder. You scared me. I'm going for a walk outside."

He snorts. "No, you're not. Try again."

I look over his shoulder, then move to his side to use him as a shield. "I had a talk with Ilya. It seems our nuptials are imminent."

The blood seems to drain from his face. "What?"

"Please don't act surprised. You know our folks see us as pawns to be used to advance their interests. Mom has been trying to shove horrid candidates down my throat for months. Ilya seems to be the winner."

"You can't marry into the Bolkosky family."

My face falls. "I don't want to, but what choice do I have? You know what Mom will do if I refuse. But I can't think about that now. I have to be somewhere."

"Let me guess. The Warriors' Christmas bash."

"Yes. I'm meeting Alex there."

"Well, let's go then."

I wrinkle my forehead. "You're coming with me?"

"Obviously." He reaches behind me and opens the door. "Go on."

"You're not even wearing a coat."

"I have a jacket in my car."

Once outside, I ask, "What's the deal, Ryder? You're not seriously thinking about crashing the Warriors' party, right?"

His expression is pinched when he answers, "Of course not. But I need to get out of here, or I'll end up punching Ilya in the face. I'll take you there, then go somewhere else."

Guilt makes my heart feel smaller. Ryder looks so sad and dejected; I feel horrible ditching him to party with his former teammates. "You know what? You *should* come to the party."

"Blair... I can't."

"Yes, you can. And you're coming."

CHAPTER 48
ALEX

I'm getting dressed in the locker room when I receive a text from Blair saying she's on her way to The Heritage.

You're ahead of schedule. I'm still at the arena.

I had to leave early. How long until you get there?

Ten minutes or so.

You'll be there before us.

Us? Who else is coming?

I have a feeling, but I wait until she confirms my suspicion.

Ryder. I'll explain when I see you.

She must have a good reason to bring her brother with her, and my gut tells me it has to do with Ilya. I knew he'd be at the party, but I tried my best to not think about it. I couldn't let worry and jealousy affect my concentration on the game. Besides, I was counting on Ryder to protect his sister.

Even though I'm still mad at him for quitting the team before the championship final, I know he isn't a bad guy. I can't simply tell him to fuck off when he drops off Blair. But I might be the only one who feels that way.

"Guys, can I have your attention, please?" I say loud enough so everyone in the locker room can hear me.

They turn in my direction, all in different states of dressing. Logan just got out of the shower, and he's still wrapped in his towel. "What's up, bro?"

"It's about Ryder."

Grunts of dissatisfaction echo in the locker room. Man, everyone is still pissed.

"What about him?" Noah asks.

"He's driving Blair to The Heritage, and I plan to ask him to join us."

"Are you crazy? He fucked over the team last season!" CJ retorts.

"I know, but isn't Christmas the season to forgive and give people a second chance?"

"Are you being serious, Alex?" Darren asks. "I'm all for giving second chances, but Ryder never asked for one."

"He won't. He's too proud, but I know he wants one and feels horrible about how things went down in Tampa."

"How do *you* know that?" Sean walks closer, making eye contact.

"I talked to him not too long ago. He had reasons to quit the team, and it wasn't by choice."

"What do you mean?" CJ furrows his brows. "Was he forced to quit?"

"I don't know everything. But trust me. Ryder isn't the asshole we thought he was."

"Let him come to the party," Noah pipes up.

His support surprises me. "I didn't expect you to vote yes."

"It's thanks to him that Gia's stalker is behind bars. I doubt he'll want to come anyway, but if he does, I won't be a dick to him."

"That's a good attitude, Noah," Assistant Coach LaRue chimes in. "But if he does come, I'd suggest keeping him far away from Coach Bedford."

Shit. I didn't think about Coach. That man can hold a grudge like no other. If we're angry to have been blindsided by Ryder, I can't begin to imagine how he feels.

"Right. Should I ask him?"

"It's okay. Leave it to me." LaRue walks out of the locker room, no doubt going to speak to Coach.

As I finish getting dressed, Logan approaches me. "What's this all about?"

"I want to know why Ryder quit the team. This could be an opportunity to get him to explain himself."

"If he was forced to quit, he won't confess to the entire team."

"Maybe not the entire team, but he might tell us."

He shakes his head. "This could backfire, bro."

"He's gonna be there anyway. And he might not even come in. But I had to prepare the guys in case he does."

"True." He rubs his forehead. "I was hoping we'd be able to relax. Now I'm all tense. Too bad there won't be any puck bunnies on the premises."

"You're hopeless. Remember that all single girls in attendance are off-limits since they're all related to someone on the team. It sucks to be you." I laugh.

"Off-limits, my ass." He heads over to his locker.

Noah steps closer to me. "What was Logan talking about?"

"You're better off not knowing."

Noah narrows his eyes. "If he has any intention of coming on to Nicole, he'd better forget about it."

"Didn't your sister shoot him down the last time she was in town?"

"Yes, but we were with my parents. Logan didn't really have

an opportunity to put on the moves. And that's beside the point! She's barely eighteen."

I throw an arm around his shoulder. "What's the matter, rookie? You don't want Logan as your brother-in-law?"

He snorts. "Like that's his intention."

"You'd better keep an eye on your sister then." I step away quickly before Noah decides to take his aggravation out on me.

I ask Blair to text me when she arrives so I can meet her and Ryder out front. I want to talk to him before he faces the entire team.

It's fucking cold outside, but the moment her text comes saying that they're parking, I head out. White fog billows out of my mouth, and to avoid freezing on the spot, I shuffle from side to side.

When I see her crossing the street with Ryder, I barely recognize Blair. She's not wearing any of her trademark bright colors. I don't know how to greet her while Ryder is standing right there. He knows I'm sleeping with his sister, but this situation feels awkward as fuck nonetheless.

"Hey. How was traffic?" I end up asking.

How was traffic? What the hell is wrong with me?

"You wanna talk about traffic while standing outside in subzero temperatures?" Ryder retorts.

"Fine. Why did you have to leave the party early?"

He and Blair trade a look that makes me even more uneasy.

"Was it because of Ilya?"

"Can we talk inside?" Blair steps closer. Screw Ryder's presence. I pull her flush against my body.

"Yes, baby girl."

"Fuck. I can't handle this. I'm going to take off."

"Ryder, come on. You shouldn't be alone tonight," Blair pleads.

"I don't think anyone will appreciate my presence." He sticks his hands in his coat pockets and does the bouncing on his feet move. The cold is getting to him too.

"They know you're coming," I tell him.

"And?"

"And I think you should come in and say hello."

He glances at the wide windows of The Heritage behind me. With all the festive lights inside, you can see everything from the street. He gets a wistful look on his face, making me curious. I look over my shoulder and realize what caught his attention. Gia. Hell, I can't believe he's not over her yet.

"I'm gonna go. You two have fun." He pivots, but instead of crossing the street, he walks down the sidewalk.

"Where are you going?" Blair calls.

"I need fresh air."

"Come on, baby girl. It's cold outside." I steer Blair toward The Heritage's entrance.

"He was planning to come to the party. I don't know what made him change his mind."

"He's not ready yet to face everyone he let down. He'll come around."

"What did the guys say when you told them Ryder was coming?"

"Most were surprised. CJ was the most vocal about his displeasure." I push the door open for her.

"I'm not surprised. He's so angry all the time."

I feel immediate relief from the cold bite of winter as soon as I step foot inside The Heritage.

"Wow. I've never seen this place look so pretty. I can hardly smell the stink of spilled beer."

Her face is full of wonder, and it makes my chest feel a little bit lighter and warmer. God, I love this woman.

"Management always goes the extra mile for the Warriors' Christmas bash. I'm fairly certain they scrub the floors only for this occasion."

She takes a deep breath. "What's that smell?"

The warm scent of spices hits my nose too. "It must be mulled wine."

"Oh my God. I'd kill for some." She begins to unbutton her coat, and I'm expecting to see a bright color pop up from underneath, but it's more black, deep maroon, and dark green.

She catches me staring and tilts her head. "What's wrong?"

"You're not wearing your rainbow colors."

"I couldn't draw attention to myself while I was trying to stealthily leave the party."

Her snug sweater has a high collar with a cutout just above her cleavage. The pendant with her initials sparkles when the small diamonds catch the light. I run my fingers over the skin showing above her breasts. "This is hot."

She pushes my hand away. "But your fingers aren't."

I chuckle. "Can I take your coat?"

"Uh, I think I'm going to keep it on for a while longer. I need to defrost."

I wrap my arms around her waist and pull her closer. "I'll defrost you in no time, babe."

"Hmm, right now?"

I give her delectable red lips a quick peck, then whisper in her ear, "Are you suggesting a quickie in the restroom, baby girl?"

She smacks my arm and pulls back. "God, no. It'd be one thing to get caught by strangers in a movie theater, quite another to get busted by someone I know."

Her outrage and explanation make me laugh. "Okay. Fair enough. Let's get some mulled wine then."

I take her hand, linking my fingers with hers, and together we walk farther into the place. A few players and staff are hanging out by the bar with their respective dates, but our friends are in the pool table area.

The first people to see us are Gia and Noah. Their attention immediately focuses on our joined hands, then snap back to our faces. Both are grinning from ear to ear.

"Merry Christmas!" Gia greets us.

We reciprocate, then Noah asks. "Where's Ryder?"

"He changed his mind about coming in," Blair replies.

The mood becomes somber, so to lighten it up again, I ask, "Where's your sister, Noah?"

He looks behind him and then around our vicinity. "She was standing right here a second ago."

"Maybe she went to the restroom."

"Funny, I don't see Logan anywhere either," I tease. I haven't really looked for my brother yet.

Noah twists his face into a grimace. "Don't even joke about that, Kaminski."

"Did I miss something?" Blair asks.

"Noah is afraid Logan will try to score with Nicole," Gia replies, trying to keep a straight face. "I wouldn't worry about her. I seriously doubt she'd fall for Logan's cheap games."

"Cheap games, huh?" Blair scrunches her nose and looks at me. "Is that what you used to do too?"

"I wouldn't call them *cheap* games. Maybe easy games." I shrug. "But don't worry, Westwood. I only have eyes for you." I tap her nose.

"You'd better."

"Oh my God, you guys are so cute together. Who'd have thought?" Gia chimes in.

"Not me." I can't help the smile that spreads over my face as I stare at Blair. The best part is that she's smiling back, and the twinkle in her blue eyes makes me want to kiss her until sunup.

"You're whipped." Noah laughs.

Not too long ago, I'd have gotten annoyed at that comment. Not anymore.

"Damn straight I am."

CHAPTER 49
BLAIR

The evening goes better than I expect. No one is surprised to see me with Alex. And to avoid getting harassed by my mother, I turned off my phone. By the end of the night, all the guys are utterly drunk. Alex is teasing Sean about something that happened during the game tonight, but I can't follow the conversation. It's all drunk talk anyway.

On the way to the car, he trips over nothing, and I steady him to prevent his fall. "Okay, big boy. Hand over the keys. You aren't driving."

"I love when you're bossy."

"Is that so?" I arch an eyebrow.

"Oh boy. I know that look."

"What look?"

"You have something naughty on your mind," he whispers in my ear.

"Maybe. But we aren't doing anything crazy tonight."

"What? Why not?"

I click the fob and unlock his car. "Because I'm spending the night at your place."

His brows shoot to the heavens. "You are? Why? Your apartment is way nicer than mine."

Since he doesn't make a move to open the passenger door, I do it for him. "Because I royally pissed off my mother tonight, and she might pay me a surprise visit tomorrow morning."

His face falls. "Oh. And you don't want her to find out about us."

"It's more complicated than that. Now get in the car. I'm freezing." I nudge him toward the opening, but he moves only because he wants to. I wouldn't be able to dislodge him an inch if he put up any resistance.

I look over the roof of the car, searching for Logan. He's all the way across the parking lot, goofing around with Darren and Sean.

"Logan! Are you coming?" I yell.

"What?"

"He's not coming with us. They're going to CJ's place," Alex tells me.

"Never mind!" I yell at Logan, and then shut Alex's door and walk around the front of his car.

I get the engine started, and Alex turns the heater to the max. "Shit. It's cold."

"Yeah." I rub my hands together, blowing hot air on them.

"Why didn't you wear gloves?" he asks.

"I was in a hurry to leave my parents' party. I forgot."

"You never told me what happened."

I put the car in drive and exit the parking spot, purposely avoiding the subject.

"Blair?"

"We can talk about that later. I don't want to spoil the evening."

He touches my leg. "Okay. We'll talk later. Did I tell you how pretty you look tonight?"

"Yes!" I laugh. "Several times."

"Well, it's true. Can I make a confession?"

My pulse speeds up a little. Drunk confessions can be the best thing or the worst thing. "Sure."

"The first time I ever saw you, I was thunderstruck. I couldn't look away."

I quirk an eyebrow. "You mean in Professor Weiland's class?"

"Yes. I thought you were the most beautiful girl in the world."

"But you were awful to me in that class!"

"Yes. I was having a bad day, and your attitude rubbed me the wrong way. I was pissed that Professor Weiland gave you a free pass for being late, whereas minutes before, he chewed my head off for the same reason."

"I was late because of my mother. I hate using my family's name to get ahead—being a Westwood has always brought me more pain than joy—but on that day, I figured I should use it to get what I wanted."

"It seems we were both fighting demons that day. I wonder if I would have fallen in love with you sooner if we'd met under better circumstances."

My heart skips a beat, and I gasp. "You're in love with me?" I stop the car in the middle of the road and stare at him.

"Baby girl, I thought I had been obvious."

I'm shaking now and trying to not freak out. "I guess… I was afraid to believe it."

He caresses my face with his cold fingers. I don't mind them now. "I love you."

A car honks behind us. Shit. I resume driving, forcing my eyes to focus on the road, but I'm quivering inside. *Alex Kaminski loves me. He* loves *me.*

But the craziest part of this whole scenario is that I love him too.

How am I going to tell him about my conversation with Ilya? He's going to flip out.

"You're quiet. Did I scare you?"

I swallow the lump in my throat. "No, I'm not scared. I just want to get us home in one piece."

"Home." He chuckles. "I like the sound of that. Our home."

The butterflies in my stomach don't give a fuck that this relationship is doomed. They're making me giddy. I like the sound of sharing a home with Alex someday. But he's leaving to play in the NHL, and I have to marry Ilya.

No. I can't marry that man. My plan to get a divorce after a year won't work. With his family, I have a feeling you marry the bullshit for life, and the only way out of the marriage is death.

"Me too," I confess.

It's the only truth I can voice out loud. Saying that I love him but can't be with him isn't fair.

"We'll have that someday, baby girl. I swear."

He rests his head against the window and closes his eyes. I let out a sigh of relief. I hope he's too drunk to remember this conversation.

I was glad Alex fell asleep in the car so we didn't have to continue our conversation. But now I have to wake him and drag his ass up to his apartment. He and Logan share a two-bedroom on campus similar to Gia's place. Alex's apartment is on the third floor, and he insists that we can take the stairs. It takes me a few minutes to convince him that the elevator is better since he can barely walk straight.

Alone in the metal box, he pins me against the wall and kisses me hard, pressing his entire body against mine. His right hand is already under my skirt, going for my ass. He's drunk, but his kisses are just as effective at turning me into jelly in his arms.

Since it's a short ride, he doesn't have time to completely annihilate my self-control. I push him off me when the bell dings and the door slides open.

"We're here," I say.

He staggers back, sporting a goofy grin. "I'm going to fuck you so good tonight, baby girl."

I shake my head. "Okay, big boy. Where's your key? There'll be no fucking if we can't get into your apartment."

"Oh, that's not necessarily true. I can push you against the corridor wall and obliterate your pussy."

Man, he's turned me into a complete nympho because my body reacts immediately to his suggestion. My clit is already throbbing.

I hold out my hand. "Key, please."

"Fine." He sticks his hand in his pocket and gets the key chain out. There are a few keys dangling from it. "It's better if I do it. This door catches."

He manages to find the hole on his second try, and then he has to jam his body into the door to get it to open.

"You should have that fixed," I say.

"I know. But that's never on our list of priorities, and we can get it open." He shrugs and opens the door wide with a flourish. "Welcome to my humble residence."

I don't know what to expect as I walk in. Usually, guys are messy, but surprisingly I don't see chaos anywhere. And there isn't a pile of dirty dishes in the sink either.

There's an old brown leather couch in the living room facing a large flat-screen TV hanging on the wall. The shelving under it has a couple of video game consoles. What's most unexpected are the potted plants by the window.

The sound of paws hitting the floor warns me my namesake is awake. She's bigger than Cookie. She jumps on Alex's legs, wagging her tail.

Alex bends over and scratches her head. "How is my sweet girl? Did you miss me?"

"I have competition," I say.

He turns to me, smiling. "Jealous?"

"No. You don't have a crate?"

"We do, but we keep her out of it most of the time. We might as well get rid of it."

"Please tell me you don't let her sleep in your bed." I get out of my coat and hang it on the rack by the door.

He rubs the back of his neck. "Eh…. okay, I won't tell you."

"Well, I'm going to bed. Which way?"

"Oh babe, I'm coming too." He turns to the pup. "You stay here tonight. Mommy and Daddy need alone time."

A burst of laughter bubbles up my throat. "I'm not her mommy. I have my own puppy to worry about."

"And who's with Cookie now?"

"My next-door neighbor. I wasn't sure how late I'd be out, and she offered to babysit."

Alex pulls a dog bed from under the coffee table and sets some plush toys and a blanket on it. "I don't see why you can't be Mommy to both of them."

"You'll have to change her name then. I'm not calling her Blair."

In response, the pup's ears stand at attention.

"She's already used to the name," he argues.

I put my hands on my hips. "That's too fucking bad. It's your fault for being an idiot."

He walks over and pulls me to him. "That was an obvious move on my part to win you over. Don't you know boys pick on the girls they like?"

"That's the most rid—"

He cuts me off with his mouth.

I'm riled up, but not enough to resist the power of Alex's kisses. I jump into his arms and let him carry me to his bedroom. If anyone asked me what it looks like, I wouldn't be able to tell. I only have eyes for him.

CHAPTER 50
ALEX

I know Blair's in my bed without needing to open my eyes. I drank way too much last night, and it was a miracle I could perform when we came back to my apartment. No matter how wasted I get, I never forget anything, and last night, I told Blair that I love her. She didn't say it back, but that doesn't faze me. She left her parents' place and came to the Warriors' party. That was a huge step for her.

I open my eyes and see that Blair is sleeping on her side with her back to me. The sheet covers her from the waist down, but I know she isn't wearing anything underneath it. I curl my arm around her body and spoon her, pressing my nose against the crook of her neck. All she does is moan softly and cover my arm with hers.

I'm already aroused, so I press my hard-on against her sweet ass while I run my hand down her belly until I find her clit. I toy with her bundle of nerves, flicking my finger left and right until her folds become slick.

She arches her back and opens her legs, granting me easier access. I switch my ministrations to her pussy hole, teasing her entrance for a little bit before inserting two fingers inside of her.

"Alex...."

"Good morning, baby girl."

I fuck her for a while with my fingers, loving the sounds she's making. But I'm burning with need for her, so I quickly replace my hand with my cock. I keep her back flush against my chest while I slowly enter her from behind.

"Fuck, you feel so damn good. I'll never get tired of your pussy wrapping around my cock."

"Good. I'll never get tired of you filling me and stretching me to the max either, big boy."

"Is that my nickname now?"

"Yes."

I kiss her shoulder before biting her smooth skin softly. "I like it."

"What are you doing to me, Alex?"

"I'm going to make you come, baby girl. Isn't it obvious?" I press my fingers over her clit while thrusting in and out of her.

"That feels good."

"Oh yeah?" Still pressing on her clit, I make small circles with my fingers.

"Yes! Yes! Oh my God. I'm coming."

Damn. That was fast. I increase my pace, fucking her harder while she rides her orgasm. I probably could go on for much longer, but the noise outside my room tells me Logan is awake.

I surrender to the moment, letting myself go. I come hard inside her, my cock throbbing as my cum fills her up. I hide my face in her tangled hair, saying her name over and over again in guttural bursts. I only stop moving when the shakes running through my body stop, and I feel the result of our lovemaking make a mess of things.

"I'm replacing my alarm clock with you," Blair says.

"I'm happy to take over." I kiss her shoulder, then pull out. "Let me get a towel."

I get out of bed and run to my bathroom. Sex without a

condom is great, but I could do without the aftermath. When I return, Blair is already sitting up, but she seems far away.

"Let me clean you, babe."

"It's okay. I can do it myself." She takes the towel from me and begins, but then stops and looks up. "Are you going to watch?"

I wiggle my eyebrows. "Yes. It's a great view."

Her face goes all shades of red. "Stop it. You're making me self-conscious."

"You're so silly. I've seen your pussy up close plenty of times."

"This is different."

"Okay, okay. I won't stare." I glance at the door. "I think Logan is up."

"Or he just got home."

"True. I didn't hear him come in last night before I passed out."

"What time is it, anyway?"

"I'm not sure. Let me check." I search for my phone and find it inside my coat pocket. "It's a little after nine."

Blair gets out of bed. "My mother has probably called a million times. I need to shower."

"What are your plans for today?"

"I'm expected back at their house tonight for Christmas Eve dinner, but there's something I need to do this morning."

"Last-minute shopping?"

She looks me straight in the eye and doesn't speak for a moment. Her gaze shows a myriad of emotions though, as if she's weighing the pros and cons of a big decision. "No. I need to visit the reason I can't escape my fate, and I want you to come with me."

BLAIR

I'm nervous about revealing my secret to Alex. My mother has threatened that if I ever tell anyone about Cory, I'll never see him again. But I need to explain to Alex that the reason we can't be together isn't because I'm weak or only interested in material things.

We get ready quickly and then leave his apartment without having breakfast first. We don't see Logan, but their dog's absence clues us in that he must have taken her for a walk.

"Do you want to stop somewhere to get breakfast?" I ask.

"Would you mind? I think I might still be a little drunk."

"Not at all."

We pick a fast-food restaurant drive-through. I'm hungry, but I'm too nervous to eat, so I don't touch my food. But I do drink the coffee.

"Where are we going, babe?"

I grab my phone and turn it on so I can type the address into the navigation system. I know how to get there, but Alex doesn't and he's the one driving. My stomach twists when I see all the text messages my mother sent last night and the voice mails.

"What's wrong?"

"My mother's blowing up my phone."

The compulsion to read the messages and listen to her voice mails is almost overwhelming, but if I do it now, it will only sour my day. I can wait until tonight to get all depressed.

"I'm sorry."

"Thanks, but I'm used to it by now."

He takes my hand and brings it to his lips to kiss my knuckles. "No one should ever get used to dick parents."

His words dispel a little bit of the darkness swirling in my chest. I set up the navigation system and then place my phone between our seats so he can see it.

"Twin Falls?" He looks at me. "What's there?"

"You'll see." I glance out the window, trying not to worry about how Alex is going to react when he learns the truth.

CHAPTER 51
ALEX

I have no idea what to expect, and Blair refuses to say where we're going, save for inputting the address on my phone. Our destination is in Evergreene, and that makes me even more curious. I know we aren't paying her parents a surprise visit, although I secretly wish we were going there to tell them they can forget about marrying her off to that Russian scum because she's mine.

One day that will be the case. That's now my mission.

I'm utterly confused when I turn into the parking lot of a place called Twin Falls Assisted Living. I glance at Blair. "Is this the right place?"

She doesn't look at me. "Yes." Then she clenches her jaw shut.

I park the car, but neither of us makes a motion to exit the vehicle. I rub my face, nervous about who I'm meeting here.

Blair takes a deep breath. "Are you ready?"

I look at her. "I am. Are you?"

She meets my stare. "I'm terrified, but I'm ready. This is a family secret I've never shared with anyone, not even Gia."

I swallow the lump in my throat and all the emotions her

confession evokes in me. I touch her face, trying to show her how much I love her. "Thank you for trusting me."

She nods, then opens the door and gets out of the car.

I follow her, zipping my jacket all the way up. She waits for me in front of the car, and I take her hand, lacing our fingers together.

My heart is thumping hard inside my chest, and my stomach is coiled tight with tension. I bet Blair is feeling the same, or worse. The fact that she's never told anyone outside her family about this—not even her best friend—speaks volumes about the magnitude of this secret.

The lady behind the reception desk glances up from her computer and smiles, recognition shining in her eyes. Blair comes here a lot.

"Hello, Blair. I didn't expect you until a bit later." She turns her attention to me. "Oh, you brought a friend."

"Yes. How is Cory? Is he up for a visit?"

My pulse accelerates. Hearing a name makes everything more real.

"He's always happy to see you, but maybe your friend should wait a bit. You know he can get agitated with strangers."

"Of course."

"I can wait here," I say, eyeing the chairs pushed against the wall.

"Oh, you can come in with me. There's another place inside where you can wait," Blair tells me.

The receptionist prints out visitor stickers for us, which we place on our clothes, and then Blair leads the way through the double doors, which open to a wide, carpeted corridor. The walls are an egg-wash color, and there are happy, pastel-colored abstract pictures hanging along the way. It's a short hallway that ends in a bright common room with several couches, tables, and flat-screen TVs on the walls.

"You can wait here while I talk to Cory. I'll be back soon."

"Okay."

She steps closer and rises on her tiptoes to kiss me quickly on the lips. "Thank you."

I smile and caress her hairline with the tip of my fingers. "You're welcome, baby girl."

A blush spreads through her cheeks, and she rewards me with a tiny smile of her own. My heart soars despite the anxiety that's swirling there. I take a seat in front of one of the TVs and try to pay attention to what's on, but my mind is working nonstop, trying to guess who Cory is and how he's linked to the hold Blair's mother has on her.

Ten minutes later, Blair returns, and I sit straighter in my seat. Next to her is a tall, wiry young man who resembles Ryder a lot. His hair is dark brown and shorter than Ryder's, but his eyes are the same shade of blue, and his jawline is the same as well. The biggest difference is his posture. Whereas Ryder and Blair have square shoulders, raised chins, and Westwood poise, Cory seems like a frightened bird, timid and unsure of himself.

His arm is laced with Blair's, and he doesn't make eye contact with me. I make a motion to stand, but Blair shakes her head.

"Cory, this is my friend Alex."

I wait for him to say something, but he keeps his gaze glued to the floor.

I'm not sure what to do, so I turn to Blair and mouth, *Can I say something?*

She nods.

"Hi Cory. Nice to meet you."

He doesn't reply, and I look at Blair again, a little panicked and asking for help with my eyes.

"Alex plays hockey just like Ryder does."

That gets a reaction from Cory. He looks at her, then turns to me. "I-I like ho-o-ckey."

"I love it. It's a great sport."

"Alex is going to play for the Miami Lions," Blair tells him.

His eyes seem to grow larger. "R-Ryder quit the—the team. He's a dumbass."

My brows arch. I want to laugh, but I'm not sure if that's okay. Cory turns to Blair. "Wh-when is he co-coming?"

"I'm not sure, Cory. Probably a bit later."

"I-I wa-want to go to my-my room now."

"Okay. I'll take you back."

"Bye, Cory. It was nice to meet you," I say, more chipper than usual to mask the fact that I'm reeling.

He waves goodbye, and then Blair takes him back. I watch them leave as I try to put the pieces together. Even though she hasn't told me who Cory is, it's impossible not to guess after meeting him.

She returns five minutes later, alone. "So that was Cory."

Now, I do get up. "Your brother."

"My twin brother."

My eyes bug out. I didn't expect that.

"He has cerebral palsy. The umbilical cord got wrapped around his neck during birth. His brain didn't get enough oxygen for too long."

"Blair… I'm so sorry."

Her eyes fill with tears. "Despite that, I've always felt a connection to Cory. He's my twin—you know what that's like."

"Yeah," I say, choked up.

"My parents don't feel that way. In fact, they lied to everyone and said he died at birth. They're embarrassed to have a child who isn't perfect." She wipes the corners of her eyes. "They hid him away, and Ryder and I are allowed to visit him only on special occasions, like holidays and my birthday and Cory's."

I pull her into my arms, hugging her tight. "It's so fucking awful. I can't begin to imagine what that must have been like for you and Ryder growing up."

"Hell, I've felt so guilty that I was spared, and Cory has to live isolated like this. He does need constant care, but he doesn't deserve to be shoved into a dark corner and forgotten."

I begin to suspect what her odious mother is doing, but I ask nonetheless. "Did your mother threaten to forbid you from seeing Cory if you don't abide by her demands?"

Blair tenses in my arms. "Yes. Not only that, she said she'd move him to a different facility out of state and that I'd never see him again."

I ease back and pinch her chin between my forefinger and thumb, raising her head. "We can't let her do that. There's gotta be a way to stop it from happening."

"What can I do? My parents are Cory's legal guardians. They can do whatever they please."

No, I refuse to accept that. There has to be something we can do to stop them from committing such a travesty.

"Now you understand why I can't fight her… why I have to marry—"

I press my finger over her lips. "No. You don't have to marry that scum, and you won't. I love you, Blair."

Tears roll down her cheeks. "I love you too."

Despite my heart being broken and bruised after learning Blair's secret, when I hear her confession, it still beats faster and lighter. I capture her face between my hands and kiss her with all my heart and soul. Now that I know she loves me, there's not a chance in hell I'm letting her go.

CHAPTER 52
BLAIR

I feel as if a huge weight has been lifted off my shoulders. I've been keeping Cory a secret for so long I was starting to think I was no better than my parents. Introducing Alex to my brother felt right, like it was meant to be. Telling Alex I love him came naturally. I'm moved by all the emotions of today. There's still fear in my chest, but peace and love are winning.

I keep stealing glances at Alex while he drives us back to Fairbanks, not daring to believe that this man, this fearsome and passionate warrior, loves me.

"What are your plans for Christmas Eve?" I ask, realizing that he never told me.

He glances at me. "Logan and I are taking Dad to a Chinese restaurant."

"Like in the movie *A Christmas Story*?"

He smiles. "That's right. We used to watch that movie every year growing up. It was my father's favorite. After the divorce… well, there weren't any more family Christmas dinners, so Logan and I decided to create that tradition with him."

"What about your mom?"

"She… doesn't like to celebrate Christmas that much. She

heads over to my grandparents'." I hear the wistfulness in his voice, and it makes my heart feel tighter.

"You don't see your mom during the holidays at all?"

"She came to Fairbanks my freshman year."

Maybe I should drop the subject. This is clearly not a happy topic for Alex, but all this time, we've only been exposed to my family. I don't know anything about his, save for the fact that my father is responsible for his father's downfall.

"How often do you see her?"

"In the summer. We spend it at our grandparents'."

I feel a little bit better that, despite the divorce, he has a stronger relationship with his parents than I do with mine. I look out the window, feeling depressed. In a few hours, I have to be with my odious parents, and that's the last place I want to be.

"What's the matter, baby girl?"

I sigh. "I wish I didn't have to go to my parents' house tonight."

"Then don't. Come to dinner with me."

I whip my face to him so fast I crack my neck. "You want me to have Christmas dinner with your father?"

"Yes, I want him to meet you."

A giant boa constrictor seems to be squeezing my heart tight. "But… he hates my family."

"He hates your *father*."

"You don't think that hate extends to me?"

He looks at me. "I want to believe it doesn't. Blair, you're part of my life now. I have to hope he can see past the Westwood name. I did."

He's trying to make me feel better, but it doesn't work. "But look how long it took."

He shakes his head. "It didn't take that long. I think deep down, I always knew you were the one for me."

I blink fast, trying to grasp his meaning. "Are you saying you had a thing for me even when you seemed to hate me?"

"I think that's why I held on to that emotion for so long. I told you before how mesmerized I was by you when you burst into that classroom. And then you wowed us all with your sharp mind."

Be still my heart and try not to melt.

"Do you want to know what I thought when I first saw you?"

"Of course."

"I knew you were Ryder's teammate, and I thought you seemed nice. I was glad, and relieved, that I could maybe have a friend in that class."

"Blair… I'm so sorry I was a jerk to you back then."

"Well, it was for the best. If you and I weren't having a bad day, who knows what would have happened? Maybe you'd have fallen in love with me then and missed the chance to fuck around for two years."

"You think I'd regret that when I could have had you this whole time?"

I tilt my head. "You'd give up all those puck bunnies for me?"

He glares. "Do you even have to ask? In a heartbeat, baby girl."

I try to not let my ego inflate, but I fail. I can't help the smug grin that blossoms on my face. "I believe you."

"You'd better." He gives my thigh a squeeze. "So, are you coming to dinner?"

My mother will have an aneurysm if I skip her dinner, but I'm already in deep trouble with her—might as well give her the proverbial middle finger again.

"All right. If you think it's a good idea, I'm game." I look at the time and curse in my head.

It didn't occur to me to get a gift for Alex—probably because I didn't know where we stood. Now there's no question about it. I must. And I also need to get Logan and their dad something.

"So I was wondering when we can try another scenario from that book of yours."

Distracted by thoughts of last-minute gift shopping, it takes me a while to understand his meaning. "Oh, you wanna role-play again?"

"I know it didn't end as we hoped, but I'd love to keep exploring. It was the hottest thing I've ever done."

My face becomes warmer. "Yeah, it was hot. I'm sorry I blew it at the end."

"You didn't blow it. If there's anyone to blame for what happened, it's me."

I shake my head. "We aren't going to try it again while we're still harboring negative feelings. If we do this, then it's a clean slate."

"Agreed. So is that a yes?"

I smirk. "Hmm… maybe that can be one of your Christmas gifts."

"Don't even joke about that, baby girl. I'm already getting a hard-on."

"I'm not joking." I slide my hand across his thigh until it's resting between his legs. The bulge is there all right.

"Blair…." he whispers tightly. "What are you doing?"

"Playing." I rub my hand over his erection, making him hiss.

"Fuck. I can't concentrate on driving while you're doing that to me. I'll stop the car though, if you continue."

Knowing I don't have much time to do what I need to do, I pull my hand away. I can't afford delays. "Okay, okay."

He turns to me. "But you *will* resume when we get home, right?"

"Do you want me to jerk you off in your car?"

He smirks. "Jerk me off, blow me, whatever your naughty heart desires."

I lean across the space between us and kiss his cheek. "My naughty heart desires many things, big boy. You'll see."

CHAPTER 53
ALEX

After I drop Blair at her apartment, I head to the mall and brave the dreaded last-minute Christmas shopping. I need to buy her something. I'm a procrastinator and horrible at buying gifts for people. When it comes to Blair, it's even more complicated. What do I get for a girl that has everything?

I'm walking past a lingerie store and naturally, my eyes snag on the garter belts displayed on one of the mannequins. Maybe I could get Blair a new one.

"Alex?" Someone calls my name.

I turn around and find Noah there, carrying a few bags. "Hey, man. What are you doing here?"

He raises his arms, highlighting the shopping bags. "What do you think?"

I shake my head, chuckling. "I'm in the same boat, but it looks like you're done."

His gaze switches to the lingerie store behind me, and a knowing smile appears on his face. "I take it things are going well between you and Blair?"

I rub the back of my neck. "Yeah, I'm way out of my depth. I have no clue what to get her for Christmas."

"It doesn't matter what you get her, as long as it's from the heart."

I fight the urge to roll my eyes. "Okay, simp boy."

He laughs. "You can always give her your jersey."

"I don't know... that seems self-indulgent. Here, babe, wear my jersey."

Noah's brows pinch. "That's true. Is there anything that represents an important moment in your relationship with Blair?"

Well, there's that garter belt, but I don't think it quite cuts it. I'm still getting her one though. It'll be more like a present for me.

I think about our moments, and one that comes to the forefront of my mind is the first time I realized Blair was more than the image she projected. It was when I caught her dancing in that gym in the arena. She was so free and happy; it moved me.

"I think I've got it," I tell Noah.

"Good. Well, I'm done here. Logan told me you're taking your dad to a Chinese restaurant for dinner?"

"Yeah, Dad's excited about it."

"Have fun. And Merry Christmas."

"Merry Christmas."

Noah turns away, and I walk into the lingerie store. Might as well get *my* present. Then I need to find Blair's. I hope they have what I'm looking for here.

I'm on my way to pick up Blair when Logan calls. I just texted him to let him know I invited her to dinner. I haven't seen him all day. Thanks to my trip to Twin Falls in the morning and then my mall adventure, we kept missing each other.

"Hey," I say.

"You're joking about bringing Blair to dinner, right?" he barks in my ear, making me grimace.

"No. She's my girlfriend, Logan. I want Dad to meet her."

"She's a Westwood! You know that's all he'll see. You're going to ruin Christmas dinner."

"You don't know that," I reply feebly.

That might happen, but I've decided to risk it. I couldn't bear the thought of Blair spending Christmas with her awful parents.

"I *do* know that." He sighs, frustrated. "Maybe don't tell him she's a Westwood."

I rub my face. I don't like that I have to hide her identity, but maybe for tonight, it's the best course of action. "Fine. I won't tell him who she is."

"Good. Are you on your way to pick her up?"

"Yeah. I'm about to park in front of her building."

"All right. I'll see you at the restaurant."

I try to not let Logan's call get to me. I can't let Blair know about this conversation. She is already hesitant about coming tonight, and I don't want her to change her mind.

She said she'd meet me outside. I text her to let her know I've arrived. A minute later, she comes out, wearing a short green-and-black-plaid swing coat with a huge bow on the front, a red beret, black tights, and over-the-knee high-heeled boots. She looks adorable and sexy as hell at the same time. It was a smart move on her part to not let me come up to her apartment. It might have made us late for dinner.

I get out of the car to open the door and take the huge shopping bag she has in her hands. It's heavy.

"What do you have here, baby girl?"

"Gifts." She beams at me.

I lean down and kiss her cherry-red lips. "You didn't need to buy anything."

"I know. I promise I didn't go crazy."

I give her sweet ass a little spank. "Get in the car before your tush freezes. I'll put this in the trunk."

She giggles. "Are we role-playing already?"

Her comment makes me stop. I wasn't even thinking about

that, but now I am. I'm looking at her and picturing her completely naked save for her harness and that collar, and my cock turns hard.

"Oh my God. You're thinking about it, aren't you?"

"I wasn't until you brought it up. Get in the car, baby girl. Please."

She flattens her mouth, but the upturn of her red lips tells me she wants to keep smiling. I put her bag in the trunk and run to get back behind the steering wheel.

She takes off her leather gloves and rubs her hands together in front of the car heater. "Boy, it got cold so fast."

"Yeah." I put the car in drive and keep my gaze glued to the road. It's not snowing right now, but it's dark, and there are patches of ice that I need to watch out for.

"How far is the restaurant?" she asks.

"It's downtown. Nothing fancy."

"Good. I'm sick of fancy places."

I glance at her quickly. "You really do mean that, don't you?"

She squints her eyes. "I know it's hard to believe I don't care about money, but I really don't. I only overspend my parents' money as compensation for all the bullshit they put me through."

"I know that now. I'm sorry I was so quick to judge."

"I don't blame you. I play the part of pampered princess pretty well."

"How did your mother take the news you weren't coming to their Christmas dinner party?"

She doesn't answer right away, so I look at her again. She's furrowing her brows and biting her lower lip. "I didn't tell them."

"You're just not going to show up?"

"Yep." She turns her face toward the window.

"What about your mother's threat?"

"She's going to take Cory away from me anyway when I tell her I'm not marrying Ilya."

My heart skips a beat only to speed up to a hundred in the next second. "Baby girl, that's the best Christmas gift you could possibly have given me." I reach for her hand and bring it to my lips.

She smiles. "But I have more gifts for you, big boy."

"All I want is you."

"Shall I find a radio station that's playing Mariah's song?"

I chuckle. "Knock yourself out."

All radio stations are playing the most popular Christmas songs on rotation, so naturally, Mariah Carey's famous Christmas anthem pops up, and Blair and I sing along at the top of our lungs. I'm in high spirits when I arrive at the restaurant, and the sense of euphoria makes me feel invincible. I'm not worried anymore about introducing Blair to Dad.

But when she doesn't make a move to get out of the car right away, I ask. "What's the matter, baby girl?"

"I'm nervous. What if your father hates me?"

I caress her cheek. "He's not going to hate you, but… I think it's better to not tell him you're a Westwood tonight."

She arches her eyebrows. "How about we never tell him?"

I laugh, shaking my head. "We won't be able to keep that a secret forever. He'll know when your full name is printed on the wedding invitation."

Her blue eyes turn as round as saucers. "Wedding?"

"Yes, wedding. You'll be my wife one day, baby girl."

She smirks. "Is that so? I don't remember getting a proposal."

"It'll come. Let's go in before Logan starts to blow up my phone."

"I left mine at home for that reason."

"Good. I don't want anyone making you sad tonight." I shorten the distance between us and give her a quick peck on the lips. "I love you."

"I love you too."

CHAPTER 54
BLAIR

My stomach is twisted into ninja knots, and it's making me feel queasy. I'm shaking like a leaf as I walk with Alex into the restaurant. My clammy hand is firmly clasped in his. I've never had a boyfriend before. Hence, I've never done the meet-the-parents thing. No, I usually met my potential boyfriend's parents before I even dated their sons.

Logan and their father turn in our direction as we approach their table. "There you are," Logan greets us, smiling, but I notice tension around his mouth. He probably believes me coming here is a bad idea.

"We got here as fast as we could, but the road conditions were poor," Alex replies.

I look at Mr. Kaminski, and our eyes meet. I can see where Alex and Logan get their looks. The man's once blond hair is now peppered with gray, and the deep creases around his mouth make him look older than I thought he was, but he's a handsome man.

Alex releases my hand and walks around the table to greet his dad, who just stood up from his chair. He's as tall as Alex, but much slimmer.

"Merry Christmas, Dad." Alex hugs him.

"Merry Christmas, son." When they step back, he looks at me again. "So you're the girl who finally set one of my boys on the straight-and-narrow path."

"That's me." I move closer, extending my hand. "I'm Blair."

"What's with this nonsense handshake? Give me a hug." He opens his arms wide, and even though I'm a little stiff, I step into his embrace.

My face is much warmer when we break apart, but when I look at Alex and see his goofy, happy grin, I forget my embarrassment. Maybe tonight won't be a bust after all.

I sit next to Logan, who's across from his dad, and Alex takes the chair opposite mine. I'm not facing Mr. Kaminski straight on, but I'm not safe from his scrutinizing stare.

The waitress comes to take our drink orders, and then Logan asks, "Could you also bring three orders of your appetizer combo?"

I quickly glance at the menu to see what he ordered, and my eyes widen. I look up. "Three? That's a lot of food. Will you have room for the main course?"

The three Kaminski men look at one another and then laugh. Yeah, my face is in flames now. Alex reaches for my hand. "I thought you were already used to my appetite, babe."

Oh my God. I can't believe he said that with a straight face. I want to kick him under the table, but I settle for a glare. Next to me, Logan chokes on his water because he can't drink and laugh at the same time.

"You have no idea how much it cost to keep these boys fed growing up," Mr. Kaminski chimes in.

His comment is meant to be light, but I notice the change in Alex's demeanor. He must be remembering the period in his childhood when his dad couldn't provide for his family, thanks to my father.

I don't want to succumb to sad feelings, but the dark cloud still hangs over my head.

"We burned up a lot of energy," Logan replies.

Mr. Kaminski stares intently at me again, and this time, he narrows his eyes. "You look so familiar, Blair. I feel like I've met you before."

Ah hell. He can't possibly know who I am. I don't look anything like my father, and as far as I know, he's only interacted with him.

"I have one of those faces. I've been told I look like the actress Ana de Armas."

"You're way prettier than her." Alex smiles.

Mr. Kaminski shakes his head. "No, that's not it."

Mercifully, the waitress arrives with our drinks, and I have a reprieve from Mr. Kaminski's probing gaze. I realize that I'm still wearing my coat, so I stand up to take it off. I'm wearing a cute red long-sleeve dress with a sweetheart neckline underneath, and I know Alex appreciates the view when his eyes widen a fraction.

The moment I sit back down, Mr. Kaminski is staring at my chest. Not staring, glowering. Does he have a problem with my clothes? My neckline isn't that low.

"Is that a *B* and a *W* on your pendant?" he asks through clenched teeth.

Shit. I totally forgot about my necklace. I've been wearing it since I was a teen and I never take it off. I cover the offending piece of jewelry, but it's too late. He's seen it already.

"Yes," I reply.

He puts his hands on the table, then turns them into fists. "You're a Westwood, aren't you?"

I should lie. There are plenty of surnames that start with *W*.

"Dad… please," Alex starts, and it's like an admission.

Mr. Kaminski turns his ire on him. "You're dating a *Westwood*, boy? After everything that family has done to us? How could you?"

"She isn't her father," he argues.

He slams the table with his fists, making me wince. "She's a fucking Westwood! They're all the same."

His outburst makes everyone in the restaurant turn toward our table. I'm mortified and feeling guilty as hell. If I'd remembered to take my stupid necklace off, this wouldn't have happened. I jump from my chair and grab my coat.

Alex looks at me. "Where are you going?"

"Home. I shouldn't have come. I'm sorry." I glance at Mr. Kaminski. "I'm so sorry."

I run from the table, trying to stop the tears forming in my eyes from rolling down my cheeks.

Alex catches up with me outside and grabs my arm, spinning me around. "Don't go. Please."

"I can't stay, Alex. Look at what my presence did to your father. This was a mistake."

"Don't say that."

"You know it was."

He runs his hands through his hair and looks away. "I'm an idiot. I really hoped you could win him over before we told him who you were."

"He's probably seen a picture of my family. That's why he thought I looked familiar."

"Maybe." He takes my coat from my hand and helps me into it. "I'll take you home."

"No! You should go back inside and be with your father. He's going to hate me more if you leave to be with me."

"You can't expect me to let you go home alone after this."

I put my hands on my hips, letting annoyance over his comment wash over me and make me forget that I'm on the verge of crying. "*Let* me? I'm an adult, Alex. I can go home by myself."

"I'm sorry. I didn't mean it like that. I just don't want you to be alone on Christmas Eve."

I wipe the corners of my eyes. "I won't be alone. I have

Cookie. You can swing by the apartment after you're done with dinner."

He pulls me into a bear hug, and I press my face against his warm chest, taking a deep breath of his cologne. I love the way he smells, and right now, I need to get my fill of everything about him.

"You don't have your phone on you. I'll get you an Uber."

I pull back and turn when I see headlights approach. "No need. There's a cab coming."

Alex flags the taxi, and it stops. I'm shocked that we could find a ride so easily tonight, but it seems the universe is giving us a break.

"I got gifts for you, Logan and your dad. You can give them to them tonight, or maybe wait until your dad's calmed down."

"We'll see. Are you sure you're going to be okay?" He looks into my eyes, searching.

"Yes. I'm fine. Go make peace with your dad." I rise on my tiptoes and kiss Alex's cold lips. "You're freezing already without a coat. Go!"

Stubbornly, he doesn't budge until I'm inside the taxi, and even after I give the driver my address and we're in motion, Alex remains rooted to the spot. My chest feels unbearably heavy. I have the grim sense this is the last time I'll see him, and the horrible sensation brings tears to my eyes again.

I'm still reeling from Mr. Kaminski's reaction when the taxi drops me off in front of my apartment. I'm not paying attention to my surroundings at all—not that I ever have any reason to be leery at night. I live in a safe neighborhood. So when a dark figure emerges from the shadows, it catches me completely by surprise.

I let out a gasp and reach inside my purse for my pepper spray.

"Good evening, Blair," Ilya says smoothly.

My heart is still going a hundred miles per hour, and I don't let go of the pepper spray can in my hand yet. "What are you doing here?"

"Waiting for you." He approaches like a jungle cat who's pursuing prey.

I swallow the huge lump in my throat. "It's Christmas Eve. Don't you have any plans?"

"I do, and so do you. We're expected at your parents' house tonight."

"I didn't know they hired you to be my babysitter."

He narrows his eyes. "I'm not used to chasing after women, Blair. But you see, your father and mine made a deal, and you're part of it."

I lift my chin higher. "I'm not marrying you."

He grabs my arm and pulls me flush against his body, trapping my hand with the pepper spray between our bodies. "Oh, but you are, sweetheart."

"You can't make me." I try to break free of his hold.

He arches his eyebrows. "I can't? Hmm, let's see. If you don't marry me, you'll be directly responsible for the end of your lover's hockey career and his brother's. The contract they're about to sign will go up in flames."

"You're bluffing," I grit out.

"Am I? Do you even know what my family is capable of, darling? Why do you think your father is so keen to partner with us?"

My stomach drops through the earth. I *don't* know why, but I do know that this deal between our families has also affected Ryder's life.

As if reading my mind, Ilya continues, "Your brother already fucked with our plans, and we're running out of patience."

"How did he do that?"

His lips curl into an ugly grin. "It doesn't matter. The important thing is that you don't."

He hasn't mentioned Cory at all. Ilya might not know about him since my parents did such a good job hiding his existence. He's not even registered at Twin Falls under Westwood. But Alex and Logan are banking on their contracts. It's their dream to play professional hockey. I can't let Ilya take that away from them. But ending things with Alex to marry Ilya feels like a death sentence, and if I tell Alex any of this, I know what his response will be. He'll sacrifice his dream for me.

"I can see the gears in your head working hard to find a way out of this, but there isn't one. Not only will I take away their chance to play professional hockey, they'll also lose their scholarships."

"What?" I squeak.

"Yes. There are many reasons a player can be kicked off the team. If the school found the mighty Kaminski twins were taking performance-enhancement drugs, for instance…"

"They aren't! You're going to set them up?"

"Set them up?" He tsks, shaking his head. "No, I'm just going to expose them for the frauds they are."

Angry tears fill my eyes, blurring my vision. Ilya is too smart to confess he'd set them up, but that's exactly what he's threatening to do. I can't marry him, but right now, I don't see any other option but to follow along with his demands.

"Release me, or I'll scream bloody murder," I grit out.

He drops my arm and steps back. Then he reaches inside his pocket and retrieves a monogrammed linen handkerchief, then offers it to me.

"Dry your tears, darling. That uncivilized hockey player is beneath you. You may not realize it yet, but you're meant for bigger things. You were born to be a Bolkosky."

I stare at him, face blank. "You might coerce me into marrying you, Ilya, but I'll always be a Westwood."

CHAPTER 55
ALEX

Dad refused to talk to me during dinner, so Logan had to play an intermediary between us. At least he didn't ask to go home after Blair left. It'll take a while to convince him that she isn't like her father. I'm not giving her up though. He either gets over his prejudice, or I won't see him as much anymore. It pains me to think that way, but Blair is my endgame.

I couldn't wait to go check on her. In fact, I barely ate my food, thanks to all the anxiety making my chest tight. I did order a dish to go because she left without eating dinner.

On the way out of the restaurant, I try to give Dad a hug, but he refuses to get near me.

"Dad, don't be like that," Logan interjects.

"Traitors don't deserve hugs," he grumbles.

Logan opens his mouth, but I cut him off. "It's okay. Give him time."

"Give me time for what?" Dad's eyebrows shoot to the heavens. "Do you think I'll ever get used to one of my sons dating a snake?"

"Blair isn't a snake. She couldn't be more different than her family. Please don't punish her for her father's sins."

He watches me angrily for a couple beats before turning to Logan, "Let's go. I'm tired."

"Okay, Dad." Logan gives me an apologetic glance before steering Dad toward his car.

I head to mine and put Blair's gift bag on the passenger seat. I didn't dare try to give her gift to Dad. He'd probably destroy it in a fit of rage.

I turn on the engine and blast the car heater to the max. Then I check my phone, hoping to see a message from her. The only new message I have is from CJ. Since he's a grump, and he wouldn't send me a text only to wish me Merry Christmas, I click on it.

> Blair just announced her engagement to some Russian asshole at her parents' party! I thought you were together???

I have to read his text several times because I can't possibly be reading that right. "What the actual fuck!"

I call him immediately, but the motherfucker doesn't answer. Then I call Blair, and it goes to voice mail too. Shit. Did she not go home like she said she would? I put the car in gear and peel out of my parking spot, taking the route to the highway.

The next person I call is Ryder. The phone rings and rings… and nothing. "Son of a bitch."

I don't know how CJ got the news. Maybe he's at the Westwoods' Christmas party. His family is chummy with Blair's parents. My heart is pumping like a factory, and my head is spiraling. Blair wouldn't have turned a one-eighty on me just because of my father. Something happened.

I think for a moment about calling Gia to ask if she knows anything, but I don't want to ruin her evening. It doesn't matter anyway; I'll find out when I crash the party Blair isn't supposed to be at.

I'm driving way over the speed limit, but it seems no cops are out yet to try to bust drunk drivers. I get lucky. It also means I arrive in Evergreene in record time.

When I approach her parents' gate, I call Ryder once again. This time, he answers.

"Alex—"

"Tell me the news I heard from CJ isn't true."

"I'm sorry. I don't know what happened."

My heart sinks. "Is Blair at the party?"

"Yes… she came with Ilya."

I pull my hair, yanking it at the strands until it hurts. "How is that possible? She went home."

"I don't know the details. I haven't been able to get Blair alone to talk to her."

"I'm at your parents' security entry."

"What? You're here?"

"Yes, make sure they let me through, or I swear to God, I'll drive through this fucking gate."

"Fuck... *fine*."

I end the call, and when the security guard asks for my name and where I'm going, there isn't an issue.

No surprise, I find Ryder waiting for me outside his parents' mansion. I park my car right at the front, blocking the driveway.

"You can't come in, Alex. You'll just make things worse."

"The hell I can't!" I try to walk around him, but he blocks my path and grabs my arm.

Big mistake. I whirl around and punch the side of his face. He staggers back, releasing me at once. Then he rubs the spot I hit. I got his mouth. His lower lip is busted and bleeding.

"You finally decked me. Congratulations. Is that your plan when you burst inside the house? Punch Ilya's face?"

"You bet your ass."

"And what do you think that will accomplish? You're not thinking, man. If Blair is there and agreeing to the engagement, it's because he's holding something over her head, and I bet a million bucks it has to do with you."

"I don't care what that asshole does to me! I won't let her marry him to save me."

He steps closer to me, invading my space even though I've already punched him once. There's no fear in his eyes though. "The Bolkosky family are criminals, if you haven't figured that out already. I won't let you put Blair's life in danger because you're a hothead."

The revelation is akin to a punch to my guts. I wince and step back. "Are they going to kill her if she refuses to marry Ilya?"

Ryder runs a shaky hand through his hair. "I don't know what they'll do. We need a plan. I'm begging you to go home now."

"You just told me Blair is engaged to a guy in the Russian Mafia, and you want me to go *home*? Are you out of your goddamn mind?"

"Nothing is going to happen to her tonight. I'll protect her."

"We both know that's a load of crap."

Now it's his turn to wince as if I punched him again. His expression falls as guilt sets in his eyes. "I fucked up. I know. Give me time to fix it. She won't marry him tomorrow or the day after. We have time."

"What do you want me to do? Just sit on the sidelines and watch her be engaged to him?"

"I'm asking you to go home and cool off. We'll talk tomorrow. Blair is going to spend the night here, and so am I. I won't let anything happen to her. You have my word."

Every fiber in me is rebelling against the idea of leaving without talking to Blair. But I can't ignore Ryder's warning. What if I put her life at risk with my presence? I'll never forgive myself if something happens to her because of me.

Reluctantly, and with my heart mangled to pieces, I say, "I'll go, but you'd better keep your phone handy and answer when I fucking call you."

He holds my gaze. "I will."

BLAIR

I was trying to keep my shit together when I saw Ryder dash across the room toward the front door. He looked nervous. My immediate thought was that Alex was here. It wasn't the most ludicrous notion. CJ is at the party. I could tell he was surprised as hell when Ilya announced our engagement during a dinner toast.

But I can't follow my brother when I'm surrounded by friends of my parents who are busy congratulating me, and Ilya is keeping a hawk eye on me from his corner of the room.

All I can do is nod, smile politely, and hope no one notices that inside my head, I'm screaming. This can't be happening to me. It's a nightmare I can't wake up from.

Minutes later, Ryder returns. He's pressing a tissue over his lips, and I think I see a blood smear on his white shirt. What the hell happened? He disappears into the hallway that leads to the staff stairs.

I excuse myself and follow him. Ilya can't say anything about me going after my brother.

I catch up with him just as he's about to enter his former bedroom. "Ryder, wait."

He stops and looks at me. "We need to talk."

He waits for me to approach and lets me go into his room first. Then he closes and locks the door. When he stops pressing the tissue to his lips, it allows me to see that there's a cut there.

My eyes widen. "Who did that to you?"

"Your boyfriend."

My heart stops beating for a second, then it lurches forward painfully. "Alex was here?"

"Yes, CJ texted him about your engagement."

My stomach dips and I feel sick. I bend forward a little, hugging my middle. "How… how was he?"

"What do you think? Berserk. He finally punched me when I wouldn't let him in the house."

I turn around, giving my back to Ryder. "He must hate me."

"He doesn't hate you. He's worried sick about you. What did Ilya say he'd do to coerce you into this sham engagement?"

My eyes burn from the tears forming in them. "He said he'd end Alex's and Logan's NHL careers, make their contract with the Miami Lions go away, and…" I stop, trying to get my words out without crying. "He also said he'd get them kicked off the team by setting them up."

"Let me guess, by saying they were taking steroids?"

I turn around and face him. "Yes. Is that what he did to you?"

Ryder freezes for a second, and his eyes are full of turmoil. "No. He didn't threaten to end my career, but that of my close friends. Jesse, for starters."

"Why?"

"Money. Dad sold me out to get a deal with the Bolkoskys. The company is in trouble, and he needs capital."

"What do you mean he sold you out?"

"He told them I could guarantee certain game outcomes."

I suck in a breath. "They wanted you to throw a game."

He nods. "The championship finals."

"And you did."

He looks away. "Yes, but not in the manner they desired. They didn't want me to quit the team. I knew that if I stayed, I'd become their puppet. I couldn't do that to my teammates. So I quit before the finals, knowing it would destabilize the team. It wasn't a guarantee the Warriors would lose. I took a gamble that worked out for those fuckers. But they were raving mad, nonetheless."

"Is that why you broke up with Gia?"

He rubs his face and looks into the distance. "Yes. I knew it was just a matter of time before they threatened to harm her too. So I broke up with her, hoping they'd forget she existed."

"Oh, Ryder…"

He gives me a wry smile. "It was for the best. She's happy with Noah now."

"But you're brokenhearted."

"I'll mend. We have to worry about you. You can't possibly marry into the Bolkosky family, Blair. It will be a death sentence."

His words feel like I'm being pierced by a spear. "What can I do? I don't have any leverage."

He doesn't speak for a couple beats, but his eyes never leave my face. "I'll find a way."

"Ryder… please don't do anything reckless. I can't lose you too."

He pulls me into a hug. "You won't lose me. I promise."

I want to believe his words, but they feel hollow to my ears. He's just as powerless as I am.

CHAPTER 56
ALEX

I haven't slept since I got back from Evergreene. I drove for hours, trying to figure out how to save the love of my life from marrying a criminal. I'm not an idiot. I know how dangerous the Russian Mafia is. We could run away, but that wouldn't solve anything. If they're as powerful as Ryder led me to believe, they'll find us anywhere. And then what? We'd both end up dead.

When I got home, Logan was already asleep. It's now six in the morning, and I'm still sitting in the same spot on the couch, staring at the wall and seeing nothing but bleakness.

Logan walks out of his room, yawning. He sees me and asks, "Did you just get home?"

He doesn't know that Blair got engaged to Ilya. He probably thinks I spent the night at her place.

"No."

"What happened? You look pitiful." He heads for the fridge and takes out the box of OJ, then drinks straight from it.

"Blair is engaged to someone else."

He chokes on the juice, spitting out half of it. "What?"

"It happened last night. Her father made a deal with the Russian Mafia, and Blair is part of the package."

"You're fucking shitting me." He walks over and takes the chair across from me.

"I wish I was. If she doesn't follow through, they might…" I get choked up and can't finish the sentence. Covering my mouth, I look away, fighting back tears.

"They'll hurt her?"

I nod, unable to say those words out loud.

"There's gotta be something we can do to stop it. Go to the police, the FBI."

I whip my face to his. "And say what? We have no proof they're doing anything illegal. Besides, Ilya has Blair's father's blessing for this unholy union."

"Are you just going to sit there and let that happen?"

"No." I run my fingers through my hair. "I have to think. Last night, I went to her parents' house, but Ryder stopped me from storming the party. He also doesn't want to see Blair marry that scum."

Logan stands up. "You haven't slept at all, have you?"

"I couldn't."

"You need to rest. You'll be able to think more clearly when you aren't running on fumes. Take a shower and try to sleep for a few hours."

Logan is right, but I doubt I'll be able to shut my eyes for more than a few minutes.

"We have Jesse's bachelor party tomorrow. Do you think you'll be able to go?"

"You didn't just ask me that. Of course I won't go."

"Maybe you should."

I get angry. "Do you think I can go to a party and get wasted while Blair is headed toward a life of misery?"

He narrows his eyes. "Have you stopped to consider that Ilya is expecting you to do something stupid? If he's Mafia, he probably has eyes on her *and* you. If he believes you don't care that she dumped you, he might back off. That's when you take action."

My brain is beginning to agree with Logan's argument, but my heart is rebelling against it. "I don't know."

"Like I said. You need to rest. Staring blankly at the wall won't do anything." He puts his coat on and grabs puppy Blair's leash. Her ears perk up, then she jumps to her paws and runs to him. "You'd better be in bed when I get back."

I don't answer him, nor do I move a muscle before he walks out. When the door shuts after him, I lean forward, resting my elbows on my knees, and let out a strangled cry.

BLAIR

When I wake up, my eyes are puffy. No surprise. I cried myself to sleep. I hear a bark, then Cookie jumps in my bed. I feel like crying once again. Ryder must have gone to my apartment to get him. I let him lick my face, then set him back on the floor to get out of bed and trudge to my old bathroom in my parents' house. Last night, Ryder stayed with me and let me cry on his shoulder until I was too exhausted to keep my eyes open. He's gone now, but I hope he's still around. I can't face my mother alone this morning.

I don't dare to look too closely at my reflection in the mirror. I brush my teeth almost robotically, feeling hollow inside. Then I return to the bedroom and search for my phone.

There are several text messages from the girls, but none from Alex. I ignore their texts. It could be about the wedding, or they've heard about my engagement. I can't deal with that right now. My heart sinks, and the urge to cry renews, but I suck in the feeling. Letting despair take control won't help me. I need to get my shit together and find a way to break free from Ilya's threats.

There's a knock on the door, and even though I don't want to see anyone, I find myself saying, "Come in."

"Good morning, miss. I brought you breakfast."

"Thanks. How did you know I wanted to eat in my room?"

"Your brother told us."

"Is he still in the house?"

"No, miss. He left a few minutes ago." She sets the tray on my desk and then pulls out a white envelope from her apron. "But he asked me to give you this note."

"Thanks."

She nods, then walks out of the room, closing the door softly. I rip the envelope open and read his message.

I couldn't risk sending you a text. I'm resorting to old-fashioned methods. I'm working on something. Don't lose hope, but also, don't try to reach Alex. I think it's wise if you don't speak to him for a few days.

Love, Ryder.

My heart is thumping loud and fast in my chest. There goes Ryder again, being all mysterious. I press my hand to my forehead. He'd better not get himself in more trouble to save me.

As much as it pains me, I do agree I need to stay away from Alex. Ilya might hurt him if I try to talk to him. I can't risk his life like that. That means I have to pretend I'm happy with my engagement in front of all my friends too. I won't involve anyone else I love in this mess.

I start by replying to texts from Gia, Ashley, and Zoey first. I give them the same lie. Things didn't work out between Alex and me, and I decided it was best to accept my fate and get engaged to Ilya.

Gia calls me immediately, making my stomach clench. Ryder broke up with her to protect her from the Bolkoskys. I can't reel her into the mess now, so I ignore it, setting the phone down. The compulsion to answer it is there, but not as strong as it usually is. Despair is trumping everything. I have to get ready to face my first day without Alex's love. The pain in my chest is so sharp it hurts to breathe.

I can do this. It's only temporary.

That's the mantra I stick to and replay in my head over and over again.

CHAPTER 57
BLAIR

I haven't seen Alex in a week, but we still have to finish our proposal for the UN. It's due the first week of January, so not communicating with him is impossible. We don't text or talk on the phone. Our convos are strictly via email, but it still hurts like a mother every time I see his name pop up in my inbox.

Since we're currently on Christmas break, I decided to stay with my parents. Now that they've gotten me to bend to their will, they aren't as controlling as before. I'm staying away from Fairbanks for several reasons. Less risk that I'll crack and go find Alex and less possibility of being cornered by Ilya when I'm alone.

He's come to visit a couple times since our engagement, but I'm never alone with him. Ryder has turned into my shadow whenever Ilya drops by. He, too, is spending the holidays at our folks' place.

I don't know what he's planning to do to save me from this unwanted fate, and my heart sinks with the possibility that he doesn't have a solution—and won't find one. I'm doing what I can by learning everything about the Bolkoskys. I've been searching articles, learning about the family tree and the companies they own, but I find nothing I can use against them. I consider spending more time with Ilya, pretending I'm resigned to marrying him, but I don't think I can be near him without showing my revulsion.

Riley's bachelorette party took place a couple of days ago, but I decided to skip it. I would have only ruined the fun for everyone, and it would have been too hard to pretend I was happy about being engaged. Plus, I'm sure the girls would ask about Alex, and I wasn't confident I could count on my poker face around them.

I heard Alex went to Jesse's bachelor party in Boston and got completely trashed, to the point he had to be carried out of the bar by Logan and Sean. Ilya made sure to rub that in when he visited, citing that Alex had already moved on and that I should too. I heard the insinuation loud and clear. But I know Alex wouldn't be flirting with other girls. He's not that guy anymore.

Even if that were true, I'd never forget him. Alex is imprinted in my heart forever, and neither Ilya nor anyone else can erase the mark he left on me. I will always love him.

I can't escape attending the rehearsal dinner tonight, but honestly, I've been counting the days. I'll see Alex in person again, and despite the danger, my heart won't stop beating faster thinking about him. The yearning is so intense I bought a bottle of his aftershave to carry around so I can smell it any time I want and feel closer to him. It's going to be brutal, being in his presence and pretending we're over. But I miss him so damn much I'm willing to deal with the pain just for the chance to look into his eyes and tell him without words how much I love him.

After spending hours getting ready for tonight, I stare at my reflection in the mirror. I run my hand over the silky, deep-blue fabric of the dress I bought for the occasion and notice it's a little loose at the waist. I've lost weight. My mother will be happy.

Bitch.

I put on my white fake fur coat and grab my purse. I'm wearing the deepest shade of red lipstick, and as I raise my chin, I pretend I'm Taylor Swift on her Fearless Tour.

I lose my bravado when I find Ilya waiting for me at the bottom of the stairs. "What are you doing here?"

He's wearing a sharp dark-gray suit, a white shirt, and a blue tie that matches the color of my dress. I bet my fucking mother gave him that information.

He looks me up and down, and his eyes widen in appreciation. "You look stunning, darling."

"You didn't answer my question."

"I'm here to take you to your friends' rehearsal dinner."

My stomach drops through the floor. "You're not in the wedding party."

His brows arch. "I'm your fiancé. I don't need to be part of the wedding party to be your date tonight."

Shit. I wasn't expecting this turn of events which, in hindsight, was fucking stupid. Of course, Ilya wouldn't want me to attend the rehearsal dinner alone, knowing Alex would be there.

"I didn't RSVP that I was bringing a guest," I argue just for the sake of it, knowing very well I won't get rid of him.

"They should have anticipated it after our engagement announcement," he fires back with a cold smile. "It's almost like you don't want me to come."

"I don't."

He narrows his eyes. "You need to change your attitude pretty fast, sweetheart. I expect a devoted wife."

Another angry retort lodges in my throat, but I swallow it down. I'm not afraid of what he might do to me. It's Alex I need to worry about.

"You'll get a devoted wife, but we aren't married yet."

"Soon enough." He offers me his arm. "Shall we?"

Ignoring him, I stride out of the house. Snow fell heavily during the day, but the sky is now clear. Our driveway is devoid of snow though, and there in front of the house is Ilya's sports car. I release a breath of relief. If he's busy driving, then he can't pay too much attention to me. The last thing I want is to be trapped in a limo with him.

Memories of my time with Alex in a limo come to the forefront of my mind. All the naughty things we did inside that car. Those memories are tainted now. It was on that evening that Ilya set his sights on me.

He opens the door for me, but I refuse his help getting in. It smells like leather and expensive cologne inside, but these scents do nothing but repulse me.

"Any particular music you'd like to listen to during the ride, darling?"

I don't want him to know anything about me, so I look out the window and say, "I don't care. Listen to whatever you want."

He doesn't comment, but a moment later, "Anti-Hero" by Taylor Swift fills the silence. Fucking great. Does he have a file on me? Probably.

His powerful car engine comes to life, and I feel it reverberate everywhere. My phone vibrates in my purse, and I immediately fish it out to see who texted me.

It's the bridesmaids' group chat. Zoey just sent a selfie, saying she can't wait to see everyone.

"What are you going to do while I rehearse for tomorrow's wedding?" I ask Ilya.

"I'll just watch you."

"Like you were watching me before your indecent proposal?"

He peels his eyes off the road and smiles at me. "Yes, but this time will be better."

"Why is that?"

"Because there will be more than watching afterward."

I press my thighs together, making sure there's no gap between my legs. The urge to run away is immense, but I can't do that while inside his sports car going almost ninety miles per hour on the highway.

He wants to fuck me, and I don't know how I'm going to escape that.

CHAPTER 58
ALEX

"Would you please stop pacing? You're making me nervous." Logan grabs my arm and makes me stop.

We're at the old Hotel McCoy in downtown Fairbanks, which is a historical landmark, and where Jesse and Riley are getting married tomorrow. Apparently, this is a coveted wedding location and gets booked years in advance, hence why they had to get married in the middle of hockey season.

"I'm sorry. Why aren't the bridesmaids here yet?" I glance at the entrance to the grand ballroom, where members of Jesse's and Riley's families are already gathered.

Jesse and Deacon look at me. "A stranger would think *you* were the groom," Deacon pipes up.

My phone vibrates in my pocket. It's a message from Ryder that makes my blood run cold.

"What's the matter, bro?" Logan asks, probably noticing the effect of what I just read showing on my face.

I meet his stare. "Ilya is with Blair."

He blinks fast. "Wait, she's coming with him?"

I clench my jaw so hard I might crack my teeth. "Yes."

"Is that going to be a problem for you, Alex?" Jesse looks

sternly at me. "I don't want any drama ruining this rehearsal."

Damn it. That's the last thing I want for them. I know how hard they fought for their love and the number of obstacles they had to overcome to get here. But I can't give him an honest answer that will put his mind at ease, so I lie. "No, it won't be a problem."

"There'd better not be a problem," Deacon chimes in, watching me through narrowed eyes.

The door opens, and in come the bride and her bridesmaids. Jesse smiles from ear to ear when he sees Riley, and he shortens the distance between them to pick her up in his arms and twirl her around. "We're getting married tomorrow!"

She giggles. "Oh my God, Jesse. Put me down."

I want to be happy for them, but I'm too much in the dark to feel any joy. Blair is the last bridesmaid to enter, and next to her is that motherfucker Ilya, looking smug as shit. I want to punch his face until it becomes nothing but pulp.

Logan yanks my arm. "Stop doing that."

"Stop doing what?"

"Growling like you're a rabid dog."

"I wasn't growling." I pull my arm free. "Shut up."

Gia and Noah walk over, both sporting concerned expressions. "Are you okay, Alex?" Gia asks.

"I'm fine."

"You don't look fine," Noah points out.

"He'll be fine as long as we keep him away from Blair's fiancé."

I glance in her direction and catch her staring. She looks so beautiful I could cry. And the way she's looking at me with so much yearning isn't helping my case. I want to go to her, take her away and never stop running.

Ilya follows her line of sight, and his eyes darken when he realizes she's staring at me. He leans closer to her and whispers in her ear, making her flinch. I make a move to go over there, but Logan blocks me.

"Don't."

The wedding coordinator draws our attention and gives instructions about where we should stand, the order of couples, and so forth. Gia steps next to me and links her arm with mine while Noah takes a seat.

After the officiant, Jesse, his grandparents, and Riley's aunt enter, it's the wedding party's turn. Jesse's baby sister Emma and her boyfriend begin the procession, followed by Gia and me, then Darren and a friend of Riley whom I haven't officially met yet, CJ and Ashley, Logan and another out-of-town friend of Riley's, and finally Sean and Blair. Zoey and Deacon are last since they're the respective maid of honor and best man.

I don't take my eyes off Blair when she walks down the aisle, and she holds my stare. My heart is running at the speed of light, and for a moment, I pretend this is *our* wedding and Sean is bringing her to me. My chest swells with emotion. I want this for us. It's crazy that I thought it would take years for me to be in this headspace, wanting to settle down with the girl of my dreams, and here I am.

Blair turns left, and I can't help but follow her with my gaze. It's only when Darren elbows my arm that I quit and focus ahead, only to find Ilya staring daggers at me. He's not sitting down like Noah, but standing at the back of the room, holding a phone in his hand.

Even from afar, I can feel his malevolence. I glower, not afraid of what he can do to me. Blair is the only person that matters, and the one I need to protect from him. Jesse's father walks Riley down the aisle, but I miss most of the rehearsal, and when I come to, it's over. I go through the motions, relying on my friends to give me cues for my next steps.

In a daze, I take Gia's arm again and move like a robot. Noah stands and joins us. The wedding party quickly forms its own circle, and the chatter is lighthearted, but Blair doesn't join us. She distances herself from the group and walks over to Ilya. A moment later, they exit the ballroom. Dinner will be served in the steak house restaurant in the hotel, but no one has gone there yet, so it alarms me that she's leaving with Ilya already.

I don't stop to think; I follow them out before anyone can stop me. They're already going through the revolving door of the hotel, which means Ilya is in a hurry to get somewhere. I sprint to catch up with them, leaving my coat inside.

When I burst through the door, I find them waiting near the valet area. There's no one around, and Ilya has Blair pulled against his body, his beefy hand clutching her chin while she struggles to break free.

"Let go of her!" I yell.

Instead of stepping back, Ilya looks at me, amused. "What are you doing here, Alex? Come to watch the show?"

He presses his lips against hers, and I see red. Rage erupts in the pit of my stomach and spreads through my veins with devastating fury. I grab him by the back of his jacket and yank him away from her. Blair staggers back, and I have only a second to spare her an apologetic glance before I punch Ilya in the face, sending him to the ground.

Blair gasps, covering her mouth. Her eyes are wide and frightened. I go to her, but she steps back, shaking her head. Her rejection feels like she yanked my heart out of my chest.

Ilya laughs from his sprawled position on the ground. "She doesn't want you, and you just ruined your life for nothing. I'll enjoy crushing all your hopes and dreams, asshole."

Blair takes a step forward. "No, you leave him alone!"

He jumps back to his feet, wiping blood from his lip. "No can do, darling. He'll learn the hard way no one crosses a Bolkosky."

"You won't touch him or his brother. If you do, our deal is off," she cries out.

I turn to her. "You made a *deal* with him?"

Regret shines in her eyes. "I had to. I can't let him ruin your and Logan's lives."

Approaching headlights draw my attention to the hotel driveway. But when the car stops at the curb, it isn't the valet who exits the vehicle; it's Ryder. He takes one look at the bleeding Russian motherfucker and then at Blair and me and draws his own conclusions. His gaze hardens.

"What did you do?" he asks me.

Before I can answer, Ilya approaches him and says in a dangerously low tone, "Your sister just signed her death warrant and her lover's."

Fear grips me, making my entire body shake. I throw my arm around Blair's shoulders and pull her to my side. She doesn't push me away, which is a small consolation considering the fucking mess we're in now.

"I don't think so," Ryder says. "Check your phone."

Ilya's brows furrow before he pulls out his device and taps on the screen. His jaw tightens, and he grinds his teeth. He looks up and locks into a staring contest with Ryder for a few seconds. Then he looks at Blair and me with so much hatred that I want to put myself in front of her to protect her from the blast.

Another car stops behind Ryder's, and this time, it's the valet with Ilya's ride. He shoves money into the valet's hand and gets into his sports car without another word. I don't breathe right until he peels away, burning rubber.

"Ryder... what did you do?" Blair asks in a choked voice.

He lifts his chin, eyes burning with determination. "I got you out of your deal with Ilya, sis. You're free."

I'd rejoice in his words if I didn't know there were strings attached. "What did you give up in return?"

He levels me with an intense stare. "It doesn't matter. It's done. For your protection, your story with the Bolkoskys is over. All I ask is that you make Blair happy. One of us deserves to be."

Blair breaks away from me and hugs her brother. "I didn't want this. You deserve happiness too."

He pats her back. "I know, sis, but for now, this will do. I'll live vicariously through you and Alex." Still holding her in his arms, he looks at me. "Don't disappoint me, Kaminski."

"I won't. I swear it."

CHAPTER 59
BLAIR

"I'd better go before someone from the wedding party catches me here." Ryder eases out of my embrace.

I'm still stunned by the sacrifice he made for me. My eyes are burning with tears that are about to spill. "They need to know you aren't the bad guy in the story."

His pupils dilate. "No. They *can't* know. This is important, Blair."

I open my mouth to argue, but Alex touches my back. "We should go in, sweetheart."

Ryder glances at him, looking relieved by his interruption. I step back from my brother, and immediately, Alex's arm loops around my waist.

"This isn't over, Ryder. We'll talk," he tells him.

In his usual fashion, when talking is the last thing he wants to do, Ryder locks his jaw, a muscle twitching.

"You two try to have fun tonight." He returns to his car, and neither Alex nor I move until he drives away.

In silence, Alex steers me back into the hotel, and the moment we're out of the freezing weather, he pulls me into his arms, hugging me tight to his chest.

"I'm so sorry, baby girl." He's shaking, and I don't know if he's still cold or if he's nervous.

"You have nothing to be sorry about."

He clutches my forearms and pushes me back. I see tears shining in his eyes. "I do. My biggest regrets are not being able to protect you or do anything besides keep my distance. You have no idea how much it killed me not to see you, hold you, and tell you how much I fucking love you. And then seeing that motherfucker put his hands on you..." He chokes up. "It took every ounce of self-control to not end him with my bare hands."

I cup his face, trying to hold my shit together and not bawl my eyes out. "Staying away was the biggest declaration of love you could possibly have given me. Knowing you were safe was my solace. I couldn't bear the thought of him hurting you or Logan. He was going to end your NHL careers and get you expelled from school."

He captures my face between his hands. "Do you think I care about any of that, baby girl? You don't think I'd trade it all to protect you, to keep you from marrying a monster? The money, the status, it's all meaningless if I can't have the most precious thing in my life. *You*."

My lips tremble, and the first tear rolls down my cheek. "I couldn't live with myself knowing I ruined your life. And Logan... he could end up hating you for taking away his dreams too."

Alex wipes away my tear with his thumb. "The only way you could ruin my life is by not being in it. As for Logan, he has the biggest heart, and he wouldn't bat an eyelash either at giving it all up."

"Yo, what are you guys doing?" the man in question asks. "I've been looking all over for you." We turn toward him, and he doesn't miss when Alex takes my hand. "What happened?"

"Ilya is gone," I say.

"For good," Alex adds.

Logan's brows arch. "I'm gonna need more explanation than

that, but later. The rehearsal dinner has already started, and I have a hot bridesmaid waiting for me."

"Who? Sophia?" I ask.

He curls his lips into a crooked grin. "I've always had a thing for redheads."

Alex snorts. "And blondes, and brunettes..."

His eyes narrow, and I'm afraid he's going to remind us that Alex used to be a player too, but he doesn't, thankfully. I'm aware Alex has a past, but I care only about his present and future.

"You know she has a boyfriend, right?" I ask.

He shoves his hands in his pockets and shrugs. "That's never stopped me before."

There's another detail that might stop him in his tracks—the fact that her brother plays for Clayton U. But I decide to let him figure that out on his own. He turns around and heads back to the restaurant.

I take a step forward to follow, but Alex stops me. "What?"

"I need to do this." He traps my face between his hands and slants his mouth over mine hungrily, possessively. It's like he's pouring everything in his heart into the kiss.

I wrap my arms around his waist, stepping closer, trying to meld myself to him and kiss him back with the same passion, matching each stroke. My skin tingles; I feel effervescent, light as air. I missed him so damn much, and I'm afraid that if I let go, he'll disappear.

Alex pulls back, pressing his forehead against mine. "If we don't stop, I'll have to blow my savings and get us a hotel room."

"Or we can find an empty meeting room." I smile.

"Don't tempt me, baby girl."

I lean back so I can look into his eyes. "I'll always tempt you, big boy. I'm not a good girl."

"But I can bring the good girl out of you." He brings his

mouth to my ear. "As a matter of fact, maybe she'll come out and play tonight."

I arch an eyebrow. "Is that so?"

He boops my nose with his index finger. "Yep."

"What if I want *you* to be the good boy?"

His brows shoot to the heavens. "That... shit... Can we go home now?"

Home. I don't care where he's referring to—my place or his—but hearing him say that word makes a crazy feeling of euphoria spread through my body. I was sort of joking about reversing the roles. I didn't expect Alex to be so on board with the idea. Now I'll be thinking about it during the entire dinner.

Then I remember I've been staying in Evergreene, and Cookie is still at my parents' house. My expression falls.

"What's wrong?" He touches the crease between my brows.

"I still need to deal with my parents. Ilya might be out of the picture, but it doesn't mean I'm off the hook with them, especially my mother."

"She can forget her matchmaking schemes. The only man you're marrying is me."

"What?" I squeak, my heart almost leaping out of my chest. "Is that a proposal?"

Alex's face goes all shades of red. "Of course not. When I do propose, it will be epic. I just want to set this in stone. You're mine, baby girl, and I'm yours."

I curl my fingers around the lapels of his jacket. "That's right, big boy. You *are* mine."

ALEX

Eventually, we joined our friends for dinner, and I tried to behave, but it was damn hard with Blair sitting next to me. Logan must have said something before we got to the restaurant because no one asked about Ilya or why Blair and I were back together.

The truth is, I couldn't wait to get her alone. I brought her to my place and asked Logan to not come home tonight. He struck out with the hot bridesmaid, so I have no idea what sleeping arrangements he's made.

No sooner do I step inside my place and close the door than I pick up Blair in my arms and press her back against the wall. She tries to wrap her legs around my hips, but her long dress gets in the way.

"How much do you like this dress?" I ask against her lips.

"I don't hate it, but I never want to wear it again."

I almost ask if she minds if I ruin it, but then I think about how much it had probably cost. Even if it was sponsored by her parents, it's still a waste. Maybe she wants to donate it to charity.

I set her down. "Take it off."

Her eyes widen, but her lips curl with mischief. "I thought we would reverse roles tonight."

My cock is more than on board with the idea, but now that I have her standing in front of me, I don't want to play games.

I rub my thumb over her lips. "If you want, but I'll be just fine making love to you nice and slow."

Her lips part, and a little gasp comes out. She grabs my wrist and sucks my thumb into her mouth. Fuck me. My heart is beating like a stampede now, and I'm so hard I could actually explode with just a little bit of friction.

"Blair..."

She pulls my thumb out of her mouth. "Alex..."

Her eyes are burning with desire, and I snap. Forget making love nice and slow. I want to fuck her hard, brand her with my cock, and fill her tight pussy with my cum. I pick her up and toss her over my shoulder like a caveman.

"Alex! What are you doing?"

"Taking you to bed, baby girl."

I kick the door to my room open and toss her onto the

mattress. She laughs and gasps at the same time when she bounces on it.

"What happened to slow?"

"Second round." I take my jacket off, and then I'm yanking at my shirt. I don't bother with the buttons, and several pop out and fly somewhere.

Blair shrugs off her coat first, but she keeps her dress on, making me frown.

"I want you to fuck me while I wear this dress." She hikes up the skirt, revealing her black lingerie, mercifully no garter belt, but still, my thoughts become feral. Thinking that when she had gotten dressed, she was still engaged to Ilya.

"Did he... I mean."

Her eyes widen as if she's reading what I'm trying to say and can't.

"I was never alone with him until tonight."

Relief whooshes out of me in a loud exhale. "Good. I don't think I could keep my distance from that asshole if he had hurt you."

"I know."

I clear my throat. "Why do you want to keep the dress on?"

"Because he thought this was for him." She rolls her panties down her legs, revealing her perfect pink pussy.

I get rid of my slacks and underwear in a split second, then join Blair on my bed, spreading her legs wide. "Never. This is all mine."

I lick her clit in a long and sensual stroke, making her gasp. Her back arches, making me ache with desire. I didn't mean to eat her out now, but I couldn't resist her taste on my tongue. I toy with her bundle of nerves, alternating between lazy circles and sucking her clit into my mouth. Blair's heavy breathing tells me she's getting close, but unfortunately, so am I. I pull back and leave a trail of kisses up her flat stomach and her breasts on my way upward.

"Mine," I repeat in a growl before I enter her with one precise push, burying myself in her all the way to the hilt.

"Yes! I missed this. I missed you." She grabs my face between her hands and kisses me hard, matching the pace of my thrusts.

"Me too, baby girl. You have no idea." I piston in and out of her as if I'm in a race to prove to myself she's not a figment of my imagination. She's truly here with me, driving me insane with need.

She cries out against my lips, falling apart under my body and sending me spiraling toward a vortex of sweet oblivion as well. I come hard inside her, my cock throbbing inside her wet tightness. I keep moving until her body relaxes under mine and I'm completely empty. But I don't pull out, needing to maintain the connection for a little longer.

"This right here was worth the angst," she whispers.

"No, it wasn't," I grumble, making her laugh.

"Okay. Fair, almost worth it."

Leaning on my elbows, I pull back so I can look at her face. I love how her cheeks are pink and her lips are swollen from all my kisses. My heart swells with an emotion that's too big to describe.

"I love you so damn much, baby girl. These past few days have been the worst of my life."

Her delicate brows furrow. "I've been a mess as well. It felt like my heart was ripped out of my chest."

"Never again. I don't *ever* want us to feel this way again."

"Me neither, but… you know we have more obstacles to face."

"You're talking about your parents?"

Her eyes grow sad, and it makes me fucking mad that those fuckers cause her so much pain. "They'll never accept that I'm dating you, and they'll still hold Cory over my head."

I've been thinking about her brother since we've been apart, predicting that even with Ilya out of the picture, her parents will still threaten to take him away from her. "I have an idea about how to solve that."

Her brows arch. "You do?"

I nod. "Tomorrow, we'll go to your parents to pick up your stuff and tell them we're together."

"They'll flip out."

"I know. I'm counting on it." I smile.

"Are you going to tell me how you plan to prevent them from moving Cory to another facility?"

"Not yet. I haven't worked out the details. But do you trust me?"

"I trust you," she replies. No hesitation, no doubt, and that speaks volumes to me.

My idea has to work.

CHAPTER 60
ALEX

I wake up before Blair so I can put my plan in motion. I can't do it alone, but after a couple of texts, I get the pieces in place. Today is Riley and Jesse's wedding, and my window isn't long before Blair and I must be at the wedding venue. I don't want her to spend another minute worrying about her parents though, so I'm getting rid of their dark cloud of gloom as soon as possible.

But the most important item on today's agenda is Blair's birthday. She claims she doesn't want anyone to make a big deal about it, but tough shit. She's my girl, and she's getting spoiled by me.

When we were in DC, she told me she wasn't a breakfast person, but since then, she's shown me that's not entirely true. So in case she's hungry, I prepare something light—Swedish pancakes with maple syrup. My plan is to bring her breakfast in bed, but she walks out of my bedroom with tangled hair, wearing nothing but my button-down shirt from last night.

"Good morning," she says through a yawn.

"What are you doing out of bed, baby girl?"

"I smelled coffee." She sits on the barstool by the counter and looks at the food. "Oh, pancakes. I'm starving."

I walk around the counter and turn her around in her seat. "Me too. Happy birthday, my love."

I kiss her soft lips, tasting the minty toothpaste on her tongue. I go from innocent pancake-making to wanting to pour maple syrup all over her body.

"Hmm... you taste good," I murmur against her lips.

"I bet those pancakes taste yummy too." She pushes me back. "We don't have much time for shenanigans. I have to be at the hotel in a few hours."

"Why so early? The wedding isn't until four."

"Well... we bridesmaids need more time to get ready."

I sigh. "Okay, fine. But we aren't going anywhere until we properly celebrate your birthday, starting with..." I walk to the coffee table and grab the two gift bags I set there.

Her eyes widen. "You bought me presents?"

I rub the back of my neck. "Well... they were originally for Christmas, but since we didn't get to celebrate it... I would have gotten you a proper birthday gift, but I was a little worried I might lose you forever."

"Alex... this is so thoughtful. But you really shouldn't stress about buying me gifts. I've got everything I want standing right in front of me."

"It makes me happy to buy things for you."

She opens the box from the lingerie store first, and when she fishes the garter belt out, she tries and fails not to show amusement. "I think this was more a gift for you than me."

I smirk. "Guilty. I couldn't resist it though. I saw it in the shop window and knew you needed to have it."

She laughs, putting the box on the counter. Then she opens the second box, and that's what makes me hold my breath. What if she doesn't like it?

She gasps when she opens the lid of the music box, revealing a little ballerina spinning to the sound of a beautiful piece of classical music.

"Alex…" She looks at me with eyes that shine even brighter. "How did you know?"

"How did I know what?"

"How did you know I used to have a music box just like this when I was little?"

"For real?"

She nods, swallowing hard. "Yes. I got it from one of my nannies after my mother insisted I take ballet, even though I was terrified of dancing in front of people and being terrible at it. My nanny bought me a music box like this and told me that if I ever got scared, all I had to do was pretend I was this tiny ballerina, spinning around in her own little world."

"And did it work?"

She smiles. "It did."

"I had no idea. I got it for you because when I caught you dancing in that gym at the arena, I saw a beautiful and free woman who wasn't hiding behind a mask. It was in that moment that I realized I was falling for you."

She releases a shuddering breath and puts the music box down. Then she walks over, and I pull her into my arms.

"Do you want to know when I knew you were more than my rival?" she asks.

"When was that?"

"When you got hurt in that game and my heart leaped into my throat. I wanted to see you to make sure you were okay. I was so scared. I couldn't sleep the entire night worrying about you."

I cup her cheek, completely taken aback by that revelation. "I cursed the gods when I got that injury, but now I'm happy I got hurt."

"I know it's wishful thinking, but… I don't want to ever see you get hurt like that again."

"I'll try my best to stay in one piece, baby girl."

"What about the gift I got you for Christmas? Did you like it?"

I rub the back of my neck. "I couldn't bring myself to open it."

She quirks an eyebrow. "What are you waiting for then? Go get it."

I run to my room and grab the bag from my closet. It's not heavy, but it's bulky. I set the bag on the counter and look inside. "You got me two gifts too?"

She nods, smiling.

I pull out the smaller of the two boxes, that's more or less the size of a shoebox. My eyes widen when I see what it is.

"It's a hockey shower-slash-tool-kit bag. I know, it's lame," she says.

I look up, smiling like crazy. "Lame? Are you kidding me? This is awesome."

"I filled it with things I thought you might need when you're on the road with the Miami Lions. Small refillable shampoo and body wash bottles, stick tape, extra skate laces. Oh, there is also a small screwdriver, helmet hardware, and shower sandals."

I pull her to me and kiss her hard, knowing she's nervous about her gift. "I love it."

Her cheeks are red when I lean back. "I'm so relieved."

"Let's see what's in the other box."

"Oh, that's an impulse buy. I saw it at the store, and I couldn't pass it up."

I unwrap the gift and pull from the box a red wool sweater with a picture of a Dalmatian puppy on the front. My face splits into a broad smile. "This is fucking awesome."

Her brows shoot up. "Really? You don't think it's stupid?"

I shake my head. "Not at all. Hey... it matches the pillow you have on your couch."

She squints. "It kind of does."

"Now, do you want to eat your pancakes or try on your new gift?" I fish out the garter belt from the box using my index finger.

She smiles. "Definitely try that on."

I snatch the maple syrup from the counter, and she arches her brows.

"What? I got a craving." I laugh.

She saunters toward my bedroom. "I don't mind. It's your bed that will get messy, not mine."

"I bet I can lick the maple syrup off your body without getting a single drop on my mattress."

She pivots and walks backward. "Another bet? What are the stakes?"

"Loser grants the winner one wish that can be collected at any point in time."

"Any wish?"

"Yes."

"You're on." She disappears into my room, and I smile.

Oh, my sweet Blair. If you only knew, you've already won this one.

BLAIR

I know I said we didn't have time for shenanigans this morning, but Alex did what he does best—stubbornly disagreed with me and showed me on multiple occasions that there's always time for *O*s. Now, instead of heading to the wedding venue, we're on our way to Evergreene to pick up my bridesmaid dress because Ryder forgot to pack it when he went there last night to get Cookie and my things. After the blowout with Ilya, he did that without me needing to ask, but it seems to me that he left the bridesmaid dress on purpose, so I'd have to visit my parents before the ceremony today.

"Are you nervous?" Alex asks.

"Yes. I know it's best to deal with my parents sooner rather than later, but I still don't know how we're going to stop them from using Cory to punish me." I glance at him. "You haven't told me yet."

"You still trust me, right?" He meets my gaze.

"Yes, but... I'm afraid. I don't want any more sacrifices made on my behalf."

He takes my hand, lacing his fingers with mine. "No more sacrifices. I promise."

I want to push the issue, but if he's not telling me his plan, he has his reasons. I also know he doesn't lie. If he says there won't be any more sacrifices, I believe him. But my stomach is twisting painfully, making me sick, and my hands are clammy. I have no idea what kind of situation we're going to walk into. My father is embroiled deep with the Bolkoskys. How is he going to react to the son of his former employee being responsible for messing up his deal with the Russian Mafia?

At the gate, the security guard opens his mouth to ask for Alex's driver's license, but I lean forward and identify myself. He doesn't ask to see my ID. He knows who I am, even though I've never seen him before in my life. It's probably part of his training to memorize the faces of the most influential residents in the community.

I don't see Ryder's car in my parents' driveway, and my stomach flips. I wish he was here, even though I didn't ask him to be.

Alex's phone dings. He looks at his phone quickly before putting it away, then he looks at me. "Ready?"

"As ready as I'll ever be."

We walk into my parents' house as a united front, and low and behold, they're waiting for us in one of the living rooms. I wonder if they were notified by security. How else would they know we were coming?

My father is standing in front of the fireplace with his back to us, and he's holding a glass of whiskey. It's not even noon yet. *Shit*. That doesn't bode well. Mom is sitting regally on the couch, her spine stiff, and when Alex and I enter the room holding hands, her cold eyes zero in on them. She snaps her gaze to mine and squints. She's like a snake ready to strike.

It's my father who speaks first though. "No."

Just one word. Hard. Final. And it echoes in my ears.

I lift my chin. "I didn't ask."

He scoffs. "Do you think because you managed to break your engagement to Ilya, you're off the hook? Your duty is still to this family."

My pulse is thundering in my ears, and my face must be red because it feels like it's on fire.

Alex squeezes my hand tighter. "Like Blair said, she didn't ask for your permission. *We* don't need your blessing."

My father turns his glare on Alex. "I tolerated your presence on the team because you're a good hockey player. And even if you do get that NHL contract and make millions, you'll never be good enough to marry a Westwood."

"Good thing I don't plan to marry a Westwood. I plan to marry the woman I love, Blair. Her last name is irrelevant. It doesn't define who she is."

"What are you going to do, Blair?" my father asks. "Who's going to pay for your tuition, your apartment, your clothes?"

I laugh in derision. "Like I care about any of that."

"Easy to say when you've never had to work for anything in your life," he barks, twisting his face into a grimace.

My blood boils to the surface. "On the contrary, Daddy. I've always had to work hard for the things that matter to me. It wasn't your money that made me top of my class."

"It was *my* money that paid for your top-shelf education! Don't forget that, you little brat."

Alex tenses. "Don't you dare talk to her like that," he grits out.

My mother waves her hand dismissively. "Don't waste your breath arguing with Blair. This is nothing but an act of rebellion that won't lead anywhere. She knows what she stands to lose."

My belly tightens. Here it comes. The threat to take Cory to a place where I'll never see him again.

"I wouldn't be so sure." Alex pulls out his cell phone and

clicks on an image on Instagram before handing the device to me.

It's a picture of Ryder, Cory, and Logan at Twin Falls, posted from Ryder's account. Cory is between them, holding a Warriors jersey. The caption says *Cory Westwood, younger brother of former Warriors forward Ryder Westwood, finally gets his jersey*.

That was Alex's plan all along—to out my brother's existence to the world. I can see now why he didn't want to tell me. I'd be afraid of hurting Cory in the process, but... looking at the happiness on his face, maybe I've been too overprotective of him.

"What are you looking at?" No sooner does my mother ask that question than her phone starts to ding nonstop.

She checks her messages and turns as pale as a ghost. Watching her freak out that her dirty little secret is out is the most satisfying scene I've witnessed in years.

"Now you can't hide him anymore," I say. "Good luck explaining why you've kept his existence a secret all these years."

Her nostrils flare, and a vein throbs in her forehead. "I hope you're prepared for the consequences of your actions."

"What? Are you going to cut me off? Go ahead. And don't bother to threaten to not pay my tuition. I know you already paid for my full ride."

"You'll get your diploma, girl. But as far as I'm concerned, you're dead to me," my father retorts. "Now get out of my house!"

I wait for the pain to come, but I feel nothing but relief. Deep down, I've always known I've never mattered to my parents. I'm just a pawn.

"Gladly. I'll just get my dress and be out of your life for good."

I tug Alex's hand, urging him to follow my lead and walk out of the living room. But he's standing frozen like a boulder, staring daggers at my father.

"Come on, babe. Let's get out of here," I say.

He finally lets me steer him away, and I can breathe more easily. It wouldn't do for Alex to land in jail for punching my father in the face.

We meet one of the maids in the entry foyer, and she has a garment bag in her hand. "Your brother asked me to give you this, Miss Westwood."

Ryder. Bless his heart.

"Thank you."

Alex takes the bag and says, "Let's get the fuck out of here."

CHAPTER 61
BLAIR

Alex barely says a word on the drive back to my place, and I can't say it doesn't worry me. He's stewing in his anger, and it's coming off in waves. His jaw stays clenched tight, and the way he's squeezing the steering wheel makes me think he's picturing it as my father's neck.

He stops in front of my building, and I ask, "You're not coming up?"

A small smile tugs the corner of his lips. "Better not. I know you need to get ready, and if I come up, I'm going to have you flat on your back again."

His words make my body come alive, and jitters of desire spread through my limbs, concentrating between my legs. "Why did you say that? Now I'll be thinking about it, and it'll be torture."

"Well… I *could* come up, but if we're late, that'll make us shitty friends."

I sigh, resigned. "I know. I guess I'll just have to use one of my toys then."

He actually growls. "Don't say that."

"Are you jealous of my sex toys?"

"No," he replies in a gruff voice. "But now I'll be thinking about you using them, and…." He runs his hand through his hair. "You need to get out of the car now, baby girl."

I laugh. "You're kicking me out without a kiss?"

"Yes." He narrows his eyes. "If I kiss you, then it's game over. Go. Before I say to hell with arriving on time to the wedding."

"Okay, okay." I open the door, but before I slip out of his car, I lean toward him and kiss him quickly on his cheek. "I love you."

"I love you too. I'll be back in half an hour. Is that enough time for you to get ready?"

"Yes."

He keeps his hungry gaze on me until I close the door, and he doesn't drive away until I'm inside the building. It's not until I'm riding the elevator to my apartment that it dawns on me—I just broke up with my parents, and on my twenty-first birthday, no less. I've declared my independence, and I'm starting to freak out.

No, Blair. There's no need to panic. You'll be okay.

Taking deep breaths, I try to calm down. Once I'm inside my apartment, I check my phone for messages and notice the bridesmaids' group chat has been very active for the past hour. The conversation is light and filled with happy energy. I begin to calm down. I have no reason to worry. I have the love of the most wonderful man in the world and a tight-knit group of friends who have my back.

There's still one thing I need to set right. I can't be with Alex in peace while his father still hates me. I need to find a way to win him over, I just don't know how yet.

But first things first. I have bridesmaid duties to attend to. I head into my room and pack a duffel bag with items I'll need. There's a makeup artist and a hairdresser on-site, so I don't have to worry about dolling up now.

I take a quick shower to rid myself of my parents' bad juju and get dressed in the custom velvet tracksuit Riley got for all her bridesmaids. It's pink, soft, and comfortable. I have ten minutes to spare before Alex is supposed to pick me up. To kill time, I take my *BDSM for Beginners* book and open it to a page I have bookmarked.

We didn't get to play last night, and I'm hoping Alex will let me be the boss tonight.

ALEX

Blair looks so beautiful that I'm having a hard time keeping my eyes off her. I almost asked Gia if she would mind walking in with Sean instead so I could take Blair down the aisle, but I decided that earning the wrath of Zoey wasn't worth it. She takes her role as the maid of honor seriously, and I almost didn't recognize her. How could such a sweet girl turn into a drill sergeant?

We've done our dance number, speeches were given, the wedding cake was cut, and now I can finally relax and enjoy my baby girl. I lean back, throwing my arm behind Blair's chair, and watch her eat a piece of cake.

"What?" she asks after she swallows a huge bite.

I smirk. "Nothing."

"Aren't you going to eat your cake?"

"In a moment. I'm content to watch you eat yours."

Her brows furrow. "Why?"

I wipe a smear of frosting from the corner of her mouth. "Because you look darn cute doing it."

"Could you please not do that in front of me?" Logan complains across from us.

"Don't be a hater because you didn't bring a date," I reply.

"Well, I had other plans." He gives Sophia a sidelong, wistful glance. She's sitting at the end of the table with her boyfriend, some arrogant doctor no one in our inner circle warmed up to.

"You knew she had a boyfriend, though," Gia pipes up.

"Yes, and I can't believe she'd rather be with him."

I roll my eyes. He's moping tonight, but tomorrow the redhead will be forgotten.

"You just want her because you can't have her," Noah says.

Logan tosses a balled-up napkin at him. "Shut up, rookie."

Ashley and her date stand up. "We're going to the bar to get drinks. Anyone want anything?"

"No. I'm good." I turn to Blair. "What about you, babe?"

"I'm fine too."

She gets the same answer from everyone besides Sean, who simply stares at her like he's having a hard time being in her presence.

"What do you guys think about Ashley's date?" Blair asks when they're gone.

"He's a moron," Sean retorts.

I'm taken aback by his reply. I don't think he said a word to the guy all night.

"I guess Brian doesn't have big brother's stamp of approval," Darren pipes up.

"Ashley can do whatever she wants." He pushes back his chair and jumps to his feet. "She isn't my sister."

My jaw drops as I watch him stride out of the room.

CJ returns to the table. "What's gotten into Sean?"

"Beats me," Logan replies.

"Hmm…" Blair hums.

"Do you have a theory?" I ask.

"Maybe. But I'd rather not talk about it now." She drops her gaze to my untouched piece of cake. "If you're not going to eat that—"

"You can have it, baby girl. You'll need the energy for later." I smirk.

She narrows her eyes. "That's not what I was going to say, smarty-pants."

"Okay, what were you going to say, then?"

"I was going to ask if you want to dance."

I lean closer and kiss the corner of her mouth, tasting the

sweetness of the frosting on her skin. "Sure, I'll dance with you, my little ballerina."

"Ugh. Now this guy," CJ complains. "It's all your fault, Noah."

"What? How is Alex's behavior my fault?"

"I don't know. You must have done something with your Canadian wholesomeness. You turned the biggest player on campus into a hopeless fool in love."

I whip my face to him. "Hey! Watch your mouth, punk."

"I'm not lying," he retorts.

"Sure, sure. It's my fault Alex fell in love with Blair. I have special powers. You'd better watch out, CJ. You might be next." Noah wiggles his fingers at him.

CJ makes the sign of the cross with his fingers and points it at Noah. "Stay away from me, Satan."

I laugh. "He's Satan now? I thought he was the poster child for Canadian wholesomeness."

"That was before he threatened to hex me."

Blair squeezes my thigh, making me forget this absurd conversation in an instant. "Do you want to dance or not?"

"Hell yeah."

CHAPTER 62
ALEX

I haven't forgotten that drunk Blair means horny Blair. Thank God we've already crossed that line many times over so I can give her what she wants. She tries to get my clothes off as soon as we enter her apartment's elevator, but I manage to keep my shirt on.

"Babe, we're almost home," I say between kisses.

"I can't help it. You're too irresistible."

"Don't make me toss you over my shoulder again."

She rises on the tips of her toes and whispers in my ear. "Please do."

The elevator door opens, and I do exactly what she asks. She giggles when I pick her up and then tries to pinch my ass. I spank hers instead. "You're misbehaving, baby girl."

"It's still my birthday. I can misbehave all I want."

"True. Now give me your purse. I need the key."

"I really need to get you a copy, although it's probably pointless. I'm sure I'll be evicted soon."

That's true. I doubt her parents will let her live here for much longer.

"You can always stay with me." I struggle with her tiny

purse, trying to find the key while holding her over my shoulder and my coat and jacket with the other arm.

"It's sweet of you to offer, but I don't want to live with you and Logan."

I finally find the key and open the door. "Why is that?"

"Because he's still a manwhore, and I don't want to be reminded of your previous lifestyle."

I lower her to the couch and stare. "It's in the past."

"I know. But it doesn't help that he looks like you."

I drop into a crouch in front of her. "Can I tell you a secret?"

"Of course."

"We never brought girls back to our apartment."

Her brows arch. "Really?"

"It was easier not to. Some of those girls got super clingy."

"Ah, that makes sense. Boy, you were terrible."

"But I'm a good boy now." I smile.

She tilts her head, then runs her fingers through my hair. "Are you? I guess we'll have to see."

"Is that so?"

"Yes. Take off your clothes."

I get back on my feet and unbutton my shirt slowly. Blair's eyes widen when I part the fabric, flexing my pecs. I toss the shirt to the side and then unbuckle my belt.

"Give me that." She lifts her hand, palm facing up.

I pull the belt out of its loops and hand it over. She folds it in half and yanks both ends, making it snap. "Are you going to spank me with that, baby girl?"

"You don't get to ask questions tonight, big boy. Now pants off. Let me see that cock I love."

Hell and damn. Bossy Blair is such a turn-on. My cock is already rock hard when I get rid of the rest of my clothes. I want to curl my fingers around my shaft, give it a few yanks, but I have to wait for her orders.

"On your knees."

I drop to the floor, holding her stare. Her eyes are pure fire, and it's so fucking hard to keep my hands to myself.

She loops the belt around my neck and uses it as a makeshift collar. Then she lifts one of her legs and presses her high-heeled shoe against my shoulder.

"Touch me."

"Where?"

"Anywhere."

I wrap my hand around her ankle and lick her calf. Blair's eyes become hooded, and her lips part. I put her leg over my shoulder so I can place open kisses up her thigh, shoving her dress upward in the process until I can see her lacy panties.

She's breathing a little harder now, so I continue until my mouth is on her pussy. I don't bother sliding the fabric to the side before I begin licking her with gusto.

Her fingers curl around strands of my hair, and she yanks. "Alex... I love the way your tongue moves."

"I love your taste, baby girl."

She shoves me off suddenly, and I fall on my ass. I'm sure I broke the rules by saying anything, but hell, it'll be worth the punishment. She joins me on the floor, straddling me. "I'm going to ride you now, cowboy, and you're going to behave."

She curls her finger around my length, then presses the tip against her clit through the panties, which are now soaking wet. She uses my cock as her own personal toy, rubbing it against her core. I grab her hips, but she narrows her eyes. "Hands off."

I drop them to my sides, but I'm not sure how much longer I can be a good boy. Even though this is hot as hell, and I love seeing her in control, she's too much temptation for me to resist. I want to touch and kiss her everywhere. I want to fuck her until she's begging me to never stop.

Her little gasps of pleasure are making my head spin. My balls are tight, ready to explode, but this is about her, and I'm not going to fuck it up.

"Are you going to behave now, big boy?"

"Yes," I hiss.

"Good." She finally pushes her panties aside and lowers her hips, impaling herself on my shaft.

I let out a loud growl when her pussy wraps around me, hot and tight. Flattening her palm against my chest, she begins to move, bringing her hips up and down slowly. I'm panting, working hard to resist thrusting my hips upward.

"Do you want me to go faster, babe?" she asks in a velvety tone.

"Yes."

"Ask nicely, and I might grant your wish." She gyrates her hips, and my hips buck involuntarily.

"Please, baby girl. I'm begging you."

Her lips curl into a satisfied grin. "I want you to fuck me like you've never fucked me before. Don't hold back."

I narrow my eyes. "And I can do anything I want?"

"Yes."

Faster than lightning, I flip us around, getting her underneath me. But that's not how I want to fuck her. I get on my knees and flip her over again, raising her hips off the floor. Blair whimpers when I slide my fingers into her wet pussy hole.

"That's it, baby girl. Moan for me."

"You're not doing what I told you to," she complains.

I grasp her hips, digging my fingers into her skin, and penetrate her with a hard thrust. "How about now?"

"*Yes*. More... harder."

She keeps her cheek flat against the rug and her eyes closed as I piston in and out of her fast and relentlessly. I'm not holding back now. I want to give her what she asked for and more. I lose track of time as I surrender to the pleasure that's coursing through my veins. Her moans become louder, and her walls clench around my cock.

"Make me come, Alex."

I slap her ass, knowing how much she loves it.

She cries out, her body trembling now. I increase my pace,

destroying the dam that was keeping my orgasm at bay. The flood breaks through like a tsunami, and I'm groaning loudly, too, as I empty myself in her.

I get lost in the sensation and don't come back down to earth until Blair says, "That's enough. I can't..."

I pull out, then pick Blair up in my arms, cradling her against my neck. "Are you okay, baby girl?"

Her face is flushed and sweaty, and her eyes are still hazy with lust. "More than okay. You're such a good boy."

I kiss her softly and slowly, savoring her sweet taste. "I'll always be a good boy for you, my love, even if you want me to be bad."

"Oh, there are many wicked things I want you to do to me."

I cup her face. "We've only just begun."

CHAPTER 63
BLAIR

Over the next few days, Alex and I take advantage of winter break to finalize our proposal for the UN. As much as we want to be with each other all the time, we've worked out a reward system. For every section of the report we complete, we celebrate in the bedroom—living room, bathroom, kitchen—whichever room strikes our fancy.

Last night, we finished the project and spent the evening celebrating, which meant there was barely any sleep. We don't even care if we win the proposal or not, although that would be nice. Despite the few hours of sleep, I'm up at seven this morning. Alex is passed out on his belly, facing the other way. The bedsheet covers only his yummy tush, so I have a perfect view of his wide back and the scratch marks I left there.

Oops. I got carried away last night—not that he cared.

I slip out of bed and decide to take a shower in the guest bathroom so I don't wake him. I'm pretty sure he'll sleep late, and I plan to use the time to my advantage.

These past days have been amazing, but there's still an issue that's been bothering me. I need to talk to Mr. Kaminski. I can't be the reason Alex isn't speaking to his father.

I get dressed as silently as I can and then do some snooping around on Alex's laptop. I need his father's address. Alex was online shopping last night, and he left the browser open on that page. I click on his account and easily see that he's sent some packages to his dad's. Jackpot.

Quickly, I write down the address on a sticky note, then return the browsing window to the store's home page. As well-intentioned as my motives are, I'm still invading his privacy. Good intentions do pave the road to hell.

Before I head out, I write him a note that I'm running errands and I'll be back soon. Cookie whines in his crate, making me feel guilty that I'm not taking him out for a walk. Maybe it's not a bad idea to bring him with me. He might help me with Mr. Kaminski. Who doesn't love a puppy?

I get his leash, then open his crate. "All right, boy. We're going on a little adventure."

The GPS takes me to a neighborhood where the houses are old and small, but I don't get a vibe that it's an unsavory place. Mr. Kaminski's address leads to a nearby trailer park. Heavy snow fell last night, and I can tell I shouldn't try to plow through it in my car. I leave the vehicle just outside the trailer park and continue my trek on foot.

I'm glad I wore my heaviest coat, but I wish I was wearing proper snow boots. Cookie is tugging at the leash, wanting to play in this winter wonderland.

"Hold on, boy. I can't run as fast."

I try to keep pace, but it's hard when the snow comes up to my calves.

I hear laughter ahead, then some taunting. "Give it up, old man. We know you've got connections. Don't your sons play hockey for that rich-people school?"

Oh my God. Are they talking about Alex and Logan?

"So? That doesn't mean I got tickets to the damn playoffs."

"Leave him alone, you good-for-nothing losers," a woman chimes in.

"Stay out of it, you old hag."

"Don't talk to her like that. Show some fucking respect."

I push through the snow, trying to move fast, and at the same time, I stick my hand in my purse and get my pepper spray out. It seems Mr. Kaminski is dealing with good-for-nothing neighbors.

"Respect? I'll show you my respect."

I round a corner and come upon the scene just in time to see a burly teen shove Mr. Kaminski against a trailer. He winces, but at least he doesn't fall down. The other teen laughs. Only two—I can deal with that.

"Hey!" I yell. "What the fuck are you doing?"

They turn in my direction, and almost immediately, their surprise becomes leering. Cookie is now barking, and it's a pity he's only a puppy and not big enough to scare anyone. I keep my pepper spray hidden behind my back.

"Oh, who do we have here?" the bigger of the two guys asks as he moves closer.

"You'd better go before I call the police."

The teen dirtbags look at each other and laugh. "The cops don't come here, bitch."

"Get out of here, girl," an old woman with all-white hair urges me.

"Oh, she ain't going anywhere." The biggest jerkface reaches for my coat, ignoring Cookie, who's pressing against my leg.

Before he can yank me closer to him, I unload the pepper spray in his eyes. He screams, releasing me at once.

"My eyes! You fucking bitch."

His friend is smarter than him, and instead of trying to grab me, he tackles me to the ground. I lose my grip on Cookie's leash, and he disappears from view.

"Get off me!" I try to push the asshole off, but he's heavier, and the snow underneath me isn't helping either.

He wraps his hands around my neck and squeezes, cutting off my air supply. *Shit. Shit. Shit.* That's not how I envisioned this visit going. Black dots appear in my vision; I'm close to passing out.

Then someone knocks him off me, and a second later, Mr. Kaminski's face is hovering over mine. I wheeze, drawing a big gulp of air into my lungs. It takes me a moment to regain focus, but at least I can breathe.

He offers me his hand. "Can you stand up?"

"Ye-yeah. I think so."

I let him help me back to my feet and then look for the two jackasses who attacked me. There's no sign of them.

"They're gone," Mr. Kaminski answers my silent question.

"Who are they?"

"Some good-for-nothing punks. They don't live here."

I touch my throat. I bet it's already bruising. Cookie barks in the distance, and I'm relieved to see the old lady holding him by his leash.

"Why are you here?" Mr. Kaminski asks.

"I came to talk to you."

His brows furrow. "I have nothing to say to you. I thought I made my feelings very clear the last time." He walks away. "Go home."

Even though my heart is still beating at breakneck speed after the attack, I try to not think about it as I follow him. "I'm not going home until you hear me out."

He stops and looks over his shoulder. "Is that so? Because you're a Westwood and I'm supposed to cater to your whims?"

"No. Because I love your son, and he loves me. I want a chance to change your mind about me."

His expression is still angry when he opens his mouth to no doubt tell me to leave again, but the old lady cuts him off.

"Stop being a grump and invite the girl inside. She just saved your ass for crying out loud."

Mr. Kaminski looks at her. "I didn't ask her to interfere, and I saved her ass in return. I'd say we're even."

"Please, Mr. Kaminski. Don't send me away."

Cookie barks as if he's pleading for a chance too. Mr. Kaminski finally seems to notice him. "Is that your pup?"

"Yeah. His name is Cookie."

"My boys also adopted a Dalmatian pup. They named it…" He glances at me, his eyes going wide. "Blair."

I smile wryly. "Yeah. At the time, Alex thought it was a hilarious joke because Blair was the only bitch in the litter."

Surprisingly, Mr. Kaminski laughs. "Yeah, that's something he'd do."

"You see, Alex didn't like me very much when we first met, and the feeling was mutual. But when we finally stopped fighting for a moment and allowed ourselves to see the other person without prejudice, something wonderful happened. We fell in love."

"Oh my God. If that isn't the sweetest story ever." The old lady walks over. "I'm Mildred, the nosy neighbor."

"Nice to meet you, Mildred."

She smiles. "Now, I don't know about you, but my ass is frozen solid already. How about a cup of coffee?"

"I'd love some coffee."

Still holding Cookie's leash, the woman heads to the trailer on our right.

"Where are you going? That's not your trailer," Mr. Kaminski complains.

"This young lady came to see you, not me. You're making the coffee."

She disappears inside the trailer like she belongs there. "Damn nosy old hag," Mr. Kaminski mutters under his breath, then looks at me. "I guess we're having coffee. Come on."

CHAPTER 64
ALEX

I have no idea what time it is, but when I stretch out, searching for Blair's warm body, I find her side of the bed cold to the touch. I turn onto my back and call her name.

Nothing.

Still sleepy, I get out of bed and walk into the living room. She's not there either, and Cookie's crate is empty. I make a beeline for the fridge, and that's when I see her note sticking to the door.

Okay then. She's running errands. I guess I could go back to bed, but maybe it's better if I don't. Oversleeping is never good.

My phone rings from somewhere in her apartment. It's Logan calling. I go in search of it and find the sucker between two pillows on her couch.

"Yo. What's up?" I answer.

"Get ready. We need to go see Dad."

Shit. Whenever Logan says we need to see him, it's never good news.

"What happened?"

"I'm not sure. I got a text from Old Mildred. She wasn't specific. She just told us to get our asses there ASAP."

"Fuck." I run my fingers through my hair. "What did Dad do now?"

"Beats me. Are you ready to go? I'm on my way."

"Yeah. I just need a couple of minutes to put some clothes on."

Five minutes later, Logan calls to tell me he's in front of Blair's building. I am already waiting for him in the lobby, so I rush out.

"Were you able to get a hold of Dad?" I ask him as soon as I slide inside the car.

"Nope. I only got his voice mail. You?" He looks at me.

"Same. God. Why can't he keep that damn thing charged?"

Logan sighs. "It's a mystery we won't ever solve. What did Blair say about you leaving in a hurry like that?"

"She isn't home. I'm glad. I still don't know how I'm going to deal with Dad hating Blair."

"We'll think of something. You flipped, and so can he."

"The big difference is that I never truly hated her."

Logan bobs his head. "True. When is she moving in with us?"

"What? Where did you get that idea?"

He shrugs. "Didn't her parents cut her off? I figured that'd be your next move."

"Sometimes I hate how well you know me," I grumble. "Anyway, I asked, and she said no."

"Really? Why?"

"Because she doesn't want to live with you."

Logan widens his eyes. "What did I ever do to her? I thought she liked me."

"She likes *you*. She doesn't like your lifestyle because it reminds her of my former lifestyle."

"I see… did you tell her I don't bring girls to the apartment?"

"Yep. It's okay. I kinda don't want her living with you either."

"Wait a second. Are you jealous of me, bro?"

"You did kiss her once, and you joked that you'd end up

marrying her and I'd have to pine from afar."

Logan throws his head back and laughs. "I was yanking your chain. I already knew you had a crush on her back then. Besides, may I remind you that she kissed me, and only to piss you off?"

I rub my face and look out the window. "I want to purge that memory from my brain."

"Good luck with that."

Despite the easy banter Logan and I share during the ride to Dad's place, I can't loosen the knot of worry in my gut. I wish Old Mildred had been more specific about why we had to see him so urgently.

I begin to get an idea of what's going on when I see Blair's SUV parked just outside of the trailer park.

"Isn't that Blair's car?" Logan asks.

"Yes."

Logan parks right behind hers since the reason she didn't drive into the park is that the road is undrivable with all the snow. Logan and I make the trek to Dad's trailer on foot.

I have no idea what to expect, but my pulse is going much faster now. As we near his place, the sound of laughter reaches us. I look at Logan, and he seems as surprised by it as me.

I walk into Dad's trailer first and find him sitting on the small couch, holding a cup of coffee. Old Mildred is next to him, and Blair is sitting on the rickety chair with Cookie by her feet.

Her eyes widen when she sees me standing there.

"What's going on here?" I ask.

"Alex! How did you know I was here?"

"I didn't." I give Old Mildred a meaningful glance.

She smiles like an imp. "I thought you might want to join us. I didn't want to spoil the surprise."

"Is this some kind of *Twilight Zone* moment?" Logan pipes up.

"I convinced your father to give me a chance, that's all," Blair replies.

"Really?" I narrow my eyes. "Convinced him how? He's the

most stubborn man I've ever met."

He snorts. "I'm not stubborn, but your girlfriend proved that she's made of better stuff than I thought."

I walk over to Blair and lean down to kiss her, and that's when I see the angry red mark around her neck. I push her hair aside. "What happened to you?"

"It's nothing. It barely hurts anymore."

"Blair… tell me."

"Some punks were harassing your dad, and Blair interfered. She took care of one with her pepper spray, but the other got his hands on her," Old Mildred explains.

I straighten to my full height, rage now running freely through my veins. "Where are they?"

"Just calm down, son. They're gone. I took care of the second bastard. They won't come back."

I see now how Blair got Dad to give her a chance. I just wish she didn't have to get hurt to prove herself to him.

"Is there any coffee left?" Logan asks.

"No. We're all out." Old Mildred gets up from the couch. "I'd better go. I have a new show to binge."

"Maybe I should go too." Blair stands.

I can hardly believe that my father and Blair are in the same room without Dad going ballistic. I need to see more of them interacting to believe I'm not hallucinating.

"Is anyone hungry? I haven't had breakfast yet," I say.

"Oh, I'm down," Logan replies.

"Sure, I can make the sacrifice and have some pancakes and bacon I definitely shouldn't be eating," Dad grumbles.

"How about you, baby girl? I know you're not big on break—"

"You still haven't figured out that was a lie?" She smiles.

"I had my suspicions, but…"

"Let's go." She jumps from the chair. "I bet I can eat more pancakes than any of you."

Chuckling, I shake my head. "You're on."

CHAPTER 65
BLAIR

It's hurricane central in my apartment. I don't want to wait for the eviction notice, so I'm moving out before my parents have the chance to kick me to the curb. They're still dealing with the aftermath of the shocking revelation of their secret son.

I'm moving in with Ashley. She shares an apartment with two other girls, but one of them is moving in with her boyfriend, so it's perfect timing. She's here helping me pack alongside Alex, Logan, Noah, and Gia.

The lovey-dovey couple is busy packing my kitchen while three puppies run around them. They thought it was a good idea to bring Marshall, not knowing my namesake would be here too. Cookie thinks it's a party.

Ashley flops on the couch and runs her hand over the soft fabric. "Hmm… I know I said we didn't need any furniture, but I'll trade my couch for yours."

"No can do. My parents bought that couch, so it stays. I'm only taking the bare minimum with me."

"That's too bad."

"What about all your clothes?" Gia asks.

"I don't have money to replace them all, and it isn't like I can go to class naked."

Alex walks into the living room at that precise moment. "What's this talk about going naked to class?"

"Never mind. What do you have there?"

"This is all the stuff that was in the guest bedroom closet. Logan is packing the bookshelf in your room now."

My eyes go round. "He's what?"

Alex's brows shoot to the heavens when he realizes what that means.

"Oh my God. What is this?" Logan asks from my bedroom.

Alex sets the box in his hand down, and we both run to my room. Naturally, Logan found my *BDSM for Beginners* book and he's now reading it.

"Put that book in the box right now," I tell him.

He glances up, his eyes still caught in a bewildered expression, until slowly, his lips unfurl into a smile. "Man, maybe I should have gone after you when I had a chance."

I snatch the book from his hand. "You never had a chance."

He makes a pout. "You wound me, Blair."

"Why were you snooping through her things? I told you to pack," Alex retorts.

He twists his face into a scowl. "I wasn't snooping. But that book caught my attention."

"What book?" Ashley asks from the door. "What are you guys talking about?"

I pivot, hiding the book behind my back. "Nothing."

She squints. "Did Logan find a stash of porn magazines and he's now giving you a hard time?"

My face gets superhot, superfast. "What? No."

She shakes her head. "There's no need to be embarrassed. I have a few, although I prefer video for my porn needs."

"Ash, shut up. I don't need that mental image in my head. Sean will castrate me if I start to fantasize about you," Logan grumbles.

She crosses her arms and glowers. "Not that I want you to fantasize about me, but Sean has no business getting all protective."

"He's your brother," Logan argues.

"For the hundredth time, he's *not* my brother." She spins around and strides out of the room.

"Boy, what's with her? I bet she's sexually frustrated," Logan pipes up.

"Didn't you just say you didn't want to fantasize about her?" I ask him.

He shrugs. "That wasn't fantasizing. I was just making an observation."

"You know what? Why don't you go help Gia and Noah in the kitchen? Blair and I got this." Alex steers his brother out of the room and closes the door.

I put the book that started it all in the box. "He's not going to forget he ever saw this, is he?"

"Unlikely. I bet he already has a copy in his online shopping cart."

"Kill me now."

Alex takes my hand and spins me around so I'm facing him. "Are you embarrassed that he knows?"

I bite my lower lip before I answer. "I'm not embarrassed, but I know he'll use that knowledge to tease us at the most inappropriate times."

He chuckles. "You're not wrong. I guess we'll have to dig up dirt on my brother then."

I tilt my head. "I can't believe you don't already have that information."

Guilt shines in his eyes. "I do, but if I use it, I'll be breaking our sacred twin bond. We need new intel."

"I'm not sure I want to go too deep into the inner workings of Logan's warped mind."

Alex loops his arms around my waist, pulling me closer. "What about the inner workings of *my* warped mind?"

"Your mind isn't warped."

"Are you sure?" He leans closer to my ear. "Because I'm about to toss you on that bed and fuck you one last time in this apartment while my brother and our friends are out there packing."

"You wouldn't dare."

He bites my earlobe. "Wanna bet?"

I'm not sure what's hotter—the little bit of pain, the promise of another orgasm, or the fact he wants to put a wager on it.

"You really know how to get me to do things, don't you, big boy?"

He pulls back and looks into my eyes. "I know you, baby girl. And truthfully, I don't think I need to tease you or dare you to do anything that might be scary or unconventional. You'll do it on your own because you're not afraid of anything, and that's why I love you so damn much."

"I love you too, Alex. And you're wrong. I'm afraid of lots of things—of losing you, for example."

He cups my cheek. "That's a fear you can strike out of your heart. You're never going to lose me."

"What about Miami?"

"What about it?"

"You'll be leaving Fairbanks when you get your contract."

"True, and I'm hoping you'll come with me when you're done with school."

My heart wants to take flight. Alex and I have been intense since we got together, but this is the first time he's actually told me he wants me to come with him.

"Oh?"

"Oh?" His brows furrow together. "You sound surprised."

"I didn't want to assume..."

"Assume? Blair, I love you. Of course I want you by my side, and if I didn't ask before, it's because I didn't want you to think I consider my future to be more important than yours. You'll have a career of your own, and maybe that will take you somewhere else."

"Times have changed. Most companies are fine with employees working remotely. Besides, I'm not sure what I want to do yet. Maybe I'll start my own business. All I know is that I want to be with you."

He smiles from ear to ear, and it brightens the entire room. "It's settled then. Now, how about that bet?"

I look at the closed door, knowing very well he didn't lock it. The thrill of a possible bust makes my skin yearn for his touch. That's an easy answer. "It's on."

EPILOGUE

ALEX

FOUR YEARS LATER

I told myself and all the guys that I'd keep my cool. Logan laughed his face off and said I haven't been able to keep my cool since Blair came into my life. He's lucky I'm bound by brotherly duty to maintain his status as my best man. Ryder was more than willing to take his place.

Bets were made that I'd crack, and as I turn around and see Ryder walk Blair down the aisle, I do lose it. The swell of emotions that start in my chest can't be contained. My eyes fill with happy tears, and I try to cover a sob with my fist.

Blair is smiling at me, and she's doing a much better job of keeping it together. Although when they stop in front of me, I see that her eyes are glistening too.

Ryder gives her a kiss on her cheek and then says, "She's all yours."

I take his place, linking my arm with hers and hoping she doesn't notice the tremors that are wreaking havoc throughout my body.

"You look beautiful," I tell her.

"Thank you. So do you."

"I guess you lost that bet, huh?" she whispers before the officiant starts.

"You knew about it?"

She laughs softly. "Baby, I'm making bank."

I look at her, and she turns. "I should have known," I say.

Unable to resist, I lean in and kiss her.

The officiant clears his throat. "We didn't get to that part yet, son."

Laughter spreads among the hundred-plus guests filling our backyard. We tried to have a small and intimate ceremony, but when you play on a team, that's a hard task. Besides Ryder and Cory, my parents and grandparents, all my teammates are here, plus coaches, assistant coaches, and every other person who's had an impact on my career. Most importantly, my closest friends from Hannaford U came, and so did Blair's closest friends. Noah and Gia's little girl is the flower girl, and Cookie and Namesake—I had to change her name for obvious reasons—are the ring bearers.

Last year, after we won the Cup, I was offered a generous three-year contract to keep playing for the Miami Lions. Logan got one too. Soon after, Blair and I bought our forever home, and on the day we got our keys, I dropped down to my knees on this very spot, facing the intercoastal, and proposed. It feels like we're living in a fairy tale. We're both doing what we love. She runs a charity foundation that focuses on helping underprivileged kids through dance and art, a path that presented itself after UN picked our proposal. We live in a beautiful city, and we got her parents to relinquish Cory's care to us. He lives in an assisted living facility five minutes from us.

"Sorry," I reply sheepishly, but not feeling sorry at all.

"No worries. Shall we start?"

"I can't wait to start," Blair replies, and I know she's not talking about the ceremony.

Our gazes meet again, and I wink. *I can't wait to start the rest of our lives either, baby girl.*

Logan stands up, hitting the side of his champagne glass with a fork to get everyone's attention. Oh boy. Here comes the best man's speech.

"Good evening, ladies and gentlemen. The moment you've been waiting for has finally arrived."

Ryder covers his face. "Oh God."

"Yeah, buddy, you should pray. It won't be easy following in my footsteps." Logan pauses for dramatic effect and gives the room a quick glance. "You probably have heard by now how Blair and Alex finally got their shit together and admitted they had been pining for each other since they first met. What only a few of you know is that it all started when my dear sister-in-law attacked my mouth."

Blair gasps in an exaggerated fashion. "I did not attack your mouth!"

Logan makes eye contact with Gia. "Hmm, am I lying, Gia? I mean, you were there."

"Leave me out of it, Logan." She laughs.

"All right. I get it. Girls ought to stick together. But anyway, I'm pretty sure seeing Blair kiss me triggered something in my brother's brain because that night, he went home… *alone*."

Son of a bitch. I can't believe he's telling this story. I'm going to kill him.

"Let that sink in, folks. My wingman deserted me, and it wasn't just a fluke. Little did I know that I had lost my wingman *forever*. After that night, there was no one else but Blair."

Blair turns to me. "Really?"

"Yeah, really," I say.

"Now, I don't know if that was Blair's master plan all along, but kudos to you, sis. It worked like a charm, whether intentionally or not, and I'm so fucking glad that it did. You make my brother a better man, but most importantly, you make him annoyingly happy. Welcome to the family. I love you." He locks eyes with me. "Both of you."

He lifts his glass. "To the bride and groom."

BLAIR

The most magical evening of my life is beginning to end. Most of the guests have left already, and it's only the inner circle now, hanging on until the last moment. Our friends from college are sitting at a table, reminiscing about our time at Hannaford U, while I dance with my husband.

"I can't believe this is our life now," I say.

"Believe me, baby girl. It's only getting started."

"Is what Logan said during his speech true? You didn't get with any other girl after I kissed him?"

"Yep, it's true. I refused to believe I didn't feel the desire to hook up with anyone because of that, but there's no denying it. He's right—watching you kiss him was a wake-up call."

"It wasn't premeditated. And for the record, I didn't feel anything when I kissed him. There were no fireworks. I only had that with you."

He touches my face. "I know. I only ever had fireworks with you too, my love. And looking back at all our dark moments, all our stupid arguments, I can honestly say I was in denial."

"In denial of what?"

"That you were the one for me. It's always been you, Blair."

My eyes start to burn from the tears of happiness that are forming.

"Don't cry," he says.

"These are happy tears, silly. Because it's always been you too."

He captures my face between his hands and presses his forehead against mine. "Always and forever."

*** **THE END** ***

Thank you so much for reading Blair and Alex's story. I hope you loved it. Please consider leaving a review.

Keep reading for a sneak peek of INFAMOUS, Ryder's story.

The next book in the PLAYERS OF HANNAFORD U series is Ashley and Sean's story. I'm sure you're curious about them. You can already pre-order their book.

A SNEAK PEEK OF INFAMOUS

RYDER

Christmastime might be the most wonderful time of the year for some, but for me, it's hell on earth. Despite being the coldest and the most heartless people I know, my parents love to pretend we're one happy family, and their Christmas party is the most lavish show in town.

I inhale my third glass of whiskey as I wander aimlessly through the crowd. The bow tie around my neck feels like a noose, and the sound of fake laughter is akin to nails scratching a chalkboard.

I cross paths with a waiter and dump my empty glass on his pristine champagne tray. I could have left the glass on one of the many tables in my path, but fucking up his tray arrangement was more fun. Now I need a new drink. I stop in my tracks and weigh my options. If I keep going straight, I'll be deep in the mingling zone. The last thing I want is to engage in pointless conversation with any of the guests. But that's where the main bar is set up with more liquor choices. My father has booze in his office, although I doubt that he left it unlocked.

While I'm busy making a list of all the places I can get alcohol without running into someone I don't want to speak to, I spot Blair in my periphery, sneaking out of the party. For once, she isn't wearing a coat in a pastel color, hence why she stood out to me. I make a beeline in her direction and catch up with her before she walks out the door to the gardens.

"Where are you going, sis?" I ask, making her jump.

"Shit, Ryder. You scared me. I'm going for a walk outside."

I snort. "No, you're not. Try again."

She looks over my shoulder, then moves sideways to use me as a shield. "I had a talk with Ilya. It seems our nuptials are imminent."

My blood freezes in my veins. "What?"

She looks me in the eye. "Please don't act surprised. You know our folks see us as pawns to be used to advance their interests. Mom has been trying to shove horrid candidates down my throat for months. Ilya seems to be the winner."

My heart is beating faster, propelled by fear. "You can't marry into the Bolkosky family."

Her face crumbles. "I don't want to, but what choice do I have? You know what Mom will do if I refuse. But I can't think about that now. I have to be somewhere."

Bitterness pools in my mouth. "Let me guess. The Warriors Christmas bash."

"Yes. I'm meeting Alex there."

If she sneaks out of the party alone and screws with our mother's agenda, there'll be hell to pay. The solution is simple. "Well, let's go then."

She furrows her brows. "You're coming with me?"

"Obviously." I reach behind her to open the door. "Go on."

"You're not even wearing a coat."

"I have a jacket in my car."

Her brows are pinched, and she keeps an eye on me as she walks out. Once outside, she says, "What's the deal, Ryder? You're not seriously thinking about crashing the Warriors' party, right?"

I grimace. "Of course not. But I need to get out of here, or I'll end up punching Ilya in the face. I'll take you there then go somewhere else."

She studies me intensely. "You know what. You *should* come to the party."

Ah hell. That's the last thing I want to do. Everyone on the team hates me, and tonight, I don't want to pretend I'm unaffected by it. "Blair... I can't."

Her eyes narrow in determination. "Yes, you can. And you're coming."

The ride to The Heritage is quiet. I open and shut my mouth several times, but the words won't come out. Guilt is sitting heavily on my mind. If hadn't tried to outsmart the Bolkoskys, my younger sister wouldn't have to marry the son of the Russian mob.

I thought I was being clever by quitting the team before the championship final. But I learned the hard way that you can't cross the Bolkoskys. They wanted another year of guaranteed results. They're arrogant to believe one hockey player can do that for them. Throwing one game is one thing, but doing it throughout an entire season? Impossible.

But it was the certainty that, if I stayed, none of my teammates would be safe that made the decision for me. Now they all hate me, and I lost Gia, the only girl who ever mattered to me.

Blair receives a text message, and I finally break the silence. "Is that Alex?"

"Yeah. He wants to meet us outside The Heritage."

"Why?"

She sighs. "I told him you were coming to the party."

I clench my jaw tight. "I see. I never agreed to it."

"But you should."

She's going to keep badgering me if I say no again. So I just shut my mouth and let her think she's convinced me.

Another five minutes, and I'm parking across the street from the popular bar on the Hannaford U campus. I used to come here often when I was a Warrior. This is the team's hangout. But I avoid the place now. I came once at the beginning of the semester with Adrian, Preston, Josh, and Hunter, the only friends I have left at school and only because they aren't on the hockey team. It was a colossal mistake.

The jacket I have in the car isn't thick enough for this type of weather, but I suck it up. We find Alex outside The Heritage, shuffling from side to side as fog billows out of his mouth when her breathes.

His entire body changes when he looks at Blair. He only has eyes for her and no one else. Last year, if he tried to score with her, I'd have kicked his ass. He and his twin brother have a reputation. But I know that's in Alex's past. He's head over heels in love with my sister. One more reason for me to get her out of that damned arranged marriage.

I expect him to kiss her hello, but he just stands there, awkward as fuck. I'd laugh if I wasn't freezing my ass off.

"Hey. How was traffic?" he asks.

What kind of dumbass question is that?

I snort. "You wanna talk about traffic while standing outside in subzero temperatures?"

He narrows his eyes. "Fine. Why did you have to leave the party early?"

Blair and I trade a glance. I'm not sure if she wants to tell Alex about Ilya.

"Was it because of Ilya?" he asks, guessing the reason in one.

"Can we talk inside?" Blair steps forward, and finally, he pulls her to him.

"Yes, baby girl."

They're about to kiss, and even though I know they're together, I don't want to witness their PDA. I've seen Alex hook up with too many random chicks, and seeing him with Blair is still weird.

"Fuck. I can't handle this. I'm going to take off."

"Ryder, come on. You shouldn't be alone tonight," Blair pleads.

"I don't think anyone will appreciate my presence." I stick my hands in my pockets and bounce from side to side. The cold is getting to me.

"They know you're coming," Alex pipes up.

I arch a brow. "And?"

"And I think you should come in and say hello."

I look behind him into the wide windows of The Heritage. With all the Christmas lights inside, I can see everything, including Gia, laughing about something her new boyfriend, Noah, said. A sharp pain in my chest makes it harder to breath. I thought I was starting to move on, but it's obvious that I have a long way to go.

Alex glances over his shoulder and then back at me, his eyes now shining with pity. Fuck that shit.

"I'm gonna go. You two have fun." I turn, but instead of crossing the street to get into my car, I walk down the sidewalk.

"Where are you going?" Blair calls.

"I need fresh air."

I don't want her to come after me, so I quicken my pace and turn the next corner. This area has other small shops and restaurants besides The Heritage, but most are already closed.

I'm shivering, and I come the conclusion that this walk was a stupid move on my part. This isn't fresh air—it's air cold enough to freeze my lungs. I'm not wearing a hat, and not even my longish hair can protect my ears. I can't feel them anymore.

I see a small convenience store that's still open and head that way. They might have coffee. I need something warm in my body pronto.

The bell dings when I open the door, and the guy behind the cash register glances at me. "We're closing in five minutes."

"Do you have a coffee machine?"

He points with his head. "In the back."

He sounds grumpy, which isn't surprising. I wouldn't want to be here either. The coffee machine is old and could use some cleaning, but at least it works. Whether the dark liquid dripping into my cup is any good will be another story.

I hear the doorbell ding again, and the guy repeats the same thing he told me.

"This won't take long," a female voice replies.

My coffee is done, so I put a lid on the cup and walk back to the cash register. I don't see the woman who came in. She must be in a different aisle.

I set the cup down on the counter and shove my hand my in pants pocket, looking for my wallet.

"That'll be four dollars," the guy says in a bored tone.

Geez. Four dollars for this sewage? I don't find my wallet where it should be. I pat my jacket pockets next, finding them all empty.

Hell. "I left my wallet in my car."

I sense someone step in line behind me. This dude's other customer.

The clerk narrows his eyes. "Sure you did. Next you're gonna ask to go grab it real quick, taking the coffee with you, and I'll never see you again."

"Do you think I want to steal this overpriced coffee? I'll pay you back."

"I'll pay for his coffee," the woman behind me chimes in.

I turn around, not knowing yet if I should accept her offer or just leave the damn coffee behind, but I end up losing my train of thought. A pretty dark-haired girl with full lips and big hazel eyes is standing there, and she catches me by surprise. I wasn't expecting her at all.

When I keep staring at her like a moron, she steps forward and puts a bottle of laxative on the counter, unfazed. Most people, especially girls, would try to hide that.

"Can I also have a couple of one dollar scratch-offs, please?"

"Can I see some ID?" the clerk asks.

She pulls out her driver's license and shows it to him. He barely glances at it.

"That'll be sixteen dollars and ninety cents."

She pays for it, and then, looking at me, she says, "Merry Christmas."

I don't know what's wrong with me, because it takes me a couple seconds to wake up, grab my coffee, and go after her. "Wait," I call.

She stops and looks over her shoulder. "What is it?"

"Thank you for the coffee. You didn't need to do that."

"I know, but you sounded desperate for it." She resumes walking, so I keep pace.

"My car is parked right around the corner. I can pay you back now."

"There's no need. Pay it forward."

"Can I walk you to your car, then? It's dark."

She chuckles. "No kidding. I expect it to be dark at night. But you can walk with me if you'd like. My destination is also around the corner."

"Oh. Are you going to The Heritage?"

She gives me a sideways glance. "Yeah. How did you know?"

"Easy guess." I take a sip of my coffee and wince. It's disgusting.

We turn the corner, and the lights of The Heritage sign shine in the distance. I begin to wonder why she's at the Warriors' party. She must be either related to or dating someone on the team. If she came with one of the players, and he let her go to a convenience store alone, he's a fucking asshole.

Jesus, I'm getting worked up over a girl I've known for two minutes.

She pauses suddenly and announces, "My pocket is vibrating." I wait for her to fish out the device and click on the screen. A moment later, she shrieks. "Are you fucking kidding me?"

I arch my brows. "What's wrong?"

"My boyfriend just dumped me. Who does that two days before Christmas?"

"An asshole." I take another sip of my coffee, trying to hide that this news pleases me. She isn't someone's date.

"That's right, a complete asshole." She looks up, and I see tears welling in her eyes.

Ah hell. I'm an ass too for being happy she's single now. "He doesn't deserve your tears."

"I'm not crying." She wipes the corners of her eyes and looks at her phone again. "I'm furious."

As she begins to type, I notice that her hands are shaking. "What are you going to tell him?"

"I don't know."

Another ping tells me she's gotten another message. Her eyes widen, and then her lips tremble. "I fucking knew it." She lifts her chin, capturing my stare again. "He's been hooking up with someone else."

"Then he's not only an asshole, he's a dumb fuck. If you were my girl, I wouldn't stray."

Shit. I don't know why I said that.

She stares at me with bright, round eyes, but doesn't say a word. I probably went too far, and now she thinks I'm a creep. Then her luscious lips curl into a wicked grin. "That's it. Let's take a selfie together."

In an instant, I'm leery. "Why?"

She steps closer and stretches her arm, pointing the camera at us. "Because I want him to know I've already moved on with someone much, *much* better. Now smile."

I don't smile. I can't, because this is absurd.

"Come on. You owe me. I paid for your coffee. Give me a kiss on the cheek."

Our gazes connect through the camera pointing at us, and the vulnerability in her eyes does something to me. Her ex was obviously someone she cared about, and she's hurting.

I sigh, resigned. "Fine." I loop my arm around her waist, pulling her closer to me. "Ready?"

"Yeah."

I press my lips to her cold cheek. Immediately, the sweet scent of her perfume invades my senses. It awakens something in me that makes me want to kiss her some more.

She takes a bunch of pictures of the same pose, but they aren't as good as they could be. Her eyes are sad in them.

"I think we can do better than that," I say.

We're still close when she turns her face to mine. "How?"

I look into her eyes, then my gaze drops to her lips. Shit. I'm going to hell for this. I set my now cold coffee on the ground, and then pull her flush against my body again.

She lets out a little gasp when I cup her cheek. "Your hand is like an ice block."

I chuckle. "Sorry."

"But… what are you doing?"

"If you want to make your ex jealous, an innocent kiss on the cheek won't cut it."

She blinks fast, getting my meaning. "You're right."

"Do a video."

She looks away for a second to change her camera to video mode, then points it at us again. When it's recording, I hold her face again and press my lips to hers, gently at first, but then she parts her lips slightly, and I forget this is only for show. I deepen the kiss, coaxing her lips open so I can play with her tongue. Hell. She's sweet like her scent, and a damn good kisser.

The temperature is still freezing, but my body is getting warmer. I tighten my hold around her waist, wishing I could flatten her against a wall and press my body to hers. It's been a while since I kissed someone who ignited this combustible reaction in me.

A car honks in the vicinity, then some idiot yells, "Get a room!"

Shit. What am I doing? I step back, feeling guilty now for

getting carried away. My make-out partner lowers her phone but keeps her now-hooded gaze on me. She's breathing a little faster.

"Do you think you have enough footage?" I ask in a tight voice while trying to force my pounding heart to slow down.

"What?"

I point at her phone.

"Oh. It should be fine." Instead of looking at the video, she closes the camera app.

Almost immediately, her phone rings. She answers but doesn't take her gaze off me.

"Hey.... I'm on my way back. Stop freaking out. I'm a big girl, Noah."

My stomach dips.

Noah.

No. No fucking way.

"Sorry. I have to run back to the party. My brother is pissed that I left without telling him. Older brothers are such a pain in the ass. Thanks for your help." She smiles.

"You're welcome," I reply, still in shock.

She sprints toward The Heritage, leaving me reeling with the realization.

I just kissed Noah Kingsley's baby sister... and I loved it.

Fuck my life.

TO BE CONTINUED...

Become a member of my Patreon to read Ryder's story as I write it, plus other bonus content, early access to NSFW art, and an exclusive Patreon serial.

JOIN HERE

ABOUT THE AUTHOR

USA Today Bestselling Author Michelle Hercules always knew creative arts were her calling but not in a million years did she think she would become an author. With a background in fashion design she thought she would follow that path. But one day, out of the blue, she had an idea for a book. One page turned into ten pages, ten pages turned into a hundred, and before she knew it, her first novel, The Prophecy of Arcadia, was born.

Michelle Hercules resides in Florida with her husband and daughter. She is currently working on the *Blueblood Vampires* series and the *Filthy Gods* series.

Sign-up for Michelle Hercules' Newsletter:
bit.ly/MichelleHerculesVIP

Join Michelle Hercules' Readers Group:
https://www.facebook.com/groups/mhsoars

Connect with Michelle Hercules:
www.michellehercules.com
books@mhsoars.com

facebook.com/michelleherculesauthor
instagram.com/michelleherculesauthor
amazon.com/Michelle-Hercules/e/B075652M8M
bookbub.com/authors/michelle-hercules
tiktok.com/@michelleherculesauthor?
youtube.com/@MichelleHerculesAuthor
patreon.com/michellehercules

Printed in Great Britain
by Amazon

26850169R00236